BLOODLINES

BLOODLINES

❦ ❧

John Jenkins
Mark Weaver

VINE
BOOKS

Servant Publications
Ann Arbor, Michigan

Vine Books is an imprint of Servant Publications especially designed to serve Evangelical Christians.

Published by Servant Publications
P.O. Box 8617
Ann Arbor, Michigan 48107

Cover design by Multnomah Graphics/Printing
Cover illustration by Chris Ellison
Text design by K. Kelly Bonar

The type face used in the diary portions of this novel is Bodoni, named after Giambattista Bodoni, a leading type designer of the early 1800s. The chiseled quality of its line strokes and the square serifs are typical of the type styles used at the time of the American Civil War.

93 94 95 96 97 10 9 8 7 6 5 4 3 2 1

Printed in the United States of America

ISBN 0-89283-825-6

Library of Congress Cataloging-in-Publication Data

Jenkins, John, 1952–

   Bloodlines / John Jenkins, Mark Weaver.
     p.   cm.
   ISBN 0-89283-825-6
   I.Weaver, Mark, 1951–   II. Title.
PS3560.E4855B56 1993
813'.54—dc20   93-25534

The heritage of the past
is the seed that brings forth
the harvest of the future.

National Archives Building.
Washington, D.C.

Thanks to Keith for the truth,
to Scott for the MPO,
to Kaycee for her support,
to Servant for their guidance,
to Harold for his criticism,
to numerous friends for numerous readings,
and most of all to our wives,
Brenda and Sally,
for their patience.

PART

 I

1

Wednesday Evening

I T WAS TIME to call the past into account.

The high-pressure system gathering over Charlestown, West Virginia, broke fully over the Blue Ridge Mountains. Heavy, frigid air poured into the Potomac River valley. High winds blustered past the historic spires of Georgetown, past the USA Today's glassy high-rise, nipping the northeast corner of Arlington National Cemetery and its seemingly endless rows of white headstones.

The cold, January winds swept through the Lincoln Memorial's tall marble columns and over the icy reflecting pool, gusting swiftly across a quarter mile of grass to the Washington Monument, the proud 555-foot sentinel whose four blinking red eyes maintained an ever-faithful vigil over the nation's capital.

Across Constitution Avenue, a New York-based Channel 13 television crew worked on the south end of the ellipse, the south view of the White House their backdrop. The camera crew braced themselves against the wind, stuffing bare hands in pockets, raising coat collars, tightening scarves. On the opposite side of the White House, a similar shoot took place at Lafayette Square, facing the north portico. A Chicago NBC affiliate completed a live newsbrief for their audience back home.

Though two weeks away, coverage of the twentieth anniversary of Roe v. Wade and the annual pro-life March For Life had already begun. The rhetoric of last year's election campaigns heightened the nation's awareness of a growing cultural divide. Washington was already tensing for the influx of protesters on this twentieth anniversary of Roe v. Wade. Memories of mass protests and arrests in Atlanta and Wichita last summer heightened fears of widespread civil disobedience.

A few minutes later and seventeen blocks north, traffic slowed to a halt on the steep hill at the corner of 16th and W, near the south end of a park. Enclosed by a tall concrete wall, a block long on each side, the park covered a grassy crest of historic land known as Meridian Hill. The park stood on the original site where, in the late 1780s, an inspired young architect surveyed and laid a meridian stone, with the hopes that the fledgling United States might not only be politically free from Great Britain, but also free from its Greenwich

9

prime meridian. Meridian Hill Park, as it was appropriately named in 1914, had as its axis a cascade of graduated pools and falls descending among basins, stepped walls, statuaries, elegant trees and dense shrubbery.

After the fiery riots that shook Washington in the summer of 1968, the park's name was officially changed to Malcolm X Park. Soon, however, the park fell from public favor and became home to dozens of Washington's homeless. Graffiti scarred its pebbled walls; the fountains and pools had been dry for many years until local activists began restoring the park to its former glory.

Meridian Hill Park, as it was still called by most, was still not a place to stroll at night. Heroin, crack, and marijuana could be bought inside any of its three entrances. One of those entrances, near the corner at 16th and W Streets, was home for three of Washington's homeless.

At 6:30 P.M. this Wednesday evening, the three heavily bundled men watched the traffic jam grow block by block. Gusting wind stung their faces. Glenn, the tallest and thinnest of the three, pulled his orange ski cap down over his matted hair. He glanced at his friend Jimmy, who sat at his regular place on the end of a curve in the low pebbled wall near the entrance to the park. Jimmy absentmindedly fingered one of the dozens of political campaign buttons he had collected during his twelve years on the street.

Jimmy's hand twitched awkwardly, twice in succession, then slipped from the button and dropped into his lap. Glenn reached down and patted him on the shoulder. "Jimmy, you OK?"

Jimmy turned and stared up at Glenn, his wide oval face uncharacteristically blank. Perplexed, Glenn rubbed his scraggly chin. Jimmy always smiled, just like all the funny faces on his buttons. Why wasn't he smiling now?

Glenn walked fifteen feet to the corner and tugged at the patchwork sleeve of his friend Larry's parka. Larry was heavyset and bald, except for a few thick strands of gray hair behind his ears that lay bunched in the open hood of his parka. Larry, once a superintendent for a county Public Works Department in Maryland, watched out for him and Jimmy.

Glenn rubbed his tongue over an infected crack in his lower lip before speaking. "Somethin's happened to Jimmy."

Larry's bushy eyebrows arched in concern.

As the men started to turn around, the sound of screeching tires snapped their heads back around to busy 16th Street.

A Cadillac limosine with tinted windows blared its horn as a broad-shouldered man jogged across the street through the middle of the traffic.

The man in the blue jogging suit raised his hands as if to apologize, then continued on to the other side.

Glenn tugged at Larry's sleeve. "What about Jimmy?"

Larry nodded. They stepped away from the curb back toward the steps and the opening to the park.

The two men stopped abruptly near the end of the low wall. Larry gnawed at his lower lip; Glenn's mouth hung open.

Jimmy was nowhere to be seen. And to complicate the mystery, Jimmy's autographed burgundy and gold Redskin cap lay on the sidewalk by the end of the wall. Jimmy, a mute, never went anywhere without his Joe Gibbs' Redskins cap. Never.

Concerned, Glenn and Larry started up the steps into the park to find their friend.

With sad eyes, the man in blue watched the two men from the other side of the street.

"Babe, I know where we are. Centreville is just over the hill and down the road a mile or so."

Mark MacDonald turned the red Chevy Blazer off the curving exit ramp down a dark ribbon of road. Shadows of barren trees darted by.

Katie sat silently, hands folded in her lap. She glanced up at her husband. He had both hands on the wheel, the green dials on the dash glowing on his grinning face. She studied her husband's profile for an instant before she closed her eyes and leaned her head against the headrest.

What would he say when she told him? Would he be happy? She remembered the excitable young man he had once been, grinning at her from between books on the shelf at the William and Mary Library. She remembered his cocky smile and his laughter. She remembered his confident walk and the promises he'd made with his twinkling eyes. How could she have helped but fall in love with him? How could any girl have helped falling in love with him?

But that had been ten years ago.

Mark ran a hand through his short, sandy hair, his grin shrinking as they continued through the wooded Virginia countryside.

Katie removed the clip holding her makeshift ponytail and shook her thick blonde hair down upon her shoulders. She dug casually through her purse, pushed aside the letter from the executors of Mark's grandfather's and aunt's estate and pulled out a hairbrush.

Mark shook his head. "We're not in Centreville, we're in Manassas. I got off the interstate a couple exits early."

"How do you know?" she asked.

"I can tell," he replied with a smile in his voice. "I can smell history. I can feel history—also, we just passed a sign."

Katie chuckled. "You nut!"

"I'm also hungry," he said. "But nothing seems to be the way I remember it."

"You're always hungry," she said playfully, patting his arm.

Mark glanced over and smiled. Katie drew back and looked out the passenger window, suddenly reminded of the playful moment four years earlier that caused the accident that changed their lives.

Katie sighed, her breath momentarily fogging the window. That summer night on a Virginia Beach street corner came back in a flash. She should have seen the red pickup. She should have paid better attention. She shouldn't have been acting playfully so close to the curb.

It was her fault they lost the baby. It was her fault that the accident paralyzed her. It was her fault that Mark had to put his life on hold for so long, that for a time his affections had grown cold.

"This move is going to work for me, Katie," Mark said softly, interrupting her thoughts. "I know it is. I can feel it. I mean, it has to be God. First, we inherit a $300,000 house, then two days later Bud Dwyer calls and wants me to be a partner with him in developing real estate. I know this is going to work and it's something I can really give myself to. Helping people buy their first home is important; I feel in my gut that this is how God wants me to serve Him."

She knew in her heart that wheeling and dealing in real estate would never fulfill Mark. His adult Sunday School classes had always been the best attended. He was a teacher. And he loved history with a boundless passion. He had plans to get his graduate degree. But then she had the accident.

"I'm happy for you. And being back in the house where you grew up as a teenager will make it doubly nice. I wish I had known your aunt a little better. And I wish I could have thanked her for taking you in when your father passed away."

"Growing up without parents was rough, but Aunt Clara did the best she could," Mark said.

Katie looked at her husband. The opportunity to work with his old friend Bud in the nation's capital had rekindled a hope in him that she had not seen since the accident.

"I wish we had more than two weeks for you to enjoy before Bud comes into town."

"Two weeks is plenty."

"I don't know Mark, there's an awful lot to do in Washington. I want to see the Air and Space Museum and go up the Washington Monument."

"Don't worry, babe. We'll have plenty of time."

Katie's mind went on silently. She would let Mark do whatever he wanted in those two weeks. She had been a burden for too long. And he deserved a little time to breathe again.

The cold wind snapped at Jimmy's pant legs and rustled his tangled hair. The intersection behind him was a blur filled with moving shapes. Breathing hard, he ran his deeply wrinkled right hand slowly over the top of his head.

Alarm showed on his oval face. His Redskin cap was gone!

With the wind pushing hard at his back, Jimmy was totally disoriented. He turned and headed down the narrow street, away from Meridian Hill Park and all that he knew as home.

Mark pulled into a parking space beneath McDonald's golden arches. He came around the Blazer to help Katie out. A gust of wind snapped at his jacket. He opened the door and reached his hand out for her to steady herself.

"Mark, please. You know I can do this myself."

"I'm sorry. Just habit." Mark stepped back.

Katie climbed carefully from the Blazer. It had been a long uphill struggle. The doctors said she would never walk again, much less be able to conceive children. The specialists said that the nerve damage resulting from the break between her sixth and seventh cervical vertebrae would leave her with a loss of lower body functions and impede her ability to conceive a child.

One quiet Sunday morning, five weeks later, after her doctors had given up hope, after Mark could find nothing encouraging to share, could find no spiritual comfort, the big toe on her left foot moved.

She felt Mark's gaze as she negotiated her way between puddles in the parking lot. He really had stopped doting over her, especially after the doctors declared her eighty-five percent recovered. In passing, most people couldn't tell she'd once spent time paralyzed in a stryker frame.

They ordered their meal and found a table. Mark ate his french fries in huge mouthfuls and sipped on a coke between bites.

Katie studied his face. Even though Mark would soon turn thirty-two, the corners of his eyes were lined with fine wrinkles. The three years of recovery and physical therapy had taken their toll not only on her, but on him as well. How many days had he rearranged his work schedule to accommodate her therapy and doctors' appointments only to make up his time on the weekends or evenings? How many times in those first few months had he carried her from room to room? And how many nights had he spent on his knees praying for her? How many nights had he not slept, but worried about her recovery or been depressed about the setbacks that had inevitably come?

"Mark, I love you."

He stopped chewing and stared at her blankly for a moment. Then he nodded slowly, smiling, "I know you love me."

Taking a deep breath, Katie reached for a french fry, munched it carelessly and said what the doctors had claimed would never happen.

"I'm pregnant."

The seconds ticked by without response and she raised her eyes to meet his. Mark's mouth was wrapped around the drink-filled straw. She watched the brown fluid slide slowly back down into the drink.

"Come again?" he asked hoarsely, looking like a man who had been awakened in the middle of the night.

"I said, I'm pregnant."

He leaned back in the hard plastic chair and grinned wildly. "You're pregnant..."

"Yes."

"How'd that happen?" he asked seriously.

Katie chuckled, shrugged and said, "Well, how do you think?"

Mark chuckled, too, his grin blooming into a broad smile on his handsome face.

He reached across the small, white table and took her hand in his.

"It's going to be good now, Mark," Katie whispered. "I'm going to make it all up to you! I promise!"

The words began to rush from her. "I'm going to be a real wife to you and do things for myself because I can walk now and I'm going to let you do things you want to do and I'll help fix up your grandfather's old house and maybe even..."

"Katie, it's OK," Mark interrupted.

She lowered her head.

He clasped her hands, then reached up and stroked her soft blonde hair. "I know how hard you're trying. Everything's going to be all right. God has something great for us to do. You, me, and the baby. Together."

Jimmy stood on a corner, his shoulders sagging and his arms hanging limply. He glanced up at the windswept night sky, rubbed his arms and stepped back into a black wrought-iron fence. Surprised, he spun around. A lifesize statue loomed above him—a man wearing a hat and cloak sat on a horse. The man held an open Bible.

The wind returned, nipping at his ears, slipping up his sleeves, sliding down his collar. The abrupt chill sharpened his focus just enough to get his arms swinging, his legs moving.

Nearby, a figure wrapped in a ragged sleeping bag atop a narrow but warm grate watched Jimmy with growing concern. "Hey—watch yo' step! A man's down here by yo' clumsy feet."

Jimmy glanced down and, for a brief moment, understood. Stepping around the sleeping bag, he stuffed his hands back into his coat pockets and started up Mount Pleasant toward 16th Street, the wind pressing against his back.

2

Wednesday Night

"WELCOME TO WASHINGTON," Mark muttered to himself. Traffic had never been this bad when he had lived in the District as a teenager. Fortunately, the townhouse was less than four miles away, situated only twenty or so blocks north of the White House. He pressed the FM button on the radio. The Blazer's speakers erupted with synthesizers and drums imitating a heart beat.

Katie turned her head as the pulsing rhythm grew louder, faster, joined by a bass guitar that vibrated the Blazer's speakers. An electric guitar shrieked out of the left speaker and echoed across to the right as a harsh chorus of male voices screamed over the crash of cymbals.

No gods, no masters! We rape, we steal, we kill!
No gods, no masters! Your blood is ours to spill!

Katie clicked off the stereo. Her cheeks were red. "I can't believe stations are allowed to broadcast songs like that!"

Mark shook his head. "Contrary to the music, this is one of Washington's nicest areas to live. The National Zoo is less than a mile away; the Washington Monument and the other—"

Katie patted Mark on the arm. "If you don't make it in real estate, you could be a tour guide."

Mark ignored her barb. His face became serious. "Rock Creek Park has a public golf course. One of my earliest memories of Washington is Dad, Grandpa, and me riding in a golf cart around the edge of a green. I think I was four. They let me chase down shots that ended in the woods. Even at the age of ninety-four, Grandpa could still sink a putt."

"You really loved your grandfather."

"Yep," Mark said with a sigh. "After I moved in with Aunt Clara in Culpeper, Grandpa would visit and Aunt Clara would drive us to the Manassas Battlefield. My grandfather could sit and stare out over those rolling fields for hours."

Mark paused, wrapping his hands tightly around the steering wheel.

"Anything wrong?" Katie asked.

15

"No, not really. I just forgot how much I miss him. After Mom and Dad died, he and Aunt Clara were all the family I had. Then he died just after I turned ten. That's when Aunt Clara and I moved to Washington."

Mark shook his head. "I'm rambling. I know I've told you this before."

"It's OK to ramble a little," Katie said, reaching over and gently rubbing his shoulder.

After several moments of silence, a thin smile returned to his face. "Y'know, that reminds me of something. Both Grandpa and Aunt Clara used to call this road Church Street. They claimed it had more churches on it than any other street in the whole world. I once counted seventeen within a one mile stretch."

Katie grinned and looked out the window. Before they had gone two blocks, she counted six churches: two Baptist, an Episcopal, a Seventh Day Adventist, a Catholic, and a Methodist.

After crossing a short bridge above a four-lane parkway, Mark waited for a line of traffic to pass, then swung the Blazer left onto a long, narrow street, dimly lit with cars parked parallel to the curbs on both sides. The street ended in a T formation.

Mark winced at the condition of the neighborhood. Across the street, empty stores were boarded shut and graffiti covered the peeled and faded paint. Windswept trash danced down a filthy sidewalk where three young men in heavy coats huddled, their hands cupped over cigarettes, a dozen empty beer bottles by their feet. Iron bars protected windows and doors.

Mark flipped his turn signal on and swung right. He eyed his wife. "Quite a change for just one block."

As they turned again onto one-way Crest Road, the neighborhood changed again. Poorly lit stores gave way to brick townhouses, then further down, to larger, better maintained buildings. At the end of the street on the left, loomed a large church made of white stone.

They stopped for a red light adjacent to the church. Stone steps stretched across the front and led to massive, two-story tall columns. Behind the columns were arched wooden doors. The somber structure's architecture was a mix of styles: Spanish roof, Greek columns, Gothic doors.

The church faced one side of a triangular park bordered by wooden benches and the intersection of three streets. The park's interior was covered with huge, square inlaid slabs of stone with a few dense trees and shrubs on the north side parallel to the townhouses. In the park's center stood a larger than life statue of a man reclining in a Romanesque chair that always reminded Mark of someone from *Ben Hur* or *The Robe*.

Mark pointed at the last townhouse on the right. "There's our new home—5133 Crest Road."

The light turned green. Mark suddenly realized that there was a No Parking sign at the curb directly in front of their townhouse. He parked on the left side of the one-way street between a beat-up Chevette and a brand new Toyota with thirty-day tags.

For a moment, he and Katie stared quietly out the window. The narrow townhouse had a small covered porch and a three-story bay topped with a conical roof and fish-scale shingles. Above the front door was a rectangular beveled glass panel that allowed them to see a brightly lit ceiling fixture inside the house.

"The executor said he'd leave the hall light on," Mark said, opening his door and walking behind the Blazer. He removed two suitcases and a make-up case. Traffic in front of the townhouse forced them to wait until the light at nearby 16th Street turned red.

As they stepped onto the sidewalk in front of the townhouse, a strong wind rustled at their backs.

Katie shivered and smiled. "Even on a cold night it's charming—just like the photograph. I'm afraid to say, but I'm already starting to like it."

The wind picked up, snapping at their clothes. They hurried up painted concrete steps to the front door. Mark fumbled briefly with his keys, then unlocked the door and swung it open.

They were greeted by a rush of warm air. After setting the luggage down on a polished oak floor, Mark closed and locked the front door, then threw the dead bolt.

The old house was just as he remembered it.

From the foyer Mark could see a shadowed parlor and wide fireplace through a cased opening to their right. A combination dining and sitting room were straight ahead at the end of a short hall. The kitchen was in the darkness beyond the dining room. To his left stood a hall tree with a tall oval mirror and brass coat hooks. Up the stairs directly in front of him on the second floor were two bedrooms and, up again on the third floor, two rooms used for storage.

"The furnace works," Mark said, unzipping his coat. "And we're in for an easy time if the movers placed the boxes where we—"

Katie slipped her slender arms up under his coat and around his back. She kissed him squarely on the mouth.

Mark pulled his head back slightly. "What's that for?"

Katie smiled. "It's for a lot of things, Mark David MacDonald: for ten years of marriage; for how hard you've worked to be a good husband; for sitting and praying with me each night, week after week in that hospital room; for never giving up on God or on me; for this chance to start over and for being the father of our miracle child!"

Her blue eyes flashed. "I think we ought to celebrate this wonderful occasion, don't you?"

"Celebrate? What do you—"

Katie brought her lips up to his mouth a second time, pausing to brush the end of her nose lightly against his. She stared deeply into his widening eyes.

Understanding, Mark grinned, flipped off the light switch and returned her kiss.

Jimmy stood in heavy shadows at one end of a narrow, unlit parking lot with a wide, three-story building on his right. On his left, a high wooden fence ran all the way to Crest Road.

His heart raced, his legs ached and his feet throbbed. White spots flashed before his eyes as he sagged back against the wall.

His hand brushed against metal. Jimmy turned and ran his hand over the surface of a dumpster. Adrenalin pumped strength into his exhausted legs. He groped around the corner to the front side.

The dumpster was open.

He grabbed the side of the opening and lifted one leg inside. His boot dropped onto a large plastic bag. He repeated the motion with the other leg—and stepped onto more bags. He almost fell.

Hanging on to the lip, Jimmy lowered himself onto the plastic bags and lay down. He rolled over on his side, drawing his knees slightly toward his chest.

Folding his arms tightly, he promptly fell asleep.

Mark woke, his eyes popping open in the darkness. He lifted his head—a siren warbled close by, and red and blue lights flashed through the lace curtains. He groaned softly. The digital clock read 12:35 A.M.

He looked over at Katie. She lay with her back to him, breathing softly, moonlight spilling over the goosedown comforter pulled snugly around her neck. He studied the upward curve of her naturally rosy lips, the pale dance of freckles across her nose and high cheekbones.

Tonight, her blue eyes had radiated a vitality that he had not seen for a few years, not since the accident that had left her paralyzed from her rib cage to her toes and had caused her to miscarry their first child. Her face showed little hint of those bitter, haunting days during her prolonged recovery.

For several minutes he just stared at her, his thoughts ranging backward three years and three months, to Atlanta, just prior to the accident, to a similar first night in a new house. Hadn't Katie wrapped her arms around him then, in the foyer by the front door, as she had tonight? Hadn't she kissed him and excitedly announced that she was pregnant?

A sick feeling stirred in his stomach. Was it indigestion or was it... fear? Fear that something might go wrong again and they'd lose this child, too. He wasn't sure he wanted to struggle with that level of pain and disappointment again. Having the foundation of your life shaken once was enough. The strain on their relationship had been formidable. After three long years, the distance and disillusionment her paralysis had brought finally seemed behind them.

Mark arched his back. The feeling in his stomach sharpened. Facing the triple bay window, he pulled back the curtain. Moonlight streamed across the bed.

The traffic on 16th Street was sporadic; the sidewalks surrounding the park and statue were vacant. The Blazer sat in shadows from the row of trees partially blocking his view of the park. He could only see the back of the statue's head, shoulders, and upper torso.

Suddenly, an old man in a waist-length coat shuffled into view from behind the statue. He stopped in the middle of the park and started to turn his face toward the statue of the man in the chair.

Mark yawned and dropped the curtain. He tip-toed across the bedroom into the hall. Reaching into the bathroom, he flipped on the light and found three large boxes stacked near the bathtub.

Now, if he could only find the antacids...

Jimmy's eyes fluttered open as wintry air brushed lightly across his face. Moonlight fell through the open door of the dumpster, illuminating the plastic bags around him. He could not remember ever feeling so warm, other than the nights he and Glenn and Larry had spent in shelters. Even his head felt warm.

His eyes darted left to right. His cap—where was his cap? He tried to lift his hand to his head, but his arms would not obey.

Then he heard the voice.

The voice had not come from outside the dumpster, but from somewhere much closer, like a whisper. Then he heard his name again—not the name everyone knew him by, but his real name.

He rolled his eyes upward. He saw no one.

"Steven, do not fear, I have come to you. Though you have forgotten my name, I have not forgotten yours."

Steven swallowed, his eyes tearing. A yearning forced itself from his mouth. His reply was slow, slurred, but fully understood by the one who listened and could hear words spoken by the heart.

"Yes, Lord."

The voice came closer. "When you were a little boy, you knew me. You spoke my name and would come to me. Then, when you were older, your illness made you forget many things, including my name. But Steven, now you know that I do not forget."

A flood of memories burst from the damaged portion of Steven's brain. He saw forgotten scenes from inside a church where the golden morning light streamed through tall stained-glass windows: a plate with broken bread and a chalice of wine, an open hymnal across his knees, and faces, a multitude of friendly faces, faces both young and old singing songs of praise and joyful adoration.

The name! Hot tears rolled down Steven's pale cheeks. The people sang songs of praise to Jesus!

"Do not fear, Steven. You were born for this very day. Now, be strong and courageous! For I tell you the truth, my son, you shall be with me in Paradise!"

Steven answered through tears as loudly and as clearly as he could with his rediscovered voice. "Yes, Lord!"

The sound of heavy footsteps outside the dumpster caused Steven to look upward. A dark silhouette of a shaggy head appeared in the rectangular opening.

"Thought I heard something. There's a wino in here looking up at me." The harsh voice echoed dully in the dumpster.

"Leave him," replied a deeper voice behind the silhouette.

"Are you crazy? No way!"

Steven listened calmly, his heart and thoughts at peace.

"All right, pull him out. Someone else will have to decide what we do with him."

Strong hands grabbed Steven's ankles and dragged him through the garbage toward the opening.

Steven closed his eyes. He felt no pain, just a penetrating warmth that spread downward from his head all the way to the ends of his toes. His mind began to click and whir and remember with the enthusiasm of youth. Instead of morning light on stained-glass windows, he saw bright, unfurling clouds of glory. Instead of broken bread and a chalice of wine, he saw Jesus, the Christ, descending from heaven, his arms opened wide....

"Steven, come with me now to Paradise!"

Mark sat on the edge of the bed, the covers draped over his bare legs. He stared out the window at the statue and moonlit park. As exciting as his friend Bud's offer was, he knew that real estate was not his true passion. You couldn't get paid to learn, read and philosophize unless you taught for a living. And that would mean graduate work—and still there were no guarantees. By the time he had secured the position he really wanted, he could be well into his forties!

His toe touched the wooden floor. The chill startled him.

He looked out over the park. The old man with the peculiar shuffle now walked slowly up the steps of the church and into the shadows behind the white columns.

As Mark's eyes moved back to the park, his attention was drawn across 16th Street to the wide, three-story building occupying the entire corner. At the back corner of the building, three men exited from a shadowed driveway spanning the alley.

Mark leaned close to the window. One man, terribly drunk, was supported under each arm by two other men. His head hung forward and the toes of his shoes dragged across the pavement toward a light colored van with two rectangular windows in the back.

One of the men reached up and knocked on the door. It opened immediately. A man with a ponytail appeared in the back of the van. He raised his arms as if to protest, then lowered them and helped lift the drunken man into the back of the van. For almost thirty seconds the van sat silent, then the tailpipe shook and spewed a dense cloud of exhaust into the air. The van pulled away.

Mark laid back and pulled up the covers. He drew a lock of Katie's hair through his fingers. He wondered about their baby, insulated from the worries of the world. This was their miracle child, the baby the doctors said Katie could never conceive.

Mark smiled and released Katie's hair. The furnace kicked on; air hissed softly through the vents in the floor. Within moments he fell fast asleep.

⋖⋗ 3 ⋖⋗

Thursday Morning

A MODESTLY SUCCESFUL ATTORNEY from the District of Columbia selected a golf club for his shot to the green.

The attorney pulled an eight iron from his bag, stepped to the ball and swung away. He watched the ball rise—and hook to the left. It struck a frozen spot near the back edge of the green and skipped down the far slope and out of sight into the trees and tall underbrush at the bottom of the bank near 16th Street.

"That was my lucky ball," he said to the others in the foursome. He pulled his wedge from his bag and looked for another one. The ball box was empty. "Hey Bob, where'd my ball go?"

His business partner pointed off to the right. "Ten feet left of that big stump, near the bank."

Bill sighed and made a bee-line through the rough into the woods. He could see the traffic moving slowly beyond the thin strip of trees. Standing up by the street was a broad-shouldered man wearing a blue jogging suit. The man stood motionless, arms crossed with his back to the traffic, watching him approach.

The attorney stepped cautiously around a large thorn bush near the rotten stump. There was no way he was going to find that ball in there. He poked his wedge into a scraggly bush and then shook his head. "Try a little more to your right," called a voice from the bank above him. He looked up. It was the man in the jogging suit.

The attorney nodded and waved a hand to acknowledge the friendly advice. Less than ten seconds later, he stood up and shot his arm into the air, golf ball in hand.

"Found it!" he yelled.

The others in his foursome laughed and waved.

Bill turned to offer his thanks to the jogger, but to his surprise, the man was nowhere to be seen. He shrugged, took three steps and froze. His voice wavered as he called out.

"Hey guys, you'd better come down here. And make it quick!"

At 8:30 A.M., the smell of cabbage, garlic, and onions browning in a cast iron skillet could be overpowering. But not this morning.

Fletcher Rivers could already taste the main ingredients in his special omelette as he stared into the bathroom mirror. He had not washed his shoulder length, slightly graying hair for three days and a thick growth of gray stubble had filled in around his closely trimmed beard. The stayed-up-way-too-late look around his brown eyes would serve him well today.

He stared into the mirror. Did the face he saw belong to a drug addict, or to a forty-year-old undercover cop? The crack and heroin dealers on the streets of D.C. would be his judge and jury.

Fletcher sniffed the air and grinned—the vegetables were pretty ripe. Walking into the spacious country kitchen, he poured three whipped eggs into a hot skillet.

He stared out the window over the sink. The clear plastic bird feeder that his wife had given him as a birthday present a year and a half ago swayed gently in the wind beneath the eaves.

Susan. Susan and her short, silky brown hair, and wide brown eyes. He remembered how they'd set up the ladder and then waited patiently as Melissa, their five-year-old, excitedly pulled the feeder from its box....

Fletcher squeezed his eyes shut, trying to force his thoughts off of Susan and Melissa.

The noisy sizzle in the skillet broke his reverie. He added the vegetables to the eggs, lifted the corner of the omelette with the spatula and peeked underneath.

Snapping off the burner, he slid the omelette onto the plate, poured himself some coffee, and headed for the round oak table in the breakfast nook.

As he set his plate on the place mat, the phone rang.

Mug in one hand, Fletcher crossed the room to the phone.

"Hello."

"Fletcher—it's Botello."

Fletcher set his mug on the nearby counter. A phone call from homicide, received at home, was more than an irregularity. A phone call meant trouble, significant trouble, likely personal trouble—even if it was a call from a friend and former partner.

"Figured I'd catch you just as you sat down to that special omelette of yours."

A short pause followed and Fletcher grimaced. Botello was generally blunt, direct. This wasn't a good sign.

"Using your crystal ball again, aren't you, Mike? Hey—never mind my breakfast. What's cooking on the streets that my phone rings this early in the morning?"

At the other end of the line, Detective Botello cleared his throat. Fletcher envisioned his friend's smooth black face lined with concern.

"Bad news, real bad. Bagged somebody by Rock Creek Golf Course. A golfer discovered the body near 16th Street." More hesitation, then, "It was Jimmy, your C.I."

Fletcher felt his knees go weak. In the hierarchy of professional tipsters that ran from the low-life snitch to the privileged confidential informant, Jimmy defied classification. He had been unique among all of Fletcher's contacts.

Fletcher steadied himself and edged onto a tall wooden stool. "You've ID'd him?"

Botello sighed. "Jimmy Carter button on his coat tags him. Sorry, Fletcher. His life's in God's hand's now."

Fletcher paused. He did not hear Botello's final comment. An uncharacteristically cold, dead sensation settled in the pit of his stomach. He faced death weekly as an undercover cop. His inability to cope now was unanticipated and disconcerting. Botello's grim announcement pierced his heart as effectively as a 9mm bullet. After shifting the phone to the other ear, he finally found his voice. He hoped that his Christian ex-partner would avoid making any sappy religious euphemisms—not that Mike didn't mean well. He knew there were important questions that he needed to ask.

"What happened?"

"Not really sure yet. Found him with his head against a concrete drain pipe. His left knee was twisted badly—most likely from tumbling down the bank. Probable death due to head injury."

"Why probable?"

Botello cleared his throat again. "I looked him over. The head injury and blood pool along the left side of his stomach tell me different stories. He could've died somewhere else and been moved."

Fletcher sorted the information. "That would help explain how a sixty-year-old man could get all the way from Meridian Hill Park to the Rock Creek Golf Course. This warrants an investigation."

The line went silent for a moment, and then Botello continued. "Fletcher, what we want don't mean diddly. Wonderboy Troy's been assigned to the case. With the big manpower drain Homicide's facing right now, Jimmy's case is gonna fall into the bottom of a deep, dark hole. I figured you deserved to be informed. I didn't want the Red Head opening him up before you heard about it."

Wiping his eyes, Fletcher breathed deeply. "Sorry for hassling you, Mike. You know I appreciate the call."

"Yeah, I guess I do. Maybe you'll be returnin' the favor. Only the good Lord knows."

Fletcher glanced at the clock above the stove. "Listen, I'm on my way downtown. Take care of yourself, man!"

He hung up the phone, flung the soggy napkin into the sink and cursed. Wonderboy Troy—the ebony Adonis of the Washington Metropolitan Police Department, a former college football lineman for USC whose moment in the sun was playing in the Rose Bowl on national television. He made final cuts with the New York Giants as a special team's wedge buster before blowing his knee out and permanently losing his opportunity for fame and fortune. Outwardly the guy looked like chiseled marble, but anyone who knew him could see the chip on his shoulder from losing his opportunity to make it in the NFL.

Fletcher grew steely eyed. In the MPD, however, seniority meant more than size, and Wonderboy was ten years his junior. The true obstacle to getting information on Jimmy's case would come from Troy's associate and rumored lover, Lt. Karla "KC" Daniels. For four months running, Fletcher and KC had successfully avoided each other: no accusations and no shouting matches in Captain Conran's office, and, more importantly, no reprimands.

Fletcher frowned. Those peaceful months were now officially over. Jimmy's death would see to that. Slipping on his jean jacket, he opened the side door to the garage. He paused, knowing that he should take the time to dump the omelette down the garbage disposal and rinse the skillet. He could be gone all day. When he got back the house would stink to high heaven.

Jimmy. Number thirty on the homicide list. Now he was nothing but a nameless statistic.

Grief crowded around his eyes. He ran a hand through his messy hair and stepped into the garage, slamming the door behind him.

Let the kitchen stink! Let the whole house stink! And why not? The city stank. His life stank!

Mark woke. A siren wailed, then abruptly stopped. He blinked his eyes, focusing on the clock. He stuffed his face into the pillow. 8:35 A.M.! Then in a flash he remembered: the baby! He turned his head and stared happily at his wife.

A car door slammed. Horns honked angrily. Katie stirred. Mark threw back the covers and swung his feet to the floor.

Flashing lights pulled his eyes diagonally across 16th Street to his right. He pushed the curtain aside. A police car was parked in front of an ugly three-story building with a gray slate roof and ornate Gothic trim. The building's facade was sand-colored stone, split down the middle by a wide bay window with a row of narrow windows on either side. The front door was under a shadowed archway to the right of the bay. The gray roof and asymmetrical placement of its windows and door gave the building a foreboding appearance.

Two policemen, one black and one white, approached the front door.

Mark rubbed his face. Last night staggering drunks, today, flashing lights and uniformed policemen. He turned around.

Even in the bright morning light, the bedroom looked cozy: the brass bed by the windows, a chest-on-chest and a gold brocade easy chair on either side of the door. Opposite the bed was a stone fireplace with a fancy wrought-iron fireshield. An oval Persian rug was centered in the hardwood floor. The walls were wallpapered.

Katie identified the informal style as Colonial Revival. Mark thought the name fit well, evoking a time when craftsmanship was driven by an artful eye, not economics.

As Mark stepped quietly around the end of the bed, Katie murmured in her sleep. Mark paused and smiled.

Since they had not unpacked, he retrieved the clothes he had worn the day before. At least he could make coffee. Their time was their own for two weeks and he was going to make the most of it. Once Katie was up and breakfast was over, they could begin to size up the house. Last night they had only made a cursory pass of the first and second floors.

Pausing in the hall, Mark glanced up the stairs at the third floor landing and the two closed doors. He scratched his chin, as a well-defined memory rushed out of the past and stole over him.

In all his visits as a young child and after eight years of living in the house, he never set foot in the two rooms on the third floor. Not even once. His grandfather, and then Aunt Clara, had always kept them locked.

Mark buttoned his brown flannel shirt and quietly slipped downstairs to make breakfast.

Across the street, a taxi pulled over to the curb behind the parked police car. An attractive woman in her late twenties wearing a pinstriped business suit swung her long legs from the car, pausing briefly to allow a tall, blond man to jog by. She stepped up to the sidewalk, the breeze flirting with her short brown hair. Her heels clicked on the sidewalk as she walked, briefcase in hand, toward the dreary clinic.

The front door was recessed beneath a high arch. On the wall beside the door, a brass plaque read AFI Women's Health Clinic. She pulled at the door handle, but it was locked.

A black police officer appeared behind the glass door, his deep voice muffled by the glass.

"Sorry, the clinic's closed right now. You'll need to reschedule your appoint—"

The expression on the young woman's face wrinkled into a frown as she pressed her American Family Institute employee card up against the glass in front of the policeman's face. Her warm brown eyes hardened with resolve.

The policeman raised his hands apologetically, then quickly unlocked the door. "Sorry, Ma'am."

"Thank you," she answered brusquely, stepping into the foyer.

The policeman locked the door. "Careful as you go and please don't touch anything. A detective will be here shortly."

Her frown returned as she looked through an open door into the foyer where a magazine rack hung by one screw, its magazines spilled onto the floor.

The policeman held out a hand. "Watch that doorframe. You don't want to get that stuff on your clothes. It might be blood."

She was glad he warned her. The metal doorframe had been brushed with a reddish brown substance which did look like blood.

She continued cautiously into the waiting room. The sofa, chairs, and end tables had all been overturned, and pillows had been tossed around the room. Scattered among the pieces of furniture were brightly colored packets of condoms. Some were open.

Regaining her composure, the woman forced a smile and extended her hand. "I'm so sorry. I've been rude. My name's Michelle Willoughby and I'm here to meet with the insurance agent. The main office wants to get the clinic operational again as quickly as possible."

He shook her hand and smiled. "Officer Garvey. Pleased to meet you. And you don't need to apologize."

Michelle opened her briefcase on the registration desk and removed a pad and pen. "By the way, where's Nurse Rollins?"

"She's with my partner, Officer Clark, in the back," Garvey explained as he opened a door to the left of the registration desk. "She's one riled up lady—blames the pro-lifers who picket the clinic on Saturday mornings."

Pausing in the hall, Michelle took notes. The magazine rack had fared well compared to the torn-down shelves that had held the color-coded patient files.

To the left, the receptionist's chair lay on its side. Items from the desk had been swept into a jumbled pile in the middle of the floor: paper clips, staplers, pens and pencils, the appointment books and cards, notepads, and plastic file trays. A wall clock that had stopped at 12:45 rested on top.

Officer Clark led Michelle to the back. Turning a corner, they passed a photocopy machine that lay upside down on the floor; Michelle made another note. As she did, an angry, middle-age nurse with white hair and wide shoulders stepped from one of the examination rooms with the characteristic sweetness of a Marine drill sergeant.

"Those right-wing scumbags are going to have hell to pay!" The nurse stopped in the middle of her tirade. She eyed Michelle. "You're from the main office. Good. This is only my second week on the job, and I'm going to be too busy to handle getting somebody out here to clean the place up."

Nurse Rollins led Michelle into one of the rooms at the end of the hall. "This is one of three rooms where we conduct our examinations. If the patient traffic is high, we can use it as an overflow room for procedures. Now we'll have to work with only two rooms until they can get this one back in operation."

After her tour, Michelle was back in the reception area. Rollins continued ranting about the picketers. The police officers listened silently.

Michelle tried to change the subject by asking a question. "The clinic opens at noon on Thursdays, correct?"

"What? Oh yes," Rollins answered distractedly. "The doctors make their hospital rounds on Tuesday and Thursday mornings."

"At least we're not faced with a line of women at the door. I'll get the repairs started immediately. Fortunately, there seems to be more of a mess than actual damage."

Rollins shook her head and waved at the doorframe. "A judge ought to force those so-called Christians who did this to come in here and clean it up, including their vile symbolism! Smearing blood over a doorframe—it's disgusting!"

Officer Garvey raised his hand. "Now ma'am, you're jumping to conclusions. First, there's no direct evidence that points to any specific group. And second, we haven't determined for sure that it's blood. When the lab runs their tests we'll know better."

Rollins scowled. "That's crap! I've been around enough blood to know blood when I see it!

"Two weeks from now, right-wingers from all over the country are going to hold their big protest on the Mall. You can bet that this vandalism is connected to the protest. When the reporter from *The Washington Post* gets here, I'll tell him so!"

Michelle started to close her briefcase, then paused. "Did you clear that interview with the main office?" Her voice revealed concern as she snapped the briefcase shut.

"Mr. Peters should be here any minute." Rollins smiled triumphantly.

Michelle was puzzled that AFI's East Coast Director would want to be personally involved in making a statement. "Don't you think that if pro-lifers were actually responsible for the vandalism, they'd avoid blatant violence just two weeks before their march?"

"They're not stupid," Rollins snickered. "They just don't believe that anyone can prove they did it. I've seen them do this in New York. As long as the Supreme Court continues to allow pro-lifers to picket and blockade clinics, they'll continue their social violence. What happened in Wichita's nothing compared to what they're planning—just wait and see."

Nurse Rollins straightened her shoulders and flashed her eyes at Officers Garvey and Clark, then back to Michelle. She slammed her fist on the registration desk.

"This little lady from the Big Apple's not taking it from those Bible-thumping bigots any longer. If it's war they want, then it's war they'll get! The next time anyone comes in here and tries something like this, it'll be over my dead body—or theirs!"

The smell of freshly brewed coffee wafted up the townhouse stairs to the second floor bedroom. Katie smiled and finished smoothing the comforter. As she passed by the window, she pulled back the curtain. Lowering one hand to her abdomen, she eagerly anticipated the morning when she'd feel the baby move for the first time.

Gray and white pigeons pecked and fluttered along the sidewalk in front of the church. A kindly-faced old man with dark black hair and a ragged waistcoat stood near the statue. Traffic was heavy on all three sides of the triangle.

Two short beeps from a horn drew Katie's eyes across the street to a taxi. A pretty young businesswoman carrying a briefcase stepped off the sidewalk and entered the cab. A white-haired nurse standing on the curb turned and headed back toward the drab building. Both looked upset.

Katie left the bedroom. Using the oak rail, she carefully descended the stairs, pausing to run her hand over the handsome wallpaper and study the delicate floral pattern. The beauty helped overcome her aversion of stairs.

She thought about last night. Mark had seemed so alive. Now, with the move and his grandfather's inheritance finally becoming his, she could see the restlessness beginning to disappear. Old fires and motivations were being rekindled.

Katie drew her lips into a thin line and continued down the stairs. She was not going to be an obstacle ever again....

As she reached the bottom, she heard the scrape of a chair from the kitchen. She passed through the combination dining and sitting room, her awe renewed by the beautiful furniture that was now theirs: a mahogany sideboard and drop-leaf table, four spindle-back side chairs, a hundred-year-old silver tea service.

Mark sat in a rocker by the kitchen window overlooking the small backyard, steaming mug in one hand, a paperback book in the other, totally absorbed and unaware of her presence in the doorway. "Good morning." Katie entered the kitchen. "And here I was thinking that I would find you engrossed in one of those ancient-looking books of your grandfather's...."

"Oh hi, babe." Mark slipped his finger into the book and glanced up. "After watching that PBS series with Agatha Christie's Hercule Poirot, I thought I might start the vacation with a little light reading. You know me, there's nothing like a good mystery!"

"I made some coffee. It's decaf, of course."

Katie smiled and poured herself a cup.

Mark returned his attention to his book as Katie sat down, sipped her coffee and looked around. The kitchen wallpaper was the prettiest in the house: climbing green ivy on a white background.

"Everything is so neat and tidy."

Mark closed the book and put it on the window sill. "Aunt Clara was always fastidious—even though she had arthritis the last ten years or so. I can hardly believe that she lived twenty-two years in this house. Never seemed that long.

"I have to admit, this house has real charm. Maybe charm isn't the right word. This house has a lot of character."

"The same goes for this neighborhood," Katie added. "It has a lot of characters. A park, a church, and sirens all night long. A homeless man in the park. Now a police car in front of that gray, dreadful looking building."

Katie pressed the warm mug up against her cheek. "Well, anyway, we're going to enjoy these couple of weeks. All we need to do is unpack a few boxes and grocery shop. We haven't had a real vacation since my accident."

Glancing at the counter, Katie noticed the stack of mail. The sight reminded her of the attorney's note in her purse. She rose from her chair and sorted through the stack. At the bottom was a yellow mailer from Rinaldi & Bell.

"Here's that package Mr. Rinaldi wrote you about."

Mark glanced up. "Mr. Rinaldi? What package?"

She explained about the letter she'd forgotten to show him. The executors had overlooked a package at the settlement of his grandfather's estate.

Mark carefully opened the mailer and removed the contents.

"What do we have here? A note and a large sealed envelope that looks pretty old." Mark's eyes darted across the page. "Like you said, the clerk who prepared our estate package overlooked a letter Aunt Clara wanted me to receive upon her death. That's odd."

He opened the envelope. He removed and unfolded three sheets of pink writing paper.

"It's from Aunt Clara—written almost twenty-one and a half years ago—October 15, 1971."

Katie leaned forward. "Don't you dare read it to yourself!"

Mark grinned and sat back in the rocker.

"Dearest Nephew Mark, When you read this letter, your grandfather Kyle and I will both have passed on to be with the Lord. I must place the burden of this letter squarely on your grandfather. What you will shortly read are his final requests concerning a disposition detailed to me just prior to his death in 1971. Your grandfather, bedridden for six days with a severe bout of influenza and too weak to write..."

Mark raised his eyebrows. "I can't make out the next word. Here, look." He turned the letter toward Katie. She squinted. "I think it reads 'charged.'"

He nodded.

"... charged me before God that I would keep this disposition from you until the day the estate became yours, or your eighteenth birthday, whichever came first."

Mark halted a second time. He looked up at Katie and frowned. "I guess the transfer didn't work out quite the way he planned it. I turned eighteen almost thirteen years ago."

He sighed and returned his attention to the second sheet.

"Mark David MacDonald is a good name belonging to a good man, a MacDonald worthy to receive my estate. James Thomas MacDonald, your father, went home to our Lord Jesus Christ shortly after your fifth birthday, without having possessed any real measure of our MacDonald legacy. I, too, now draw near the day when I will shed this earthly dwelling, and I have become painfully mindful that I have left you as unaware of the MacDonald bloodline as your father was.

"I could speak of other colorful MacDonalds who helped pioneer this nation, but instead I will begin with Eli, a faithful man of God, who died in 1856. Eli served among the Indians at Shawnee Mission, Kansas. Eli had two sons. The eldest, my grandfather John Ezra, was a good man who, like Eli, remained faithful to the Lord all of his days.

"However, it is the name and legacy of Eli's second son, Samuel Mark, that I must reveal.

"At last I have told you! Perhaps, in that day when we come face to face again on heaven's streets of gold, you will forgive me for withholding Sam's name from your father and from you. Perhaps now, your forgiveness can come sooner, for in giving you his name, I am also giving you the story of the MacDonald bloodline, a two-fold cord of good and evil.

"Aunt Clara will provide you with instructions regarding my great uncle's two 'knapsacks from the war,' as he was so fixed in calling them. By God's providence, the knapsacks survived the 1917 fire and no longer possess the heavy scent of smoke.

"I have done what I must do. I have passed on our legacy. Forgive your Grandpa Kyle, as I hope you so fondly will always remember my name."

Mark looked up, his face troubled. "Grandpa Kyle—"

His voice broke. He rose and stood by the window. He reread each letter. "I don't know what to make of this. A legacy? A cord of good and evil? And where are the instructions about the knapsacks—or whatever he called them? This is crazy!"

Katie pushed herself from the chair, took the letter from Mark and read it. "I guess you'll just have to drop your book and start working on a real mystery. Let's starting looking for the knapsacks. Maybe Aunt Clara lost the instructions, or maybe the attorneys still have them. Twenty-two years is a long time. Obviously things got a little mixed up."

She grabbed his hand and placed it on her stomach. "Just imagine! One day you'll tell your children and grandchildren about the mystery your grandfather left you to solve."

Mark slowly turned his head until their eyes met.

He leaned back against the window sill, breathed deeply and crossed his arms. He took the letters from Katie. He studied the pages a third time.

He looked up abruptly, his eyes flashing. Had Grandpa Kyle and Aunt Clara stored the knapsacks upstairs in one of the locked rooms on the third floor where he had never been allowed to explore?

Staring up at the ceiling as if he could see straight through it, a child-like grin crept onto his face.

Katie laughed nervously. "What are you thinking?"

Mark's grin widened into a smile. "Maybe we won't need any instructions after all!"

4

Late Thursday Morning

MARK SAT ON A STURDY, but narrow wooden box with a scabbard across his knees. He wiped his hands on a towel. Katie sat opposite him on a wobbly metal chair.

Against the walls were clothing racks and dozens of old suits, shirts, pants, blouses, and dresses—fashions spanning an entire century. Numerous boxes of old shoes, boots, and hats were stacked against the wall beneath the window. The closet held more cardboard boxes. Only the center of the room was clear of old furniture and household furnishings.

Mark stood up and carefully drew the three-foot-long sword from the scabbard. He smiled and fingered the blade, then slashed the air in front of him. "Reminds me of a cavalry sword. Wonder where Grandpa picked it up?"

Katie folded her arms and grinned. "Well, at least you found something interesting."

"Yeah, I guess," Mark said. "I really thought the knapsacks would be up here. These rooms were always locked and off-limits."

They stepped from the bedroom across the short hall. Mark returned the sword to its scabbard.

The other third-floor room turned out to be a study, facing the front of the house like their bedroom below, with a fireplace and mantle on the left side. Mounted above the mantle was what looked like an empty gun rack. A six-foot trestle table with lamps at each end stood beneath the windows.

Glowing swirls of diffused sunlight drew Mark's and Katie's eyes to a slant-front bureau desk on the right wall. The walnut desk sat atop a three-drawer chest with brass batwing pulls. The desk's open interior revealed tiered drawers, pigeonholes, and a six-inch-tall central locker. An old fountain pen and a dry ink well stood in one corner. By the desk was a leather upholstered chair.

"Do you want to check the cellar again?" Katie asked.

"There's nothing there but canning jars and old pots." Mark sat down and leaned the scabbard against the wall. He opened one of the small desk drawers and fingered a stack of yellowed receipts.

Katie ran her hand slowly over the top of the desk. "Most of the furniture in this house dates around the turn of the century. This desk is older. No nails. Reminds me of the chancellor's desk at William and Mary from the 1700s."

Mark stared. "No way! Before George Washington?"

"I think so."

"Well, now we've got a sword and an old desk, just no knapsacks," Mark frowned.

Katie rubbed Mark's shoulders. "I'll call the attorneys. If they misplaced a letter, maybe they misplaced the knapsacks, too."

"Sounds like a long shot."

Katie wrapped her arms around his shoulders and squeezed.

Mark smiled as she left the room and headed down the steps. He turned his attention to the mostly empty desk.

The top drawers and pigeonholes contained a few pieces of memorabilia: four Washington Redskins ticket stubs from the 1954 championship game with the New York Giants, receipts from household repairs, local tailors, and a shoe repair shop.

The bottom drawer held an old Bible and a thin bundle of envelopes tied with string. Glancing at the envelopes revealed that the letters had been written by Kyle and addressed to Sam, in Manassas, Virginia. He removed the Bible and the letters.

The Bible was cracked and faded, the pages heavily worn. He opened it to the first page: The Revised Standard Version, First Edition.

His eyes darted down the page to the copyright. 1884!

He looked at the date again and noticed an ink stain showing through from the other side. He turned the page and found a neat handwritten inscription.

To my great uncle, Sam. Your faith and courage inspire me. I hope you enjoy this new translation of the Bible as much as I do. Always, with deepest affection, your nephew, Kyle.

September 15, 1884.

Mark calculated rapidly. Kyle was born in 1870, so he'd been fourteen years old when he gave the Bible to his great uncle.

Mark glanced briefly at each of the five letters. They had all been written between February of 1892 and January of 1893, four by Kyle and one by his wife, Mary. All Mark remembered about his grandmother was that she died one day shy of their twenty-fifth wedding anniversary in 1917.

A bell rang in Mark's memory. He had seen a reference to the year 1917 sometime recently? But where?

Mark pulled his grandfather's deposition from his shirt pocket and opened it. Yes—there it was—there'd been a fire in 1917. Did the fire have anything to do with his grandmother's death? His grandfather had never talked about it if it did.

He shrugged and read the other letters. It had taken Kyle all summer and fall to convince Sam to move from Manassas and live with them.

The room darkened suddenly. Mark looked out the window. The sun had slipped behind low, gray clouds creeping in from the west.

Mark closed his eyes. Sam had lived in Manassas, then here, in this very house! For how long? A week? A month? A year or more? Who was Sam MacDonald? Why had Kyle been so secretive about his life?

Mark opened his eyes and shook his head. He was sure there were answers to all of these questions, but to find the answers, he had to find the knapsacks! And he and Katie had checked every closet and every box big enough to hold two canvas knapsacks!

Knapsacks from the war?

Sunlight breaking through the windowpane warmed his bare forearm as details from his Civil War studies percolated through his thoughts. Maybe he and Katie had looked for the wrong thing. Civil War knapsacks—if they were medical knapsacks—were actually canvas covered...

Mark spun from the window and found Katie standing in the doorway with a saucer of cookies in her hands. "The attorneys don't have any more information. I didn't want to return empty-handed."

Mark smiled and grabbed a cookie, kissed her on the cheek, then stormed from the room, pulling her in tow. He crossed the hall to the back bedroom and halted abruptly in the doorway.

Katie ran into Mark's elbow. Cookies tumbled from the saucer, four of them shattering instantly at her feet. One, however, rolled lazily into the room, halting beside a sturdy-looking wooden box about a foot-and-a-half tall, a foot wide and eight inches deep—the same box on which Mark had sat twenty minutes earlier.

Mark slipped his arm around Katie's shoulder. "I think I may have solved our mystery."

Mark centered the wooden box in the middle of the table. The brass latch on the front of the box was tightly sealed with wire. On each end were two screw holes where handles had once been.

Mark leaned over the table, holding a pair of needle nose pliers. "Well, here goes nothing!"

"I don't know what I will do with you if there's something in there other than what you expect," Katie said wryly.

Mark released the loose end of the wire and looked up for a second, a wrinkle creasing his forehead. "Now that's an interesting thought. What do I expect to find? Diaries? Papers? A book?"

Katie laughed. "I'll finish unpacking then go to the store. I've already written you off for a couple days—and don't fake how you want to help! I know how much you love this kind of thing."

Mark turned and raised his eyebrows. "I don't want you lifting groceries by yourself now that you're pregnant."

"If I need help, you'll be the first to know," Katie replied determinedly. "You organize Sam's stuff—I'll organize the kitchen. At dinner you can fill me in."

Mark smiled and watched her leave the study.

There was no reason to delay further. His hands trembled as he reached for the latch.

"This is crazy," he said softly to himself. "I'm nervous about opening a box!"

The lid swung upward and his nervousness evaporated. Tightly organized and packed with leather-bound journals, envelopes and magazines, the box was crammed full—except for one open slot where a plain white envelope was pressed into the corner.

Mark's eyes shifted from the slot and the envelope to an old Bible nestled neatly in the center. He carefully removed it.

The old King James Bible's black leather cover was faded and heavily cracked with age, its pages worn smooth and thin. Mark slowly opened the leather cover into which a name and a date had been tooled.

Sam MacDonald, April 15, 1856.

Mark whistled. He placed the open Bible on the table and sat down. For a few minutes he did nothing but stare out the window.

He mused about the study, the handsome old desk and chair, and then about Grandpa Kyle's crazy message through Aunt Clara and the single thread that ran maddeningly through them all.

The mystery of a man called Sam.

5

Thursday Afternoon

M ICHELLE GALANCED UP as her assistant placed a thick file folder on the corner of her mahogany desk. Julie, the sharp, twenty-one-year-old from Account Temps had proved an able replacement for a junior accountant who was in her second week of maternity leave. She saw a lot of herself in the enterprising college graduate. Julie was not the prototypical 90s woman AFI liked to hire—a well-versed feminist and pro-choice advocate. Julie had come from a sheltered rural town in southwestern Virginia to attend nearby George Mason University and to land a job in the big city. Having someone else in the office with traditional values was refreshing.

"Thanks, Julie. By the way, you're doing a great job."

Beaming, the young blonde turned to leave the office.

Michelle glanced back to the computer monitor. "Could you please close the door on your way out?"

Julie glanced over her shoulder and smiled. "By the way, I'm heading out to lunch. My boyfriend called."

"Sounds fine."

As the door closed, Michelle lifted the cumbersome folder and placed it in the middle of the desk. She turned back to the monitor and reviewed her spreadsheet on the Crest Road clinic. She picked up her mug of tea and cupped it tightly in her hands.

Michelle studied the figures for the third time. She did not like what she saw. The numbers in the fixed asset ledger supported the hypothesis she had formed in the taxi on her way back. All the evidence pointed to an inside job. Had AFI vandalized AFI?

Her phone buzzed: line number two, an internal call. The smoker's cough from the other end of the line drew a sigh from Michelle. "Yes, Carol, what can I do for you?"

"Your carpenters failed to show up and they've got a back-log of girls."

Girls. Carol's use of the word made Michelle frown sharply. "I'll find out what happened and notify the clinic."

Another cough. "Good. That Rollins woman's a real bear. Explain the delay. I want this mess totally cleaned up by the time I get back from my house-hunting trip next week. My plane leaves in less than two hours and I don't want to be bothered by her again."

"Absolutely," Michelle replied. "Call before you leave. Bye."

Michelle punched an outside line and placed a local call. The phone rang four times before someone answered.

"Hello." The man sounded winded.

"Dan, I'm sorry. Did I catch you at a bad time?"

"Michelle, is that you? Hey, it's really great to hear from you! Don't mind my huffing, I just got in from a jog. What's up?"

"Something's come up." Michelle lowered her voice. "It could mean trouble for Kent and our picketers at the Crest Road clinic."

Dan was silent for a few seconds. "How about lunch. I can be there by one? Will that work for you?"

Michelle sighed. "Thanks, Dan."

"Don't thank me, Michelle—you're the one who deserves the thanks! See you there, kiddo."

Michelle hung up the phone. She opened the thick file folder in the center of her desk.

AFI vandalizing AFI. The prospects were promising!

Closing the door behind him, Detective Fletcher Rivers stepped from the examination room where Jimmy's cold, naked body lay beneath a white sheet, peaceful and untroubled.

Fletcher folded his jacket neatly over his arm and pressed his back against the cool wall tiles. He massaged his closed eyes with his fingertips, and then recrossed his arms. He drew a deep breath, exhaled slowly and repeated the action until he felt control return to his arms and legs.

He had just committed a crime.

Searching through Jimmy's clothes in a basket by the examination table, he discovered a tiny but crucial piece of evidence that had been overlooked in Jimmy's initial once-over by Botello. Using tweezers from the medical chest on a nearby counter, Fletcher had removed the evidence from Jimmy's sock, dropped it in a plastic vial—and walked out with it.

And he wasn't sure why!

His hand moved toward the thumb-sized plastic vial hidden in his jacket pocket. The vial felt like it would burn a hole right through the cloth and into his heart. He resisted and forced his hand down into a pant's pocket instead.

A door directly opposite the examination room opened abruptly. The coroner stepped halfway into the hall, and then paused and spoke quietly to someone still in the room.

Fletcher pushed himself from the wall. An irrational fear of being discoved swept over him, the way it occasionally would in the middle of a drug bust or when he thought his cover had been blown.

The coroner closed the door and faced Fletcher. Bill Matthews was in his early fifties, thin as a reed with a short red flattop. Fletcher knew that in his twenty-four years as Coroner, Matthews had seen it all—forensically speaking.

"So, did you get to see your C.I.?" The tone of Matthews' question showed genuine concern.

Fletcher nodded and glanced down at his feet, searching for words. He kept his voice low. "Yes I did. I think somebody stuck Jimmy in a car trunk and then rolled him down that bank by the golf course. But even if you can show probable cause to keep the case active, Wonderboy's been assigned to the case. He won't bust his butt for someone like Jimmy."

Looking up, Fletcher avoided Matthew's gaze. "So, I was hoping that you might copy the results of your autopsy for me, as a favor. Jimmy was—let's just say, special—not to anyone else, but to me."

Matthews frowned. "Pursuing it on the side, huh? You like to put me on the spot, don't you?"

"You're an institution. What would they do, slap your hand?"

"All right, but stay low," Matthews replied reluctantly. "I don't want Conran the Barbarian blasting me about this."

Fletcher stared at the ceiling and thought about how angry Captain Conran could get.

Matthews frowned again. "That's what I'm afraid of—now get out of here before someone sees you hanging around my office!"

Fletcher's stomach flip-flopped uncomfortably as Matthews entered the examination room. The vivid image of the vial's contents hidden in his coat pocket refused to fade.

What a fool he was for stealing evidence from the examination room! Why did he always have to be so complusive? Shifting his coat over his arm, he slipped his hand into the pocket and wrapped his hand around the vial.

A metal trash receptacle stood nearby. He crossed the hall, pushed open the small swinging door and calmly dropped the plastic vial inside.

Heading toward the pair of shiny elevator doors at the end of the hall, Fletcher breathed easier now. Even though he couldn't—wouldn't—undo his mistake, at least he wouldn't compound his error by keeping it. Between seven and eight that evening the cleaning crews would permanently correct his gross blunder.

As he approached the elevators, the doors swished open. Two women stepped out, dressed down for the street. They were both officers from the Morals Division. Karen, a California, silky-haired blonde, said hello as she passed by. Fletcher nodded, but his thoughts were focused on the angry woman blocking his path to the elevator.

Lt. "KC" Daniels' oval, mahogany face was stiff and her normally full lips were drawn into a severe line. She folded her muscular arms sternly across her chest. Her avid devotion to weight lifting made her five-foot-eleven broad-shouldered frame and perpetual glare even more imposing. No corn rows today; her hair was simply pulled back. Her thick eyebrows arched upwards sharply.

"What are you doing down here, Fletcher? Did you decide to drop in for a friendly chat with one of the Red Head's cadavers?"

"Back off, KC!" Fletcher exploded. How quickly old wounds were reopened! KC had been involved in all three of Fletcher's official reprimands, hindering his advancement and once, jeopardizing his career. She would never forgive him for the bust that sent her younger brother to prison with a five-year sentence. Never mind that Jamal had been guilty—never mind that he was up for early parole.

She flashed a big white smile. "Let me tell you who's going to back off. I'm down here doin' you a favor, tryin' to keep you straight. The one thing you don't need is another reprimand."

Fletcher stared fiercely into her dark eyes.

Her smile widened. "You'll stay completely out of Troy's case. The alternative is a memo to Captain Conran about your incorrigible tendency to impede homicide investigations that don't involve you!"

Fletcher fought back the words that burned like coals on the tip of his tongue. His hands tightened uncontrollably into fists.

KC laughed in his face. "Come on, turkey, say something, do something! Deck me—just like you slugged my partner two years ago! Go ahead and knock out my pearly whites while you're at it!"

Fletcher's arm shot out from beneath his jacket with lightning speed, then pulled sharply back in a perfectly harmless motion. Surprised, KC flinched. As she did, he slipped around her and pounded the elevator button. The elevator issued a soft tone and the door on the right opened. He stepped into the empty elevator and smacked the lobby button with the side of his fist.

As the doors started to close, KC spun around, aimed a forefinger straight between his eyes, thumb raised. She fired two imaginary rounds in swift succession.

"Pow! Pow! Gotcha, Fletcher!"

Mercifully, the doors slid shut.

By 1:00 the line at Wendy's was subsiding. Michelle stepped from the counter with her salad and drink. Off in a corner on the second level, she saw a slightly balding man with light brown hair. She smiled. As she approached the table, he looked up.

"I'd recognize the sound of that determined step anywhere." Dan rose part way from his seat as Michelle slid into her seat across from him. Dan was in his late thirties, of average height and build with a neatly trimmed beard. He wore a light green ski sweater and jeans. He had already eaten.

"So, what brings my favorite Christian mole out of her lair within the American Family Institute?"

Michelle grimaced. "Christian mole! I'll never get used to hearing you call me that."

It was Dan's turn to smile. "Whatever the term, it can't obscure the fact you're a feigned radical feminist accountant by day and a pro-lifer by night and weekends."

"A stranger in a strange land," Michelle said with a fierce grin. "I bite my tongue each and every day, and I'm tired of tasting blood. Soon, it'll be their turn."

"So what's up?" Dan asked, unfolding his hands. "You mentioned the Crest Road Clinic and Kent."

Michelle drizzled dressing over her salad. "The clinic was vandalized last night—shelves yanked from the walls and files dumped on the floor—but the only real damage was to a four-year-old copier. Here's the funny thing—early last week the clinic put in a requisition for a new copier."

"An inside job?" Dan asked.

"AFI's pulled this trick a half-dozen times since they started franchising clinics six years ago, but nobody's been able to prove it. I've been worried ever since Planned Parenthood started distancing themselves from AFI."

Michelle sipped her Diet Coke. "With Carol out, I'll be Acting Director and overseeing the casework. It's great for the newspaper exposé and book I'm working on, but bad news for our church. AFI's never forgotten how you were on the evening news complaining that they used their dumpsters to dispose of aborted babies."

Dan's eyes suddenly lit up. "Makes sense. The March for Life's just two weeks away. The press gets excited and we get a black eye for something we didn't do."

"Exactly. And here's another twist." Michelle explained how the perpetrators tried to imitate the Passover symbology by painting animal blood around the door. "But their analogy breaks down—the blood was to protect, not destroy. So, when you put it all together:

no substantial material damage, the timing, and the misused symbology—the finger points back at AFI. Now that they've helped elect a pro-choice president, they're going for our throats. The word's out how they're going to push the Freedom of Choice Act through Congress. And if they can keep the public from focusing on details of the legislation, all the better."

Dan nodded. "And this will be the first time we've marched in front of a pro-abortion White House in twelve years."

Michelle nodded. "The public is polarizing—anyway, that's how the press is painting the picture. By the way, did you find out about AFI's permits for their counter rallies, specifically the one they've got planned that weekend before the march?"

"I got a call from the District Building right after I spoke with you. Supposedly, the city issued the permits on a restricted attendance of fifty thousand. But my contact says don't be surprised if they draw a quarter-million. It may be the first time *The Washington Post* will downsize headcount for a pro-abortion rally."

Michelle frowned. "Like I said, I don't like the way this thing's developing. The town's already a pressure cooker."

Dan tapped Michelle on the arm. "Changing the subject for a moment, you said you're Acting Director."

Michelle smiled nervously. "Carol made it official and gave four weeks' notice. She's off house-hunting in the Midwest. I'm still the front runner for the position. To be perfectly honest, I can hardly control myself. I'll have access to every financial transaction, past and present, from AFI Eastern district. For two-and-a-half years I've been working for this. Give me six months as Director and my friend at the *Times* and I will have what we need to win a Pulitzer."

Her smile faded. "This vandalism's really thrown a hitch in my plan. I can't let AFI get away with it, but on the other hand, I'm not going to blow my cover, not when I'm this close."

Dan turned his head and stared for a few moments out the plate glass window overlooking Georgia Avenue. "Have you considered the police's Anonymous Tips Hotline?"

Michelle pushed her empty plate to the side. "Not really."

"It might be an avenue," Dan suggested. "It's anonymous so people can squeal on their friends and neighbors without fear of identification or reprisal."

Michelle chuckled. "I'll think about it, OK?"

Dan continued, his voice softening. "Each morning Joyce and I pray that your heart will stay clean before the Lord. You know how much I want to see AFI's days come to an end. But the price you're paying—sometimes I wonder if it's worth it. Make sure you stay in the center of the Lord's will. Don't get too far out of balance."

Clenching her fists, Michelle leaned forward. "Balance? Dan, we've had this conversation before. The churches are losing the battle because we're always so concerned about staying in balance! AFI's not balanced! The nurse at the clinic this morning isn't balanced! Our opposition is far more dedicated to their beliefs than we are. Tell my sister and thousands of others like her about balance."

Michelle fought to keep her frustration in check. "You know I can't sit back and wait for AFI to blow it. People need to know the truth and understand what AFI's really doing. My work can make a difference and I'm not going to put it in jeopardy."

Dan did not lower his gaze. "You know I appreciate your activism. Women deserve to know how these clinics exploit them, especially our teenagers, but they need more than knowledge, Michelle. They need someone to connect with them right where they are. An exposé of AFI isn't going to alleviate their hurting."

Dan paused and smiled sympathetically. "It hasn't alleviated yours."

Michelle felt her pulse jump, but she folded her hands in front of her and held back. Dan was one of a handful of people in the church who supported her unequivocally. And he was sincere.

Dan turned sideways in his seat and spoke quietly. "Just remember, Joyce and I are always available."

Michelle broke eye contact and glanced at her watch. "Well, my time's up for today, anyway. A prospective director's got to show some ability to regulate her time."

"The Lord be with you, Michelle."

She returned a thin smile and picked up her tray.

"I'll take that for you," Dan offered. "You know how we pastors are paid to clean up other people's messes."

She could not hold back a laugh. "Bye, Dan. I'm a big girl—I can handle my own mess."

She turned and headed for the door.

Mark leaned over the desk. The writing on the back of the receipt was faint. The pensive scribblings were distinctly unnerving.

Unde malum—the phrase still haunts me after forty years. As I rub my hand over this antique desk, I am reminded of a period of history which has slipped far into the past. No one lives today who witnessed the poignant, private dramas which may have been recorded upon this desk's handsome surface. Why are we so adept at passing our possessions from generation to generation, and yet so unfaithful to learn from the trials and sufferings of those who passed into death before we were ever thrust from our mothers' wombs?

Is this not the testimony of the gleaming, sin-stained blade of my grandfather's Long Knife? Is this not the Devil's fiendish, eternal scheme to scar God's creation with a bloodline fashioned from human life?

Does not God require that which is past?

At the bottom of the note was a date: January 21, 1893.

Mark reread the words on the aged receipt. The note struck a chord of apprehension. His eyes surveyed the piles and stacks positioned around the now empty wooden box: the books, the newspaper articles, the diaries, the maps and correspondence. The items were arranged chronologically—twelve years worth of observations and reflections of a man who lived through one of the most trying times in the history of the nation, the Civil War.

What had happened from 1853 to 1865 that caused Sam, some forty years later, to write this ominous note? And what did the ominous phrase *unde malum* mean?

Mark carefully folded the note and put it in his shirt pocket.

Sam's words. He stared at the neatly arranged stacks and piles of history witnessed by Sam's eyes, heard with Sam's ears, and sifted and sorted through Sam's mind.

The thought brought a smile to his face. He remembered when Katie found him in the kitchen reading Hercule Poirot. Well, Katie was right—thanks to Grandpa Kyle, he had a real-life mystery to solve.

Mark turned his attention to a journal lying all by itself at the left end of the table. He would start at the beginning. He would walk with Sam, step by step, thought by thought, day by day, just as Sam himself made the journey almost four decades before the note on the back of the receipt had been written.

He picked up the diary dated 1856 and cradled it in his lap. He scratched his head, took a deep breath and began to read.

6

Late Thursday Afternoon

27 April 1856, 4:35 P.M.
Washington City, Sheppard's Boarding House

Take Up the Pen

I sit in the windowseat of my small, second story boardinghouse room overlooking Pennsylvania Avenue, one block west of the White House. A new journal is propped against my knee and open to the first, empty page. Tucked beneath the journal are three, unopened telegrams from Kansas.

Be still, O my soul. Trust in God.

I shall not open the telegrams yet. First, I must record my account of the Lord's recent work in my life.

Like my heart, winter has turned to spring and the breath of God is everywhere. Washington evenings are cool and pleasant to both soul and body. Below my window the street bustles with horses, carriages, and wagons. Fine ladies dressed in hoop skirts and bonnets parade with their gentlemen, showing off the latest fashions; shopkeepers have opened their doors to the spring breezes and new customers; children play kick-the-can in the grassy field across Pennsylvania Avenue; bright flowers bloom everywhere; hope is alive.

I have a clear view of the unfinished monument to President Washington. I see the seemingly ill-fated structure as a symbol of our nation's unfinished dreams. Are we not like men who began to build but did not count the cost? Is this not a work of the flesh, rather than the will of God?

Like the unfinished monument, I, too, am incomplete. For two and a half years, bitterness hardened my heart, quenched my faith and bridled my joy. I cannot recount those years. They are lost, except for the lessons You have taught me, Lord, from my own failures, from my own sin, and from Victoria's innocent blood.

Ah! At last I have written her sweet name.

But the pen must wait. Mrs. Sheppard has rung the dinner bell. Latecomers are always sent to eat in her kitchen. I must hurry.

Words of Wisdom

The clock in the hall chimes 7:00 P.M. I have returned from a fine dinner of beef stew, greens and drop biscuits prepared by Mrs. Sheppard. Several new faces were present, and an old one, Toby Sikes, a free Negro, was there, too. He keeps a room down the hall from me. He purchased his freedom four years ago and is presently employed by the wagoneer who once owned him. With my help, Toby has taught himself to read. He is a fast learner and is now well-versed in a variety of topics. We discussed the current political situation. Old party lines are breaking down, the issues have become muddled and no one sees clearly anymore. But like always, the unavoidable subject of slavery hung like a plumbline through the middle of every conversation. Indeed, it is a peculiar, addicting sin.

Now to the task at hand. I recall my grandmother's words: "If you forget the lessons of life, you will repeat them; if you forget the blessings of the Lord, you will forget Him." I will record the lessons that You have taught me from both the failures and the blessings which You bestowed upon me.

August, 1853

My thoughts lead me back to Charleston almost three years ago. I kissed Victoria goodbye that hot, South Carolina morning. My work at the *Charleston Observer* stretched into the early afternoon. After finishing my weekly article for the newspaper, I bid our Managing Editor, Mr. Pitkins, good day.

The sun was still high in the sky as I rode my chestnut steed up a grassy slope bordering the northern end of our property. As I crested the hilltop, I noticed the wheels of an upturned wagon in the gully beside our private road.

I reined in my horse harshly. Was that Victoria's wagon in the ravine?

I kicked my heels, my heart pounding in my chest. Was that her bonnet lying in grass? A desperate prayer for God's mercy exploded from my mouth.

I leapt from my steed at the edge of the ravine.

At the bottom of the hill, beside the slow moving creek, I spotted Victoria. Her slender legs were trapped beneath the upturned wagon. A pool of blood had already dried and darkened on the wide sheet of gray rock beneath her shoulders and head. Her filly lay crumpled and still in the stream beyond the wagon.

I stumbled down the bank to her side. "Victoria! Victoria!" I screamed, pushing the wagon off her broken and bloody legs and into the creek.

She did not respond. Her blue satin dress was torn at the sleeve, her dark hair disheveled. Her gentle brown eyes stared blankly into the sun.

I placed my ear to her motionless chest.

My Victoria was dead.

It was not an accident as so many claimed it to be. Victoria was an excellent driver, always cautious. She worked all of her horses with a trained hand. No, it was premeditated murder, retaliation for my outspoken stance against slavery and for my wife's devotion to me!

A young slave claimed that he had seen Seth Beaumont, a critic of abolition, riding with an unidentified man across our property that very morning. Of all our detractors, Beaumont had been the most vocal, and the most hot-headed, prone to indulgence, much like his father and grandfather.

Later that day, I barged into Beaumont's tannery, wild with anger, bearing a loaded pistol. Beaumont's two brawny sons restrained me and seized the gun. Beaumont, whose standing on the city council was influential, took advantage of the situation. He threatened to have me jailed unless I left Charleston for good. His only concession was to grant me time to bury Victoria in her family plot overlooking Charleston harbor.

My employer, Mr. Pitkins, offered me an opportunity to become the Observer's Washington correspondent. With elections and slavery issues becoming so crucial, the Observer needed its own source for news in the capital city. I packed my personal belongings and left immediately.

In Washington City, I became a slave to bitterness and grief. Resentment was my daily companion, whispering potent lies in my ear. Why Victoria? The question haunted me. But in my heart I knew. It was I who had cut against the grain of Charleston society; it was I who urged her to sign the emancipation papers for Jethro and Liza, her kindhearted slaves. Victoria's family had owned slaves for several generations. She wanted to please me, even if it meant hurting her parents and friends. She rebelled against all they believed in; she rejected Charleston society and culture. I had not considered the cost to her.

Her untimely death led me down a path of deep depression, so unlike my God-given nature. I had always been level-headed, optimistic, hopeful. But in reality I was naive, believing that I could change the minds of Charleston's elite. But, I had deceived myself. I had wanted to change the world, to right the wrongs of slavery and bring light to those who walked in the darkness of pride and greed. But God did not answer my prayers. I almost convinced myself that sin had left this human race in such terrible disrepair that even God himself could not fix it. I was wrong! And I almost lost my faith in God. I had taken a stand for Truth! Why had He not protected my precious wife? How could He have let this happen? I rejected His grace and embraced my new companions, Bitterness and Resentment. I surrendered fully to my grief. I would not release Victoria to Him and so my longings for her ached with me these three years.

What good are the works of the flesh? They bring only heartache and pain.

It's been over two years since I moved to Washington City. It was good for me. I made new friends and accepted new challenges. But still, I could not face my bitterness.

Road to Renewal

O, how good God is! He knew exactly what I needed and extended His grace to me. Last December I received a letter from my long-time friend, John Kline, an elder and respected leader in the Church of the Brethren. He is sensitive to the Holy Spirit and asked me to come with him on his late winter circuit through the Shenandoah Valley. John knew of my situation, how I had not found God's grace and how my heart groaned daily to be free from the tormenting memory of my murdered Victoria.

I telegraphed Mr. Pitkins, requesting a temporary leave of absence. Mr. Pitkins, a gentleman and a friend, granted my request. I told no one of my intentions, excepting Mrs. Sheppard, to whom I advanced three months rent to keep my second floor room.

In early February, I met up with John on the road, a man forever "on the stretch for God." Silhouetted on horseback by a setting sun, his riding cloak hung from his square shoulders and covered all but his upper calves and boots. A broad-rimmed hat hung low and shadowed his face. An open Bible lay across one of his hands. At first glance, John is an imposing figure, but a closer look reveals a humble countenance and ever-compassionate eyes.

For the next ten days, John and I rode south through the Shenandoah Valley. John warned me about my rebel heart, how I had chosen not to relinquish Victoria. He told me that the Devil comes to men in many forms and ways, to delude and then to destroy. First they come as one or two, but then as legion. The

Devil learns to know every place of vulnerability. To the brother who is fond of ardent spirits, he comes behind the deceitful smile of the rumseller. To the brother who is covetous, he comes behind the nefarious grin of the slave auctioneer.

We crossed the mountain west of Harrisonburg and proceeded north along the Potomac River to Fort Seybert and Bethel Church. Here stood the center of John's deepest burden and ministry. His parish sat between the road and the river. The welcome sign posted on a tree along the entrance road read: "Whosoever cometh unto me I will in no wise cast out." John 6:37. New hope arose in my heart.

We did not stop at the church but continued northward, with the flow of the river, along the road which led deeper into the valley. Snow had been falling intermittently for several days. The valley was tranquil, unperturbed by the growing political unrest in nearby Washington and throughout the nation. Anyone would feel peaceful here in this late winter Eden, but especially one who had an appointment with God.

The Cowger Homestead

John arranged my stay with the Cowger family. They made their home about three miles from the Bethel Church. We forded the Potomac three times, tacking from bank to bank until we reached their home. The Cowgers, some of John's most faithful parishioners, were beginning another spring planting. Matthew, his two sons, and Bones, their old Negro, had a new field to clear. John told Matthew that he had found a willing helper and insisted we would share the slave quarters with Bones. The Cowgers strongly protested but John would not hear it, and that was that.

Bones' quarters were very modest. He had four walls and a roof over a plank floor, two narrow beds, two Shaker chairs, a small table, and a black iron stove. Bones insisted that he would not have friends of his master sitting on the floor, and so the chairs became ours. As we bedded down for the night, both Bones and I tried to give John one of the beds. But John folded his arms across his barrel chest, insisting that he would sleep on the floor. Besides, he added, he would be leaving in the morning.

God is wise to store His glory in different vessels. When John rode away the following dawn, he knew that I had lessons to learn in that humble room from a humble servant of God.

Bones

The weeks progressed with long days of hard labor in the fields, pleasant evenings of songs and prayers in the main house with the

Cowgers and Bones, and quiet walks along the valley road. Day by day I came to a clearer realization that it was God, not John Kline, who had arranged this visit, especially my time with Bones.

Bones was a gangly old soul with many missing teeth. At the foot of his bed rested a guitar, which he played often and well. He expressed deep faith in his Savior, Jesus Christ. His faith was adorned with much joy and exuberance, and I was constantly moved by his confident assurance.

Every Sunday after church, Abigail, the Cowger's nine-year-old daughter, visited Bones and read to him from the Bible. Bones had memorized a large number of Scriptures and had put numerous verses to music. His rich tenor voice soothed my heart and brought tears to my eyes.

I had never cultivated a close relationship with Jethro or Liza. In Bones I saw a quiet resolve, a peace that I personally had never known. My conscience was pricked. How could Bones, who lived only to do another man's work, be so at rest, so tenderhearted?

The answer came the next day when John Kline stopped by. It had been nearly four weeks since he had left me at the Cowgers. We met that afternoon and rode together for several hours along the ridge overlooking the valley.

"Bones is a freer man than you, Sam," John said as we stopped at a rocky overlook above the Cowger's farm. "He's learned what it means to forgive—and he's surrendered his anger to the Lord."

John's statement surprised me. I pondered it for several days. What makes a slave and what makes a free man? The Apostle Paul found grace enough to rejoice in a prison cell. Bones, a slave for sixty years, served the Cowger family without bitterness. I was bitter because I had lost Victoria. The two and a half wonderful years we had spent together had ended so violently, so unjustly. Even so, did I have the right to nurture animosity toward God?

Several days later after John left again, I asked Bones how he had come to such peace about his station in life.

"Mistah Sam," he said, "I's been owned by somebody alls my life. Been a slave o'er sixty year and never been my own mastah like you or Mistah John or Mistah Cowger or any other white folk. Never known no other way. Had no choice and couldn't do nuttin' 'bout it. It ain't been easy, Mistah Sam. And it ain't been fair.

"Hatred run my life for many year. When I's younger, I hated Mistah Cowger's pappy. Hated livin' in an ole shack back up near the hill.

"Now they's been some good things, too, like my wife, Natty, God rest her soul. We had some good years together, Mistah Sam. Lordy, how I loved that woman. And Mistah Cowger, after his pappy died, he treat me pretty good, better than some be treated, so I hear.

"Mistah Sam, I ain't bitter no mo'. Didn't come easy to me, no suh. I done fought it many a year. Hatred eat me alive. And then one night after wrestlin' with God, I chose to forgive. I feel better now, like a man who's free in his insides.

"Life ain't perfec', no suh. I gets lonely. I miss my Natty. And Mistah Cowger he still work me but he knows I be gettin' old so he don't work me too hard no mo'.

"I sees you in pain, too, Mistah Sam. You lost somebody you love. You miss her. I can see that in your face. Let her go now. You can't be hatin' them people what took her. It'll eat you alive jes' like it done me."

Beneath The Oak

Bones' words pierced my soul. Later that afternoon while out riding and thinking, I had my own wrestling match with God. Like my heart the weather couldn't decide if it was winter or spring. March weather is so unpredictable. The snow would blow in across my face for a few minutes and then the sun would appear as bright as a midsummer's day.

I was riding along a path beside the southern end of the Cowger's fields when I stopped and reached into my pocket for the small apple that I'd brought for my horse, James Madison. As I pulled my hand free, something hard slipped through my fingers and fell onto the ground. I looked down, but the grass was thick and dusted with snow, so I could not see what I had dropped. I climbed from the saddle, squatted down and poked in the grass. Two nails had fallen out of my pocket—one straight, one bent. The nails had been in my pocket from a few days before when I had helped Mr. Cowger build a new grain shed.

Two nails. Do you remember that moment, Soul? Do you recall the bright sun, the gust of wind that rustled suddenly through the trees and the two nails that seemed to burn in the palm of my hand?

Squatting in the grass beside the rocky path, I found myself overwhelmed by a wave of shame and grief. I looked up. In my mind's eye I saw You, O Lord, suspended on the cross, nails driven through Your bloodied wrists. You had chosen to give Your life for someone like me. You had surrendered Your will, and embraced the will of Your Father.

If You "who knew no sin" could become "sin for us," who was I to hold You responsible for taking my Victoria? She was never mine; she was always Yours. On our wedding night I thanked You for bringing her into my life. We consecrated our relationship to You and prayed that You would set us apart for Your use alone. Eye to eye, heart to heart, and hand in hand, we said "Yes, I will" to each other and to You.

Suddenly I was on my knees in the snow. Beneath that gnarled oak overlooking the Cowger's freshly plowed field, I gave myself to You. With a great outpouring of tears, I chose to forgive Seth Beaumont and any others who might have been involved in Victoria's murder. I chose to repent of my bitterness and resentment and bring it to Your cross. I laid my vision for the healing of our nation's darkened heart at Your feet.

Nails clutched in one hand, I bowed my head and said "Yes, Lord, Yes."

My remaining two weeks in the valley were halcyon days, with summer-like weather and an occasional afternoon thundershower. Peace like a deep river coursed through my soul. One exceptionally sunny afternoon, Bones and I took off our shoes and walked through the freshly turned field. The rich soil squishing between our toes felt comforting to the bottoms of our bare feet. We were like young boys celebrating a new spring, a new day, a new beginning. It reminded me of my boyhood days in Ohio and of working with my father at the Shawnee Mission in Kansas.

Finally, the time came to return to Washington. God had accomplished a work in me through John Kline and Bones. All things seemed new. My deliverance from bitterness brought John unending delight. For the remainder of the journey, deep meditations occupied my thoughts. We parted on the outskirts of Washington City, on the banks of the Potomac. I thanked this wondrous man of God for all he'd done. Across the river, the ugly stump of Washington's half-finished monument rose above the tops of buildings and trees, my ever-faithful reminder of what can happen to one who builds without counting the cost.

The Telegrams

Mrs. Sheppard greeted me at the boarding house door. Her thoughtful eyes searched mine as she handed me three telegrams from Shawnee Mission, Kansas dated March 15, 19, and 23.

God favored my decision to record my days in the valley before reading the telegrams. As I suspected, my father has departed this earth.

My father, Eli, I thank the Lord Jesus for you, for your faithful stewardship over your small piece of God's earth and over our family inheritance. After Grandpa Will's death in 1813, you traveled thousands of miles to settle title disputes and tomahawk claims on land that he had pioneered. You worked tirelessly in your Virginia mill and then in Grandma's fields in Ohio. In Kansas, you sowed your last twenty years to the Shawnee, serving those dispossessed people who traveled to the plains of Kansas from their homelands of Ohio on the banks of the Little Miami. Now, the harshness of the very land on which you labored so self-lessly for the benefit of others came like a thief in the night and claimed you.

I could not be present with you in your last days. I cannot recall you from heaven to tell you the things a son might say to his father. God in his wisdom chose your time. Your faith shall endure unto your children's children's children. God has revealed His wisdom in His manifold mysteries.

Lord Jesus, like my father, I commit myself to Your will and purposes. Amen.

My pen has spilled the testimony of my heart. The night has nearly drawn to a close, the sun will soon warm my windowpane. My soul's dark night is over, too. I have wept, but joy cometh in the morning! I have buried the two souls dearest to me and I now taste the power of His resurrection! The winter is passed, the spring has come. My debts have been paid.

I am free again, alive in Your glorious new dawn, O Lord!

I will say Yes, Lord, Yes!

7

Thursday Evening

MICHELLE CLOSED THE FRONT DOOR to her second floor condominium and set her briefcase by the table in the foyer. She slipped off her high heels and took a deep breath, and then headed straight to her bedroom, shoes in hand. After a quick change into a sweater and jeans, Michelle passed through the kitchen, poured herself a glass of cranberry juice and made a beeline to her recliner.

The recliner was her chair for reading, thinking, and praying; this evening her thoughts whirled around and around in her head like a never-ending carousel. The vandalism, her lunch with Dan, his suggestions and her objections, all rose and fell in alternating cycles—doubt and fear of discovery if she were to blow the whistle, then a growing conviction that she should use her knowledge to help bring the truth to light.

Doing nothing could have disastrous results.

What if AFI's attorneys used the vandalism to manipulate a partisan judge to place restrictions on the upcoming March for Life? Or what if her church, Agape Christian Fellowship, became implicated in a crime for which they played no part?

On the other hand, doing something could have equally disastrous effects to her personally. If AFI somehow discovered that she gave information to the police, she would be instantly terminated. It had happened to others before, and for less cause. Within AFI's management were ideological opportunists who cared little about mercy.

If she lost her job, she would lose three, hard fought years of her life—three years dedicated to her little sister, Anne. How she had loved this gregarious and intelligent sister. But as a junior in high school, she made the mistake of getting pregnant and then compounded the mistake by hiding it. Instead, she sought advice from her high school health clinic—a new AFI clinic.

An exam and an abortion had been arranged and performed without parental consent. Anne developed a serious infection that led to complications. Now the scar tissue in her Fallopian tubes would prevent her from ever having children.

Michelle sipped her juice and considered the tragic irony.

Both she and Anne had been raised in a Christian home by loving parents who were consistent role models—Dan would have considered them well-balanced.

Not long after Anne's complications, she remembered how she first met Dan who, at that time, worked with Campus Crusade for Christ. She was attending a night class at the University of Maryland. They soon became fast friends, remaining so even after Dan married, went to seminary and returned to pastor Agape Christian Fellowship.

During her master's studies at the University of Maryland, the church had became involved with the pro-life movement. And it was a research paper on the government funding of private, non-profit companies in the abortion industry, focusing on Planned Parenthood and AFI, that inspired her to use her newly developed accounting and finance skills to expose those who had robbed her sister of her "reproductive rights."

And now, almost three tough years after graduate school, she was finally within reach of her goal. She couldn't jeopardize her opportunity to access the critical financial information that was inaccessible even to Congress and the IRS!

And yet, what if Dan and Kent and others in her church were jeopardized because of her decision to remain silent?

The carousel of arguments would not release its dizzying grip.

She had to do something, but at the same time, she could not put her job or possible promotion at risk. Whatever she did, she had to remain absolutely unknown. Invisible. Anonymous.

She had only one viable alternative to silence.

Dan had always given her sound advice in the past, why doubt his wisdom now? She climbed from the recliner and headed toward the kitchen phone.

Katie walked to the edge of the dining room, stuck her head around the corner and called up the stairwell a second time. Over five minutes had passed since she had first called Mark.

"Dinner's served!"

She smiled. She had her own interesting historical fact to share over dinner.

The rumble of feet preceded Mark as he spun around the post to the bannister. In one hand he held a ragged black Bible.

"Wash your hands," Katie said. "You're all dusty."

"Good idea." He placed the Bible on the mahogany sideboard and hurried into the kitchen. "I'm sorry for staying upstairs all day."

Katie took her seat at the table. "I doubt you're all that sorry. Anyway, I told you not to worry about helping me. Enjoy your liberty."

Mark returned from the kitchen and sat down. He unfolded his napkin. "Whose turn to pray?"

"Yours, I believe."

They closed their eyes and held hands across the table. Mark paused, rubbing his thumb gently over the tops of Katie's fingers.

"Lord, Thank you so much for ordering our steps and providing for our future and giving us a child to continue the MacDonald line. We pause now and acknowledge your providence and your sovereignty. We lift our hearts and say, Yes, Lord!"

He opened his eyes.

Katie was smiling at him curiously. "And Thank You, Lord, for this food. Amen," she added, smoothing her napkin.

Mark grinned and reached for a hamburger. After several minutes, he reached back and grabbed the Bible from the sideboard. He opened the tattered cover and showed her the inscription from Kyle to Sam.

Katie's eyes lit up as she read Kyle's words. "How endearing."

"Uhm, huh. Here's something else." He pulled an aged piece of paper from his shirt pocket.

"It's a receipt from the antique dealer who sold the desk to Kyle. It's dated January 16, 1893, a week before Sam moved from Manassas to Washington."

Katie laid her fork across her plate, then studied the receipt. "Then the desk was a welcoming gift! Wow! That must have been an incredible amount of money back in 1893."

Mark nodded. "Look at the dealer's claims. The desk and chair are 18th century pieces, purchased in Alexandria, Virginia, at an estate sale in 1781, from the grandchildren of a plantation owner who lived in Richmond. Work it backwards—it's probable the desk and chair were built before 1750, just like you guessed."

Katie grinned. "They're museum quality."

"More valuable than that, since we know about the history surrounding them. But that's not all—read the back."

Katie turned the paper over. "Sam?"

"Could be his last words—of the writings that survived."

Katie read down the page. "This sounds kind of ominous. What does *unde malum* mean?"

Mark shook his head. "It's Latin, I guess. Pretty dark stuff—a sin-stained knife, Devil's plans."

Katie forked several carrots. "Tell me about his diary."

"At first, I felt odd reading a dead relative's private thoughts. But after a while, Sam didn't seem dead any more. When he writes, it's like he's talking, sometimes to God, sometimes to himself, and at other times, well—it's like he's speaking to me."

Katie wrinkled her nose. "You've read Civil War diaries before. You never made any comments about those books."

"Reading about Sergeant Rice Bull is interesting, but it's not the same. Sam's flesh and blood."

Mark proceeded to tell Katie how Sam had been a reporter for a Charleston newspaper and how in 1853 his wife, Victoria, died in a wagon accident—an accident that Sam believed was murder.

"Vigilante reprisals were commonplace in the 1850s, particularly in the South when slavery was involved."

Katie listened patiently as Mark finished his story about Sam's sabbatical on a farm west of the Shenandoah and how an old slave named Bones helped Sam recommit his life to the Lord.

"Do you mind a tangent?" Katie asked.

Mark chuckled. "What—me, the master of tangets? Go ahead."

"This afternoon I took a walk in the park. That statue out front is a memorial to Cardinal James Gibbons. Does his name ring a bell?"

Mark shook his head.

"He was born in 1834 and died in 1921. He was quite a luminary in his day."

"How could you tell that from the statue?"

Katie grinned. "Well, the dates were on the statue. Then I looked him up in Grandpa Kyle's encyclopaedia! He was a pastor and chaplain in a Baltimore Civil War hospital. In 1917 he was proclaimed by Roosevelt as the most respected, venerated, and useful citizen of the United States. I thought you'd like to hear about one man who left a mark on his generation—even if he's not remembered today."

The gleam in Mark's eyes turned thoughtful. "Cardinal Gibbons and Sam both lived through the war. I wonder if they knew each other?" He rose and carried their empty dishes into the kitchen.

Katie grinned and leaned against the doorjamb.

Mark filled the coffeepot with water. A crease formed between his eyebrows. "You know, after looking through that box of journals I find myself growing a little resentful toward Grandpa Kyle. How could he do such a thing? Maybe he was getting a little senile near the end."

"Hey!" Katie said with a frown. "Pretty strong language about someone who's been so good to you."

"It has nothing to do with Grandpa being good. I just want to know why he hid Sam from the rest of the family."

"You've only begun reading Sam's journals. Think about that note—maybe Sam started off solid but later slipped into something weird."

After a moment of silence, Mark nodded. "You're right."

Katie rubbed his tight shoulders. "There's got to be a simple explanation for his reluctance to tell us about Sam. And knowing you, it won't be long before you've found the answer."

A smile returned to Mark's face as he wrapped his arms around her waist and pressed his body tightly against hers.

"You're buttering me up."

Katie responded, brought her mouth close to his ear. It seemed like a long, long time since they'd been free to enjoy each other. "Don't lie! You love every second of it!"

"Yeah, well..."

Katie's grin widened, her voice whispery, "Now, how about that cup of coffee you promised...."

"What's your pleasure? Another beer?" The buxom, red-headed waitress bent provocatively over Fletcher's left shoulder. He ignored her and watched a rock band road crew arrange equipment on an elevated stage across the room. She was so close that Fletcher could read the hands on her watch—7:45 P.M. He pulled his head back and looked toward the door.

"Yes, please." He replied flatly.

In less than ten minutes one of his informants for the 16th Street and Florida Avenue corridor would arrive. Carlton Glaze worked the upper end of Fletcher's current jurisdiction. There was a remote possibility that Jimmy's role as an informant had been uncovered and his death was retaliatory. By hitting Carlton early on, he hoped to discover new information related to Jimmy's death. Substance abusers like Carlton had short-term memory problems. A word heard on the streets might be forgotten with his next fix.

Fletcher picked up the burgundy and gold Redskin cap from the corner of the table and stared at the magic marker signature of Redskin's Head Coach Joe Gibbs. Jimmy had loved the cap more than any other possession, even his assortment of campaign buttons. No one knew or understood Jimmy like Fletcher had, not Glenn, not Larry. Jimmy's closest friends only knew him through his humorous, silent antics, through the honest smile that he always wore. Fletcher had known his fears, his dreams, and aspects of his tragic past. Glenn and Larry did not know that hidden part of Jimmy, because neither spoke Jimmy's language.

They could not sign.

The waitress returned and set the beer on the table. Fletcher tossed three one-dollar bills on the tray, then slowly poured half the beer into his glass.

Fletcher's knowledge of sign language had pierced through the forgetfulness that hung behind Jimmy's eyes. Once unlocked, Jimmy's trapped memories of signing returned, and within two months he fully remastered the art. Fletcher tried to get him to use his rediscovered skill and reenter the workplace, but Jimmy wouldn't budge. The streets belonged to Jimmy, and Jimmy to the streets. Too many years had passed to change that. But he did make Fletcher a counteroffer: he would become an informant.

Fletcher studied his glass. Five beers in a half-hour. How long had it been since he had downed so much alcohol so fast and risked loosening the internal walls he so carefully constructed to shield his thoughts from the past? Seven months? Yes—that Friday night Susan and Melissa flew out of National Airport for Iowa.

He shook his head, fought back the memories, and drained his glass.

Jimmy's familiar face drifted through his thoughts. Jimmy's theory was correct: no one paid attention to an old homeless man, particularly one who was disabled. For all intents and purposes, he was invisible. Thus, Jimmy had personally witnessed scores of drug-related activities—including the cocaine bust when Jimmy's, KC's, and Fletcher's lives became so fatefully entangled. But that was over now. Jimmy was gone forever. Not only were local drug dealers and their South American suppliers potential suspects, KC was too, having motives against both Jimmy and Fletcher.

But something in the back of Fletcher's brain simply said it wasn't so. KC wasn't a murderer.

How then had Jimmy died?

An image from the morgue stabbed through him like a finely honed stiletto. He could still visualize Jimmy's body beneath the white sheets, the basket of Jimmy's clothes he'd searched through, the grimy sock he'd found—and the pieces of a fetus he had found.

He still could not believe he had removed evidence from Jimmy's body. He had pulled a few stunts over the years as an undercover policeman, but never as blatantly stupid as removing—and then discarding—material evidence in a potential murder case. He wanted to blame his irrationality on the fact that Wonderboy Troy had been assigned to the case.

The case. He'd thrown away a potentially key piece of evidence. The tiny foot directly linked Jimmy's death to the clinic vandalism. But if he showed up in homicide and tried to explain what he'd done, his already tarnished reputation would be destroyed and his days with the MPD would be history.

Why then had he broken the rules?

As he poured the last of the bottle into his glass, he forced his thoughts back to the specifics.

Jimmy could have had a seizure of some kind, and then worked his way along his familiar route up 16th Street to Mount Pleasant. It wasn't that improbable of a scenario.

Six blocks from Meridian Hill, at the corner of Crest Road and 16th Street, was a woman's health clinic. Less than two months ago, the health department had cited them for improper disposal of the aborted babies. The clinic took exception to the word babies, but agreed to pay closer attention to health department guidelines. Had Jimmy climbed into one of their dumpsters and inadvertently snagged the fetus in his grimy sock?

The overhead lights dimmed noticeably over the stage and a round of loud applause and catcalls sounded across the club.

Five seedy young men with shaggy, unkempt hair who were dressed in dark leather and silk took the stage, hands raised high above their heads. Catcalls turned into rowdy cheering as the band broke ranks and ran toward their respective instruments. A thin, white hand touched Fletcher's right shoulder.

"Yo' Fletch, it's 8 o'clock and life's a charm. What's cookin' for yours truly?" Carlton Glaze slipped into a chair. His face was pale and pock-marked. His brown hair had been shaved close to his skull. Though Carlton was six feet tall, he did not weigh more than a hundred and thirty pounds soaking wet.

Fletcher held up empty hands. "No handouts tonight. I need information." Fletcher studied his snitch's reaction.

Carlton's face twisted with mock disgust. "Man, oh man. You're one cruel dude! The Glaze don't need your problems. The Glaze needs a little satisfaction!"

"Yeah, well, then I guess I'll be seeing you later, Carlton, Fletcher said as he started to rise from his seat. "Like the song says, 'I can't give you no satisfaction.' Hope you can make your next rent payment."

"OK, OK. Ask me." Carlton raised his hand. "Maybe I've got a few answers."

Before Fletcher had an opportunity to probe his informant further, the band began to play. The room vibrated with the melodic hum of a synthesizer and a rhythmic bass line that evoked a slowly beating heart. The crowd roared their approval.

"Hey, that's heavy!" Carlton turned halfway in his seat and glanced toward the stage. The waitress approached the table. Fletcher pointed at his bottle and held up two fingers.

"Who are those guys?" Fletcher asked. The music was peculiar, arresting.

Carlton shrugged.

As the lead guitarist gyrated back and forth, he signaled the other band members with a subtle flick of his head. The pulsing rhythm grew louder, faster, his triangular black guitar now wailing over the pounding synthesizer and bass. Cymbals crashed and the three guitarists began to sing in ragged harmony over the thunderous sound of a heartbeat.

No gods, no masters! We rape! We steal! We kill!
No gods, no masters! Your blood is ours to spill!

The guitarists moved as one and belted the savage chorus a second time.

A cold sweat broke out across Fletcher's forehead. He gripped the edge of the table and leaned back in his chair. He recognized his illogical reaction to the song, but that did little to calm his stomach.

The room shook as the the drummer's hands swept in a blur over drums and raised cymbals; the black guitars screamed deliriously. Three wild faces stretched toward their microphones. As they began to harmonize, the music slowed into the hum of synthesizers and a solitary, rhythmic bass line that thumped like a human heart.

We are the children of the earth! We are the world's destiny!
We are the past giving birth! We make the future history!
We are the children of the earth! We are the world's destiny!
The strong! The valiant! The mighty!

The lead guitar wailed long and hard, followed immediately by the other instruments in a dissonant rhythm.

The sound, like the tragic cry of a lost child in the night, resurrected the guilt that haunted Fletcher so mercilessly.

Dear God! How could he have been so naive and unprepared! Susan had never forgiven him—would never forgive him for letting Melissa walk the hundred feet of dark sidewalk up the cul-de-sac alone that cold January night. He was a detective for the Washington MPD! He was supposed to know better!

Fletcher rose to his feet, his stony heart cracking. An unexplainable panic crept over his body like a thousand black spiders. He seized Carlton by the arm and yanked him from his seat as he tossed a ten dollar bill into the center of the table.

Carlton looked dazed as he tried to rip his arm away. "Heeeey, chief! What the—"

Fletcher pointed a finger in his face. "Shut up! We're not finished, not yet. What we are doing is leaving—right now!"

Carlton blanched. "OK, OK, just let go of the arm!"

He released his grip. Carlton rubbed his bicep and started for the door. Fletcher snatched the Redskin hat, his stomach boiling. He kept one eye on Carlton as he moved between the tables in front of them toward the red exit sign and the club's muscular bouncer.

He took one last look at the band. The guitarists rocked to the pulsating thrum of the electronic heartbeat. Fletcher shook his head in disgust, turned around and found himself standing almost toe to toe with a wiry fortyish-year-old man with neatly styled, shoulder-length, black hair.

To his surprise, the man smiled and extended his hand. "I hope it's not the music that's sending you away." Fletcher shook his hand and noted that the man's voice hinted an Irish accent.

Fletcher stuck the Redskin cap under one arm, then stuffed his hands in his coat pockets. He nodded his head back toward the stage. "You responsible for those trashy lyrics?"

The man laughed. "I promote the band, not write their songs."

Fletcher caught the almost imperceptible narrowing of the man's gray eyes before he laughed a second time. But Fletcher had the alcohol from six beers flowing through his veins and into his brain. Eight years of undercover work on the streets let him pick up the fleeting display of apprehension, but his reasoning faculties could not process its meaning into a memory.

"Yeah, well, you and your band are really sick!"

"Perhaps we are." The gray eyes did not flinch. "But you are really drunk. I suggest you let your friend drive. Pardon my forwardness, but I wouldn't be able to forgive myself if I read about you in *The Washington Post's* obituaries tomorrow."

Fletcher clamped down on his tongue and turned angrily toward the exit. Imagine! A forty-year-old leftover from the sixties lecturing an undercover narcotics officer on substance abuse! How had he gotten himself into a mess like this? Had he lost his mind?

Lost his mind, maybe—Fletcher looked around—lost his informant, definitely.

Carlton Glaze was nowhere to be seen.

Fletcher shouldered open the door and stormed outside onto the sidewalk, looking quickly in both directions. He was immediately struck full in the face by a frigid gust of wind that kicked up a wall of dust from the sidewalk. He turned from the wind. As he did, Jimmy's cap popped from beneath his arm and bounded down the sidewalk into the darkness.

Fletcher spun around, his vision blurred. He rubbed his eyes, took two short steps and then stopped. Several cars turned the corner. The wind buffeted his coat and pants, snapping his hair about his head. Pursuit of the cap would be hopeless.

Fletcher turned away dejectedly and headed back into the gusting wind.

Once again, the sudden feeling of *deja vu* was overwhelming. He lowered his eyes and stuffed his hands back into his coat pockets just as he had done on a similar cold night nearly a year ago, when the wind had snapped his five-year-old daughter's pink snow cap from his frozen fingers and spun it into the darkness.

As he made his way up the sidewalk toward the parking lot, his heart ached and broke once again into a kaleidoscope of painful memories of the family he once had.

Melissa, my little one!

Where are you and your mother now? Are you happy? Do you miss me?

Fletcher stuffed his hands into his coat pockets and stared straight into the stinging wind.

8

Thursday Night

THE VAN NESS GARDENS TENEMENTS in southeast Washington were built in the late sixties, one of the first government-subsidized apartment complexes constructed in the District. Due to their hasty construction, the three-story apartments soon fell into disrepair; by the mid-eighties they became home to many of the District's poor and unemployed. Unlike other apartment buildings in the city where inspired vigilante groups roamed, Van Ness Gardens simply slipped into filthy obscurity.

From her red 1990 Camaro parked across the street, KC drew deeply on her cigarette. Her eyes followed a thin young man with close cropped hair as he sauntered up the short flight of concrete steps into the building and up a brightly lit stairwell to the third floor.

She exhaled smoke and glanced down at her watch—he'd returned earlier than expected, almost half an hour earlier. Not that it mattered. What would happen would just happen a little sooner, but her role would not change. She would watch with the skillful eye of an undercover policewoman. She laughed silently at the thought.

The two men waiting inside the apartment were no different than the young man who fumbled with his keys at his apartment door— they were all drug-sucking, needle-marked scum.

KC sucked on her cigarette and blew the air in a thin white stream toward the narrow opening in her driver's side window. In a courtroom, however, her presence here made her as guilty as the two druggies hiding in the apartment.

She put a hand to her mouth and coughed. Growing up in D.C. had attuned her to the violence and the death. She was taught to walk on concrete and had scraped her knees early—and often. She fought to stay clean through high school. Her hard work paid off. She went to Howard University on a scholarship. Again, her dedication to her studies paid off. She graduated in the top ten percent of her class and joined the Metropolitan Police Department full of determination and vigor.

Jamal, her younger brother, walked a different path, succumbing to the power of the streets. While she studied her way though Howard, Jamal was an understudy of a different type—a go-fer for a high-level dealer for a Colombian drug ring. How peculiar a family: brother and sister working on opposite sides of the law! For two years she looked the other way and ignored her brother's fine jewelry, bulging wallet, and sporty new car. Then came the inevitable. Ignoring her warning, he found himself as one of the targets in a bust near Meridian Hill Park, compliments of Fletcher Rivers and his deadbeat informant. Jamal went to prison with the bad boys—the really bad boys.

She never forgave Fletcher for what he'd done. The kidnapping of his little girl only temporarily softened the hostilities between them.

Fletcher did not know that Jamal's arrest indebted KC to the Latinos who lost over two hundred pounds of high-grade cocaine. She suffered through two and a half years of blackmail—looking the other way or making timely phone calls to dealers when a key bust was about to go down.

Fletcher did not know that, three months ago, the Columbian's demands ended abruptly with a phone call from a man whose face she had never seen and whom she knew only by the name, True Believer. And with his call came money—enough money for her own gold jewelry and a fully-loaded red Camaro. No more turning her head at drug deals. No more hurried phone calls. Now she was asked to recruit a fellow police officer to cross the line, tap police telephones, manipulate and delete computer data and alter case files, provide biographies of fellow officers, or like tonight, babysit a murder.

The apartment door opened and closed. KC watched the two killers casually walk down the stairs. She tossed her cigarette out the window, started her engine and backed down the car-lined residential block. At the intersection she snapped on her lights, made a lazy U-turn and drove away.

As the Camaro's red taillights shrank in the distance, an athletically-built man wearing a black leather jacket, jeans and rubber-soled sports shoes stepped from the shadow of a wide oak tree. His shoulder-length black hair was pulled tightly against his head in a ponytail. Deep set, serious eyes stared out of a rugged, masculine face and followed the red tail lights until they disappeared around a corner four blocks away.

The street light momentarily illumined his face: the faint wrinkles in the corners of his gray eyes hinted at his age, but his slender, muscular physique belied whatever his eyes revealed.

An image of a chess board formed in the mind of the man who

called himself True Believer. The opening moves of a strategically important game had been made by invisible hands—his hands. Pawns moved into position, protected by powerful pieces that were protected by even more powerful pieces. Through careful planning, he now controlled the center of the board.

But planning was only half the equation—implementation was the other. In the bloody streets of Belfast, Londonderry, and Dublin, he had mastered both skills and learned to leave nothing to faith or chance. He had learned how to recognize opportunity when it presented itself, as opportunity had revealed itself this night. The unexpected had occured and he met his opponent, face to face, in the least likely of circumstances.

A thin crescent smile flashed briefly across his otherwise grim visage. Carlton Glaze, a snitch for detective Fletcher Rivers, was an inconsequential player. A message had to be sent, one that only the detective would understand.

Studying KC's profile of Rivers convinced him that the street-wise, forty-year-old narcotics officer would indeed grasp the implications of the murder.

Slipping his hands into his jacket pockets, he turned and walked down the heavily shadowed sidewalk toward his car.

Sam's next six journal entries covered April 29th to May 6th. He did not return to Kansas after his father's death but left his father's affairs to his older brother, John Ezra. In a letter from Shawnee Mission, John Ezra wrote how he left Elizabeth, his wife, and his seven-year-old son, Thomas Peter, in charge of the farm in Adams County, Pennsylvania.

Shawnee Mission. Mark lifted the map of western Missouri and the Nebraska Territory toward the light. He recognized names: Saint Joseph, Independence, Osawatomie. Shawnee Mission was about twenty miles west of Independence, north of the Santa Fe Trail.

Placing the map off to the side, Mark turned his attention to a second journal that now lay open on the table. Not only had Sam resumed writing in his personal journal, he had begun a second and concurrently written work entitled: A MacDonald Family History.

The family history, Sam noted on the very first page, was a collection of vignettes about the MacDonald line, based on his memories and the collected narratives of relatives.

The Scriptures teach that the effects of sin can be passed from one generation to the next. "I will visit the sins of the fathers upon the third and fourth generation of them that hate Me." These sins are

handed down as a legacy from father to son to grandson, and to successive generations. I reflect on the violence that has altered the course of my life; how my heart became like stone toward those responsible for my wife's death. I even became hard toward You, O Lord. I am convinced that my present situation is bound to my family's past by an invisible cord, a legacy that I cannot yet understand.

The Scriptures also teach that blessing can be passed from one generation to the next: Abraham blessed Isaac who blessed Jacob who blessed Joseph. Abraham was "blessed to be a blessing."

Our family was bound by a two-fold cord: the curse of sin entwined with the blessing of grace. O Lord, may grace triumph over sin and blessing over curse! "Lead us not into temptation, but deliver us from evil!"

I will use this companion journal to explore the relationship between blessing and cursing, and how it has affected our family's heritage. I do this for myself and for any MacDonald who shall follow.

Any MacDonald who shall follow!

Mark lifted his eyes as goosebumps rippled along his arms. He reconsidered his Grandpa Kyle's puzzling behavior. Had his grandfather read this very same page, these very same words?

The question Katie raised prodded through his frustration and sank home painfully. Maybe there was a yet undiscovered logic behind his grandfather's mysterious treatment of the knapsacks. Order and reason had always been his grandfather's *modus operandi.*

Mark sat up in the chair. Did his grandfather's decision have something to do with the violence that altered the course of Sam's life and affected the family's heritage?

The goosebumps returned.

The family history journals continued to prove enlightening. Mark was astounded to learn that Thomas Henry, the first MacDonald, set foot on American soil in 1607 with Captain John Smith and the newly formed Virginia Company. Three ships brought 144 aristocratic Englishman to settle at Jamestown, Virginia, the first permanent English settlement on American soil. Miraculously, Thomas survived the first year when over two-thirds of the founders perished from sickness and starvation because they were too proud to work the soil. Fortunately, Thomas' sons and grandsons learned from the founder's mistakes. In 1692 one of Thomas' great grandsons, Richard Samuel, moved to the Northern Neck region of Virginia and established himself as a miller. Richard's only son, Matthew, followed in his father's trade.

Joseph Hosea MacDonald, Matthew's son, purchased land in Culpeper County, Virginia and built his own mill in the foothills of the Blue Ridge Mountains. Joseph had four sons, but Sam mentioned only the youngest: Will, born in 1757. He noted that Will became an Indian fighter who, in a providential twist, married the Indian princess Nikitchecame, half-sister to the great Indian chief, Tecumseh.

Sam then continued with his thread about the miller's tradition, revealing that Will's son, Eli, had not followed his father's path into the wilds but labored as a miller. He had worked his trade at the Sudley Mill from 1819 to 1827, near the settlement that would later become Manassas, Virginia, the birthplace of his son, Samuel Mark MacDonald, in 1820. Sam's birth, however, was not without great cost. His mother, Sarah Ashby MacDonald, died a few days later from infection and high fever at the age of twenty-five.

Mark paused and stared at the ceiling as an old ache in his heart thumped painfully.

Mother. He knew the word, but not the emotions.

He and Sam shared a common tragedy—a mother who died in childbirth. Mark knew how hard it was growing up and never knowing what it was like to have a mom. Aunt Clara had always been kind, but Mark was sure it wasn't the same as having a mother's love.

Returning to the journal, a date and a name arrested Mark's attention: June 12, 1838, Stuart and Lincoln, Attorneys at Law.

Flabbergasted, Mark read quickly down the page. Sam noted how a once insignificant lawyer from Springfield, Illinois—now an old friend and source of frequent correspondence—had helped in the sale of two thousand acres of land that Will MacDonald had originally staked out in 1790, the year Eli had been born. The sale of the land would provide funds for Sam to attend medical school.

Abraham Lincoln! The lawyer and an old friend!

The chime of a wall clock below announced it was midnight.

Grinning uncontrollably, Mark set the family history off to the side. He stood up and stretched, and then went downstairs to the kitchen and grabbed a soft drink from the refrigerator.

He tiptoed quietly back up the stairs past the bedroom. It had been a long day for Katie. He wondered if the pregnancy would moderate her new and stubborn determination to do everything by herself. Probably not! Behind her sweet disposition was an iron will forged by dependence on God—tempered only by occasional bouts of doubt and fear that her disability had burdened his life and hurt their marriage.

Mark continued up the stairs.

Pausing in the doorway to the study, he visualized how the room might have looked when Sam lived there—the desk and chair, perhaps a brass bed near the windows, the crackle of burning oak in the fireplace, a photograph or an old daguerreotype on the mantle. The only thing out of place was the empty rack above the fireplace.

Mark's eyes moved to the old sword standing against the desk. Why not? He grabbed the sword and placed it on the rack.

A handsome stone fireplace and an old sword. Perfect!

He sat down and opened Sam's personal journal, transporting himself once again to a boardinghouse room and window seat where Sam sat with an open journal across his knees.

❧ *9* ❧

Shortly after Midnight, Friday Morning

7 June 1856, 8:15 P.M.
Sheppard's Boardinghouse, Washington City

Bloodshed in the Capitol

Violence has been loosed in our city. Madness has seized the hearts and minds of my countrymen.

At first I ignored the <u>New York Herald's</u> report that our senators and congressmen were carrying knives and guns on their persons in the halls of Congress. I dismissed it as an outrageous fabrication of greedy newspapermen. Then, late this afternoon, I received word of the outrageous thrashing of Senator Charles Sumner from Massachusetts by Congressman Preston Brooks of South Carolina. The thrashing occurred on the Senate floor in retaliation for his May 19th speech. Sumner had slandered Brooks' uncle, Senator Butler of South Carolina, and all of the South.

"Murderous robbers and hirelings picked from the drunken spew and vomit of an uneasy civilization," Sumner had bellowed from behind his desk. He raved on, arguing that the whole history of South Carolina should be blotted out, for its "shameful imbecility toward slavery confessed throughout the Revolution." He scurrilously compared Butler to a whoremonger whose whore was slavery, and said that Butler, like the Egyptians, "worshiped divinities in brutish forms."

Brooks pummeled him until he was nearly unconscious. Sumner has a concussion, and his scalp has been torn open all the way down to his skull.

Bloodshed in Kansas

This morning I received a letter from an old friend of the family, Mrs. Doyle. Her husband, Jim, and their two sons had been murdered at their homestead near Pottawatomie Creek in Osa-watomie, Kansas, some forty miles southwest of Shawnee Mission.

She claimed that her family, as well as three other pro-slavery farmers, had been butchered by the abolitionist John Brown and a small band of violent men armed with swords. The murders were in retaliation for the actions of the Border Ruffians, a pro-slavery lynch mob which had swept into Lawrence, Kansas, the day following Sumner's speech. They laid waste to several free-state printing presses and a half-dozen private homes, killing five men in the process.

As Brown and his murderous crew dragged her husband and sons away, she begged him to release them. He retorted with Scripture: "An eye for an eye, a tooth for tooth." Within minutes her husband and sons were dead. O God, I pray, help her to forgive, like You have helped me.

There is one final piece to this story worth noting. As Mrs. Doyle wept over her dead loved ones, she claims to have seen a wiry, dark haired man on horseback appear from the shadow of nearby trees. A crescent moon emerged from behind a bank of clouds and illuminated his face, a cruel face with a long dark scar. He watched briefly, then snapped his reins and rode off in the same direction through the prairie grass Brown and his gang had departed. She does not know who he was or why he was there, but that his presence filled her with great fear.

What will heal Kansas now that her ground is stained with the blood of innocent men?

Tertullian's Riddle

The events of that bloody week in May have driven me to reconsider a question voiced by the early church theologian Tertullian over seventeen hundred years ago: underline malum.

Whence comes evil?

Without doubt it is a deep mystery. I ask You, O Lord, what is in the hearts of men that leads them down the path of violence and bloodshed? And Lord, what does Your Church have to say in this matter? Will we arise with the voice of truth to deliver this nation from the seeming inevitability of separation? Or will Your Church follow this troubled union down the dark path of trial and suffering?

Despite the fear that seeks to grip me regarding our rising sectional differences I must continue to trust in the Lord and His hand of Providence. Yes Lord, You control all things.

"New Directions"

John Kline appeared at my door two days ago. He told of Bones' passing and how Mr. Cowger found him resting peacefully against the old twisted oak. Bones had left instructions with Mr. Cowger to give me his guitar. The Cowgers were kind to see his request fulfilled.

After an evening of prayer with John, I have decided to once again pursue my original course of studies at the University of Pennsylvania Medical School in Philadelphia, studies I began nearly twenty years ago before taking up the rallying cry of the abolitionist. I now have no obligations to keep me here in Washington. Mr. Pitkins of the Charleston Observer has agreed to publish an extensive series on recent advances in medicine and surgical procedures.

I will return to school following the harvest at John Ezra's farm. Corn, late beets, carrots, and winter squash will need to be gathered in. I look forward to working my hands in the soil and watching God's creation make its quarterly changes.

Indeed, my brother, John Ezra, is one of the most blessed men on earth. With the psalmist, he can say, "The lines have fallen to me in pleasant places." No one could ask for a better wife and companion than Elizabeth Rachel. Their son, Thomas Peter, now age seven, is already helping with the farm. Adams County, Pennsylvania, must be the garden of Eden.

Fletcher Rivers lost the battle to block the guilt.

Tchaikovsky's *Violin Concerto in C major* played softly in the dark living room. The clock on the VCR read 1:35 A.M. He leaned back into his sectional sofa, his socked feet propped on the edge of an oval oak table. His gaze followed the intermittent pattern of headlights from the nearby highway gliding up the wall and across the ceiling.

Two-day stints that ended in a late-nighter had never been kind to him.

After a long weekend seven months ago, he had come home to a completely dark house. Taped to the refrigerator was a terse note from Susan. She couldn't handle the fear any longer. She and Melissa had been followed again by two Latinos in a strange car, so she packed her and Melissa's suitcases and returned to Iowa.

"Don't try to contact us," the note had read in closing, "if you care anything about the safety of your daughter."

Fletcher rubbed his eyelids. Her remark had been double-edged, not just a caution for the future, but a bitter reminder of the past and his failure for allowing Melissa to walk alone up a dark sidewalk three houses to visit a friend. Susan had come home from the grocery store to a brightly lit house with two Fairfax County police cruisers parked out front. He intercepted her on the front porch with their daughter's pink snow cap clutched in his hand.

Susan understood before he said a word.

Then they hunted—how they hunted for their daughter!

Fletcher wiped a tear away, but as soon as he did, others followed, trickling slowly down into the corners of his mouth. He shook his head slowly from side to side.

It had been chance, only chance, that Melissa's life had been spared.

Seventy-two hours later, an alert Texas state trooper pulled over a pickup truck with expired tags just seven miles from the Mexican border.

Two men broke from the truck and made a run for it across the mesa, leaving a cold and terrorized five-year-old girl sitting in the middle of the front seat with her hands tied against her sides and her mouth taped shut.

Within the hour the two men had been apprehended. Facing kidnapping charges of a minor, they talked freely.

It was then that Fletcher and Susan learned that Melissa's kidnapping and planned trip into the dark heart of South America, was retaliation for his involvement several weeks earlier in one of the MPD's largest cocaine busts ever.

The devastating news was temporarily offset by Melissa's safety and well-being. Though severely traumatized by her three-day journey with the coarse drug runners, the men had not abused her.

That cataclysmic line between Melissa's ragged, emotional anguish and the absence of abuse kept Susan from leaving him right then and there. Heightened neighborhood patrols by the local police had only temporarily soothed her fears and made it tolerable for her to stay.

The strange car and the two Latinos. Had they really been following her? The odds were against it.

Fletcher lowered his head. No doubt about it. This was like the night Susan left and the night Melissa vanished. The tears just kept coming no matter what he said to himself and no matter how he tried to rationalize his emotions. He had shed more tears in the hours between his daughter's kidnapping and her recovery than in all of his earlier adult life.

His eyes roamed over the shelf unit that housed his stereo components, his television set, his VCR, and videotape editor. His collection of family videotapes spanned the five-foot-wide shelf beneath the VCR. The videos of better, happier times comforted him and tormented him with equal force.

He massaged his eyes and tried to shut out the images of his shattered, sobbing wife's face as she listened to him explain how their little girl had vanished and later, when she pounded her fists uncontrollably on his chest in anger and disbelief.

As he did, an image of Jimmy's ashen face in the morgue unexpectedly transposed itself over his wife's face.

Fletcher grimaced as he slammed a fist against the top edge of the sofa. Why did Jimmy have to die? Why not one of his other informants, like that slimy, no-good wimp, Carlton Glaze?

He wiped his eyes. They were all gone—everyone he really cared for—gone.

Exhausted and drained to the core, he closed his eyes, letting the focus of his attention rise and fall with the passionate strains of Tchaikovsky's lead violin.

Like a shot in the dark, the telephone rang, dissonantly piercing the andante. Fletcher lurched to his feet. The phone rang again as he staggered down the short hall to the kitchen.

"I'm coming!" He leaned over the counter and yanked the phone off the hook. "It's 1:45 in the morning. What could you possibly want?"

Fletcher's ingrained professionalism finally regained full control of his thoughts. He pushed himself erect, his body suddenly tense.

"Say again?" He rotated his shoulders, shedding the layers of weariness that had accumulated over the past seventeen hours.

"No, I don't need any directions. Tell whoever's on the scene that I'm on my way out right now."

Fletcher slowly hung up the phone, then turned and walked back into the living room. He snapped off the stereo and grabbed his jacket from the sofa. A wave of guilt washed over him. He desperately wished that he could retract the wishes that tumbled through his mind a few moments earlier.

Carlton Glaze had just been found dead in his apartment.

He hurried out the door to the garage, analyzing the ten minutes he and Carlton had spent together at the Bayou. But no matter how he dissembled the conversation, there was nothing Carlton had said or done that was out of the ordinary.

Fletcher backed his TransAm down the driveway and into the cul-de-sac, the double garage door closing behind him.

In a rundown efficiency apartment in northeast Washington, filled with dirty brown shag carpeting that had survived the tread of numerous, month-to-month renters, Harold Wertman opened the refrigerator door and looked inside.

The white light illumined his long, triangular face and scraggly, salt-and-pepper beard. His dark, almost black eyes searched the near empty shelves. He let his lanky frame sink slowly into a squat, his hand on the open door. He scratched his chest through his Cal-Berkeley Class of '70 T-shirt. The open can of spaghetti smelled funny; the small block of cheddar cheese had hardened into an umber brick. He opened the vegetable crisper on the bottom. The half-dozen carrots felt rubbery, like giant, orange pencil erasers; the last two clumps of seedless red grapes were covered with white mold. So much for going organic!

He rose from his squat and closed the door. On the counter next to the refrigerator sat two, room temperature Cokes in twelve ounce cans he forgot to chill. He shrugged, popped one open and returned to the sagging, green sofa in the living area of his one-room efficiency. The only light came from a lamp sitting on a box by the end of the sofa. Dirty yellow curtains hung crookedly over the sliding balcony door. In the middle of the carpet sat three cardboard boxes filled with loosely packed books.

What did the Scriptures say? The Son of Man had no place to lay his head? Harold leaned back and celebrated his present suffering. Two thousand years ago, Jesus had no pillow; today, Harold's refrigerator was empty, just like his wallet. Such were the sacrifices of visionaries throughout the millennium who dedicated themselves to better the world!

Returning to his book, Harold felt a warm tingle spread from the base of his neck to the middle of his back. The feeling slid exquisitely down his spine, around his chest and rib cage, down into his legs. Had other heroes in ages past known this sublime rush of glory? He was sure they had, for such were the rewards for those who abstained from worldly pleasures.

His stomach growled noisily. He glanced up from his book to his watch—it was almost two a.m. and time for his Sponsor's call about tomorrow's payment of a thousand dollars—in cash. All the wondrous glories notwithstanding, his refrigerator and his belly needed replenishing. He was two weeks behind on rent, as well. He returned to his book again, his eyes searching for where he left off reading. He found his place when the phone rang. He jumped up.

"Hello—" He fumbled and dropped the phone. Cursing, he snagged the cord before it hit the floor. He snatched it up and put it back to his ear.

"Anything wrong at your end?" The Oriental, female voice sounded apprehensive.

Harold gripped the phone tightly. "I just dropped the stupid phone, that's all."

"I called to notify you we're going to delay our meeting until Monday or Tuesday."

Harold caught the emphasis on Tuesday. "You promised me a thousand dollars last Monday or Tuesday! I'm out of food and my rent's overdue! What's the big deal about advancing me a thousand against the twenty you owe me?"

The soft voice interrupted gently. "Hold on. Where's your patriotic spirit, Harold? Do you actually think you're the only one suffering tonight? So you miss a meal or two! Think of all the unborn babies who will never eat a single meal while the stinking capitalistic doctors stuff themselves in their big houses! People like me, people like you—we're the only ones who really care. The rest are infidels, pretenders who will be forgotten. But in the ages to come, we will not be forgotten!"

Harold shuffled his feet. He started to reply but the woman cut him off.

"This coming weekend is very important to the Sponsors. You must intensify your activity at the picket. The time of victory is coming, Harold, and you have been chosen to participate in that victory. While others sleep, you will labor for the triumph of the people!"

"OK, but just remember—the laborer is worthy of his hire. I've got to have my money by Tuesday!" He slipped a hand up the front of his T-shirt as his stomach growled. "You're not supposed to muzzle the ox while he's working."

The phone was silent for several seconds before the voice returned. "Very well. Remember, we are counting on your ability to complete this phase of the work. Harold—sleep well."

"Yeah, good night to you, too." He placed the phone on the receiver and walked slowly back to the couch, rubbing his stomach. Tuesday. If he had to crawl, beg or steal, he would find some way to make it to Tuesday and his reward. He picked up his book and fell back into the couch. His eyes scanned the title written on the spine with a sudden surge of pride.

To Purge this Land with Blood was a biography of John Brown of Osawatomi. In 1859, Brown changed the course of history and accelerated the social forces that helped put an end to slavery. Almost a century and a half later his body was probably still a molderin' in the grave—not over the issue of slavery, but over those despicable, degenerate, capitalistic, lake-of-fire-bound baby killers! But now it was his turn to be the John Brown of the nineties! It was his turn to purge the land of blood, to help reroute the crooked course of history again—just like he'd done with the *Save the Whales* campaign some years back in San Francisco. He turned and propped his feet up on the couch, opened the book, and began to read.

Carlton Glaze lay flat on his back in the middle of the parquet floor, his eyes rolled upward into his head with an euphoric smile frozen on his face. There was no evidence of trauma, just a blank, happy stare.

Fletcher had seen it before. Carlton had been the unwilling recipient of a hot shot, a fatally potent heroine injection. It was a pleasant way to die. There was a rush of ecstatic warmth that quickly spread throughout one's body—followed by a numbing darkness and death.

Carlton's death could be written off as an overdose, the result of a hasty fix by an overstressed addict, but it was a weak argument. Never mind that the syringe and spoon on the table nearby would have his fingerprints on them. Anyone could have rolled his pliant fingers across their surfaces after he was dead. It was a moot issue anyway. A gas chromography test of Carlton's blood would reveal the concentration of the overdose. Fletcher was counting on Botello to get him a copy of that report.

Stepping around a paramedic, Fletcher glanced into the kitchen on his way to the balcony door. Carlton's teenage brother and girlfriend were still answering questions in the kitchen. They claimed Carlton had told them he was leaving for Baltimore around midnight. Having let themselves in with a key he had given them, they expected to find an empty apartment. Instead they found Carlton, his body still slightly warm and their opportunity to use his bedroom ruined by a hot shot.

Fletcher slid open the balcony door, then stepped outside. He gulped in cold air, then braced himself against the rail. For a moment he studied the police cruisers and the rescue squad with their flashing lights.

Fletcher leaned back against the rail and rubbed his face. Just four hours ago they had sat together in the Bayou. And even though Carlton ran off, Fletcher thought little about it. Carlton had always been a bit shaky. But now, just hours later, he was dead with a macabre smile on his face.

But why? Carlton was only a tiny fish in a very big pond. Fletcher had no doubts that his informant might die on the streets of Washington, but not from a hot shot in his apartment.

A coldness settled over Fletcher, slipping through his coat and beneath his clothes, chilling him to the bone. The coldness was not from the wind, but from the realization that Carlton's death could have been orchestrated for a different reason. What if someone wanted to send Fletcher a warning? First Jimmy, then Carlton. Both were Fletcher's informants. Had they been uncovered? It was a possibility. Or was someone telling him not to pursue investigating Jimmy's death? What did someone fear that he might uncover? And did it have anything to do with Jimmy's body being taken from a dumpster and dropped onto the Rock Creek Golf Course?

What had Jimmy seen?

Fletcher took a deep breath of the frigid air and considered the situation. First, he needed to get his hands on Jimmy's autopsy report. Second, it was possible that whoever knew about Fletcher's potential involvement with Jimmy's case had been willing to commit murder to keep him away. If that were true, Jimmy and the clinic could be linked. Media coverage of the vandalism implied that radical Christian activists had been responsible. Vandalism was one thing, but murder?

Fletcher shook his head, pushed himself from the rail and sauntered wearily back inside.

Standing on the sidewalk below, a broad-shouldered man with shoulder-length blond hair watched Fletcher leave the balcony. Slipping his hands into the pockets of his blue jogging suit, he nodded and started across the parking lot.

❧ **10** ❧

Early Friday Morning

MARK TURNED ONTO HIS BACK and opened his eyes. The room was dim. Pale morning light contended with a low, gray cloud cover that had drifted over Washington during the middle of the night.

"Murderers—you're all a bunch of murderers!" boomed a deep, metallic voice outside. A loud, ragged chorus of voices followed immediately afterward, echoing the metallic voice word for word.

Mark's eyes popped open.

"Killers—you're all a bunch of baby killers!" The ragged chorus repeated the angry refrain.

Rubbing his eyes, he glanced in disbelief at the clock. It wasn't even seven o'clock! He threw back the covers. His eyelids felt heavy; last night's reading marathon had taken its toll.

He looked sleepily over his shoulder at Katie. Her blue eyes were wide open, staring straight up at the ceiling.

Katie turned on her side to face Mark, propping herself on an elbow. She brushed a drooping strand of blonde hair from her face.

"That building on the corner is an abortion clinic."

Mark rolled over and sat up. He pulled back the curtains. A line of thirty to forty picketers marched back and forth along the sidewalk in front of the building, waving tall homemade signs and placards. One small knot of picketers stood on the corner with their heads bowed.

His thoughts drifted to Sam and his day, to how the country was so divided in its views on slavery and state's rights. Mark wondered if Sam and Lincoln had corresponded on the subject. He turned half way around, resting one knee on the edge of the bed, and told Katie about Sam's true-life pen pal.

The metallic voice barked again and drew Mark's attention to a tall young man with his hair pulled back into a ponytail. Wielding the bullhorn, he continued his monotoned barrage while waving a black poster cut in the shape of a swastika.

Remembering another important point, Mark turned back to Katie. "*Unde malum* appeared in an 1856 journal entry. Sam attributed the phrase to Tertullian, one of the early Church fathers. I don't know if you remember, but I taught about him in a Sunday school series on the Church fathers.

"Anyway, *unde malum* is actually a question that translates whence comes evil?"

Katie bunched her pillow beneath her chin and sighed. "The receipt you brought to the dinner table last night was dated 1893. That means Sam wrestled with *unde malum* for almost forty years. I wonder if he ever came up with an answer?"

The bullhorn and chorus continued their crude, antiphonal refrains. Mark stood up.

"Better question. Should I make some breakfast for you and baby MacDonald?" he asked, slipping his hand beneath the sheet and gently patting her stomach.

"Not yet," Katie answered, lifting his hand away as she slowly swung her legs over the edge of the bed. She pushed herself upright and slipped on her bathrobe.

The bullhorn blared. Strident voices rose and fell.

"All of a sudden, I'm not very hungry."

There were only three logical routes that Jimmy could have taken to reach the Crest Road Clinic. Glenn had little information to offer other than that Jimmy had started twitching just before he disappeared.

Fletcher rubbed the sleep from his bloodshot eyes. He was going to conduct his own investigation regardless of KC's threats and the message intended by Carlton's death.

The light turned green. Fletcher darted through two lanes of traffic and pulled his TransAm in front of a No Parking sign on the Mount Pleasant side of a tiny park bordered by a waist high, black wrought iron fence. He nodded and smiled. His hunch paid off: lying on a grate in the sidewalk was an old black man bundled in a sleeping bag and army blankets. They were alone, except for a broad-shouldered man in a blue jogging suit who stood silently near the end of a wooden bench on the other side of the tiny park.

Fletcher stepped up onto the curb and squatted down a few feet from the old man's curly head. The man's eyes popped open at the sound of the detective's shoes on the cement.

"Don't worry, I'm not after your grate." Fletcher stuck a ten dollar bill down into the top of the sleeping bag. The old man followed the crisp new bill with wary, bloodshot eyes.

"I need information. And if you can help me—I've got another one of those," he said, patting his shirt pocket.

The black man's widening eyes and nodding head were the only things that moved.

"Two nights ago, did an old man—short, big green coat with buttons on the front—pass by here?"

He nodded, then his eyes narrowed. "I seen somebody, pale as a snowflake, by the end o' my grate beneath the preacher. He was a twitchin'. Then he looks up at the preacher and suddenly his shakin' went away!"

The muscles in Fletcher's jaw tightened as he glanced up and followed the man's eyes to a tall bronze and marble statue. He stuffed the second ten dollar bill into the sleeping bag.

Fletcher studied the life-size statue of a man sitting on a horse. He wore a wide-brimmed floppy hat and a huge cloak that hung down to his knees. His bronze face was resolute, and in his right hand he held a Bible. According to the bronze plate on the marble base, the preacher had a name: Francis Asbury.

Fletcher vaguely recognized the name as images were dislodged from forgotten childhood memories: sitting at a table with other young children; a middle-age man with a huge smile who told stories from the Bible and about modern-day heroes of the church; hot summer days and a paper cup of lemonade beside a stack of vanilla wafers. He remembered folding his hands and interweaving his fingers a certain way while saying: "This is the church, This is the steeple, Open the doors and see all the people!" He also recalled walking down the long aisle in the middle of the church with other kids his own age, surrounded by smiling faces, lifting his voice and singing with all of his heart, "Fairest Lord Jesus."

The images shifted pleasantly through his thoughts. Yes, come to think of it, the name Francis Asbury did ring a bell. He was a hero of the Methodist Church.

Focusing his thoughts back to the business at hand, Fletcher walked back to his car. He climbed in, opened the glove compartment and removed a handheld mobile phone. He dialed Botello's office number. The phone rang once and was answered.

"Time for the morning news!" Botello boomed.

Fletcher listened carefully as Botello read the results of the autopsy report. The coroner's conclusions were not all that surprising after listening to Glenn and the old black man.

"An embolism killed Jimmy, not the blow to the head," Fletcher verified, nodding. "Then there's no case—you can't kill a dead man."

Fletcher's eyes lit up as Botello gave additional details. "A pamphlet stuffed up inside under the sweater, that's interesting. And what about Carlton?"

His eyes opened wider as Botello explained that the concentration level of heroine in Carlton's body was over fifty percent. Fletcher shook his head—the overdose was no accident.

"Botello, I owe you one. Talk to you later."

As he returned the phone to the glove compartment, he realized that he was only three blocks from the clinic and dumpster where Jimmy had probably died among piles of trash, aborted fetuses, and discarded AFI literature.

Died, not murdered, drifting off into a warm, eternal sleep.

Unexpected joy stabbed at Fletcher's heart.

Breakfast consisted of croissants, and a pot of brewed coffee. Mark picked up a section of the newspaper and began reading. "Katie, there's an article in the Metro section about the clinic across the street. It was vandalized late Wednesday night. We must have slept right through it."

Mark looked back to the paper. "Without directly accusing anyone, the article speculates that there might be a connection between the vandalism, the church groups that are picketing and the upcoming March for Life. I always felt the *Post* was biased."

"Speaking of the March for Life," Katie asked, "do you think we should participate? You've always said if the opportunity arose, you wanted to go."

Mark folded the paper and stared silently out the window into the backyard. Abruptly, without answering her question, he rose from his chair and took her hand.

Smiling curiously, Katie set her mug on the table. They went upstairs to the second floor. Mark led Katie to the bedroom window.

Mark drummed his fingers on the window sill. "I never told you that I woke up Wednesday night and watched three men cross the driveway at the back of the clinic. One looked really drunk and was carried by his buddies. A guy with a ponytail stood in the back of the open van and helped load the drunk guy in. Then they drove off."

"You think they had something to do with the vandalism?"

"Maybe. The article said that medical equipment was destroyed. One of the men could have hurt himself."

"Sounds far-fetched," Katie answered, "but you never know."

Mark stood up. The number of picketers had increased dramatically; now it stretched all the way around the corner to the driveway where he had seen the three men.

"I could go to the police. My statement might help the police find out who really did it."

Katie smiled. "You've never done anything like this before."

Mark shrugged. "Blame it on Sam. Maybe his boldness is rubbing off on me a little." He walked around to the other side of the bed and picked up the phone from the nightstand.

"Let's find out where I've got to go."

The hardest part about getting into the District Building was finding a parking space. Situated in Judiciary Square just one block north of Pennsylvania Avenue and in sight of the U.S. Capitol, the daily fight for parking spaces between tourists and federal employees from the nearby Labor Department was fierce. After almost ten minutes of frustration circling nearby streets—the drive from the townhouse had only taken seven minutes—Mark finally found a space across the street from the National Gallery of Art. He walked a block and a half back to the busy municipal complex, where a uniformed policewoman gave him directions to the office of homicide detective Troy Martin.

The detective's small office barely had room for a desk, two chairs, a three-shelf bookcase and a pair of metal filing cabinets. On one corner of the desk was a computer. On the stark white wall behind Detective Martin's desk hung his diploma, a bachelor's in criminology from the University of Southern California. The only picture in the room was an eleven inch by seventeen inch photograph of the 1987 Trojan football team. The thick-chested, ex-college football tackle peered over in-baskets on his desk and raised his bear-sized paw to interrupt Mark.

"Now hold it right there—I can only write so fast. How many men climbed into the van?"

"Three men, the fourth was already in the van—the one with a ponytail. Don't you guys have a tape recorder for statements?"

The detective continued making notes. "Is there anything else you'd like to add?"

Mark closed his eyes and pictured the scene in his mind. "The van's rear bumper was sharply curled." He opened his eyes and smiled eagerly. "That should help in identifying the vehicle."

The ex-tackle placed his pen on top of the note pad. "There are more vans in the District with curled bumpers than you might think," he said rising from his chair. He extended his huge hand.

Mark shook it, confused.

"If we need any additional information, we'll give you a call. Thanks for taking the time to come down and give a statement."

The detective sat back down, tore the page from his notebook and slipped it into a folder.

Mark spoke up, his voice testy. "It took me longer to park than for you to take my statement. I've given you information that could have a bearing on your investigation, including a decent description of what the men looked like and what they were wearing."

Detective Martin rose to his feet and folded his arms in front of him. "Yes, I remember. We'll call you if we need anything more. Do you need help finding your way out of here?"

Mark frowned. "I can find my way."

Troy sat down and leaned back slowly into his chair. Yesterday he received a statement from the Anonymous Tips program that pointed the finger at the AFI for vandalizing its own clinic. Now, a local stops by and identifies four males and a van at the scene.

He frowned sharply and snatched up the phone. His thick black finger punched a four-digit number.

The phone rang once and was answered. Troy sighed deeply.

"KC, it's me. A second lead just came in on the Crest Road case. Some guy just moved into a townhouse across from the clinic near the corner of 16th and Crest. He claims he saw four male suspects and a van leave the clinic."

Troy listened silently. He raised a hand and loosened his collar, then closed his eyes and nodded.

"I understand. I'll notify you if anything else comes in." He hung up the phone.

At times he hated that woman! Sometimes he wished that he had never gotten involved with her or her friends! He didn't want to admit that she had used him, but that's exactly what she had done. A knock at his door startled him.

Fletcher Rivers opened the door and poked his head inside. "Hey, Troy! How's it going?"

Troy bristled, his rising anger covering his alarm. Fletcher's tone was lighthearted, but his eyes were bloodshot and serious.

"You've been warned about sticking your nose into this case."

Fletcher flashed a humorless smile. "Two of my informants found their way into the morgue. I just stopped by to say I was happy that the cases were in such good hands—you know what I mean? As a former offensive linemen, I'm sure you had a reputation for not letting anything get by you—like the fact that Carlton died of a hot shot or that a pamphlet was found stuck up Jimmy's sweater."

Troy thrust up a hand. "I've got more important work than to worry about scum who dig around in trash cans or pump their brains full of dope. Take my advice: don't start treading on quicksand."

Fletcher smiled, backed out of the office and shut the door.

Troy grabbed his phone and started punching in a number.

Unexpectedly, the door burst open. "Sorry—but I forgot to mention something," Fletcher said sheepishly, poking his head into the office.

"I stopped by the Crest Road clinic this morning and asked for some free literature. A crotchety nurse told me the pamphlet I wanted was temporarily out of stock. Seems their recent order had misprints and was tossed—into the dumpster behind the clinic."

Troy slammed the phone down, his face red with anger.

"Get off my case!"

By the time the ex-tackle stormed his way around the desk, Fletcher had already slammed the door and disappeared.

The trip to the police station had basically been a bust, Mark reasoned, as he reached the light at the corner of Pine and Crest adjacent to the deserted church. At least the parking space across from their townhouse was empty—a small consolation!

Stepping onto the curb, Mark was surprised to see Katie in her jacket and gloves standing in the park, watching the heavily bundled picketers sing and wave their signs across the street.

Katie turned and waved. Mark joined her by one of the benches.

The tall, lanky man with the ponytail carried a bullhorn in one hand and a black swastika poster in the other. He stood toe-to-toe with a beet-faced nurse in uniform. The nurse's mouth worked furiously as she wagged her finger back and forth an inch from his nose.

"I've been out here ten minutes," Katie explained as she slipped an arm through Mark's. "Everything was going smoothly until a handful of some counter-protesters showed up with their pro-choice sign. They weren't here three minutes before Mr. Ponytail blasted them with his bullhorn around to the other side of the building.

"Then the nurse came out. I'm surprised there are no TV crews taping this. Where is Mr. Ponytail coming from? He's hurting the pro-life position and negating the other picketer's efforts."

Mark nodded but his thoughts were elsewhere.

A man with a ponytail. The image of the van's open rear door flashed through his thoughts. Could he be the same man from Wednesday night who stood in the back of the van?

The nurse shook her fist. Mr. Ponytail waved his sign.

A slender, young Oriental woman in a blue parka stepped between the combatants, placing her hands firmly against the ponytailed man's chest and tiptoeing to speak in his ear.

He started to argue, then stopped abruptly. The young woman walked away and Mr. Ponytail followed, his head lifted high.

The nurse cursed him repeatedly.

The picketers, reacting to the nurse's outburst, began a rousing chorus of *Amazing Grace*.

Obviously disgusted, the nurse threw her hands over her head and stomped up the sidewalk to the clinic.

Mark rubbed his chin, the image of the open van still in his thoughts. He couldn't decide if the man with the bullhorn and the man in the van were one and the same. Because of the angle of the street light, he'd seen more of a silhouette than details.

"Mr. Ponytail looks like one of the men I saw Wednesday night, but I can't tell for sure. The man in the van was about the same height, only a lot thinner."

"How did it go with the police?" Katie asked.

Mark shrugged and recounted the trip in detail, including how it took him longer to find a parking space than for the detective to record his statement.

Katie squeezed his arm. "You did your duty. Now it's up to the police to figure out what's useful in solving the case."

Mark nodded. "I'll shut up about it—for a while."

They stopped in front of Gibbon's statue. The marble base was almost six feet high, upon which rested a bronze chair and the larger than life-sized cardinal. The royal figure wore a long robe that covered his legs down to his shoes. His right hand was slightly raised, palm down as if to bestow a blessing; his left hand was closed on a crucifix that hung around his neck.

Katie pointed and showed Mark the inscription and the dates.

The wind kicked up suddenly, rustling the pines behind the statue. Katie shivered. "Let's go inside."

As they crossed the street in front of the townhouse, the picketers began to sing another chorus, waving their banners as they lifted their voices.

Stand up! Stand up for Jesus! Ye soldiers of the cross!

Sitting in the passenger seat of Harold Wertman's van, Kim Park smiled and made eye contact with her operative.

"Harold, you did a fine job today. The Sponsors will be pleased," she said enthusiastically, unzipping her parka. She picked up a bag from the floor. "Do you want another donut?"

"Now that you mention it, I'm still kinda hungry." He reached into the tall white bag that Kim placed between the bucket seats and grabbed two jelly donuts. "You know, I just hate those Nazis! They pollute the earth with their capitalism. We're going to change that—right?"

He bit into the first donut with a vengeance.

Kim reached into her coat pocket, pulled out a crisp, new one hundred dollar bill and dropped it into the bag of donuts. "The Sponsors have authorized me to advance you this money. They are aware of your need and don't want you starving before Tuesday."

Harold set one donut on his leg, then retrieved the bill. He stuffed the money into his pants pocket.

"Tell them I appreciate it," he said through a mouthful. "They won't be disappointed. One way or another, I'm going to hang right in there all the way to the end—you tell them that."

"The Sponsors believe you—I believe you." Kim reached over and gently touched his arm, smiling coyly. He was so blind to what was really going on. True Believer had done an excellent job in finding such a dupe.

"Next week, when I return from New York, do you think you might have some time to spend with me—at my apartment. Would you like that, Harold?"

His widening pupils told her what she wanted to know.

He stuffed half a donut into his mouth, then drummed excitedly on the steering wheel.

⫷ **11** ⫸

Friday Afternoon

B Y NOON, THE PICKET HAD BROKEN UP. A handful of diehards continued to march back and forth in front of the clinic with their
posterboard signs. Mr. Ponytail had not returned. Mark was sure that
his absence had a lot to do with the peacefulness in the air.

Standing at the end of his sidewalk, Mark noticed a young couple
with heads bowed, sitting in the middle of the long row of benches.
Two identical posters that read "ADOPT, not ABORT" stood against
the benches nearby.

They're praying, Mark realized. He zipped up his coat and started
across the street.

The man was about his age, of average height and build, with
light brown hair and a well-trimmed beard. The woman had medium-
length brown hair and also looked to be in her early thirties. The
man's quiet prayer was marked with obvious concern.

Mark paused, second-guessing his intention to introduce himself,
but the man lifted his eyes and spotted him standing nearby. He
stopped in mid-sentence. His wife looked up.

Mark smiled. "Sorry to interrupt."

The man smiled back. "That's OK. What can I do for you?"

Mark hesitated, then decided to dive in. "My wife and I just moved
up here from Atlanta—into that end townhouse. We're Christians. I
just thought that I should introduce myself. The name's Mark Mac-
Donald."

"Kent Watkins, nice to meet you. This is my wife, Mary. I'm the
associate pastor at Agape Christian Fellowship. I'm also the picket coordinator, except for when Harold Wertman decides to use his bullhorn and dominate. The regulars ignore him. It's the new people I
worry about. Most see through his antics and maintain a good attitude. Some have bad manners to begin with and he just makes it
worse."

"He doesn't listen to you?" Mark asked.

"It's a difficult situation. I have strong convictions about being a
public witness for the Lord, but Harold's extremism only fuels the
opposition—like today. He heightens our opponents' belief that we

condone violence. Today was a particularly bad day for his out-bursts, especially on the heels of the clinic vandalism. There's a possibility our church will be investigated."

Mark breathed deeply, then dove in and explained what he'd seen Wednesday night. He also told them about his earlier meeting with the detective in charge of the case.

Kent's eye's brightened. "Troy Martin—you say? He's the detective who called and asked for names of people in our church who are involved in the picket. I really appreciate you telling me about this. We may need your testimony before it's all over."

Mark nodded. He liked Kent. "Where's your church located?"

"Right out 16th Street and Georgia Avenue and across the Beltway. If you'd like to attend our Sunday services or weekly home meetings, we'd love to have you. We place a strong emphasis on God's Word, corporate worship, and evangelism in a variety of forms—including the picket." Kent removed a business card from his jacket pocket.

"We participated in a Life Chain a couple times back in Atlanta," Mark explained. "And we want to attend the March for Life. Picketing, now that's another issue. My wife and I are not sure where we stand—no offense to you or your wife."

Mary smiled. "No offense taken. Whatever you decide, do it out of conviction, not compulsion, and make the Scriptures the basis for your convictions. If we had just one volunteer from each of the eight hundred churches in the D.C. metropolitan area, we could close this clinic. Right now, our most regular supporters are a small but dedicated group of Catholic charismatics. Really solid brothers and sisters in the Lord."

"That's wonderful," Mark said. Then he turned to Kent. "By the way, since you've been working with different groups in the area, what's up with the church across the park? It looks vacant."

"Used to be an independent Bible Church." Kent sighed. "About a year and a half ago, the pastor passed away. After several months of internal struggles, the congregation just up and dispersed. It was pretty strange—sad, too. They were always supportive of the picket. They're still trying to sell the property.

"We've got to go," Kent said as his wife smiled and grabbed his arm. "We're overdue on our babysitter. Hope we see you Sunday!"

Katie met Mark on the front porch as the Watkins climbed into their car. "I saw you talking to that couple. Who are they?"

Mark explained, his eyes wandering to the vacant church, then back across to the clinic. The two buildings juxtaposed themselves in his mind: light and darkness.

"Maybe we'll find ourselves a church home," Katie said with a grin. "It's not always easy to see in advance what the Lord has in mind, is it? Roots springing out of dry ground; new friends found in picket lines."

As he followed Katie into the foyer, a gust of wind slipped in behind him through the open door. He glanced back over his shoulder. The homeless man in the tattered jacket shuffled slowly along the top step of the church.

Mark shook his head and closed the door behind him.

From the corner of Lamont and 16th Street, just one block south of the clinic and in clear view of the park, Harold Wertman finished the last of the half-dozen jelly donuts. Using a pair of army surplus binoculars, he had watched the picket coordinator and his wife break away from the man with sandy hair and cross the park and street to their car. Now he was glad he read the book about the original John Brown. Old man Brown was cunning and suspicious. His instincts served him well and helped him avoid many dangerous situations in those violent years before the Civil War.

Harold could not explain what had kept him here in the van, maintaining his vigil long after Kim had called it a day. Maybe it was because he was so close to the pay-off. Maybe it was memories of past glories, like in '69 when he successfully orchestrated sit-ins at Cal-Berkeley to oppose the Vietnam War. Or maybe it was simply fate, the destiny that was his for the taking, just like the cagey John Brown of old!

He shook his head. What had the picket coordinator discussed with the man who lived at the end of the street? Maybe it was harmless conversation, or maybe, the newcomer was a police plant sent to undermine the Sponsor's operation. He would call Kim.

He put his binoculars on the seat and started the engine.

Michelle opened the upper-left drawer to her desk and stuck her purse inside. For her lunch hour, she had slipped on her walking shoes and taken the Metrorail to L'Enfant Plaza for a long stroll around the National Air and Space Museum. The walk had given her time to pray and seek the Lord.

One of her inside telephone lines buzzed noisily. She grabbed it. "This is Michelle."

The voice at the other end belonged to Carmen, secretary to Mr. Peters. Mr. Peters was the silver-haired East Coast AFI Director. Michelle did not know him well. Though his office was here in Washington, he was often on the road. Numerous conferences, seminars, and speaking engagements kept one of AFI's few golden-tongued and dignified promoters booked solid.

Carmen explained Mr. Peters' problem.

"I'll do what I can." Michelle waited as Carmen transferred Mr. Peters to her extension.

"Hi. I'm in the Blue Room and I need a check. Carmen says that you're the only person in the office right now with signing authority. What's your limit?"

"$25,000."

The line was silent for a moment. "OK. Cut two checks for $25,000 each."

Michelle made notes. "Who's the recipient?"

"Parallax, Ltd. Code both checks under Marketing and Consulting. Do you need me to co-sign?"

"No sir, but please have Carmen dash off a memo authorizing me to write these two checks. I don't want it to show up on an audit that I attempted to circumvent my authorization levels."

"No problem."

Five minutes later with checks in hand, Michelle opened the mahogany door to the main conference room. Blue walls and carpet encompassed a long, rectangular mahogany table and twenty leather armchairs. At the opposite end of the room was a huge window overlooking a park. This was John Q. Public's view of AFI, whether neighborhood groups, school boards or remote television crews.

This afternoon the long mahogany table was covered with a half-dozen, large posters. Standing over the table was the handsome, fifty-year old Mr. Peters in his three-piece suit, and at his side, a second gentleman who Michelle vaguely remembered seeing once or twice before. The visitor looked to be in his early forties and was of medium height with straight black hair that fell onto his shoulders. He wore baggy gray pants and a loose-fitting plaid jacket that made guesswork of his actual build; his tie was a thin streak of bright red down his white shirt.

She approached the table and glanced at the posters. A triangular black guitar was the primary foreground image on each one. She held back her surprise at what appeared to be promotional pieces for a rock group. But before she was able to get a closer view, Mr. Peters and his guest looked up and turned from the table.

"You're prompt. I like that." Mr. Peters took the checks.

"Will there be anything else?" she asked, finding her eyes drawn to Mr. Peters' guest who preempted the Director with a reply.

"I can think of plenty else."

The odd turn of phrase with its clear insinuation arrested her attention. Their eyes met and she felt an uncomfortable rush in her cheeks and neck. She knew she was blushing. She had to force herself to break contact with his deep gray eyes.

Mr. Peters laughed. "Now, Brian, be good and don't frighten away our Controller. In a month Michelle may become our Finance Director and then she'll be signing all your checks."

"What a pleasure that would be," Brian replied, his eyes searching.

Michelle forced a smile and excused herself. Stepping into the hall, she heard a sudden burst of laughter through the wooden door.

She blushed deeply as her embarassment turned to anger. Women's rights advocates—what hypocrites! She hurried past the receptionist toward her suite of offices at the opposite end of the hall, relishing in advance the supreme humbling that her exposé of AFI would one day bring.

⋙ **12** ⋘

Late Friday Afternoon

MARK OPENED THE STUDY DOOR. Bright sunlight slanted across the room and onto the fireplace, the mantle and the antique sword. Light shimmered off the sword's pommel and caught his eye.

He lifted the sword from the rack and slid it out of the sheath. The grip felt cool in his hand. Pointing the sword toward the window, his eyes followed the play of light up and down the silvery length of the slightly curved blade.

Returning the sword to its sheath, he placed it on the rack. A wave of confusion rolled through his thoughts. Why, Grandpa Kyle? Why did you hide these fantastic things from our family?

As Mark turned toward the desk, a smile crept across his face. It seemed like ages since he last read Sam's journals, though he knew barely twelve hours had passed since he had crept quietly down the stairs and joined his sleeping wife at 1:30 A.M. in the morning.

He lifted the leather-bound journal from the table, pulled the chair up to the desk and sat down. At the top of the page, Sam had penned a simple header.

Family History
<u>The Two-Fold Cord:</u>
<u>The Christian and the Savage</u>

No story in my family history, however fascinating, can compare with the story of the two-fold cord, the marriage of my grandparents. The ill-fated entwining of these two souls entangled our family bloodline in the discordant strands of evil and grace.

My grandfather, Will MacDonald, was raised in a Christian home in Culpeper, Virginia, but his own yielding to sin led him to become a savage in the Kentucky wilderness. Because of his rebellion, the strand of evil entered our family line.

The abundant grace that entered the MacDonald line came through my grandmother, a young Shawnee princess. Raised as a savage in the Ohio wilderness, she abandoned the gods of her fathers, knelt before the cross, and became a Christian.

Nikki, short for Nikitchecame, My Peaceful Lake, was the daughter of Pucksinwah, the Shawnee Kispotha chief, and the half-sister of Tecumseh, the great Shawnee leader. Nikki was born into the kingdom of darkness in 1770 along the banks of Ohio's Little Miami River in Chillicothe, literally The Place, the center of Shawnee life and culture. Nikki was born again into the kingdom of light in Lexington, Kentucky, in 1791 through the preaching of Francis Asbury, the tireless Methodist circuit rider.

In 1785, at the age of fourteen, she was presented as a "gift" to Will MacDonald, a wily frontiersman who had saved Tecumseh's life.

In 1828, long after my Grandpa Will had died, my father, my brother John, and I came to live with Grandma Nikki in Springfield, Ohio. For eight years we helped with her farm. Although she was a full blood Shawnee, over forty years of living in a frontier community, adopting the ways of the white man, and demonstrating Christian love and charity opened many hearts to her. God graced her devoted life, and she had many fine white Christian friends.

In the afternoons Grandma and I took walks along the edge of the forest, and in the evenings she told stories to all of us. Sometimes, I would lie on the warm stone hearth, watching embers pulse in the fireplace. Those were days I shall always cherish.

Saturday mornings we sat on the porch and she shared from her heart. These were special times. Her silver hair shimmered like the moon and her eyes danced with the joy of Christ. She gently rocked in her "oaken, broken" rocker, with a quilt draped over her knees. Her thumb marked a place in her old worn Bible. She was a woman deeply devoted to God, one who had come to understand the blessing and the curse.

During these sessions, I generally whittled at an old stick of sycamore or beech. Dad perched himself on an old log stool, puffing on his pipe, while John leaned against a corner post, his arms resting on his knees.

One special morning we took our usual places. I was sixteen and John Ezra was eighteen. Grandma had something very important to tell us.

"Boys, your father and I agree the time has come for you to hear the story of your Grandpa Will, his lie, the stolen knife, and how he fell into the darkness and brought a curse on the MacDonald line.

"Your Grandpa Will's father, Joseph Hosea MacDonald, was a bitter man. He treated Will badly and Will hated him. In '74,

Joseph's cousin, Colonel Angus McDonald, paid a visit to your Grandpa's house in Virginia. Angus was a legendary frontiersman and spun some tall tales of life in the wilderness. Will, only seventeen at the time, hung on every word. Came time for Angus to leave and Will decided to follow. Didn't tell his folks; just slipped away late one morning. Now Angus tried to talk him into going back but your Grandpa Will showed him his father's "Long Knife," that silver sword which had hung over the family's fireplace mantle. Will convinced Angus that his father had sent him, and told him that the Long Knife was a gift, a sign of his father's blessing.

"It was a lie, boys, a boldfaced lie," she said, pumping her oaken rocker back and forth. "Well, your Grandpa Will never saw his folks again. Never saw Virginia again. Spent the next few years roaming the wilds of Kentucky, staking land claims. Never did honest work. Even after we were married, after he traded for this land, after he built this house and settled down for a short while, your Grandpa never did take to working the land like most. Half our meals came from the hills or the woods. In spite of his wandering ways, God still allowed your Grandpa to make a tidy fortune in land.

"Well, boys, back in '77, there was a lot of new folk coming down the Ohio; seemed like every day they was coming. Most of them was heading for Kentucky. This place was the hunting ground for both the Shawnee and the Cherokee. But the white folk, they wanted to stay there, live there, build houses, plant fields, and graze cattle. At first your grandpa and his buddies helped the folks coming down the Ohio as best they could, helped start new towns, helped build forts.

"But after a while, the white folks got to fighting the Indians. They was all ranging through the woods—burning, scalping, looting, and taking prisoners. There was a lot of hate in those days, boys, on both sides.

"Your Grandpa was no stranger to all this. In fact, he was a big part of it. In '78, the killings and the violence got so bad that folks called Kentucky the dark and bloody ground.

"In '85, your Grandpa saved my half-brother's life. He shot a tomahawk out of the hand of a frontiersman who was about to lay it into Tecumseh's skull. Don't exactly know what drove him to do that, boys, only know that God had his plans. If Will hadn't saved his life, we never would have married, he never would have dragged me off to Lexington, I would have never met Francis Asbury or my Savior Jesus, your father Eli never would have been born and neither would you."

She smiled and winked at us, a momentary respite from her otherwise grim tale.

"1790 started off to be a right good year for us, boys. Why, that was the year your daddy was born, and that was the year I met my Savior. And I even got your Grandpa to go to some of brother Asbury's meetings. Why, I thought for sure that Will was gonna give his heart to Jesus, too, just like I had done.

"But then, only ten miles north of our cabin in Lexington, a tragedy plunged your Grandpa deep into a prison of hatred. One afternoon in late December while out on a hunt, your Grandpa happened on an Indian raid. Nine Shawnees fell on a small cabin, pulled the family out into the open and began to torture them. Tied up the whole family first, and then laid a tomahawk right into the father's skull. Next, they took two of the three children and scalped them right in front of their mother. Will listened to her screams, but knew he was outnumbered, so he just hid at the base of a big oak tree, horrified. Your Grandpa knew the Shawnee, and what would happen next.

"One of the warriors grabbed the woman, ripped her clothes off, then stuck his knife into her belly. The Shawnee took the last child captive and then burned the cabin and barn. Your grandpa waited in the woods several hours, to be sure that the Indians were gone. Then he walked down to the site of the raid and spent the next day burying the victims. His heart grew to hate even more than ever before, and he vowed to avenge their deaths.

"News about the brutal Shawnee attack was all over these parts. I tell you boys, as a full blood Shawnee, I was scared for my own safety. But brother Francis helped to calm down the townspeople and convinced them that I was not their enemy.

"Several days after he seen that brutal murder, your Grandpa came to get his things and told me he was a leaving for good. Treated me real bad that night. Hit me in the face and knocked me down. Your daddy was just a baby at the time. I was scared for him, too.

"Never saw your Grandpa Will again after that night."

Nikki shifted in her rocker and started up again. John and I had not moved, our eyes glued to her dark, sad face. "After your Grandpa left, I guess I could have gone back to my people, but I had made so many good friends at church, and they loved me and took care of me and your daddy after your Grandpa left. I just realized that these people were my true family.

"Six years later, in 1797, a group of us moved here, to Springfield. Then, twenty-two years after your Grandpa left, your grandpa's old buddy, Jasper, showed up on my porch. And he told me a tale about your Grandpa Will that I still have a hard time believing, boys. And if Jasper hadn't told me personally, I still wouldn't believe it.

"Seems that two years after the brutal murders in Lexington, your grandpa was out hunting with Jasper and a couple of his other buddies. It was early February '93 and a blanket of snow was on the ground. They spotted a small band of Indians—a family, maybe seven or eight of them. Will and the others decided to hold a raid of their own that night. Well, they snuck up and murdered them in cold blood. Even took some scalps. And after all the blood, boys, as they was a getting ready to leave, your Grandpa seen a young Indian woman hiding in the woods. She had new life in her belly."

Grandma's eyes narrowed and she focused in on me. My small knife was now on the ground next to the whittling stick. "Now, boys," she said, "this ain't too pleasant to hear, but you need to hear it, so listen up careful. All that hatred and anger that had been building up inside your Grandpa Will took hold of him, drove him to chase that young woman down and plunge his Long Knife into her belly. She screamed. He reached into her womb and pulled out the baby. Left them lying on the ground to die.

"Jasper said that after this happened, something changed in your Grandpa. Said he seemed possessed by the Devil. And after a while, Jasper left your Grandpa to hisself. Said he couldn't stand to be with him no more.

"Jasper told me that in those years after he killed the pregnant woman and her baby that nothing could stop your Grandpa from murdering Indians.

"In fact, Jasper said your Grandpa was a butcher.

"Jasper told me that he met up with your Grandpa again in 1813, up north at the Battle of the Thames on the same bloody field that my brother Tecumseh died on defending his people.

"Your Grandpa was killed in that battle, too."

Grandma sat quietly for a few moments. None of us knew what to say. Finally, she threw off her quilt and went back inside the cabin. A moment later she returned with a sword in one hand. "Sam, the Lord has shown me that I should give you this. You must stand against the evil that wrought this sword and redeem what your grandfather lost."

Grandma looked straight at me. "The day that Jasper came by and told me the sad story about your Grandpa, he gave me back the Long Knife that you now have in your hand—the sword Will stole off of his father's mantle, the sword he used to brutally murder the pregnant Indian woman and her baby, the sword that butchered so many innocent people. Jasper said that as your Grandpa lay dying on the battlefield, he made Jasper swear that he would return the sword to the MacDonald family where it belonged. I was the only family Jasper knew of.

"Just remember, boys, it all started with your Grandpa's little lie—the lie he told to Angus when he ran away with him. But that little lie was the first fruit of something dark within your Grandpa's heart—his wanting to live his life his own way, to be his own god."

I remember exchanging glances with my brother John as I held the sword. We didn't know quite what to make of Grandma's words.

"Now I know this sounds like something you'd hear on Sunday morning. I've rocked in this chair for thirty years, watching my people driven from their lands. I've read the Scriptures and thought about your Grandpa Will. He and the other frontiersmen came west to claim the land they thought was theirs. They believed their destiny was to possess this land from sea to sea. But their spirit of adventure turned to murder and violence.

"Before long, tens of thousands were streaming westward on foot and horseback, in wagons, flat boats, and steamers to possess the wide green land that flowed with milk and honey." Grandma's face was filled with pain. "Chiksika, one of my half-brothers, said 'the white race is a monster who is always hungry, and what he eats is land.' Think on it and ask yourself if it ain't so."

Not too long after Grandma told us this story, her life came to a quick and violent end. Always concerned about others, she was helping the underground railroad get runaway slaves into Canada. My father warned her of the potential dangers, but in her usual fashion, she insisted that this was what God wanted her to do.

One evening, three bounty hunters came to her cabin looking for a runaway. Of course Grandma wasn't about to give them any information. One of the men pushed her down and her head hit the porch steps. They set fire to her cabin and rode off. John and I were with our father in a field just beyond the ridge and saw the smoke rising. By the time we arrived, Grandma was groggy. We were able get her to safety, but the cabin burned all the way to the ground. Father carried her to the barn where she told us what happened. She prayed that God would forgive the men for what they had done, and that the slaves would find freedom.

To my surprise, Nikki told my father and brother to leave the barn. She pulled on my shirt and brought my face down close to hers in the cool semi-darkness. Her round black eyes stared into mine.

"Remember the Long Knife, Sam. And remember what I'm going to tell you. For fifty-one years I've lived the life of a white woman. Been a good life, and I've come to know the white man's God, and His Son, Jesus. I believe He's the one true God."

She coughed, then continued to speak. "I still remember my days as a maiden, playing with my brothers and sisters along the banks of the Miami-se-pe. How I long to go home to the wigwam of my mother, to run my fingers again through her hair as I did as a child.

"I'd tell her about the Son of God, Sam, for I fear I won't see her in heaven. But I know this can't be."

Grandma Nikki's eyes were moist with tears; she coughed again and tightened her grip on my shirt. I shall never forget that moment, staring into the face of a woman now so close to Christ and to heaven, yet suddenly and painfully so distant from her family and home. She swallowed hard and closed her eyes. I leaned closer and squeezed her hands in mine.

"The day of our wedding, my brother Tecumseh grabbed your Grandpa Will by the shoulders and stared into his eyes. Then he spoke a word to him that you must now hear. 'You have shed innocent blood. But because you saved my life and are my friend, I have prayed to my god, Moneto. I asked that he would tell me what to say to you. Moneto was silent for three days. Then, at dawn, I heard a voice more powerful and more clearly than I have ever heard before.

"'Out of your loins will come two men with strong medicine. With their lips they will drink from a bitter spring. With their ears they will hear the cry of the blood. With their eyes they will see the dark root of evil in men's souls.'"

Grandma spoke through her pain. "Wasn't old Moneto that spoke to my half-brother, boys, but the Lord, himself. He knew in advance about that Long Knife, that sword of sin, and how He'd work healing for the blood it would shed."

Her hands loosened from my shirt, and she died on the barn floor. I wept.

I think often of Grandpa and Grandma, the savage and the Christian, the two-fold cord. Grandma Nikki died, hoping that the curse of sin and the chains of darkness that sought to entangle the MacDonald bloodline would one day be broken by the blessings of grace. Her legacy of faithfulness must never be forgotten, lest the Devil find a way to revisit his curse upon us.

Mark looked up from the journal.

Katie called from the bottom of the stairs. "Dinner! Five minutes!"

Mark hardly heard her. He straddled two worlds a century and a half apart, one foot in a barn with Sam and Grandma Nikki, the other in his study. His gaze was drawn above the fireplace and mantle to the silver-pommeled sword. Though he had no proof, somehow he knew that it was no cavalry officer's sword, but a frontiersman's sword! Will's Long Knife, that sword of sin and source of violence that somehow reached through the generations and altered the course of Sam's life!

A queasy feeling wormed through Mark's stomach. He had handled that sword!

Without thinking, Mark wiped his hand on his pant leg, and then remembered something else Sam had written about the sword. He reached across the desk and pulled the yellowed receipt from the center pigeonhole containing what may have been Sam's last recorded words.

Is this not the testimony of the gleaming, sin-stained blade of my grandfather's Long Knife? Is this not the Devil's fiendish, eternal scheme to scar God's creation with a bloodline fashioned from human life? Does not God require that which is past?

Each word flamed with both meaning and mystery, stirring emotions that he could not name. A prickly sensation ran down his right arm and across the palm and fingers of his right hand.

Mark laid the receipt face down in the middle of the open desk. He pushed himself from the straight back chair, then turned and stared again at the journal entry one last time.

Her legacy of faithfulness must never be forgotten, lest the Devil find a way to revisit his curse upon us.

Mark stuffed his hands in his pockets. Grandpa Kyle's hiding of Sam, Nikki, Will, and his sword had kept the MacDonald family line unaware of their past. Sam clearly wrote that Nikki's legacy of faithfulness must never be forgotten.

For all intents, wasn't Grandpa Kyle's hiding Sam's writings the same as making them forget?

He left the study, not sure at all that he liked the answer or the sudden, bitter taste at the back of his mouth.

Traffic heading northbound out of Washington was light.

Michelle accelerated her Toyota. After recovering from being embarrassed by Mr. Peters and his consultant, the balance of her day's work went by swiftly. She finished compiling the numbers for her forecast and helped Julie get started on reorganizing the accounts payable files. The Crest Road clinic was fully operational again: carpets cleaned, file shelves rehung, the defunct photocopier replaced —by the copier ordered a week and a half ago.

The final version of her preliminary expense forecast was nearly completed for Monday's 10:00 A.M. meeting. That forecast would be her excuse for coming in to the office Saturday morning. No one else would be down in her end of the Finance and Accounting suites.

Michelle's smile hardened. The transaction that she had witnessed earlier in the day between Mr. Peters and the consultant set her mind in motion over an obvious and routine business principle: services performed required payment. In the AFI's case, millions of dollars flowed from the federal government and private industry into their coffers to supplement the graduated payments made by AFI's patients. The younger and poorer you were, the greater the supplement. While superficially compassionate, this logic gave thousands of teenagers access to free contraceptives, consultations, and exams —and more often than John Q. Public could possibly suspect, abortions without parental consent. Did anyone stop and consider what *without parental consent* really meant?

AFI did. And they meticulously recorded each and every service they provided. As a result of their fastidious accounting, perhaps the funds used to finance the vandalism had been recorded, too. All they'd have to do was set up a dummy account to pass the monies through, not in a single, traceable payment, but several small payments that totaled a significant amount. Crime was expensive.

And if an audit trail for those payments existed, she was going to find it—one way or another! If not tomorrow, then next week or next month. Once she had Carol's position as Director, she would doggedly follow every crooked turn in the very crooked maze of AFI's financial history until she had them, hands down—signed, sealed, and delivered between the pages of an investigative story that would make the Conservative Bookclub's bestseller list!

Six months! That's all she would need to expose AFI for what it really was—an enterprise whose primary goal was to push aside the Judeo-Christian view of parental authority and human rights. The East Coast and West Coast clinic-based Goliath was an organization that sought to destroy life, rather than to nurture it. Their growing franchise operation would soon have clinics in every state, misleading teenage girls with their own evolutionary interpretation of the biological facts of conception while hiding the potential physical and emotional dangers involved with an abortion.

Michelle gripped the steering wheel until her hands ached. She forced herself to stop rehashing her conservative rhetoric against the AFI. Once begun, her mind would replay the same sequence of wrongdoings over and over like a tape deck with auto-reverse.

But AFI was worse than anyone's rhetoric! Even Planned Parenthood offered a wider range of services than the American Family Institute! AFI talked education and family planning to preserve their non-profit status, but their efforts were actually focused on one specific mechanism for preventing live births.

Still, dwelling on the negative merely fueled the anger and bitterness that day by day sought a foothold in her heart. She could not lose her edge—not now. For her sister Anne's sake, and others who suffered far worse than she, Michelle knew she had to find a way to endure until she could expose AFI and its sprawling empire of death and deception.

She turned right onto Colesville Road toward Silver Spring. There was a war going on and she was behind enemy lines.

Fletcher pulled his TransAm into the garage and cut the engine. The garage door rumbled shut. He lowered his head against the steering wheel. Over the last two days he slept a total of four hours. His emotions were stretched taut, making the four hours feel like none at all. He knew he needed a good eight hours of undisturbed sleep to clear the cobwebs from his brain.

Something was wrong with the way Troy was handling the two cases. Fletcher's nose had been glued to the streets for too many years not to recognize the smell of corruption—but he was too exhausted to analyze the scent properly. KC was involved, too. With Botello's help he was going to stick his nose down into the refuse until he got to the bottom of it. But not tonight.

He climbed wearily from the car.

Mark and Katie cleared the dinner dishes from the dining room table. After they were done, Mark closed an overstuffed garbage bag with a twist-tie.

He unlocked the back door and switched on the porch light. He pushed back the curtain and looked out the rear bay window into the darkness. "Look's like the porch light's out."

"I'll put bulbs on the grocery list. I'm going shopping again tomorrow," Katie answered.

Plastic bag in hand, Mark descended the concrete steps, his thoughts already elsewhere, leaping backwards through time, weighing the generational sin that a crusty frontiersman's bloody sword had brought to the MacDonald family....

13

Friday Evening

A TLANTA HAD NOT BEEN SO COLD IN JANUARY, Katie thought, as she stared out the window at the park below. In D.C. a waist-length ski jacket just wouldn't do, particularly now that there was another MacDonald who also needed to be kept warm. Katie decided to go shopping in nearby Georgetown for a full-length red wool coat.

"No, you cannot go with me. I want to have fun!" she had said five minutes earlier with a short laugh, punching Mark in the arm. "Baby MacDonald and I can handle ourselves just fine, thank you. Whatever virtues you have disappear the moment you set foot in a women's clothing store."

He watched Katie enter the Blazer and drive away. He dropped the curtain and sat back down at the desk, his thoughts returning to the journals.

Glancing at the heading to Sam's next journal entry, he was thoroughly puzzled. From June of 1856 to July of 1858, Sam had not penned a single entry. Two years. The huge gap in time was unsettling. Would Sam explain why he stopped writing?

Mark glanced up at the Long Knife above the fireplace and mantle, and then back to the journal.

16 July 1858
Baird Hall

Twenty-two years ago today Grandma Nikki died. I am no longer the wide-eyed, sixteen-year old who knelt beside his dying grandmother as she spoke that incredible prophecy. After twenty-two years of wandering, I have returned to the very city and university where I first began to explore the implications of God's sovereign calling.

So, on the anniversary of that fateful day in Grandma Nikki's barn, I ask: What lessons have I learned in these past twenty-two years?

Strong Medicine

During the cold, winter months of 1833, my father suffered from a severe attack of influenza. Martin Dawson, Springfield's only physician, attended to his illness. I am certain God used him to save my father's life. Deeply touched by his Christian benevolence, the seeds of a healer were planted in my soul, even though I was but thirteen at the time.

Following Nikki's death in '36, when our family visited with Dr. Dawson, I shared my desire to enter the University of Pennsylvania Medical School. I received an immediate and hearty "amen" from Dr. Dawson. Father had just accepted an invitation to Shawnee Mission, Kansas, to assist in mission work among the Indians. Without me, many of the burdens of everyday life would fall upon John Ezra's shoulders.

But my father saw the fiery vision in my eyes. The next morning he blessed my request to leave home. I arrived in Philadelphia in the fall of '38, my heart afire with vision. I wanted to become a man of strong medicine—not yet realizing just how that desire would be fulfilled.

The Bitter Spring

In 1838 when I climbed into the wagon bound for the University of Philadelphia, I distinctly remember feeling a peculiar, harsh sense of loss. I had only felt it two other times in my life: first at age six, when I learned that my mother had died bringing *me* into the world, and second, when Grandma Nikki died in my arms. As I waved goodbye to Father and John Ezra, I had no idea why I felt so troubled. Perhaps it was but a foretaste of the even more bitter suffering that would eventually be mine.

The sorrowful account of my beloved Victoria's death, my former hatred for Beaumont and the loss of nearly three years of my life already fill many journal pages. O how that bitter spring deceived me, first tasting sweet, and then poisoning my soul. At last I have been healed of its acrid contaminations, cleansed by the dayspring and filled with living water. By grace I have gained the freedom of forgiveness and yielded to the work of the Cross.

The Cry of the Blood

I had chosen the field of medicine for my life's service but I did not suspect that You led me to Philadelphia for a different purpose. From the window at the end of this hall, I can see the stone wall where I first sat in the spring of '39, over nineteen years ago. There I reflected upon the words of the outspoken abolitionist,

Dr. Theodore Weld. His words deeply affected me, an impressionable zealous youth. He recounted Senator Daniel Webster's speech before the Senate, a speech which Mrs. Criswell had once instructed our entire grade-school class to memorize:

> While the Union lasts we have high, exciting, gratifying prospects spread out before us, for us and our children. Beyond that I seek not to penetrate the veil. God grant that in my day at least that curtain may not rise! God grant that on my vision never may be opened what lies behind! When my eyes shall be turned to behold for the last time the sun in heaven, may I not see him shining on the broken and dishonored fragments of a once glorious Union; on states dissevered, discordant, belligerent; on a land rent with civil feuds, or drenched, it may be, in fraternal blood.

Fraternal blood! May it never be, Lord!

Mrs. Criswell also required us to memorize William Lloyd Garrison's inflammatory diatribe concerning Nat Turner's ill-fated revolt in Southampton, Virginia.

> The first drops of blood, which are but a prelude to a deluge from the gathering clouds, have fallen.

My original interpretation of the prophecy, and its enthusiasm for "strong medicine" and my medical studies became supplanted by what seemed a much loftier goal, to use my pen to bring an end to slavery before our land became bathed in blood.

Try as I might to apply myself diligently to my subjects, I could not shake the fervent words of Weld and others. My heart was filled with indignation toward my Southern brethren. I joined the American Anti-Slavery Society in the spring of '39 and wrote several abolitionist pamphlets.

Later that year I received my father's urgent appeal to come and aid him at the mission in Kansas. It was not difficult for me to leave Philadelphia. I arrived in Kansas in the spring of '41, anxious to devote all my efforts toward strengthening the abolitionist movement in Kansas.

My zeal quickly turned to discouragement when I learned that the Reverend Thomas Johnson, founder of the Shawnee Methodist Mission, was not only a strong defender of the "peculiar institution," but a slaveholder himself. Imagine the conflict which arose in my heart! I struggled with his contradictory testimony. He had established a school to teach the Shawnee boys and girls English, farming, household skills, and religion while forcing his Negroes to labor in the fields.

I turned to my pen, writing short articles for the <u>Anti-Slavery</u> <u>Bugle.</u> Amazingly, the <u>New York Tribune</u> picked up some of my work. Within weeks I received an invitation to work as a regular reporter in Kansas. I was given assignments for special essays and with little effort began earning $35 a week. Buoyed by my success with writing, I purchased an old, used printing press and established the <u>Methodist Register</u>, a small but influential news organ which reached many readers in eastern Kansas and western Missouri.

In the spring of '46, zealous and determined, I dedicated myself to the task of preventing the cry of the blood that I feared would one day echo across our land.

The Dark Root of Evil in Men's Souls

Throughout the latter forties I not only wrote for the abolitionist cause, but I also began to write about the unprecedented growth taking place in the Kansas-Nebraska region.

Then, in 1849, I witnessed the dark root of evil sprout its gilded shoots from American soil. Gold had been unearthed at Sutter's Mill. "Westward Ho!" the settlers cried, rushing down the Santa Fe Trail, the California Trail, the Gila Trail, dusty arteries that led thousands to their dream of instant riches. As a reporter, I covered the Oregon Trail, from its point of origin to Fort Kearny, Nebraska, just south of the mighty Platte.

The western sky is dark. The white man's insatiable pursuit of gold and land, his determination to accumulate wealth, is truly fierce! The Founding Fathers sacrificed their lives, fortunes, and sacred honor for fundamental truths. We have replaced their original goals of religious liberty with our own, a civil religion based on selfish ambition.

Our altar is the land and its resources; our sacrifices are the Negro and Indian; our sacraments are the inventions of our own hands: the steam locomotive, the telegraph wire, and the cotton gin.

Is not the dark root that which brings forth the cry of the blood?

Full Circle

What have I learned? When I was young, I spoke as a child. I saw through a glass darkly, knowing only in part the mysteries of God's will that are bound up in His call upon my life. The bitter springs have not stopped flowing, the cry of the blood has not ceased and the dark root of evil in men's souls continues to spread like madness across the land. Sectional pride, malice and greed course through our veins! If this nation is to be saved from "civil feuds" and the shedding of "fraternal blood" as Webster so feared in 1830, then it needs strong medicine, as I have noted profusely in my research on the Founding Fathers.

Kim Park hung up the telephone and stepped from the phone booth. The Oriental young woman wearing tight-fitting jeans and a red cashmere sweater opened the passenger door to a silver Ferrari and slid into the deep bucket seat. She glanced to her left.

Kim Park met True Believer's cold, gray eyes squarely.

"Everything's arranged. They will be there."

She leaned back into the leather seat, rubbed her arms and looked away from the man who controlled her while she was assigned to the U.S., a man whose real name she would never know.

She watched silently as True Believer turned the key and glanced over his left shoulder. The Ferrari roared to life, and then slid effortlessly into the Friday night traffic and headed into Georgetown.

A mile further on, he slowed momentarily at a busy corner lined with shops and clothing stores. A smiling young woman wearing a new red, full-length wool coat slowly crossed the street to her Blazer.

⇜ **14** ⇝

Friday Night

R ESEARCH ON THE FOUNDING FATHERS! Mark glanced back to the last sentence in the journal entry.

So, Sam had more than one writing project! That explained why there were such large gaps in time between entries in his personal journals! He wasn't just writing about his family, but the nation, too! His personal history was nothing more than a microcosm of what was happening all across the country. If the MacDonald family line struggled from being a two-fold cord of good and evil through Nikki and Will, what did that say about America and its founding fathers?

Mark's newfound excitement faded abruptly as it began. Now a second, more problematic mystery arose. What had happened to Sam's Founding Fathers' research? And what about all the correspondence with Lincoln? Had the research and the letters been lost? An anxious thought dogged Mark. Lost—or intentionally removed by Grandpa Kyle?

He didn't want to consider that possibility.

A faint smile crept back onto Mark's face as he returned to the journal and Sam's neat, dark script. Twenty-two years. Sam had come full circle in his understanding of the meaning of the prophecy and God's will for his life—accepting the bitter springs, responding to the cry of the blood, resisting the dark root of evil and becoming a man of strong medicine, a man of physical and spiritual healing, a man determined to have an impact on his generation.

Mark picked up Sam's second journal.

The next entry was dated December 3, 1859. Sam began by noting Mr. Pitkin's request that he write a feature story about a small, but important munitions factory nestled among steep, rocky cliffs at the joining of the Potomac and Shenandoah rivers in northwestern Virginia.

Mark scratched his right ear.

Harper's Ferry. A decade of high school and college history lessons came rushing back. Harper's Ferry was where John Brown—abolitionist and angel of God to the North, madman and the Devil incar-

115

nate to the South—led a small band of insurrectionists in a fateful attempt to ignite a slave rebellion.

Was this another way Tecumseh's prophecy about the cry of the blood and the root of evil in men's souls would find fulfillment in Sam's life?

The booths at Max's Seafood Grill on Maine Avenue near the Washington Marina were tall, dimly lit, and private if privacy was desired.

In the next to last booth at the far end of the bar, KC and Troy sat across from Kim Park, a thin Oriental who wore a sheer red blouse and a black silk pants suit. In the middle of the table was a half-filled pitcher of beer from which Troy freely filled his mug.

"It is very important that we keep our Sponsors informed of any developments in either case, no matter how insignificant they seem," Kim explained in a serious tone, brushing her straight black bangs from her eyes.

"The critical aspects of the venture begin next Tuesday. We cannot afford problems that will lead to delays. If you are unable to handle those delays, tell me immediately."

KC raised her eyes to meet Kim's. "You can reassure the Sponsors that Troy's on top of both cases—but I'm surprised they don't know that already. Whoever pulled our captain's strings pulled them quietly and effectively."

The ex-tackle wrapped his huge hands around his beer. "The only real problem we face is a loose cannon by the name of Rivers—it's in the report." He placed a white envelope on the table.

Kim's eyebrows arched sharply and her small hands clenched into fists. "Your instructions were explicit! Notify me immediately of such developments—not days later and in a report! The Sponsors will find this unacceptable."

Troy raised his huge hand and pointed a thick finger at Kim, the muscles in his thick neck and jaw tightening. "Look, we've got our hands deep into a couple of very special cookie jars. We told you about Mark MacDonald the same afternoon he came in. Same with the anonymous tip. If the Sponsors are not satisfied with the level of risk that KC and I take on their behalf, then tell them they know what they can do!"

He lowered his hand. "Or else sweeten the pot."

Kim's face paled. "You are being compensated well for what is asked of you. Don't jeopardize our relationship with loose words."

KC smiled sardonically, put her hand on his wrist and held it down. "Our relationship has jeopardized our careers. The information that we provide carries a heavy price tag—instant dismissal and criminal charges—if we're caught."

In the tall booth directly behind Kim, True Believer sat with his back pressed into the corner of the wall, unseen, listening carefully as KC argued her point. His gray eyes stared thoughtfully into the semi-darkness as he considered the cost of doing business with people who found motivation solely in material gain. Success was synonymous with sacrifice, and sacrifice was based on selflessness—an invaluable quality possessed by so few of his American operatives.

Seasoned mercenaries—like the three ex-Marines who staged the vandalism and completed the critical insertion at the clinic—were professionals and an exception to the norm. His 70s Cal-Berkeley radical and self-proclaimed visionary, Harold Wertman, could not seem to look beyond the next meal. Still, using people like Harold, KC, and Troy had certain other benefits. Small amounts of money could purchase their eyes, ears, feet, hands, and knowledge plus allow him easy access to information, people and places beyond his sphere of influence. But more often than not, they were shortsighted, even blind, to the important values in life and to the global dynamics that made the world turn round.

KC, Troy, and Kim's conversation ended with an exchange of plain, white envelopes across the table. True Believer listened to the shuffle of money, the click of KC's cigarette lighter that always marked the completion of their transaction. He ignored the despicable smell of smoke as KC and her detective lackey slid out of the booth and walked away.

True Believer lifted his glass of Irish beer and sipped it slowly. Seconds later, Kim stepped around the corner and scooted into the booth across from him. She placed a white envelope on the table in front of him.

"Bonn and Geneva will be pleased," she said, with a smile.

3 December 1859, 4:25 P.M.
Sheppard's Boardinghouse, Washington D.C.

John Brown's hanging has given newspapers from Boston to Atlanta the occasion to rehash his ill-fated plan to free the South of slavery. I have heard that Harper's Weekly is already considering a biography. History will reserve a generous portion for this man, although whether as a champion or damnable villain has yet to be decided. My contribution to this debate has been delayed. I lost two journals that chronicled my eight weeks in Harper's Ferry and Charlestown, drafts of newspaper articles and my copy of John Brown's last written words.

In those journals I not only recorded my interview with John

Brown in his prison cell, but the astonishing story told to me by the hunchbacked priest, Father Gibault.

I had made such copious notes, giving tedious attention to both detail and accuracy. Tomorrow I shall contact the B&O railroad and request a search be made for the journals. I fear this is a vain measure, for journals do not simply fall out of a securely closed book bag.

Be still, Soul! Does not God Almighty guide the affairs of men? Does a sparrow fall without His knowledge? Has He not numbered even the hairs of our head? Is there not purpose in all of His ways?

Father in heaven, I ask for the ability to remember what has been lost, lest your humble servant, Father Gibault, shall have lived a life of suffering and trial in vain.

John Brown

Two days before John Brown's hanging, John Avis, Charlestown's jailer, escorted me to the condemned man's cell. It was the first time I had seen the white-haired bearded man since his November 2d sentencing. I found him resting quietly on a narrow cot, the same cot on which he had lain during most of his trial, stricken with fever. He awaited his execution with the peaceful repose of an angel.

As I entered he sat up, chains clanking. Those same passionate eyes I had seen at his sentencing were now focused on me. I recalled his final oration before Judge Parker, the jury, and a packed courtroom.

"I see a book kissed, which I suppose to be the Bible," his voice rang out in the courtroom, "or at least the New Testament, which teaches me that all things whatsoever I would that men should do to me, I should do to them. It teaches me further to remember them that are in bonds, as bound with them. I endeavored to act up to that instruction."

As I faced him in the cell I was unprepared for what proved the most peculiar interview of my journalistic career. No sooner had the cell door closed behind me, than did John Brown place a hand over his heart and begin to speak.

"Christ is the great captain of liberty, as well as of salvation, and who began his mission, as foretold of him by proclaiming it, saw fit to take from me a sword of steel. But he has put another sword in my hand, the Sword of the Spirit. I pray to God to make me a faithful soldier wherever he may send me.

"Tell your fellow Southerners that the gallows do not frighten me. My value to the cause of righteousness, the cause of Christ, is much greater as a corpse swinging from a rope, than any other fate. Tell your readers also: let them fear what God shall do to them in their sleep."

The force of his presence and his shrewd insight amazed me. He had hoped to exploit the greatest fear of a Southerner's heart: the fear of a Negro uprising, of knives, axes, hoes, and picks wielded in the deep of the night against their masters; of men, women, and children slain in their beds while they slept and dreamed—a fear that drove normal, family men to a blood frenzy. Yes, John Brown understood the mechanics of fear.

I squatted down and leaned back against a wall, scribbling his words without a reply. When I raised my pencil from the page, John Brown lifted his fiery eyes heavenward.

"If I must sacrifice my life for the cause of justice, and mingle my blood with those upon whom this wicked curse be laid, let me do so to the Glory of my God and Savior."

I write hastily now as the Lord's Spirit brings his words again to my memory.

Did this man cry, "Yes, Lord! Yes!" just as I had when I knelt beneath an old oak tree three years ago? To which lord had he submitted? The Lord in heaven, or the Devil? I wanted to tell him of my own distress, my own anger! I too had suffered loss in my attempt to be a faithful soldier of the Lord. I wanted to tell him of Nikki, of Victoria, of how she freed her slaves, how my family paid the price of liberty with blood!

But to John Brown, I was a Southern reporter. He would not accept my motives for remaining a son of the South who, in his judging eyes, was like Ishmael, the unfavored son.

When I looked up, I found him again staring straight into my soul; in his terrible eyes I saw elements of both brilliant light and deep darkness.

I broke my gaze from his, looked down and transcribed his words.

There was a pounding on the cell door: my time was up. John Avis ushered me out. I paused and gazed back one last time into those incredible eyes that followed my every step.

Two days later he swung from the rope.

John Avis approached me and gave me a copy of a note John Brown had written on the way to the gallows:

"I, John Brown, am now quite certain that the crimes of this guilty land will never be purged away but with blood. I had, as I now think, vainly flattered myself that without very much bloodshed it might be done."

Where does his soul now rest? In comfort in the bosom of Abraham? Or in the agony of Hell's fire?

Unde Malum

I reflect on John Brown's final words. Was he correct that the land must be purged of its sin through the blood of men? Does he imply a righteous judgment in this bloodletting? Or is his prophecy nothing more than a rallying cry for war?

Is this Your plan, Lord, to set brother against brother? Could You be the author of such a thing?

I now believe that these questions were answered in full through my encounter with an old, hunchbacked Catholic priest.

Father Gibault

I recall him shuffling toward me, just as it happened that bright noon following John Brown's hanging. The priest's black habit and dark hair rustled in the wind as his arms and hands reached out, his eyes open wide and wild with emotions. He stopped and leaned wearily on the end of the wall where I sat. I could tell from the way he moved that walking hurt him but the furtive look in his eyes was not the result of physical pain.

"You are a Christian, no?" he said, pointing excitedly at my Bible which lay open on top of the journal in my lap. I had been reading Ecclesiastes and meditating on my copy of the grim, prophetic note John Brown had written on his way to the gallows.

"You believe in God, in a living Christ?" he asked, wagging his finger.

"Yes," I said, caught completely off-guard. "I'm a Methodist."

The priest's deep blue eyes brightened as he studied my face. He clasped a small crucifix that hung around his neck, his eyes narrowing. "And what of the Devil, my brother? Do you believe in him?"

"Yes, I do!"

"Miraculous—a Protestant who still believes in the Devil!" The priest eyed me warily, his voice cracking. "It must be God, then, who brings us together! He has answered my prayers."

He stepped closer, placing his freckled hand gently on my arm. "I am Father Gibault."

"The name's Sam—Sam MacDonald." I mumbled, still utterly astounded.

"Will you follow me to my chapel?" the priest asked. "I have a story to tell you."

I closed my journal and followed him to a secluded stone chapel nestled on a rocky hillside.

The smell of burning wax filled the simple, rectangular room lit only by candles behind the altar at the opposite end. Directly above the altar hung a huge wooden crucifix suspended by wire cables. An altar stood at the head of a narrow aisle that ran down the middle of four rows of wooden benches.

He led me to the front row and instructed me to sit. To the left was a small table with three candles which he paused to light. Beside it stood a simple, ladder-back chair which the priest took for himself. His eyes followed my hands encouragingly as I opened my journal and prepared to write.

"I am a Frenchman, born in France's darkest days, the days of the Revolution! And it is of a most fateful day in my country's history, that I must tell you.

"On January 21, 1793, King Louis XVI was sent to the guillotine. I was but seven years old, the third son of a poor Parisian shoemaker. He was not so poor, however, that he could not close his shop and take his son to the execution. I remember that cold, foggy January day as I pushed my way through the crowds. Such crowds they were, thousands upon thousands, all swarming like bees to honey! This was a special day, when King Louis would pay for his injustice against the citizens of France."

The Frenchman clapped his hands together, startling me. I sat erect on the bench.

"If you have never stood in the Place de la Revolution, you cannot appreciate that moment when a sea of men, women, and children swept into the square surrounding the tall scaffold and guillotine, much like the scaffold on which John Brown was hung. I worked my way to a place directly in front of the guillotine. The king stepped from the carriage less than twenty paces from me. The chief executioner, Charles-Henri Sanson, allowed the king to make a final statement to the people. I shall never forget his words.

"'I am innocent of all the crimes laid to my charge; I pardon those who have occasioned my death; and I pray to God that the blood you are going to shed may never be visited on France.'

"Being but a young child at the time, I did not really understand what an execution was all about. I played a foolish, little game, my friend. I watched and imitated Charles-Henri's every move. It was a silly pantomime, perhaps the very thing that attracted the attention of someone I wish I had never met.

"Copying Sanson, I tipped my hat and rubbed my hands up and down the front of my coat. Then the king was forced into the guillotine. I stood below the scaffold, in front. I could see the king's eyes staring into the red wicker basket. Then Sanson pulled the lever that released the tranchoir. Like the executioner, I pulled my own imaginary lever. Then suddenly, my childish play ceased.

"The real blade did not completely sever the king's head.

Sanson and his son, Henri, had to force the blade down. The king's head popped off and fell into the wicker basket. A sickening feeling knotted in my stomach and I touched my cold fingers to my neck.

"Sanson's son grabbed the king's head and excitedly paraded it about the scaffold for all to see. I tell you, he was filled with madness!

"The Captain of the Guard rode in front of the crowd and started a chant. 'Vive la Republique! Vive la Republique!' Charles-Henri stood paralyzed by the maddening crowd. The sound of thousands of voices grew with each passing moment. Then, a handful of men and women broke ranks and ran beneath the scaffold.

"I was knocked to the ground, then helped up by an old, gray-haired man in a tattered coat."

Gibault's eyes narrowed. "He is the one I wish I had never met. He led me forward, between the soldiers and cannon to a spot beneath the guillotine. The king's body had been left in the guillotine and his blood had begun to seep between the planks in the scaffold's floor. I watched in horror as the crowd lifted their hands and washed them in his blood!

"The old man, his hand resting upon my head, looked down at me and said, 'Yes, Thomas Gibault, it is like washing your hands.'

"His hand felt like hot wax on my head as he turned to me, his dark, piercing eyes staring into mine. He quoted Scripture about the crucifixion of Jesus and of Pilate. Then, as the blood began to drip through the floor above us, he rolled his eyes up into his head and said, 'His blood be on us and on our children.'

"I backed away and ran through the ring of cannon and soldiers into the crowd. From a distance, I turned and watched. The old man's features changed before my eyes, his face sharpened, his nose now looked like the beak of a bird and his unkempt hair as black as coal. The old man cupped and lifted his gnarled hands, then drank the blood of the dead king. Then I knew that it was no mere man who could read my thoughts and tell me my name, but the Devil himself!

"You do not believe this old priest," Gibault said, his despairing eyes searching mine. "Let me finish before you judge my words!"

"I uttered the Lord's Prayer. When I finished, I looked up, but the old man had disappeared. I turned my eyes toward the scaffold on which the king had lost his head. And then I saw the old man again, standing beside Charles-Henri Sanson, the chief executioner of Paris. Charles-Henri had a hungry, ravenous look. and a long, dark scar ran from the corner of his mouth to the corner of his left eye. He stared toward the west.

"Then, someone in the crowd bumped against me. I momentarily lost my concentration. When I returned my gaze to the scaffold, the old man was gone, vanished, I tell you. Into thin air! Charles-Henri stood alone! And there was no scar on his face. Did my eyes somehow deceive me?"

Father Gibault unfolded his hands. The fearful look on his face deepened.

"You must believe me when I say that the Devil, the old man, has come to this place, today. I saw him this very afternoon, under the scaffold where John Brown's body hung. And behind him I saw a dark, wiry man with hungry eyes and a red wound on his cheek!

"Did my eyes deceive me again? As I stood this afternoon, paralyzed by the Devil's presence, a soldier crossed in front of me. When he passed, the old man was not there. The dark, wiry man turned and walked away before I could see his face a second time.

"Surely God himself has revealed the Darkness to me! Has not the Devil come to shed blood in this land as he did upon France's soil? He has come to profane our nation, our government, our people, to desecrate God's Holy Church, the Bride of Christ! And he moves openly, because the Church denies his very existence. But he has not changed; he has been a liar and a murderer from the beginning."

The Frenchman's voice softened, he lowered his head and stared at the wooden floor. "Because of what happened to me sixty-six years ago I left my home, vowed myself to God and to His Holy Church. Though I served God with a simple-minded devotion and a reverence for the Scriptures, I learned that those who ruled over me were of a different faith. They were an apostate priesthood who were devoted to accumulating wealth. And because they did not know God, or understand His ways, they could not shepherd France, their Holy Charge, but left it prey to the Devil who came through an open gate to ravage and destroy the Master's flocks.

"God would not be mocked. When I was ten, at the height of the Terror, our monastery was burned to the ground, our bishop and priests killed. I was spared the guillotine, though I was whipped so brutally that I have been crippled ever since.

"My faith was not deterred. I maintained my love for God, and continued to serve him. I left France and came to America in 1824 in obedience to him. When I moved to Charlestown in 1850, it was solely at his direction. Now, nine years later, at the hanging of John Brown, I am called by God to witness the old man, the Devil, once again. At my moment of dismay, I saw you seated on a low, stone wall, Bible in hand, your eyes fixed on the word of God, rather than John Brown's body as it swayed beneath the scaffold.

"The guiding hand of Christ has remained faithful to the end." The old Frenchman turned his head and stared briefly into the candles, his eyes gleaming in their light. He looked up, his eyes locking with mine.

"Throughout my life I have been ridiculed for my belief in the Devil. Now, old and crippled, I am ready to go home to God. He has given me an audience who has ears to hear, eyes to see, and a heart to believe."

We sat in silence for a few minutes. His eyes were clouded with tears. He seemed certain that I believed him, sure that Providence had brought us together. He breathed deeply, then rose from his chair. He seemed taller, more erect. Perhaps it was only a trick of the flickering candlelight.

As we stepped outside onto the cobblestone walk, he put his hand on my shoulder. "Sam MacDonald, you have my testimony concerning our adversary. I have nothing more to offer you, no other words that could add wisdom to your knowledge. I have been but a watchman on Jerusalem's walls, and I have sounded the trumpet lest the blood be on my own head. The defense of God's Holy City belongs to another generation. I will pray for you, that they who sleep within her walls will awaken.

"Do not let men deceive you. The Church Fathers have a saying, Nullus diabolus nullus redemptor: no Devil, no Redeemer. If the Devil can be excised from the Scriptures, then Christ will be soon to follow! Au revoir, mon ami."

And with that, he turned on his heel and slowly walked back inside the chapel through a sudden gust of wind that snapped the bottom of his black habit against his ankles.

Reflections

I am conscious of Grandpa Will's Long Knife which rests in the corner of the room. His sword is an ever-present reminder of the sin and destruction birthed in the hearts of men and nations.

O that the Church would be the conscience of this Nation! But no—the Southern churches use their pulpits to justify their injustice to the Negro. And the Northern churches preach the shedding of blood to preserve the Union. We worship the same God, yet we accuse each other of being the Devil's servants. We read the same Scriptures, but only to justify our own consciences. We have become two separate nations, two separate peoples, two separate faiths.

Solomon was the wisest man in all the earth, yet his kingdom was severed in two. He was seduced by the Devil's children—Milcom, Ashtoreth, Chemosh. The unfaithful kings of Judah and Israel caused their children to pass through fire, fashioned idols, practiced sorcery and divination.

King Louis XVI's final, impassioned plea could not save his nation from the bloodbath that followed. France submitted its members to her enlightened god called Reason, butchering herself with the guillotine and tumbling into chaos and anarchy.

What bloody sacrifices will the gods of our own making require?

❧ **15** ❧

Late Friday Night

TRUE BELIEVER PARKED HIS FERRARI in the lower level of the South Plaza Condominiums' parking garage, removed a black canvas sports bag from the back seat, and then locked the door. He walked to a brown metal door marked with the word ELEVATORS in faded yellow.

Tonight, Kim would sleep in her own apartment.

About forty-five seconds later, he exited the elevator into his private penthouse hallway. The walls were stark white and without decoration. Across from the elevator was a plain gray metal door. He punched in a five-digit code at the touch pad by the door. The door unlocked with a heavy, dull click. He entered a dark room, then closed the metal door, the deadbolts locking automatically.

He flipped a switch, and three floor lamps softly lit the large living room. He placed his canvas sports bag on a glass-topped chrome table in front of a U-shaped sectional sofa. Facing the sofa and table was a floor-to-ceiling entertainment unit built around a studio-quality television monitor and videotape editing deck and controller. On the opposite wall, a large rectangular window overlooked the nation's capital. A steady stream of headlights crossed the Theodore Roosevelt Bridge and wound around the Kennedy Center. Bright patchworks of lights from the USA Today Building and other high-rises in nearby Virginia cast their reflections on the shimmering Potomac.

True Believer headed down a wide hall, past a spacious kitchen to the left and dining room to the right, past his library and guest bedroom in the middle to the master bedroom suite at the back.

Entering the bedroom, True Believer stripped off his clothes. After slipping into light gray sweats, he returned to the living room and sofa.

He unzipped his sports bag and pulled out a portable telephone, followed by a notebook-sized, RISC-based computer. With its internal modem, True Believer could plug his laptop into any standard telephone jack, linking his computer with other personal computers and mainframes around the world. Data security here in the U.S. was not a problem. All sensitive material was stored off-line in a desktop workstation over two thousand miles away in southern California, accessible both physically and electronically to less than fifty people in the continental U.S. His remaining data was stored in a second computer that was far less accessible. He could count on two hands the men and women whose computers could talk to Global Two. Via Global Two, his laptop was an electronic window to a vast universe of public, restricted and top secret information maintained by numerous universities, private corporations, hospitals, and both science and medical research facilities on every continent, including Antarctica. Tonight, however, he was not delving into that universe, but adding to it. In less than fifteen minutes, he had entered and encrypted his weekly report. Another fifteen and he had downloaded the data via modem and AT&T's ever reliable phone lines to his remote, state-side workstation.

Once the transmission was complete, True Believer connected his portable telephone to the laptop with a thin cable. He reclined slowly into the deep sofa. He closed his eyes and laid his head back against the soft cushion waiting for the important telephone call he knew would come shortly.

Mark looked up from the page and glanced at his watch. It was 11:35 P.M.

His mind was in hyperdrive.

The incredible events over the last six weeks of Sam's life not only linked his personal trials with the trials of the nation, but now linked him with history and nations on a larger scale, crossing the Atlantic into eighteenth-century France.

Victoria's murder. Nikki and Will. Long Knife and an Indian's prophecy. The brandished swords of an impending Civil War.

And now, an old priest's account of the Devil appearing in human form at the both beheading of King Louis XVI and the hanging of John Brown.

Mark blinked—and found himself staring at his own reflection in the dark windowpane. He arched his back, glancing around the heavily shadowed room.

A knot formed in his stomach.

The hunchbacked priest's account of the French Revolution would not be found in a classroom history course or a Sunday sermon. Could the priest's story of the Devil's bloody venture into the physical world at King Louis' execution and John Brown's hanging be trusted?

Sam seemed to accept the Devil's physical presence in history at face value.

Should he?

Mark tapped the journal page with his forefinger. He thought back to an outline from an Adult Sunday School class he had taught some years back just prior to Katie's accident, a four-week survey on the Devil and the nature of evil. He had traced the Christian's changing views from early New Testament days to the Middle Ages, from the Reformation to the Renaissance and on through the colonization of America and into modern times. One theme had clearly emerged: through the centuries the Devil had become less a living being and more a symbol or metaphor of evil. After the witch trials of the seventeenth century, the idea of a personal Devil and demons became intellectually unfashionable, supplanted by an enlightened emphasis on reason and objectivism. That evil existed in the world, no one would deny. That evil with a capital E walked, talked, and had a will of its own—that was a different matter.

Mark chewed lightly on his lip. He taught that the Protestant Christians' belief in the Devil reached its lowpoint in the early 1800s, the generations just following the founding of the nation—the same generations preceding the Civil War.

What had the old priest exclaimed to Sam? Finding a Protestant who still believed in the Devil was nothing short of a miracle!

He rubbed the side of his face. Though there was a resurgence of belief in spiritual warfare and demon possession over the past fifty years, that resurgence was limited primarily to Evangelical, Charismatic and Catholic circles. Belief in the Devil had made a strong comeback—not that a Bible-believing Christian needed a whole lot of theology upon which to base his belief! A casual look at America's declining culture and social mores was all anyone needed to perceive the ever-widening scope of the Devil's presence and handiwork.

Perhaps Father Gibault's testimony actually reinforced his own views. Certainly he believed the Devil was more than an impersonal, evil force. The Devil had a spiritual body and an individual consciousness. He ruled a kingdom of darkness populated with other supernatural beings, a third of all the angels God had originally created. These fallen angels had individual personalities and wills. Some were given positions of great authority and power—rulers, principalities, and thrones. The weaker ones had been placed over direct control of vast demonic legions whose charge was to stimulate every conceivable vice, foible, and temptation known to man. Their goal in life was to separate men from their Creator by bringing them into progressive bondage and sin, and ultimately, spiritual death.

What better situation for the Devil than to convince the world, unbeliever and Christian alike, that he no longer existed.

Or, that he was someone other than who he actually was.

What had the old priest said? Mark flipped back a page in Sam's journal.

Nullus diabolus nullus redemptor: no Devil, no Redeemer.

And the rest simply falls into place.

The expected telephone call came precisely at 11:45 P.M. True Believer leaned forward on the couch and pressed a button on the top of the portable phone connected to his computer.

"Good evening—hold the line, I'll connect us," he said and with the touch of a second button put the incoming call on hold. He entered an overseas number. Twenty seconds later, he had successfully connected and encrypted a three-way conference call between Washington, New York City, and Geneva, Switzerland—the joys and privileges of twentieth-century technology!

"We're up. As required, this call is being encoded and will be archived to Global One." True Believer waited for the required acknowledgements. The encryption/decryption process made the male voice sound flat, electronic.

"True Believer, project status please," New York asked.

"The insertion was completed as planned and Phase I is a go," he replied, irked by New York's request for the obvious. He gave New York and Geneva a three-minute summary of the details.

Geneva broke in. The encrypting did not do her silky voice justice. "And your operatives?"

"Kim is most effective. Wertman suspects nothing. Our police detectives have operational control. They have, as I warned the Council earlier, demanded greater compensation."

"So you need additional funds?" New York asked, a slight hesitancy in his voice.

"Yes, two units, please." True Believer refrained from sarcasm. What else could he have meant when he said they had demanded compensation!

"I will notify our AFI Director to transfer units on Monday."

True Believer drummed his fingers on the arm of the couch. New York had total authority to select the route by which the funds would be dispersed. Had the decision been his, True Believer would not have chosen to use the same route twice.

Geneva spoke up. "How is Peters adapting to his role?"

"He uses his influence well; however, his expertise is in marketing our vision, not operations. In the future I would restrict his role as such. He carries his concern too visibly."

"Noted."

"What about Phase II?" asked New York bluntly, his voice taking on a harsh edge.

True Believer smiled as his well-aimed dart hit its mark. Over his objections, New York had successfully lobbied for Peters' involvement.

New York did not wait for a reply. "I remind you that London made his request two weeks ago. You've had more than enough time to finalize your target."

True Believer waited several seconds, hoping Geneva would intervene. New York, who lived and worked in a thirty-story glass tower high above downtown Manhattan, measured success by how well he forecasted stock market trends or how shrewdly he invested the profits from his international portfolio of high-tech companies. New York was a paper shuffler who could finance a local chapter of the Irish Republican Army for an entire year. But could New York point a gun at a man and pull the trigger? Could he place a bomb in a revered national landmark filled with tourists as True Believer had done in the Tower of London in July of 1974, or in a pub packed with men and women whose lives were snuffed out in a terrifying explosion of flames and flying shards of glass, metal, and wood?

No! The high-rolling financier could not understand the violent, shadow-world in which True Believer had lived daily.

Three seconds passed and Geneva remained silent. True Believer gripped the phone tightly. So! New York had convinced Geneva to side with London! What promises had he made?

True Believer could barely contain his rage. His head began to pound painfully. London! How long would that city and those people be a thorn in his side?

"How often must I repeat myself? I will determine an appropriate target based upon the developments which immediately follow Phase I. No sooner."

"That would be your prerogative in a standard operation," replied New York, "but next week's schedule and events will not afford you that opportunity, particularly while you're on my turf, using my funds and my network. You and I are jointly accountable for the success of this operation. I repeat: I want a target."

Geneva cut in, her voice seemingly unruffled by the venomous atmosphere. "Bonn gives her support to New York, True Believer."

True Believer rubbed his forehead. To force the issue with Bonn would not be wise. He had been checked—for the moment. He would let the financier bask briefly in his victory. Then, after Saturday, True Believer would have the final say. London and New York would pay dearly for their interference.

"You will have your target by Sunday, 2300 hours." True Believer responded flatly.

"Noted," replied Geneva, cutting in before New York had an opportunity to assert himself any further. "Understand, both of you, Bonn is focusing on our project. As you are aware, there is a debate within our organization over our western hemisphere directives. Several influential factions still cling to the belief that we should advance our agenda through judicial mechanisms, while a growing number press for more direct legislative action. With cultural antagonisms between secular and religious forces so heightened by last year's U.S. election campaigns, Bonn believes now is the time to begin the social restructuring for which we have all so long aspired. Never again may such a clear opportunity to sweep the Judeo-Christian ethic out of public policy present itself. I cannot represent her views more strongly than to remind us all that in the larger scope of our organization's goals, even we are expendable. Do I make myself clear?"

The line was silent except for the soft hiss of electronics that secured their conversation from the rest of the world.

True Believer waited five seconds. "Any last questions? Very well then, until Sunday."

He pressed a key on his computer and broke the connection.

16

Early Saturday Morning

TRUE BELIEVER ROSE FROM THE COUCH and stormed toward the bedroom and a shower.

How little real faith London, New York, and Geneva possessed! Why couldn't they give him the latitude he needed to properly implement the tactical details of Bonn's plan?

He did not challenge their goals to control world population through genetic engineering, abortion, euthanasia, and other eugenic mechanisms. Unlike the genocidal tendencies of the primitive Serbians in Yugoslavia and the Khmer Rouge in Cambodia, strategists like Bonn and Geneva were geniuses at achieving cultural cleansings—with public support and funding—through a variety of judicial and legislative means.

He shook his head. They could not fully trust him because they did not know the level of his own expertise. The global network to which they belonged compartmentalized itself through protocols that guaranteed autonomy and secrecy. Thus, his co-conspirators only superficially knew about his upbringing in bloody Ireland.

Only Bonn knew his real name, Ciarin Fein, because she was the one who had recruited him from the ranks of the IRA. Only she knew how his father, a staunch Catholic, civic leader and eventual political prisoner, had been murdered in an internment camp in Curragh, Ireland, in 1957. Only she knew how his mother, in January of 1972, had been murdered by British paratroopers at a civil rights rally in Londonderry. Only Bonn knew of his first act of terrorism at the age of twenty-two in his execution-style killing of two policeman from the Royal Ulster Constabulary in 1969. Only Bonn knew how, just two days after his mother's death, he had organized and incited the burning of the British Embassy in Dublin. Only she knew of his news-shattering bombing of Westminster Hall in 1974 and later, of his involvement in the bombing and assassination of Britain's war hero, Earl Mountbatten of Burma, in his fishing boat in 1979.

Only Bonn knew how his life had been hardened by the bloody fire of religious and political sectionalism. Bonn understood when traditional forms of social transformation could not achieve one's required goals and objectives, there were those who could fashion and shape history through more direct means: those who truly knew how to use terror, violence and bloodshed.

Twenty minutes later, True Believer stepped out of his shower. The night was still young, and despite the unpleasantries of the conference call, he still had his rounds to make.

He opened his walk-in closet and selected his evening attire. The dark slacks and leather jacket he wore earlier would be replaced by baggy gray pants, a white, open-necked silk shirt, and a loose-fitting, double-breasted, black silk evening jacket.

His clothes were not all that had changed. His open shirt revealed a thin gold chain and crucifix. Blow-dried, raven-black hair styled thick and full, fell upon his shoulders. He even wore a softened expression around his gray eyes and mouth.

His paramilitary demeanor metamorphosed into the casual indifference of an entertainer. When operating under his state-side identity, Brian Fein, he was an entirely different looking man, with a different name and career—a rock group promoter.

Tonight, Brian would spend some time with the boys in the band. Through the help of the record industry's best writers, AFI's best lawyers, and New York's money, he had helped promote five hard-rock flunkies into one of the hottest heavy metal groups in the nation, Legacy. Now that royalties from their hit CD, *Earth Lords*, were beginning to pour in, more funds would be available to Bonn and Geneva for developing new mechanisms to reach young people.

However, his usefulness to them was coming to an end, and vice versa. He did not need to leverage his successes with Legacy. His bulging Swiss bank accounts would not only purchase his freedom, but would meet his every need for decades to come.

Once free, New York, and London and others in the networked organization which had no name would cease to control him and would no longer have power over his future.

The pieces on the chessboard were moving, and he was in solid control of the game. It was up to Kim, Troy, and KC to make sure that Mark MacDonald's and Fletcher Rivers' involvement in the cases yielded no unexpected effects.

Ciaran flipped off the bedroom lights, checked his coat pocket for Legacy's weekend supply of crack. Every detail was in place for Tuesday morning. Egomaniacal Harold Wertman couldn't see the forest for the trees!

He packed the sports bag containing his field attire—dark slacks and sweater, leather jacket and rubber soled shoes—and headed for the living room. Later he would change clothes again, change his demeanor, change his persona. Months of planning and maneuvering were at stake, not to mention his future if he were to fail in executing his plans.

And so, while his enemies slept soundly and securely in the warmth of their beds, he would work.

Brian snapped off the lights, then slipped quietly into the hall, the metal door's heavy bolts locking silently behind him.

Having completed another journal, Mark picked up the next one in sequence from the shrinking stack. He set it on the desk and opened it to the first page.

Mark's stomach tightened as he lowered his eyes to the page and scanned Sam's next section. The handwriting was sharply angled and dark, as if written in haste.

December 1859
2:00 A.M. Sheppard's Boardinghouse

I have slept little during the past seventy-two hours, but during the time that I did, I repeatedly experienced a most extraordinary dream. It is imperative that I record the images before they fade. Was the dream a revelation from God, the fruit of an exhausted mind, or a torment bestowed upon me by the Lord's Arch-Enemy working to do wrong within my soul?

When the dream began, I stood at the edge of a bright, frosty white glen encompassed by tall, black-barked trees. Hearing a woman's terrified scream, my eyes were drawn to a young Indian who stumbled and fell into a thick blanket of snow no more than fifty feet away. She tried to climb to her feet, but fell a second time with a cry of pain—she had twisted her ankle and knee. Looking back, her face became wild with fear. I followed her trail through the snow to the edge of the glen.

A brawny frontiersman broke furiously through the line of trees and brush, his beaver-pelt cloak flapping off his shoulders, a menacing sword in one hand. A triumphant whoop exploded raggedly from his lips as his eyes locked on his struggling prey.

The woman screamed again. There would be no escape. She pulled a small knife from a sheath on her hip and rolled to face her attacker. Her defense was in vain. The frontiersman slapped the knife from her hand with the end of his sword. The woman tried to back away. The frontiersman reached down and grabbed her long black hair, yanking her head back. She grabbed his wrist with both of her hands. A cruel smile formed on his face as his eyes dropped to the woman's writhing torso—and the huge bulge beneath her loose fitting garment. The Indian woman was heavy with child!

I still flinch at the revelation of that dire moment. I still recoil at the discovery that the frontiersman was my grandfather, Will Mac-Donald!

"No, Grandpa! No!" I tried to scream, but no words would come out of my mouth.

I broke from the edge of the glen. I tried to reach him, to grab his arm, but deep snow had drifted about my legs and I could not move. So I watched, helplessly frozen in place, transfixed as Will raised his shining sword and mercilessly plunged it downward. I could not turn my eyes away as he completed his murderous deed, separating the unborn child from its mother and dropping it into a bank of snow. The expression on his face was one of supreme satisfaction. He stooped, wiped his sword clean on the woman's garment, then turned and disappeared into the forest.

Feet and legs freed at last, I approached the dying woman. She moaned weakly, life draining swiftly through her open belly. Blood was everywhere, forming into rivulets that trickled toward me.

I stopped and looked down at my feet. As I gasped for breath, my eyes beheld Tertullian's riddle, UNDE MALUM, drawn in red by an unseen hand!

The words melted the snow and formed red rivulets flowing past me. I turned, only to discover that they had merged with other rivulets, widening into a stream.

The setting changed instantly to a hot, summer day. Now I stood at the edge of an oddly familiar road bounded on one side by a deep ravine and by cotton fields on the other. I peered over the edge and my stomach turned sickeningly. The ravine was filled with rushing torrents of blood!

A dull, crashing sound drew my attention upstream. Something large moved just beneath the rolling red surface. Moving toward me, it rammed into the sides of the ravine. My hands and legs trembled. I recognized the narrow road near Charleston. Another crash drew my eyes downward. In the ravine a wagon tumbled over and over in the turgid flow! Victoria's wagon! My heart was crushed, wrung by invisible hands. I collapsed to my knees.

On the other side of the ravine, two men sat motionless on horseback. I recognized Beaumont's brawny frame at once; the dark-haired man beside him, with cold, hateful eyes and a scar on his left cheek, I had never seen before. The scene changed again.

The ground about me shook violently. The men disappeared. The sides of the ravine peeled back, like a bloody open wound. The narrow flow widened into thunderous red rapids, spewing and kicking. The cotton fields lurched toward the sky, transforming into tall, rocky bluffs looming above me. I recognized them instantly. I was back in western Virginia near a second town named Harper's Ferry. And it was no longer Victoria's wagon that tumbled by, but a hangman's gallows. Slowly, inexorably, the rapids pushed the huge structure past me, rolling it end over end. The broken and blood-soaked body of John Brown was tangled in the rope and scaffolding, disappearing as the gallows plunged beneath the surface only to reappear moments later, like Melville's doomed Captain Ahab on the broad back of Moby Dick.

The nausea returned, stabbing at my gut. I shut my eyes, knowing that the dream had yet to run its full course. Even as I did, the roaring and grinding stopped abruptly.

My eyes popped open; my heart sank and all strength drained from my limbs. Whoever or whatever had taken me on this morbid journey had transformed the rapids into an exceedingly wide river, smooth like glass and impenetrably crimson. There were no sounds, not from the river, not from the grassy hills or groves of oak and maple behind me, nor in the air above. And as in each of the previous scenes, my location was painfully familiar. I knelt on an elevated bank of the Potomac River just south of Washington City, the stump of Washington's unfinished monument in view.

As my gaze moved downstream, I spied an object in the center of the river. Compelled, I climbed wearily to my feet and stumbled forward along the edge of the riverbank on wobbly, unresponsive legs. As the object grew larger and clearer, my fear grew as well. The object was a man. He clung to a squarish wooden stump, pulling himself upward as the glistening scarlet river slowly rose about him.

Somehow cued by my presence, the man turned his shoulders and head toward me. Grief impaled my heart. It was the old French priest, Father Gibault! And it was no ordinary stump that he clung to, but the crosspiece of a nearly submerged cross!

How much grief can a man bear? Did I not nearly faint from despair?

I must rest again.

Mark raised his hands to his face and rubbed his temples. Thoroughly exhausted, the current of raw energy that repulsed the weariness was now gone.

He returned his eyes to the journal, but try as he might, he couldn't keep the words from shifting in and out of focus.

He pushed himself from the seat and propped his arms on the edge of the desk. The abrupt onset of weariness, combined with the play of light and darkness, made objects in the room appear fuzzy, surreal. The tips of his fingers tingled as they brushed over Sam's open journal.

He snapped off the lamps at each end of the table, plunging the room into darkness. As he turned around, his eyes followed a pale yellow swath from the street light that illumined the lustrous pommel of the Long Knife.

A cold shudder ran the length of his spine. Images from Sam's dream replayed themselves in his mind: the Indian woman running, falling; Will standing over her, grabbing her hair, plunging his sword....

Mark drew a deep breath, tearing his gaze from the Long Knife. He left the study, but the images followed him out into the hall: *unde malum* written in blood; Victoria's wagon tumbling down the ravine; Father Gibault clinging to the crimson crosspiece of a nearly submerged cross.

Halfway down the stairs to the bedroom, Mark paused, his hand tightening around the smooth wooden rail. The images continued to assail him.

In his mind's eye, he found himself standing next to Sam, watching the priest struggle to stay above the steadily rising river. Mark's field of vision narrowed, zooming telescopically across the wide river and focusing on a small, shuffling figure on the opposite side. The hairs on the back of his neck rose and goosebumps raced up his arms as the shuffling figure stopped abruptly and turned to face him. It was a hairy old man in a tattered coat who had beady black eyes and a nose like the beak of a bird. His hands and mouth were smeared with blood!

Mark shook his head, surprised by the clarity of the image. Then he froze in place, the surprise turning to alarm. This wasn't part of Sam's dream! It was his own vision!

His body tensed as his ears became attuned to every creak in the old house, to every night sound. His eyes strained to see through the murky blackness at the bottom of the stairs. Shadows seemed to move within the darkness.

Chill out! Mark chastised himself, running a hand through his hair and squeezing his eyes shut. It's late and you're tired—get a grip! He drew another deep breath and opened his eyes. He stared over the rail and concentrated on a faint line of yellow light under the bedroom door on the second floor.

Slowly, determinedly, he descended the stairs into the darkness, one step at a time.

17

Saturday Morning

A T 6:30 A.M., AFI was as silent as a tomb. Michelle shifted her coat and briefcase to her left hand and unlocked the door to her office suite. Before entering the outer office, she paused and glanced furtively over her shoulder down the long, semi-dark hall. Though Michelle had an iron-clad reason for being in the office, her feelings and actions betrayed her conscience.

Calm down! This is what you've been working so hard for—a quiet Saturday morning alone!

She flipped on the lights and hung her jacket behind the door. Michelle smiled as she crossed the room. Julie had neatly arranged a dozen tall stacks of hanging folders around her desk.

Michelle unlocked the inner door to her private office and swung it open. After setting her briefcase on her desk, she stepped back into the doorway between the offices and leaned against the doorframe. She considered her strategy one last time.

She pushed herself from the doorframe with a gleam in her eyes.

The soft light of dawn slanted through half-closed Venetian blinds into the study, casting an alternating pattern of gold bars and black shadows on the hardwood floor.

Fletcher set his cup of coffee on the coaster in the corner of his rolltop desk as he spun the swivel armchair and sat down. He yawned, pushing his damp hair back off his shoulders; the alternately hot and cold shower had barely cut the hunger for sleep that preyed upon his eyes. He finished buttoning his flannel shirt, then turned toward the desk and the task at hand.

He was tired because he hadn't slept, and he hadn't slept because Botello had stopped by around midnight with stolen photocopies of Jimmy's, Carlton's and the Crest Road Clinic's updated files. Botello, in his usual nonchalant manner, had downplayed the seriousness of his surreptitious, nocturnal activities at HQ.

"Somebody's working these cases real smooth," Botello explained as he handed Fletcher the copies, his eyes flashing angrily. "And with all the fresh bodies piling up in the morgue, Jimmy's case is all but officially closed."

Fletcher shook his head. What still had everybody on edge was the inexplicable surge of random shootings and stabbings outside the drug community. No one had yet been able to establish any patterns to the crimes. Washington's bad reputation was not improved as January's numbers made national news.

After Botello left around 1:00 A.M., he laid everything out and went over each piece of information, slowly sorting and collating the material into relevant stacks. Now, some six hours later, he had isolated the pieces of data pertinent to the case.

He pushed his weariness and the rest of the material to the side, and started to make notes.

For several confusing seconds, Mark dreamed he was up in the study reading Sam's journals. He turned his head to the side and into sunlight that fell across the bridge of his nose and eyes. He woke, facing the bedroom window, a bullhorn crackling noisily below.

"Christ is the great captain of liberty, as well as of salvation, and who began his mission, as foretold of him by proclaiming it, saw fit to take from me a sword of steel. But he has put another sword in my hand, the Sword of the Spirit. I pray to God to make me a faithful soldier wherever he may send me."

Mark stilled instantly, his eyes popping wide open. The bullhorn erupted again.

"I, John Brown, am certain that the crimes of this guilty land will never be purged away but with blood! I had as I now think, vainly flattered myself without much bloodshed it might be done!"

Mark bolted upright. Katie rolled over. "Something wrong?"

"Nothing's wrong, just weird," Mark answered, rising from the bed and slipping into his jeans. He moved to the window.

"What's weird?" Katie asked as she stretched and yawned.

"Let's talk about it over breakfast," Mark stuttered out as a sudden chill slithered down the center of his back.

The piles of printouts on Michelle's desk were now six inches high and the folders by her feet reached halfway up her calf. Her computer monitor displayed a portion of a report that was over forty pages long. The accounts payable ledger and check log were covered with yellow Post-It notes.

Two hours of in-depth research had revealed a startling mountain of information that might be useful—no—would be useful when she and her friend at the *Times* sat down to compile material for their newspaper series and follow-up book. But in regard to the vandalism, she found nothing that would point to wrongdoing. It was like trying to find the proverbial needle in a haystack, only harder. She didn't know what kind of needle she was looking for!

All the way to the office she had prayed, seeking God for wisdom and guidance in her work. By the time she had stepped from the elevator into AFI's offices, she was joyfully confident that the Lord was with her.

Now several hours later, that feeling had faded. Instead, she felt as if she stood in an endless maze with paths leading in dozens of directions. At the rate she was making progress, she could work every Saturday all year without finding her answers!

She had never realized just how compartmentalized her own job really was, cloistered in a private little world of coding and costing clinic expenditures, analyzing statistical compilations of patient data, and providing Carol, her boss, with stacks of monthly reports. She had not been exposed to the vast private and public funding pools from which AFI drew—and subsequently spent—on marketing, advertising via newspaper, magazines, and television, public relations, grants and sponsorships, and a myriad of other intangible expenditures. So much potential for good, yet so much deceit, abuse and exploitation.

She lowered her head into her hands. Her joy had been crushed under an overwhelming sense of helplessness, her confidence obscured by clouds of self doubt. She needed help to find her way, but there was no one to whom she could turn. She couldn't risk involving others now that she was so close.

Michelle dissembled her work and put everything back in place.

Fletcher looked at the three pieces of information which stood out above all the others. First, all three cases were now in Troy's hands. With Homicide so overloaded and the three cases so relatively unimportant, no one raised an eyebrow. Just the fact that Troy was given all three cases justified linking the vandalism of the clinic with Jimmy's and Carlton's deaths.

Equally important was his discovery of an eyewitness. A new resident, Mark MacDonald of 1533 Crest Road, had come down to headquarters on his own initiative and filed a report. He claimed he saw three men leaving—one being carried—from the clinic's rear parking lot and entering a van.

The third piece of information was a cryptic tip about the vandalism. Though he had read it three times, he was sure that he was missing something important, something right there in the text.

Fletcher picked up the photocopy. What was it? A sentence, a phrase? He stared at the three paragraphs of typewritten transcription. He read the words over and over until they just didn't communicate anymore. He rubbed his temples; his head felt empty. He looked down into his coffee cup—it was empty, too. He pushed himself from the chair.

As he passed the tall bookcase that stood near the door, he glanced at a row of three pictures on the bookcase: to the left, Susan hugging him affectionately at his thirtieth birthday party; to the right, Susan posing proudly on the steps to the redwood deck they had built all by themselves; and, in between, Melissa's kindergarten photograph.

What started visually as a painful tug on his heart unexpectedly gave way to anguish, draining what little reserves of emotion remained.

One negligent act had robbed him of his family. Susan had never shaken the fear that haunted her every time Melissa disappeared from sight for too long or woke up screaming from nightmares.

Nor did his rehabilitative work with Jimmy fix the broken things in his own heart. He found himself spending more and more time on the streets, trying to help the helpless and to find peace within himself—at the brutal expense of his marriage and his relationship with Melissa.

They tried to make it work. For two months they went to counseling with both police and child psychologists, but the wedge in Susan's heart drove deeper and deeper until it split their marriage in two.

Susan and Melissa were somewhere in Iowa where she believed they'd be safe.

Jimmy was dead.

And he was alone.

The picket line stretched around both sides of the clinic. Signs of various shapes and sizes bobbed up and down along the sidewalk bearing the same fundamental message: STOP KILLING THE CHILDREN! Most of the red-cheeked men, women, and children in the picket line wore gloves and hats to stave off the wind and cold. For the first time, Mark noticed a woman who stood on the corner and faced the oncoming traffic with a sign that read: HONK IF YOU LOVE CHILDREN! Beside her stood two little girls, carrying small signs that simply said: I'M GLAD I'M ALIVE.

Katie, wearing her new red coat, curled her legs under her on the bench beside Mark. She watched the line of picketers move steadily back and forth in front of the clinic where Kent, the picket coordinator from Agape Christian Fellowship, pleaded with Harold to stop using his bullhorn. The light wind rustling through the park brushed her hair across her face.

"I'll admit, it's strange hearing him quote stuff straight out of Sam's journal."

Mark nodded and locked his fingers through Katie's. The tone of his voice was thoughtful. "You know, we've only been living here three days, but in that time I've witnessed a crime, read Grandpa Kyle's confessional, and uncovered Sam's journals. Then to top it off, we live across the street from the busiest abortion clinic in D.C. with its own, self-appointed prophet who thinks he's the reincarnation of John Brown."

Katie forced a thin smile and squeezed his hand. "But you're also the descendant of a man who personally knew Abraham Lincoln and the owner of an eighteenth-century desk and chair."

Mark grinned briefly, but his eyes remained pensive.

"Even better, you have a patient wife," Katie continued, bringing her face close to his, "who let you hide away in your study like a monk. Come to think of it—you owe me, big time. You haven't been keeping me up with what's going on in Sam's journals."

Mark briefly shut his eyes. For a third time since they climbed out of bed, he debated whether or not he should tell Katie about Sam's bloody dream and his own strange vision on the stairwell. The gruesome murder of the Indian woman and her unborn child, the streams of blood and Victoria's tumbling wagon—she didn't need such stressful, frightening images replaying themselves over and over inside of her head now that she was pregnant.

He patted her hand. They sat quietly for several minutes as the picketers began another rousing chorus.

Would you be free from the burden of sin?
There's power in the blood, power in the blood!
Would you o'er evil a victory win?
There's wonderful power in the blood!

Mark continued to listen, his gaze wandering across the park to the statue of Cardinal Gibbons. One of Gibbon's hands was raised to bless, the other clutched a crucifix that hung around his neck.

An image transposed itself over the park.

Morning light became the flickering glow of candles. Gibbon's sober, stone face blurred into grief-lined flesh, his gray, marble robe into a black, cloth habit. The hand on the crucifix moved and tightened. The old French priest, Father Gibault, leaned forward on the edge of his chair. He was no longer looking and speaking to Sam, but to Mark, recounting his story of the old man, the Devil, and his plan not only to destroy the fledgling Republic, but also the Bride of Jesus Christ.

Shaking his head, Mark dispelled the disconcerting image.

Rising from the bench, he took Katie by the hands and slowly pulled her to her feet. Katie put an arm around his waist as they strolled across the park. Over her shoulder, Mark's gaze rose to the vacant church with its red tile roof, tall white columns and dark doors. Empty. Silent. Lifeless, like a tomb.

Movement behind the far right pillar of the church caught Mark's eye—he briefly saw a shuffling old man with scraggly raven hair and a nose like the beak of a bird. He wore a tattered coat snapped by the wind....

Mark gasped, words forming silently on his lips. Could it be?

At the same time, Katie stopped abruptly in front of the statue, jerking her arm free from his.

Startled by her sudden movement, Mark turned around. As he did, his revelation of the old man's true identity was snatched from his conscious mind.

One hand to her mouth, Katie stood and pointed.

The statue had been defaced. Two bright red words had been painted below Cardinal Gibbon's name.

His throat constricting, Mark stepped forward for a closer look. He shook his head from side to side as he ran his fingers over the two words painted on the marble. His eyes were not deceiving him.

Mark shook his head as the sky and clouds started to rotate oddly above him; the concrete seemed to jerk beneath his feet. He rocked back onto his heels, his legs giving way. He reached out and grabbed Katie's hand to maintain his balance. Deep down in an indistinct region of his heart, where his spirit discerned the natural from the supernatural, the rational from the fantastic, his comfortable, familiar way of perceiving reality crumbled and gave way to an overpowering fear and otherworldly presence.

Mark dropped to one knee as the wind kicked up around him. The shapes in the park melted into a glen surrounded by tall dark trees; a blanket of snow instead of concrete. Somewhere nearby, he could hear the mournful sobbing of a dying Indian mother.

He stared down at the ground by his knee with morbid fascination as two malformed crimson words were drawn in the snow by an invisible hand.

He blinked. The glen vanished. All that remained were two crimson words painted on the marble statue directly in front of him.

Unde malum.

PART

❧ II ❧

18

Sunday Morning

KIM FACED HER DRESSING TABLE AND MIRROR. On the table was a thin, black leather wallet, a money clip holding several crisp one hundred dollar bills, loose change and two thin gold chains—chains she'd seen True Believer wear around his neck. Connected to one chain was a crucifix and to the other one, a small, numbered brass key. The key's unique shape brought back memories of her days as a courier, when she handled all of Geneva's sensitive banking arrangements and lock box transactions.

A sound from behind her made her look up. She stared into the mirror and watched True Believer step out from behind the bathroom door and approach her.

Two muscular arms slipped around her waist. A smooth shaven chin edged its way into the crook of her neck and shoulder.

"I am well pleased," whispered a deep voice into her left ear. "You have served me most efficiently. I now understand why Geneva so desperately wants you back in Europe."

Closing her eyes, Kim laughed nervously.

His lips touched her ear. "My time here is almost finished. Soon I will be free. London, New York, or Geneva—they will have no power over me. Return with me to Ireland. I will make you free."

Kim partially opened her eyes and peered into the mirror. The face of a man whose real name she did not know nuzzled her neck beneath her short black hair, his breath hot in her ear. Contrary to the softness of his voice, she was not sure if she wanted the kind of freedom he offered. His changing temperaments confused her. An amorous embrace might be followed by a cold, distant reply; a longing stare might shift to an unfocused gaze rimmed unexplicably with anger.

She pulled away and studied his face in the mirror. His chin rose slowly from her shoulder, revealing a long, pink scar that angled sharply across the curve of his left cheek.

She blinked and tried to focus her eyes. A scar? She'd never noticed a scar before!

A prickly sensation raced down her back all the way to her feet. Upon second glance, there was no scar—only smooth shaven cheeks and dark, hungry eyes.

Mark blinked. He stood at his bedroom window. The park and side streets were enshrouded with shadows and nearly deserted—except for the revving of an engine off to his left near the church.

The scene changed abruptly. Mark found himself standing on the curb as the green traffic light at the corner turned yellow. In the distance he noticed that a red pickup accelerated up Crest Road.

Memories from a summer evening four years earlier exploded before his eyes....

Katie's accident replayed itself. He no longer stood at a dark, Washington intersection, but on a sandy street corner in Virginia Beach just after sunset. It had been a gorgeous time for a walk on the first day of their vacation.

Katie stood in front of him, one foot on the curb, the other in the street. She wore a pleated blue dress and leather sandals. She turned on her heel, laughing and reaching out for his hand. The green traffic signal above her shoulder turned yellow.

The revving of an engine made Mark turn his head. A red pickup truck accelerated to beat the yellow light. At the last moment, it swerved left to avoid her, overreacting, braking, and fishtailing uncontrollably—the rear bumper catching Katie's extended left leg.

She spun away like a lifesize doll into the middle of the street....

Mark's scream died in his throat.

The scene faded and Mark found himself standing once again on the night-darkened curb in front of his townhouse.

Katie stood with one foot on the curb. She wore a long, red winter coat over jeans and snow boots. She turned on her heel, laughing and reaching out for his hand. The green traffic signal above her shoulder turned yellow.

Out of the corner of his eye, Mark noticed a red pickup bouncing up over the curb, its front bumper less than ten feet away. His eyes zeroed in on the vanity license plate heading straight for Katie's legs—on it, two Latin words in the color of blood!

Mark woke with a start, flat on his back with his hands cupped over his face. Through his fingers he could see the yellow glow of the streetlight outside his window. He slowly lowered his hands to the bed; the sheets and pillowcase were damp!

He snapped his head to the left. Katie! The red pickup!

But this was no street corner. Katie slept blissfully with her back to him. Mark licked his dry lips as the nightmare replayed itself in the darkness: the roar of the pickup; Katie turning, reaching, the license plate.

He lifted his eyes from Katie to the shadowed ceiling, then turned on his side and faced the window, staring ruefully at the dimly lit curtains, trying to focus his heart and mind upon the Lord. Images past and present spun kaleidoscopically through his thoughts. Merging, overlapping and then breaking apart, the dizzying, frightful patterns played hauntingly in his mind.

Thirty minutes later, he drifted into an uneasy sleep.

Katie turned onto her side and watched Mark's chest rise and fall. Sunlight filtered softly into the room. Her eyes roamed to his tousled, sandy hair and then to his closed eyes. She pulled the comforter up around her neck, brought her lips together and held back a sigh.

Saturday afternoon and evening had passed without a hundred words between them.

Katie propped herself on an elbow. Her movement caused Mark to stir, then wake. He cracked open his eyes, then turned his head toward her.

Their eyes met. She smiled and gently touched his forearm.

For a second, she saw a glimmer of warmth in his eyes, then the glimmer faded. The grin that started to curl across his face drooped sharply.

Katie squeezed his arm. She hoped that a good night's sleep would snap him out of his growing despondency. It didn't. She stared right through his scowl. It had been a long four years, rebuilding their marriage and their faith. Wednesday night had seemed so hopeful. Now...

"Honey! You've got to snap out of this."

Mark blinked, his forehead lined with anguish, his eyes suddenly cloudy with tears.

His tortured expression startled her. She had seen his face like this only once before, in the Norfolk emergency room when the doctors had immobilized her and told both of them that their unborn baby was dead. Stunned, Mark had collapsed in a chair, his countenance falling, breaking. A part of him seemed to die.

Katie reached out with her hand a second time.

A huge tear rolled down Mark's cheek. He wiped it away with the corner of the sheet, then reached out and clasped her hand tightly in his. Words tumbled from his mouth.

"Babe, only heaven knows how much I love you."

Katie pulled his hand to her cheek. "I know you love me." She closed her eyes and silently prayed, tenderly squeezing his hand as her heart uttered a desperate request for guidance.

Mark glanced at the window, then back to Katie. Light from the window warmed their bed. He returned the squeeze, his voice slightly above a whisper.

"You're right, of course—I can't pretend that nothing's happened. It's just that..."

He paused, as if searching for acceptable words. "Finding *unde malum* on the statue changes everything—it's no longer a harmless mystery about a dead man's journals. Maybe what happened to Grandpa Kyle is starting to happen to us."

Katie studied her husband's face, her blue eyes thoughtfully searching his. "What haven't you told me about Kyle or Sam?"

Mark rolled over on his back and stared up at the ceiling.

Katie watched his eyes move quickly back and forth, as if he scanned images in his mind. Looking over at her, he forced a look of stern resolve to hide a shiver that made him arch his back and raise his chin.

Katie started to frown, but Mark reached over and put a finger on her lips. "There are things you need to know. But first, what do you think about visiting Agape Christian Fellowship? Then later this afternoon, I'll catch you up on everything."

Katie considered his offer, her countenance brightening. She smiled and sat up abruptly. Without warning, she fell across his chest, playfully digging her fingers into his ribs. Mark's eyes opened wide. He let out a yell—she had almost tickled him right out of the bed!

He grasped her wrists and held her at bay.

Katie's eyes flashed excitedly. "Your offer is accepted! Believe it or not, I'm just as interested in those journals as you are! Maybe I shouldn't have let you hide away alone with Sam's writings. If I'd been reading them with you, maybe I'd be a little more sympathetic or even scared myself."

She lowered herself between his arms and kissed him lightly on the lips before he could reply. "Now, let me go! We've only got forty-five minutes to get ready if we want to be at church on time."

Mark grinned at last and released her. He threw back the covers and climbed from the bed. He stretched and glanced out the window across the park.

Katie stepped to his side. Just beyond the statue of Gibbons, an old man in his tattered coat shuffled slowly between the vacant church's tall white columns toward the middle doors, ignoring the wind that snapped at his clothes and long hair.

Mark glanced upward, drawing Katie's gaze with them. A thick layer of slate gray clouds crept over the city out of the west. The dark edge was moving slowly but steadily across the blue sky. The tops of the fir trees lining the park across from the townhouse bent sharply in the gusting wind.

Katie turned from the window. "That's right, old fella. Head for cover. There's a storm on the way."

Michelle shook the raindrops from her shoes. She twirled her umbrella and then closed it. Stepping into the foyer of the Rockville Heights Community Center, she returned a warm smile to January's greeters who stood at the opening of the large meeting hall.

Out of the corner of her eye, she saw Dan and Kent standing by the tea and coffee service. Dan was shaking hands with a couple in their early thirties whom she had never seen before.

The man talking with Dan was of medium height and build with sandy hair and serious eyes. His wife, who stood close by with her arm tucked securely through his, had shoulder-length blonde hair and an engaging smile. Dan was nodding appreciatively. Michelle grinned. She'd seen that nod so many times before. Dan was always quick to give encouragement or let you know when he was thankful for something you had done.

An acoustic guitar, keyboards, and a violin began to play *Holy, Holy, Holy* quietly in the background. A drummer and bass guitarist would join them when praise and worship began.

As she approached Dan, he turned toward her, his wide, surprised smile and sparkling eyes communicating as thoroughly as any words.

The frustration that had been building for three days broke. Michelle fought back the tears.

The videotape was still as clear and sharp as the day it was taken a year and a half earlier.

A five-year-old girl with soft brown hair and freckles wearing a one-piece, royal blue bathing suit stood on the bottom step of a wooden deck and smiled timidly. Raising her small hands to her eyes, she touched her index fingers to her thumbs and raised them to her eyes.

"Do you like my glasses, Daddy?" she asked excitedly. "Do you? Mommy says she does."

From behind the smiling girl at the top of the steps, Susan sat with her arms folded across her knees and laughed quietly.

"Daddy loves your glasses, honey," replied a happy, disembodied voice. "Can I borrow them?"

The little girl lowered her hands and scrunched up her nose as she considered the odd request. Suddenly, her face broke into a wide smile. She stepped forward, giggling. She raised her hands and touched her fingers to her thumbs. "I'll give Daddy's camera some glasses!"

Her small hands grew large and out of focus as she pressed them against the lens of the video recorder. The picture swerved up and down as father, mother, and daughter all began to laugh. The camera came back into focus and then froze. The small girl's happy face and hand-covered mouth filled the screen.

Fletcher leaned forward in the recliner and stared at the videotape of Melissa on her fifth birthday. That weekend in early June was to be the first of many happy weekends that summer. They finished the three-tiered deck on the back of their house, took a week-long vacation at Disney World in Orlando and another week at Myrtle Beach, South Carolina. Then in the fall, he and Susan had spent a memorable, ten-year anniversary weekend at a friend's condo on Maryland's beautiful eastern shore.

Now, his free weekends were anything but memorable. He spent his time grocery shopping, or cleaning the house, doing the laundry, or simply being all alone with only the television and the videos to keep him company.

This was when Melissa's and Susan's absence hurt the most. And watching the videos did not help the loneliness one bit. Fletcher punched the remote and turned off the VCR and television.

"So, this is what it's going to come to, huh, Fletch?" his conscience chided. "Watching the videos and becoming a human slug feeding on dead memories."

He studied the remote in his hand, then placed it on the end table beside the chair.

Yes, watching videos was safe—reducing his life to minimal risks. Minimal risks. . .

Arms propped over his knees, Fletcher sat in silence and mulled over his current predicament. If he disregarded the grim warning behind Carlton's staged death, he was exposing himself to a much higher level of risk. He'd already found ways to lose his family, threaten his sanity, and jeopardize his career.

But what about his life? Did he really want to take that step?

Fletcher shook his head. He faced similar risks every day on the street, didn't he? Hanging out in dirty rooms filled with spaced-out dealers armed with guns or crashing through doors with a battering ram, not entirely sure what those on the other side were holding in their hands.

He closed his eyes and leaned back into the recliner.

Dan stepped to the podium as the deacons took their positions at the ends of the aisles to receive the tithes and offerings. He brushed his hand over his beard and smiled.

"The choir is going to sing a song, to inspire us for the important week that lies ahead. As most of us are well aware, this year's annual March for Life has added significance. Everything related to the march has come under extreme scrutiny. The vandalism of an AFI clinic earlier last Wednesday night only exacerbated that scrutiny and gives substance to the pro-abortion coalitions who seek an injunction to restrict—or if possible—stop the march."

A shrewd grin broke across Dan's face. "Not a bit surprising is it? These kinds of tactics have only been going on for almost two thousand years. If we say we belong to Christ, we will find ourselves at odds with the world and Satan.

"But it's better to resist evil than succumb to it, for as Proverbs 25:26 says, 'Like a muddied spring or a polluted well is a righteous man who gives way to the wicked.' That's one of the reasons why Agape supports the practice of peaceable picketing. It's the Christian's task to sound the warning and God's task to convict the listener.

"Now, as the choir sings an old, familiar hymn, I urge you to reconsider the eternal truths captured in these words originally written in 1697. Yes, 1697. Perhaps they are even more meaningful to us now than to those who first heard them."

The mention of the year 1697 sparked Mark's interest—that was five or six generations before Sam was born. From his seat in the back of the congregation, he uncrossed his legs and raised his eyes to the front of the room. Earlier, while everyone around him so easily entered into praise and songs of adoration to Christ, he had struggled to lift his voice to the Lord. The words had blurted clumsily from his mouth rather than flow from his heart. Now, the guitar and violin tugged compellingly at his melancholy spirit, centering his gaze on the choir as they sang.

Be still, my soul, the Lord is on thy side;
Bear patiently the cross of grief or pain;
Leave to thy God to order and provide;

Mark's perception of the room narrowed abruptly as his eyes fixed on the choir's upturned and expressive faces. The words of the hymn shined a light into his fearful heart. He wondered if Sam had ever sung this song.

In every change He faithful will remain.
Be still, my soul: thy best, thy heavenly Friend
Through thorny ways lead to a joyful end.

Mark breathed deeply, drawing each line of the hymn into his soul. He felt Katie slide her arm through the crook of his elbow, then gently, determinedly, entwine her fingers through his.

With all of his heart Mark wanted to believe that those words were for Katie and him.

Be still, my soul, thy God doth undertake
To guide the future as He has the past.
Thy hope, thy confidence let nothing shake;
All mysterious shall be bright at last.
Be still, my soul: the waves and winds still know
His voice who ruled them while He dwelt below.

All mysterious shall be bright at last! The lyrics pierced to the core of his fear. White hot and pure, the song echoed the assurance of God's unfailing love and providence that felt so distant.

The instruments quieted; the choir sat down. Dan took the podium with a huge smile, adjusted his tie clip and microphone, and organized his sermon notes.

Mark lifted his eyes toward the ceiling. He thought back to Sam's first journal entry, when Sam had knelt in the wet snow beneath an old oak tree, two small nails clutched in one hand, his head lifted toward heaven, his heart broken with grief, his voice crying out with all the force of his being—a cry that Mark wanted to be his very own.

I will say "Yes, Lord, Yes!"

Mark mouthed the words, but in his heart, he knew they were not yet his own.

19

Sunday Afternoon

FORTY-FIVE MINUTES LATER, Fletcher pushed himself up from the recliner, rubbed his unshaven face and stepped to the living room window. Though the sky was still overcast and gray, the winds had subsided and the rain was falling gently.

Fletcher's face reddened. He really had become a slug.

If Jimmy were still alive on this cold, wet January day, Fletcher knew that he would have already been on the road with something hot to eat and drink for Jimmy and his friends. Larry and Glenn would be just as cold and wet if Jimmy were still alive, huddling inside one of the concrete alcoves on the south side of the park.

Fletcher drew a deep breath and headed down the hall to the kitchen, wishing he could bring Larry and Glenn something more than just food. The pang in his heart became an ache. He wanted to bring them a genuine sense of hope and confidence that they would not be forgotten.

But gifts like those were not so easily given. The giver had to sufficiently possess them first, and he was in extremely low supply. Fletcher sighed, emptied a large can of stew into the pot on the stove, snapped on the burner and pulled a big wooden spoon from a nearby drawer.

For now they'd have to make do with the help he had to offer.

Undoing the strap on her umbrella, Michelle headed for the door, stepping in behind the couple she had seen talking to Dan and Kent just before the meeting began.

Michelle thought back. Kent had pulled Dan and her to the side and told them about his meeting with Mark on Friday afternoon. He and his wife, Katie, lived across the street from the clinic. He also explained how Mark witnessed an incident related to the vandalism and was willing to testify if needed.

Michelle pursed her lips. Just what or whom had he seen? Someone's identity she'd recognize? She wanted to speak to him so badly she felt she would burst!

Somewhere behind her toward the back of the line a baby began to cry. Mark turned his head and glanced back. His eyes met hers briefly. Michelle started to speak, then held back, instead offering a smile that passed unnoticed as Mark looked toward the front.

She watched him pop open his umbrella and slip his arm around his wife's shoulder. Michelle sighed, opened her own umbrella and followed them silently out into the gently falling rain.

Fletcher found Larry and Glenn just as he had expected, huddled in a concrete alcove on the south side of the park. Their canvas duffel bags were packed tightly around them to help hold in some of the warmth generated by their bodies.

There was no extra room in the alcove, so Fletcher served them from outside, placing the pot of beef stew on top of one of the duffel bags. He knelt on a narrow strip of concrete; the light rain pelted softly against the hood of his vinyl rain gear as he poured them steaming cups of hot cocoa with a smile. After handing them the styrofoam cups, Fletcher reached into his plastic bag for one more item: a package of Oreo cookies.

Glenn's face lit up.

Mark leaned his head back against the cool stone of the fireplace, Sam's fourth journal resting open across his lap. Sam's earlier journals and Family History were stacked on the floor by his feet.

"So—those are the highlights, from April 1856 to December 1859. They cover Sam's life from his sabbatical in the valley to the beginning of the Civil War and his dream about the river of blood. But there's still one thing I need to tell you."

He breathed deeply, then recounted his dream about the racing red pickup in front of their townhouse.

Katie sat in the straight back chair beside the mahogany desk. She crossed her blue-jeaned legs, her eyes running back and forth over the neatly arranged stacks of material on the long table in front of the bay windows. "You should have told me about these things yesterday, even if you thought they might upset me."

Mark's head bobbed slowly up and down in agreement.

Katie tried to smile. "I'm sorry. At least now I know why finding *unde malum* on the statue was so rough for you. When I encouraged you to find Sam's knapsacks I had no idea—"

Mark turned around and placed his hand on top of the journals. "Katie, it's nothing you did. Finding the knapsacks was an inevitability. They've been in our family over a century."

His eyes narrowed. "I've got a feeling that evil is stalking us. I've got to get over it. There's something crucial for us in those journals. His writings have become dark and portentous, but at their core, I think they're full of truth."

Katie pushed herself out of the chair, crossed the room, put her arm through his and laid her head against his shoulder. Mark placed his hand over hers. "You were correct from the very beginning when we read Aunt Clara's letter. My grandfather bequeathed us a mystery. Like it or not, we may be into something that's over our heads—I don't know. But we can't stop reading Sam now, *unde malum* or no *unde malum.*"

Katie slid her hand back under his arm, stared longingly up into his face. "How did those words get onto the statue?"

"I don't have any reasonable answers—just unreasonable ones."

Katie sighed heavily and chewed at her lower lip. "I guess I should be more scared by what's happened than I am. Maybe it doesn't bother me quite as much as you because I've already faced the most frightening thing in this world."

"What's that?"

"Dying in a hospital room and leaving you." Katie forced a grin. "God knew you were going to need me. And you do need me—to help you keep your balance until we get to the end of this thing."

Mark put his arms around her. For several minutes they simply clung tightly to each other.

"Why don't we head out for a nice dinner?" he finally asked, lifting her chin with his hand. "We can dive back into the journals, together, when we return."

"Sounds wonderful," Katie replied. "I'll go and change."

Mark glanced out the window, then exhaled forcefully.

Katie paused at the door. "What now?"

He frowned and rubbed his arms. "It'll pass."

He stepped up behind her and slipped his arms around her waist. "Why don't you start thinking about what you'd like to have for dinner?"

A half hour later, Mark closed Katie's door, walked around the Blazer and climbed into the driver's seat. He buckled his seat belt and started the engine. After glancing in his side view mirror, he carefully pulled into the street, then stopped immediately for a red light at the corner of Crest and 16th Street.

He was so intent in figuring out which direction he needed to go, he did not notice a forty-year-old man with a salt and pepper beard wearing a Redskin jacket who leaned against a light pole less than six feet from the Blazer.

The light turned green.

Fletcher leaned against the light pole on the corner, folded his arms across his Redskin jacket and scratched his beard. He watched the Blazer drive several blocks before turning down a side street and disappearing. He frowned, turned around and headed back across the park toward his car.

Five minutes later and two blocks away, Fletcher stopped at his favorite hole-in-the-wall Greek deli and ordered a cup of coffee. He found a narrow booth in the back, pulled a photocopy from his pocket and spread it out on the vinyl table-top.

He skipped down to the second paragraph. He finally figured out what bothered him about the anonymous tip.

> *There was animal blood sloppily painted on the sides and top of the door frame, an obvious Judeo-Christian reference to the Passover. The blood symbolized the work of Jesus Christ to deliver man from God's judgment against sin. For Moses and the Hebrews, the blood would protect them from the destroyer who would come to claim the firstborn of every family. The use of this symbol in connection with the vandalism is a farce and plainly reflects someone's attempt to implicate Christians in the crime. Rather than looking for suspects among local pro-life groups, the police department should focus their efforts on the American Family Institute itself. Close inspection of the so-called vandalism will reveal that little material damage was actually done to the clinic. The AFI, rather than the local churches or the Christian pro-life groups gathering for next week's annual March for Life, profits the most from the vandalism.*

Fletcher sipped his coffee and reconsidered his analysis. First, the tipster had been inside the clinic shortly after the vandalism. The use of the word "sloppily" was a visual indicator far too precise for someone who had merely watched a newsclip or heard a radio report. Confirming this assumption was the tipster's reference to *little material damage*. For some reason that phrase reminded Fletcher of something a professional might say—someone who had been inside and seen the damage.

This led directly to point number two. Why would someone intimate with the internal workings of the clinic, want to speak out against their employer? Pro-choice and pro-life groups were diametrically opposed. It was also highly illogical to think that someone who worked at the clinic would try to point the finger at themselves.

Complicating the issue, the tipster appeared religious, maybe even a Christian. The author was clearly familiar with the Bible.

Maybe the tip came from a carpenter or painter involved in repairing the damage. That idea held more promise than a clinic or AFI employee, except for that peculiar turn of phrase.

Little material damage—it was not the language of someone in the service industry. Fletcher pulled his fingers slowly through his beard. Looking up at the counter, he waited until he caught the owner's eye, then signaled for a refill.

It was dark outside by the time he had finished his second cup. The more he considered the evidence—the more he was sure Christians were not involved in the vandalism, nor in moving and dumping Jimmy's body onto the golf course. Christians and pro-lifers might be bigoted, as the television reporters had repeatedly stated, but Fletcher just couldn't believe that they would brutally take a life of someone like Jimmy while trying to save babies.

He climbed out of the booth, peeled two bills from his money clip and threw them onto the middle of the table.

What was the world coming to? Was there no justice for the murders of harmless old men and innocent babies? Even Carlton, in his own way, was an innocent victim, used as a warning. A warning to stay away. From pursuing Jimmy's death or the clinic vandalism? Was the connection important enough to kill someone for?

He pulled his cap snugly onto his head, adjusting the visor downward to shade his red eyes as he pushed open the door. If the tipster was correct and AFI was involved, then Carlton's murderers could be linked to AFI. Further, with all of the cases having been given to Troy, he was implicated, too. And if Troy, then KC. She was the first to threaten him, outside the morgue.

The potential of a conspiracy chilled him to the bone.

As Fletcher turned left down the sidewalk toward his car, he passed a tall, blond broad-shouldered man, wearing a blue jogging suit, who was standing at the bus stop in front of the deli, his back to Fletcher. The man's hands were loosely linked behind his back.

A man with blond hair and broad shoulders? Fletcher slowed his pace. He had seen this man before, recently. He glanced casually over his shoulder, then stopped suddenly. Slowly, he turned around.

The sidewalk was empty. The wind skipped a piece of trash by the bus stop sign. Had the man stepped into the deli?

Fletcher was tempted to look inside. But to do that would expose his awareness, if indeed someone had him under surveillance. He shook his head, spun on his heel and started quickly back down the sidewalk toward his car, every nerve, every muscle in his body instantly alive, keenly aware of sounds, of movements.

From now on, he would have to be careful to watch for the man in blue—very careful.

But even as Fletcher approached his car, the focus of his concern—the man in blue—faded from his mind as if it had never been there.

While unlocking the door and climbing inside, his thoughts skipped backward and replayed themselves over...

... from now on, he would have to be careful—very careful.

Fletcher checked his rear view mirror, then started the engine.

The man in blue stepped down from the curb into the parking space and gently patted the TransAm's right rear fender as it edged out into the street.

The wind brushed his blond hair back from his sober, attentive face. He folded his arms across his chest as the vehicle accelerated away from the deli.

His earnest blue eyes followed Fletcher Rivers, the man to whom he had been assigned as guardian.

Yes, you must be careful—very careful....

20

Sunday Evening

MARK AND KATIE RETURNED FROM A LOVELY EVENING. The weather had added its own special touch, with clearing skies, warming temperatures, and only the slightest hint of a breeze. Even the neighborhood seemed brighter, more cheerful.

They met their next door neighbor for the first time. Jonah Washington McKenzie was a thin, elderly black man with a smile as bright as a crescent moon. Born and raised in the Mount Pleasant area, the eighty-six-year-old local was greatly pleased to see that "Miss Clara's" house had been left in the care of such a "kindly young nephew." His serious eyes twinkled suddenly when he discovered that Katie was pregnant. "Well, well. God bless the both of you, and the little one, too," he had said with an understanding smile, as he opened his door and went inside.

Twenty minutes later, with Katie seated contentedly in the cushioned armchair he had brought up from their bedroom, Mark lowered himself into his familiar chair by the desk.

Katie folded her hands in her lap. "What a nice man, that Jonah McKenzie. I wonder if he has anyone to look in on him?"

"Maybe we'll get a chance to befriend him," Mark said as his eyes darted to the stack of Sam's journals on the end of the table.

He reached across the table and picked up a thin stack of envelopes. He shuffled through them and sighed. "OK. When I left off reading yesterday, Sam had just finished writing down his dream. After I put my books away, I peeked ahead—"

Mark raised a hand to hold off Katie's sudden frown. "Trust me. I only checked the date of his next entry—that's all. I saw the year and closed the journal. This time Sam skips all the way to August, 1862, over fifteen months after Fort Sumter."

Katie leaned forward with a quizzical look, folding her arms. "Was Sam working on his Founding Fathers Journals again?"

"I guess." Mark started to open the journal, reconsidered with a growing smile, then left it closed. He stood up, crossed the room to Katie's chair and held out his hands.

Katie grinned questioningly and put her hands in his.

He pulled her up from the chair, then wrapped his arms around her waist.

"Are you sure you want to read?" he whispered. "Haven't we heard enough about the Devil and his plans for one day?"

Katie's smiling face was inches away. He stared into her searching blue eyes and brought his lips to hers.

The soft hiss of electronics behind the silence over the telephone line told True Believer everything he wanted to know. He glanced at his watch: 11:01:40. The conference call with New York and Geneva was less than two minutes old. After logging in each participant, he cut straight to the issue and revealed his target for Phase II.

Sitting on his living room couch and flipping a small brass key over and over in his hand, True Believer relished every passing moment of silence.

Selecting a target for Phase I, a women's health clinic, had not raised an eyebrow. All agreed, including New York, that his plan to use the vandalism as a cover to insert a bomb had been a stroke of genius. The vandalism would prime the news media's pump, so to speak. While AFI's Peters knew about and understood the strategic value of blowing up the clinic and the ensuing loss of life, he knew nothing of the greater destruction that would soon follow.

But now the hissing silence revealed his compatriots' weakness. Accustomed to order, wealth, and comfort, they were ill-prepared for the violent realities of social restructuring through terrorism. Men like New York were used to more subtle methods of change, some of which were no less costly to the American public than what True Believer planned. For years New York and America's liberal left had attempted to anesthetize the nation's collective mind. Six days from now, in one short hour, True Believer planned to deliver a critical blow directly to its head.

New York was the first to respond, and rightly so. "You're—you're kidding. Bombing a clinic was one thing, but your target for Phase II is unacceptable!"

Geneva interrupted. A harsh grin spread across True Believer's face as the New Age biotechnologist reproved the financier. "We do not play games. You were the one who convinced Bonn to accelerate the decision on selecting a target. If you wish to indulge your emotions, be thankful that True Believer did not designate your Lady Liberty as our target."

"I'm grateful, yes," New York replied in a subdued voice. "But the Statue of Liberty sits alone in the harbor, unprotected and accessible from any direction. His recommended target is one of the most prominent landmarks in D.C. Besides, have we forgotten what two events take place that Saturday and then on Wednesday?"

Geneva answered, to True Believer's growing delight. Any fears that he had of New York manipulating the Swiss Ph.D. were quickly vanishing. "No one has forgotten. The irony is intriguing. There will be no doubts against whom the target was intended, and who was responsible. If some of our people must be sacrificed, so be it."

"Your use of 'our' is deplorable," New York said forcefully. "There won't be any of your people at the pro-choice rally."

True Believer could not refrain any longer. His eyes roamed across the dark room. "Ah, yes. We are heartless, aren't we? You disapprove of Geneva's terminology. It is not Geneva or Bonn who allowed your former President to stack your Supreme Court with yet another conservative. Surely you must accept that judicial opportunities for change are no longer viable. The Supreme Court has demonstrated it will not choose sides in the debate. And we all know that this is far more than a debate."

New York replied nervously. "I just don't want the record to show that our U.S. operations have failed in their part. In last year's election, we've estimated that thirty-five percent of the Evangelical Christian vote went to our candidate. Our problems can clearly be traced to a much smaller coalition of traditional family and pro-life activists. Our opponents are becoming as socially responsive as our best people, even though they are underfunded, have splintered leadership, and are despised by a majority of their own. They're a thorn in our side, a slow bleed."

True Believer replied sarcastically. "And we are here to staunch the flow and save the world from the Christians. I think you make excuses. You've allowed the Savings and Loan crisis and banking scandals to diffuse your focus from Bonn's plan."

Geneva cut in. "Enough! Our objectives no longer hinge on the potentialities of Roe v. Wade. We've weakened the old ethic based on Judeo-Christian values. Now that ethic must be thoroughly expunged. Indeed, the future of all humankind depends upon our success in reversing world population growth and evolving our race unfettered by religion.

"True Believer's plan for Saturday leverages a unique opportunity. Next week, every Senator and Congressman will be in Washington, as well as public officials from all over the country. November's election proved that the U.S. electorate are fed up with the demagogy of the religious right. Bonn believes True Believer's plan will energize Congress to action. Restoring federal funding for abortions through Medicaid will be one of our first objectives. We expect this to reduce the annual population growth by an additional one million. Then we can move ahead with the next phase in our social restructuring and depopulation initiatives."

"Agreed," was New York's only reply.

True Believer waited for a moment, and then spoke up, his voice sharp-edged. "Are there any further questions or complaints about my target that cannot wait until Tuesday night?"

Once again the soft hiss of electronics behind the silence told him everything he wanted to know. He hung up the phone, staring out his large window past the brightly lit Kennedy Center to the Lincoln Memorial.

He smiled and pocketed the numbered brass key he played with throughout the conversation—his key to freedom—*after* fulfilling his contractual obligations to Bonn.

If they refused to listen, he would expose their global-spanning powers with one turn of a key, one phone call, one password. Their invisible empire would be forced into the light!

His smile darkened. Soon, they would have no power over him.

Very soon.

Within twenty minutes True Believer had completed his end-of-day computer updating. He retreated into the bathroom for his ritual, late night shower. Half an hour later, he fell into an uneasy sleep. And, for the first time in over ten years, he dreamed of Ireland's troubles.

Londonderry, twenty-four years earlier. Dark cloudy skies and narrow cobblestone streets. British paratroopers in combat gear with automatic rifles pushing through a frantic crowd. Shouting. Pushing. Cursing. A bottle arcing over his head. A small stone church and tall steeple, an open square with a dry, broken fountain adorned with plump cherubim, a sidewalk littered with dead bodies.

True Believer tried to turn away, but a force stronger than his aversion compelled him closer to two of the bodies. He wanted to raise his hands, but the force kept them pinned to his sides.

Revulsion gnawed at his stomach.

And suddenly he was there, standing above Coleen and Aiden, his fair-skinned and dark-haired cousins who had been like sister and brother to him, innocent bystanders gunned down at the civil rights protest across the street. Coleen was sprawled on her back in the gutter, her head angled horribly against the brick curb, Aiden crumpled close beside her with his arm draped grotesquely over her shoulder, their clear blue eyes staring blankly into his, the fronts of their wool sweaters stained with an impossible amount of blood. Around Coleen's neck was the thin gold chain and crucifix her father had given her as a Christmas gift the year before.

His eyes were drawn to the crucifix, to a growing crimson pool in the middle of Coleen's chest...

Lurching forward, muscles knotted and his body drenched with sweat, True Believer awoke with a howl, his head arched back and hands to his face, cursing God.

21

Monday Morning

HAROLD LOOKED UP from his empty bowl and shook the box of cereal a second time. The box was as empty as his bowl. He pushed the bowl away, closed the book he was reading, and picked up a folded, age-yellowed page of newsprint.

He could survive one more day—besides, he was going to spend the night at Kim's. What a babe! Just thinking about it was driving him crazy. Tonight he'd have her. Tomorrow he'd get paid.

He was so close to the $20,000 he could taste it! Twenty-thousand dollars! He hadn't seen that much money since his college days at Cal-Berkeley when he banked his grandmother's inheritance check.

Harold carried his book with him into the living room and smiled. He spent a couple of hours Sunday afternoon emptying his large box of jumbled books into a neat, six-foot-long row against the wall opposite the couch. Walking to the right end of his new library, he stooped and slipped the biography of John Brown into its place at the end of the row.

He moved to the living room window. Holding the newsprint in one hand, he inched back the curtain with the other. To purge this land with blood. If that's what it took to cleanse the country from the blight of the greedy capitalistic abortionists, so be it.

Peering outside, he searched the street below for any suspicious-looking persons or cars. The Sponsors really didn't give him the credit he deserved—like spotting the picket coordinator talking with the new neighbor.

In fact, his investigative skills were so sharp, that he was certain that he had uncovered one of the Sponsor's identities!

Sunday night he connected a face to a voice, the face of a former college acquaintance and the voice of the man who recruited him to picket the clinic. The same man who paid his way from Los Angeles to Washington and who gave him instructions before Kim had been involved.

He let go of the curtain, then leaned back against the wall and unfolded the newsprint. He smiled broadly.

As he sorted through the cardboard boxes of his old college text-books and laid out his library on the carpet, the face became perfectly and visibly clear.

The yellowed, front page from the Cal-Berkeley student newspaper, dated May 1967, had fallen out of a World Religions textbook.

A picture in the center of the page showed three smiling students sitting atop a low brick wall outside the newspaper's campus office —the top three winners of the newspaper's annual short story contest. On the left was the third place winner—himself, Harold Wertman. In the middle was the grand prize winner, a red-headed babe by the name of Stella. And on the right, the second place winner, Brian Fein, the dark-haired student from Ireland. Brian had been the first full-blooded Irishman to win the short story contest. They had been treated to a dinner. After several pitchers of beer, the dark-haired Irishman began to slip heavily into his native brogue. After that night, he had always been able to pick up Brian's lilt, no matter how carefully the Irishman tried to suppress his accent.

But that had been twenty-six years ago. Without the picture he would never have made the connection.

"Brian Fein," Harold said beneath his breath, pulling at the ends of his beard. "It's you, man, I know it's you. Gotta be! But don't worry. No one will ever know. I promise."

Harold grabbed his coat and bullhorn from the end of the couch and headed for the door. Great men in history took great risks, and it was his turn to be great, just like the John Brown of old. Just like Jesus Christ. And if he were arrested, they could say or do whatever they wanted, but he would never divulge any information about Brian or the Sponsors! Bring on the FBI and the CIA!

Harold stepped into the hall and closed the door to Apartment 2, twisting the knob to make sure it was locked. When he reached the bottom of the stairs, the door on the right opened suddenly.

A broad-hipped, elderly woman with frizzy gray hair stepped into the hall. Her beady eyes peeked out over puffy cheeks with a look that could kill. Her voice was raspy, a longtime smoker's voice. "Today's the day. Ante up with three weeks rent or you're out of here."

"Tomorrow—Mrs. Grimwald, tomorrow's the deadline. We agreed, remember?" Harold replied, stepping around her and slowly backing his way toward the apartment doors.

Mrs. Grimwald frowned, then waved him off in disgust. She turned and headed back into her ground floor apartment.

Harold pushed open the front door. "Tomorrow—I promise!"

From her Camaro down and across the street, KC watched Harold exit the rundown boardinghouse and walk down the short flight of brick steps to the street. He climbed into his van and maneuvered out of his space into the narrow car-lined street. When the van turned the corner and disappeared from sight, KC exchanged glances with Troy who was already zipping his jacket. They were dressed for the street: jeans, sweaters, winter jackets.

"OK. Time for our little talk with Mrs. Grimwald, then let's see what there is to see."

"Kim better keep Brown away until tomorrow morning," Troy said as he picked up a small duffel bag from the floor of the car.

They popped open their doors, and started casually across the street toward the crumbling brick row house.

Mark left the study with one of Sam's journals and Sam's old King James Bible tucked under his arm. As he started down the stairs, he paused. Now there were no dark shadows, no supernatural presences or sensations of staring eyes. Late morning light from the study behind him filtered evenly across the landing, reflecting softly off the walls and down the stairs.

He continued down the stairs, through the dining room and into the kitchen.

Katie, in blue sweats, sat at the small table by the window, sipping a cup of tea. A second cup sat steaming on the place mat across from her. On the floor by her feet was the morning paper.

He took his seat, placing the journal, Bible, and letter in the middle of the table.

Katie lowered the cup from her mouth. The sparkle in her wide blue eyes instantly gained his attention, and the play of morning sunlight in the waves of her hair sustained it. The dance of freckles across her cheeks and nose, the familiar smile on her lips—the smile that said thank you for loving me, thank you for sharing important things with me—refused to release his eyes.

She reached out and covered his hands with her own. "Last night, after you built that wonderful fire, when we held each other close, praying for the baby, I was struck all over again with just how much we're indebted to your family—this great old house, all the furnishings, Sam's writings. I felt that way again this morning. I leaned back against the counter, placed my hands on my stomach and began praying quietly. I don't know how to explain it, except to say that I've never felt so intimately aware of God's presence! It was like a Sunday morning in church."

Katie searched Mark's face. "Before we read Sam's journal, I want to spend time praying. I want to pray for our family, this neighborhood, our new friends, next week's march—whatever the Lord brings to mind. I believe we need to—desperately."

Mark blinked. Like a lightning bolt out the blue, he remembered his dream of the red pickup, screeching tires, Katie's outstretched arm and hand. He lowered his eyes and forced a smile. Pray about a dream? He stared thoughtfully out the kitchen window at the frost covered back yard and silently reached for his cup.

Mrs. Grimwald closed and locked the door to Apartment #2, maneuvering her wide frame in the narrow hallway to face the policewoman and her impatient, hulking partner.

She pushed her thick gray bangs from her eyes while wrinkling her nose. "He's done something wrong, hasn't he?"

The policewoman shoved her gloved hands into her jacket pockets. "Ma'am, we're just not free to say at this time. When the investigation is complete, you'll be one of the first to know."

The policewoman's partner leaned forward and wagged his thick finger in her face. "If you tell anyone about our visit, we'll slap you in the can right alongside him."

Mrs. Grimwald dropped her hands, retreated a step and bumped into the wall. Who did these people think they were, intimidating her like that? Why would she want to help the jerk who owed her three weeks rent? She swore quietly and edged toward the stairs. "I stay in my apartment and watch my television. All day. I don't see nobody; I don't see nothing. Period."

Exchanging glances, the two police officers seemed satisfied with her answer. They stepped around her and hurried down the flight of stairs without saying another word.

As she had locked the door to the apartment, she realized that they didn't have the small duffel bag they'd brought in with them. Had they accidentally left it inside, in one of his rooms?

No way was she going to help. Not now. Not after the way they had treated her. She didn't care if they messed up the entire investigation! She turned away, primped her frizzy gray hair, and lumbered down the stairs and back to her morning movie.

When Julie first stepped off the elevators into the AFI executive office suite, Michelle could tell that her new friend was stressed. However, there was little time to talk about it. The receptionist had called in sick and Human Resources pulled Julie to handle the phones and other minor, administrative duties until they could get someone in later that morning. Of course, she'd agreed, as long as she would be allowed to bring her regular work to the front desk.

Michelle looked away from her computer screen at the foot-high stack of file folders and reports on the floor by the end of her desk. With Carol out, the workload had grown dramatically. However, her concentration level had not risen commensurately. On the front page of the Metro section in the newspaper, another blistering pro-choice article had appeared, condemning next week's March for Life and threatened rescue missions. The article contained an overly simplified graph that plotted a five-year history of pro-life protests, rescue missions, and vandalisms against D.C. clinics. It would only inflame the already negative situation.

Michelle turned her attention back to the computer screen, only to be interrupted by a knock on the door. It was Mr. Peters. He was impeccably groomed as always, with carefully styled silver hair, smooth clean-shaven face and broad white smile.

"Yes, sir. What can I do for you this morning?"

He raised his hand slightly. "You need to prepare two checks, similar to what you did for me last week. Incidentally, do you know when Carol is expected back?"

"No one's heard from her," Michelle answered, picking up a pen and sliding her notepad in front of her. "But I'll notify Carmen the moment I find out. About those checks, same consultant?"

A moment of hesitation preceded his reply. "No. Make them out to Harbinger Ltd., one of our ad agencies. I'll have Carmen dash off a memo authorizing you to make the transactions."

Michelle finished writing his request, then glanced up. Their eyes met briefly before she looked away. Something was amiss behind Mr. Peters' flawless exterior. On the surface he seemed calm, collected, but underneath, uncertainty bubbled and brewed.

He broke eye contact with her, and with a wave of his hand stepped out of the doorway back into the hall.

Michelle appraised his expression—the slight tensing of his thin lips, the narrowing of his gray eyes, the tiny wrinkle between his eyebrows. What had she seen? Stress? No—his countenance had revealed something else. Stronger. Distress? Revulsion?

She shook her head and turned back to her computer.

Whatever had bothered Mr. Peters had troubled him deeply, cracking his immaculate demeanor. She hoped he hadn't picked up on her interest in his hesitant response.

The phone buzzed, drawing her thoughts away. She picked up the receiver, surprised by the familiar smoker's voice. It was Carol calling from Phoenix, just letting Michelle know that she was going to extend her house-hunting vacation to the end of the week. After chatting briefly about her problems locating an affordable house, the discussion turned to business.

Carol listened to Michelle's summary of the week's activity. "You're completely in charge, and I expect you to hold down the fort as Acting Director. You're next in line anyway—unless you screw up royally! And don't forget to inform the powers-that-be of my change in plans."

"Yes, of course, I'll let everyone know. Goodbye." Michelle hung up the phone and smiled. Carol's continued absence would give her further opportunity to investigate the vandalism.

Michelle picked up the phone and dialed Carmen's extension. "Hi, it's Michelle. Tell Mr. Peters that Carol called. She's going to be out until Monday. Thanks."

She hung up the phone and eagerly turned to her work.

Nurse Rollins unlocked the little-used storage closet at the end of the short hall behind the reception area. Standing in the doorway, she flipped on the light and stuck her clipboard under her arm.

Taking an inventory of AFI literature was not the reason Nurse Rollins had unlocked the storage room. Her immediate task was to verify the status of the large wooden box in the front corner of the closet—the box that entered the clinic under the cover of the vandalism.

Rollins leaned over the crate and looked into a thumbnail-sized hole in the top. A small red light blinked rhythmically.

She would relay her confirmation of the package's readiness to her superiors in New York. Phase I of the operation was definitely a go. Tomorrow morning she would arrive late, victim of a flat tire on the Beltway. Everyone would say how lucky she had been.

As much as New York detested True Believer, he had been forced to acknowledge the man's genius.

Rollins smiled, her thin, hateful lips curling upward like a scythe.

⇜ 22 ⇝

Monday Afternoon

TRUE BELIEVER REACHED ACROSS THE DASH and snapped off the Ferrari's stereo. His dry run for Phase I had proceeded flawlessly. The digital display on the small handheld radio transmitter/receiver told him that the package hidden inside the clinic's hallway storage room was still in perfect working order. Phase I was less than twenty-four hours from execution.

His hand dropped from the stereo to the CD player. He removed Legacy's demo disc and slipped it into his coat pocket. The group's weekend practice session had been exceptionally focused as they prepared for their upcoming concert at Saturday's pro-choice counter-rally on the Mall, which appropriately, was being sponsored by AFI. His cover as Brian Fein, rock band promoter, and his presence at the counter-rally was impenetrable. Legacy would be performing from a stage set up at the foot of the Washington Monument, facing the reflecting pool and the Lincoln Memorial, before a hundred thousand supporters.

His thoughts moved beyond the events surrounding Phase I and Phase II to his freedom, now only five days away.

Freedom. For all of their rhetoric, New York, London, Geneva and Bonn actually cared little for individual freedom. They craved political power and unflaggingly pursued their tri-part creed: evolution, survival, and transcendence. Ironically, it was for those very reasons Ciarin had originally accepted Bonn's offer and allowed her to purchase both his freedom from the Irish National Liberation Army, releasing him from his father's parochial vision for their native Ireland.

Ciarin thought about his American operatives. Were they any different? The policewoman was a slave to her resentment—just as his father had been. Black or white, Protestant or Catholic, such distinctions did not matter. Anger and bitterness, coupled with extreme economic inequity, was a potent elixir.

In the burned, bomb-blackened buildings in downtown Belfast, in the shadows of the Peace Line that separated the city into Protestant and Catholic sections like the old Berlin Wall, Ciarin had forseen his own demise, his own Hell on earth, a timeless engagement from which there was no solution and no escape. Ireland was no different than Iran, where Sunnite fought Shiite, or Palestine or Bosnia where nations were torn asunder, religions divided, and brother set against brother.

Ireland held no hope of survival and no hope for peace. Both of his parents had been sacrificed to the gods of violence. His father was a victim of the bloodshed he helped to spill. But his cousins had not deserved to have their chests torn open in a filthy Londonderry gutter.

He remembered that bitter, agonizing moment as if it had happened yesterday. He felt the hatred rise up within him, filling him, energizing his resentment and overflowing through his mouth in a virulent stream of curses at God and the church who could bring no peace to his devastated world. From that moment forward, his life had been focused to but one end.

It was their senseless deaths, not his father's, which created the open wound in his own heart. Ireland's troubles only acerbated Ciarin's hatred and drove him to greater and more daring extremes, expanding the limits of his prowess but destroying the essential inner part of himself that once knew kindness and compassion.

And a decade later, the open wound had made him an easy catch for the woman he had come to know simply as Bonn. While purchasing a cache of automatic weapons for the INLA in West Berlin, Ciarin had met this extraordinary woman who first seduced him with her bed, and then with her knowledge—a startling, intimate familiarity with his personal history, his family and his terrorist activities.

Bonn had introduced Ciarin to the equally extraordinary organization to which she belonged, an organization with enough resources to deliver him from the iron claws of the INLA. Bonn herself negotiated his freedom—funneling the INLA a quarter of a million dollars to relinquish all rights to his services.

In the months that followed, she continually sought to open his mind to the possibilities of a new world order that would transcend Ireland's troubles, Islam's jihads, Marxism's revolutions and Democracy's freedom, an order freed from nationalism while committed to radical evolution and eugenic perfectionism.

He, Ciarin Fein, using all of his former expertise and skills, would augment the organization's traditional methods of social and political transformation. And so, in late winter of 1984, the man known as True Believer had been born, with his cover as Brian Fein, rock band promoter.

Only now was he able to see that he had merely transferred his allegiance from one master to another, from the petrol bombs and the INLA to an organization which facilitated death on a global scale.

With a rare sigh, True Believer rested his arms over the steering wheel and stared out the window at the triangular park and statue of the priest.

The roar of an engine caused him to glance up. A gray van shot across the intersection, pulling into the side street directly in front of the deserted church. He glanced at his watch—10:00 A.M. Wertman was right on time. Bullhorn in hand, he crossed the park.

True Believer's eyes were drawn to a second person who entered the park from the other side and paused to study Harold. The man had brown hair and a closely trimmed beard. Something about the man was extremely familiar—

Then he remembered, as he always remembered the name of someone he had spoken to face to face. Fletcher Rivers!

The ominous portent of the detective's presence blossomed in fulfillment as he turned and walked directly toward the last townhouse on Crest Road—the MacDonald residence.

A cold rage swept through True Believer like a fierce winter wind. His hands contracted into fists. For Rivers to know about the witness meant that a leak had developed. Someone from within the police department was forwarding Rivers information on the clinic case.

Steely logic clamped down on his rising passion—these were not the streets of Belfast—not yet. Retribution would be served in a less direct fashion.

True Believer turned the ignition key and gunned the engine. He pulled out into the traffic flow, made an abrupt move into the left lane, then made an equally abrupt U-turn.

He did not need to retaliate with violence. Fletcher would be dealt with expediently; one phone call to KC and she would set into motion a series of departmental procedures that would effectively remove Rivers from the case—and his career—for good.

As for the young couple who lived in the townhouse, they had become far more entangled than he had ever anticipated. Had they heeded his warnings? Phase I would be their litmus test and would enable him to measure the degree of difficulty he would have extracting them from the clinic affair.

True Believer shifted gears. The silver Ferrari accelerated past the park, the detective, and the pawn with a startling burst of speed.

Fletcher walked up the steps and approached the front door. He knocked firmly three times.

The front door opened. Fletcher smiled. The man now standing in the doorway wore a blue-green flannel shirt and jeans, was medium height and build with serious blue eyes, short sandy hair and an inquisitive expression.

"What can I do for you?"

He pulled his right hand out of his coat pocket and flipped open a small leather case, revealing a shiny detective's badge.

"Hi, I'm Fletcher Rivers, Narcotics Division. I understand that you were a witness to the clinic vandalism last week. I'm hoping that you'll be willing to answer a few questions for me."

Fletcher watched Mark's eyes for a reaction.

The moment of hesitation on Mark's face evaporated into a smile of his own. "Sure. Come on in."

Mark took the policeman's jacket and hung it on the hall tree, then introduced him to Katie. They sat down, and Katie served them coffee. Fletcher explained how he had become personally involved in a separate homicide case involving a homeless man named Jimmy, a case that was now all but officially closed. Finally he told them why he believed the case was related to the clinic vandalism.

"Right now, you're my only real link to what actually happened to Jimmy. The death of an old homeless man won't raise an eyebrow in this city, not right now anyway. I don't know how close you've been following the news, but we've had a two hundred percent increase in homicides over last January." Fletcher watched their reactions from his position at the left end of the couch. Katie sat at the other end; Mark sat in an antique wing chair to the right of the fireplace.

"If he'd actually been murdered, I might have been able to force the issue. But he wasn't murdered; he died of natural causes."

Fletcher returned his empty mug to the small tray on the living room table between them. He sighed inwardly, relieved by their openness and receptivity—so far. It was obvious that these were genuinely nice people, a couple he might enjoy getting to know under normal circumstances. The coffee and plate of cookies made him suddenly realize how long it had been since he had spent any time socializing. After Susan and Melissa left, everything had revolved around work and taking care of Jimmy. The few friends he had outside the force fell by the wayside.

Mark looked up at Fletcher. "What specifically are you asking of me? You must have read my testimony. I don't have anything else to add."

Fletcher nodded. "Don't misunderstand. As I said a moment ago, I believe there's a crucial link between the vandalism and the fact that Jimmy's body was dumped over an embankment some two miles away. Ordinary vandals don't play games with bodies. And I don't buy the media's opinion that the break-in was the work of anti-abortion groups. Those kinds of people don't have a profile that includes body snatching. I believe that those men you saw are involved in something larger in scope.

"And that's where you come in. Given that perspective, I'd like both of you to take a minute or two and think back. Is there anything unusual you've noticed going on in or around your neighborhood since Wednesday—anything you consider out of the ordinary? Walking up here I noticed that you have a great view of the park and side streets. I realize that you're new in the area, but I'd still—"

Fletcher paused, glancing at Mark and Katie. When he mentioned his objections about the media's opinions, their faces lit up like a Christmas tree. Quite possibly, they were concerned opponents of abortion, or maybe even Christians. The Bible lying on the table in front of him supported his guess. Now, however, Mark's smile had crumpled into a frown, his forehead creased with worry. Katie sat impossibly still, staring at her hands folded in her lap. What had he said to create such a negative reaction?

Then in a flash Fletcher understood. Mark and Katie were reacting to his last question—they had seen something! Something that deeply disturbed them—at least Mark anyway.

Fletcher watched as Katie looked up, her eyes shifting intently to Mark's face. He had seen that look when interviewing other couples before. The wife was waiting for the husband to speak, further confirming Fletcher's guess that they had something more to tell.

Mark looked to Katie. Their eyes met. She nodded. The room was so quiet that he could hear the tick of a wall clock in the dining room.

Fletcher shifted his position on the couch and spoke up as if on cue. "Don't try to sort it in your head. Just get it all out. Don't worry, anything you say will remain strictly confidential, unless the case is revived and one day makes its way into court. Then I hope you'd be willing to step up and testify."

Mark leaned forward and propped his elbows on his knees. He raised his hands and slowly massaged his temples. So you want to know what I've seen! Mark thought to himself. OK. I'll tell you. You seem like a reasonable guy. Let's see what you make of *unde malum.*

Fletcher positioned a miniature tape recorder on the table between them.

Mark grinned. "Do you have an hour to spare?"

Fletcher glanced at his watch. "Sure."

Mark sat up abruptly and smiled.

KC hung up the telephone and pushed herself from the bed in one motion. Troy was three steps ahead of her, slipping on his shirt. She padded across the thick carpet to the walk-in closet and yanked a wool sweater from its hanger.

Fletcher was meeting with the MacDonalds!

KC smiled and considered their turn of good fortune—Fletcher, you just couldn't keep your nose out of the case, could you? I've waited two years for this kind of opportunity. We're going to crucify you right on Captain Conran's office wall, nail you up nice and high for everyone to see.

Troy's heavy footsteps preceded his voice. "Fletcher's going to have the dubious honor of being the male lead in our new 8mm cam's maiden video."

KC pulled her sweater down over her head, then pulled her thick hair free, her smile widening maliciously.

"Sweet justice. Yes, how sweet."

Fletcher studied Mark's and Katie's faces. They revealed an honesty Fletcher was unaccustomed to. Their gaze was direct, sincere, like Jimmy's had been, which made it all the more difficult for him to discount the fantastic story that Mark had finished just moments earlier.

"Story" wasn't really the correct word. Spread out on the living room table in front of him were old journal books written by Mark's grandfather's great-uncle. In addition to the journals, there was a fascinating letter from Abraham Lincoln when he was a young lawyer in Illinois conducting title searches for one of Mark's ancestors. It appeared genuine. But the kicker was the two Latin words Mark and Katie had shown him on the statue of the priest in the park. Fletcher had no good answer for that coincidence.

And that was the problem he faced: the relevant information for the case was meshed oddly together with a great deal of supposition and inference from the past. Mark sure had a picturesque way of interpreting events—and that was putting it mildly! The Devil's appearance at a French king's beheading in 1793 and his reappearance at the hanging of John Brown in 1859 were a prelude to America's bloody Civil War.

The only link that Fletcher could see between the disparate aspects of Mark's stories was the coincidental timing of the vandalism with the upcoming pro-life march, which had already focused a lot of negative attention on various pro-life groups. Mark believed that the Devil was scheming behind the scenes to discredit the Christian Church.

Though he could not see the connections the way Mark seemed to, the fantastic elements of his testimony were balanced by his eye for detail and logical thinking—traits and abilities that Troy Martin could use more of! Mark had already analyzed and concluded that the ponytailed man he saw Wednesday midnight helping Jimmy into the van was not the same man picketing the clinic, based on his memory of the man's height and build. Many witnesses would have been fooled by the distinctive ponytail.

Mark rose from his wing chair and started to pick up the empty mugs. Katie slapped his hand and motioned him back to his chair.

Fletcher smiled and let his gaze wander across the open journals on the table. On top of all the things he'd heard, equally fascinating was the story of Katie's accident, her miraculous healing, and recent, unexpected pregnancy. He never would have guessed her left side still suffered from the effects of inoperable paralysis almost four years earlier.

"So, what do you think?" Mark asked softly after a minute of silence. "I guess I carried on a bit."

Fletcher shrugged. "Truthfully? I'm not going to discount anything you've said. Not that I share your views or insights into history or the unexplainable."

Mark cocked an eyebrow. "By unexplainable, do you mean super-natural or providential?"

Fletcher laughed. "Sorry, those words aren't in my vocabulary. Let me put it this way: just because I don't understand how or why something mysterious happens, I don't attribute every activity di-rectly to God or the Devil the way those television preachers do."

Mark laughed sharply, then waved off Fletcher's confused look. "No—that's the truth! We Christians deserve a little critical commen-tary for some of the things we say."

"What's going on out there?" Katie asked as she leaned against the archway between the rooms.

"Just some well-intentioned banter."

Suddenly, Katie moved her hands to her stomach. Smiling, she tilted her head slightly to the side, as if she was carefully listening. "That was either a growl, or the baby moved."

"It's too early for the baby, isn't it?" Mark asked.

Katie sighed and nodded. "Right now, he's about this big," she said, raising her hand and bringing her thumb and forefinger about an inch apart, "according to my book on child development. It'll be a couple more weeks before the limbs fully develop, and then a couple more to form the little fingers and toes."

Listening intently, Fletcher felt that same vulnerability as when he had watched his video of Melissa and Susan or found the tiny foot in Jimmy's sock.

He paled, gripping the arm of the couch. The room started to whirl with Katie's face its focal point. Mark and the wing chair were angled sharply across his field of vision.

Katie leaned forward, her voice marked with concern. "Are you OK?"

Fletcher swallowed hard, his color slowly returning. He breathed deeply. "Sorry about that folks. Too many long days and an equal number of sleepless nights." What a lie!

Mark nodded understandingly. "Hey, I can relate to that—just ask Katie. Like I told you, I've been staying up late and reading Sam's journals. I know the feeling."

Glancing at his watch, Fletcher forced a grin. "I'd like to go back over your testimony once more while I have the opportunity." Fletcher pulled a small notepad from his shirt pocket and reviewed the list of key questions he jotted down during Mark's seventy-minute soliloquy.

Katie sat down on the other end of the couch and folded her arms over her knees. She noticed a wedding band on his left hand. "I see you're married. Just how does a wife handle being married to an undercover detective? I imagine it must be difficult."

Fletcher froze. He tried to figure out how she knew he was married. He glanced down. The ring, of course! He ran his thumb over the thin, gold band and carefully considered his reply. Why hide it? His conscience softly chided.

He turned his head and looked Katie straight in the eye.

"I'll be blunt, Mrs. MacDonald. After twelve and a half hard years, my wife gave up trying to handle the pressure. Seven months ago, she went home to her parents in Iowa. My long days and restless nights had slowly become hers. I had—and still have—a tendency to bring my crises home with me. Not that Susan and I didn't try to work things out. It's been tough."

Clicking his pen, Fletcher looked from Katie to Mark, suppressing the painful expression moving across his face.

"Now, if you both don't mind, I'd like to get on with Mark's testimony."

Ten minutes later, Fletcher excused himself for taking so much of their time. He thanked them for their help and showed himself to the door. As he left, he paused and handed Mark his business card. "If you think of anything else, just call. You'll hear a series of beeps, then leave your number."

He shook Mark's hand.

"Nice man," Katie said quietly as Mark shut the door. "But obviously troubled. It's more than just his wife leaving him."

"I agree. I was really surprised when he didn't react negatively to anything we said."

"I'm sure he's heard his share of wild stories," Katie suggested. "He's a professional."

Mark shrugged. "Yeah, probably so. I really like the guy. He reminds me of me, a man in search of something that he's lost, something far more elusive than the identities of those who vandalized the clinic."

"And what is that?"

"Answers to his own personal *unde malum*," Mark said as he slipped his arm around her waist.

From the sidewalk in front of the AFI's clinic, a broad-shouldered man with blond hair watched Mark and Katie reenter the townhouse and close the door.

His unblinking, serious eyes moved away from the townhouse to the statue of Cardinal Gibbons, beyond to the vacant white church, and then slowly back across the park to the townhouse.

He lifted his noble chin slightly, his eyes narrowing. Though his confidence was unflagging, he could not ignore the increasing pressure in his spirit. His Archenemy approached; he could sense it!

He waited patiently in the gusting winds that swirled around his feet.

✧ **23** ✧

Monday Evening

Troy connnected the video cable from the handheld camera to the
VCR, then pulled a chair beneath him.

KC pressed the play button on the infrared remote, and then fast-
forwarded, skipping over useless pedestrian activity in and around
the park in front of Mark MacDonald's row house. She pressed the
play button again when the door of the row house opened.

Fletcher paused in the doorway and handed something to Mark
MacDonald. The camera zoomed in. Faces could be seen clearly.

"Troy, I'm going to nominate you for Best Producer, and myself
for Best Director."

The ex-football player folded his arms over his chest. "And I'm
going to nominate Rivers for Best Actor. Maybe the award will help
when he starts looking for another job."

KC froze the picture as the two men shook hands. Her grin
stretched into a contented smile. She raised her left hand and aimed
a forefinger straight at the back of Fletcher's head, her thumb raised.
She squeezed the imaginary trigger. "Pow! Pow! Gotcha, Fletcher!
Just like I said I would!"

She tossed Troy the remote, stood up and reached over his desk
for the telephone. She punched in the number for Internal Affairs.

"Hey, Bill. This is KC. Troy and I would like to spend a half hour
with you. Got the time?"

After locking the door to her office suite, Michelle paused to rein in
her thoughts and force herself to stay calm. A local television news
crew hustled their video equipment into AFI's main conference room
at the opposite end of the hall. Mr. Peters, wearing his television
blue three-piece suit, stood near the open double doors and watched
the procedure.

He looked over his shoulder down the long hall at Michelle, his
face etched with concern. A question from the conference room
turned his attention back to the television crew.

Michelle faced her adminstrative assistant who struggled with her winter coat—her hand repeatedly missing the opening to her sleeve. Julie was close to the point of tears for the third time. Her frightened look was strangely disconcerting. "Thanks." Julie grinned half-heartedly after Michelle helped her on with her coat. "It's been that kind of day. First the fiasco with the conference room. Then lunch with Tom. I caught it from both directions."

Michelle nodded sympathetically. She struggled all afternoon upon learning that Julie was pregnant. Julie's boyfriend's response was predictable: get an abortion or get out of my life. Michelle's sister, Anne, had suffered through a similar decision—with devastating results.

"I admire your desire not to abort the baby. I hope you stick with it."

Julie stared down the hall toward Mr. Peters.

Michelle caught the movement, followed it. "Forget about the conference room mix-up. No one told you about the news conference."

"I've never seen Mr. Peters so mad," Julie explained. "I'd freak if I lost this opportunity to be employed full-time. I've got college loans and a car payment. If I keep the baby, I'll need to find my own apartment."

"How about dinner at my place?" Michelle said, lowering her head until she could see Julie eye to eye. "Let's talk about it over a hot meal. I've got a pan of lasagna in the fridge."

Julie smiled, pulled a Kleenex from her coat pocket and wiped the corners of her eyes.

Out of the corner of her eye, Michelle saw Mr. Peters enter the conference room. As Mr. Peters' moods went, so went the office, and today he was tense. Barking at Julie over the conference room mix-up was atypical. A news conference rarely raised an eyebrow, so why now? Maybe it was just the escalating apprehension created by the upcoming March for Life.

As they approached the elevators, the twin, burnished aluminum doors slid open. Out stepped a ruggedly handsome man in his early forties with shoulder-length, black hair—the stylish consultant who had been in the offices last week. Today, he wore a pin-striped charcoal gray suit, a thin red tie, and matching handkerchief.

His gray eyes met Michelle's as they passed in the hallway. A knowing, intimate smile formed on his lips—the same look he had given her on Friday in the conference room.

Michelle looked away as she entered the elevator. A chill slid down the middle of her back. Blushing, she felt unclean, as if his glance had somehow violated her. Julie leaned toward Michelle as the doors slid shut and angrily punched the Lobby button.

"Wow! Did he ever give you the once-over!"

The elevator began its descent, but Michelle hardly heard Julie's comment. The charcoal suit! The black hair! Her thoughts flashed back two hours, to Mr. Peters' office and the two checks for Harbinger Ltd. Someone had been sitting in the highbacked arm chair facing Mr. Peters' desk. She had only seen the top and back of the visitor's head—his long black hair—and a sleeve and hand on the chair arm as Mr. Peters came to the door and took the checks from her hand, quickly excusing her.

As the door had closed behind her, she had heard a laugh, a soft, mocking laugh just like she had heard last Friday afternoon when she had taken two checks to Mr. Peters' in the conference room for the man with the disgusting, intimate smile.

Stunned, Michelle leaned back against the elevator wall. Was this the big break she'd been waiting two and a half years for?

Mr. Peters and two sets of checks cut to two different companies: Parallax, a consulting firm, and Harbinger Ltd., an ad agency. Four checks totaling $100,000 had been written within four business days; all four checks had been given to the same man.

Goose bumps ran up her arms. Was the sudden turn of events a series of coincidences? Or Providence? She felt lightheaded. Not only had she inadvertently stumbled across an incriminating clue into potential misdealings and violations that might threaten AFI's non-profit, tax-exempt status, but she could access the financial data and records to substantiate her claims.

Mark carefully handed Katie two thin sheets of paper. "Here's a letter Sam stuck in the front of his journal."

Katie gently laid the sheets on her knees and studied them. "It's faded badly."

A bittersweet smile broke across her face. "The letter is from Sam's brother. Do you want me to read it?"

"Sure, why not," Mark replied. "It'll be a nice change of pace to start our reading with something a little less portentous."

Katie straightened the letters.

"My dearest brother, Sam. Elizabeth Rachael and I continue to devote resources to aid in the freeing of the Negro. Tom Cartwright, a prominent member of the Methodist Church here in town, recently traveled to Alexandria, Virginia. At a slave auction Tom purchased five blacks and bought their freedom. We have hired two of them, a mother and daughter, to help us here at the farm. Violet and Angelina are hard workers and we are very pleased with them. Angelina, an eleven-year-old, is quite spirited.

"In response to your recent letter, Elizabeth and I must confess that your words astound and confuse us.

"You must forgive me my dear brother, I am a man of the soil, not of ideas. I am not endowed with the tools required to measure the truth of your words. You write of kings and princes long since dead, the Crusades, King Richard's triumph at Constantinople, the French Revolution—these things are beyond me!

"You pen ancient Latin riddles. You write of John Brown as if he were a madman. Yet, I am forced to question whether you, my brother, have yourself been overcome with madness of a sort. For if the Devil roams freely about the world as you insist, then what has become of God's Providence over history?

"You seek to understand the past through a hunchbacked priest's private revelations! I advise you to leave these matters alone and proceed with your research on the Founding Fathers. Frankly, Elizabeth and I are concerned over what appears to be a harmful brew of history and theology pouring from your letters. Are you certain that you have not drifted into a gloomy lagoon and out of the mainstream of Christian thought?

"Not only that, but you continue to press me for a response to the prophecy. I recall our youth, playing behind Grandma Nikki's house, when we swam, fished, and climbed trees together. Yet, we were so unlike one another. You were concerned with the future and the past, but rarely did you savor the moment at hand. As you know, I have always found simple pleasures in the practical present.

"On the day Grandma Nikki died, it was to you that she gave the sword and spoke the prophecy. You believe that you are one of the two. I repeat what I have said before: I am not the other man.

"Finally, brother, we hope for your success and pray for your protection. Elizabeth and Thomas Peter send their love. Continue to write, but take heed how you influence even young Angelina, whose letter I have included. She sits by the hearth and listens to me read each and every one of your letters, envisioning you as her venerable knight in shining armor.

"Your loving brother, John Ezra."

Katie grinned and shuffled the letters.

A sharp winter wind rustled the line of fir and pine trees behind the statue of Cardinal Gibbons and broke the concentration of an old man in a tattered waistcoat.

The wind scooped up loose debris near the base of the trees, lifting it from the ground and throwing it upward and outward into the park, spinning the tiny fragments of dirt and broken pine needles counter-clockwise in a distinct conical pattern. The twisting cone grew and widened until it reached the center of the park where, as if on some unseen cue, it whirled its contents straight up into the air— and then dissipated.

The tiny particles pattered softly across the old man's shoulders and scraggly raven hair, striking his sharply featured face and hollow cheeks.

The old man arched his wrinkled neck and stared wrathfully at the heavens, and then turned abruptly and shuffled across the pavement toward his haunt in the deserted church.

11 April 1861
Elkin's Boardinghouse, Charleston, South Carolina

I have returned from Victoria's parents' home. The Moores offered me Victoria's room for the length of my stay in Charleston, but I could not accept. Memories summon her face before mine, captured by the daguerreotype taken on our wedding day. O Soul, I admonish you! Let Victoria sleep peacefully in the Great Shepherd's arms!

Gazing out at the harbor, I see a small white church and graveyard, enclosed by a low, rectangular stone wall. Inside its wrought-iron gate, a small, marble memorial honors the ground where I laid Victoria in 1853. Victoria! Eight years have passed since her death, five since I buried my bitterness. Yet, like a storm in the night, memories return to buffet me.

I am reminded of the words of Ezekiel, the words that You made so real to me following my recommitment to You in the valley: "Son of man, behold I take away from thee the desire of thine eyes with a stroke: yet neither shalt thou mourn nor weep, neither shalt thy tears run down."

Never have I felt so alone. For twenty-three years I have carried Tecumseh's prophecy close to my heart. Now, Lord, I am tempted to ask if the words of this Indian chieftain are words from You? I know that You spoke through Baalam's donkey and You revealed the future to Pharaoh in a dream. You gave Nebuchadnezzar a vision and wrote on the wall at Belshazzar's feast.

Could you not speak to me clearly? Who is the second man?

Your word teaches that "two are better than one; because they have a good reward for their labor. For if they fall, the one will lift up his fellow: but woe to him that is alone when he falleth; for he hath not another to help him up."

Beaumont's Flag

Contrary to John Ezra's reservations, my studies in history and theology have proven fortuitous.

Yesterday, Mr. Pitkins requested that I meet with Miss Elkin and compose an article for the <u>Observer</u> about the flags she is distributing to the volunteer regiments. So, after leaving Victoria's parents at Moore Hill, I proceeded to her boardinghouse. Needing lodging, I took the room where I now write. Long-limbed with fiery red hair pulled back into a braid, Miss Elkin stood on her porch, dispensing flags to passing South Carolina volunteers. The flag is comprised of blood red material with a small white star sown in the center and a white crescent moon in the left corner.

Even in the darkness, I see the new state flag, proudly hung by Miss Elkin, the boardinghouse owner, rustling in the night breeze on its pole just below my second-story window. It is not the breath of Your Holy Spirit that blows through Charleston this night, but I fear it is the Spirit of the Anti-Christ, the Devil.

The flag bears the same colors and markings as that of the former Ottoman Empire, the Moslem Turks, whose violent rule once extended across three continents. These symbols promoted by Seth Beaumont represent the enemies of Christ!

With these discoveries crowding my thoughts, I descended from my room to interview the vivacious Miss Elkin. She suggested we retire to the more intimate surroundings of her private parlor.

Closing and locking the door behind us, she sat beside me on the couch, placing her hand on my arm. Her cheeks were flushed, her eyes staring deeply into mine. My heart skipped a beat. I feared a most compromising situation, but I was wrong in my vain estimation of her interest in me. It was of the flag that she wished to speak.

In spite of Miss Elkin's forward behavior I was still unprepared for her most extraordinary revelation: Seth Beaumont had designed the flag! Beaumont had provided her a detailed sketch. She gave it to me for the article. Since secession night nearly four months ago, Miss Elkin had recruited a half dozen women to aid in the fabrication of the flags. While Miss Elkin labored in her parlor, Beaumont articulated his philosophy. I was astonished at how freely she spoke in my presence. The wine she had served at dinner, it seemed, had generously loosened her tongue. Her eyes became spirited.

Seth explained the meaning of the star and crescent, how it was the emblem of the Cavalier and the Confederate Soldier. His faith in Rebel superiority was so inspiring. He said there would be war, revolution, and bloodshed when the South rose to carry the standard of Christ.

Her face beamed with pride as she told me the very minute and hour the batteries would open fire on Fort Sumter. Then she even went so far to explain how Seth served in the Confederate Army's Secret Service, reporting directly to Jefferson Davis. She believed that there was no more loyal a Confederate in all of Dixie!

I was shocked by her boldness. Then the Lord gave me understanding. The brazen, haughty look in her eyes told all. She and Beaumont were lovers!

I admonished Miss Elkin to reconsider her infatuation with this married man.

She would not receive those words from me. I fear for this woman's safety, for if Beaumont knew that she was disclosing this information to me, she would be in grave danger.

Morning comes. The moon has nearly finished tracing its course across the sky. I see the lights of Castle Pinckney directly before me, casting their reflection upon the water of Charleston Harbor. I see the distant light from the fires at Fort Moultrie. No light is visible from the Union stronghold at Fort Sumter. My pocket watch tells me that the moment draws near. It is 4:25 A.M.

There is nothing to do now but wait and pray. I ponder if Beaumont's infernal red flag is but a manifestation of the already inflamed hearts and minds of rebellious South Carolinians.

Momentarily, the sound of a hundred cannon will waken this land to a frightening new day. Mr. Pitkins has assigned me to cover Virginia's army because I am a Virginian. I also know Jackson and Lee from my stay at Harper's Ferry and Charlestown.

The second hand ticks—it is time! It is 4:30 and the War begins!

My window pane rattles from the sudden thunder of cannon fire! The boardinghouse shudders with every clap from Charleston's batteries.

The heavens outside my window are aflame! Does the Devil dip his sickle through the sky? What hellish evil is now unleashed by this fury? Are spirits of violence and destruction let loose on our land? Will the grasslands of Virginia become the plains of Armageddon? How deep will the blood flow? Are we now reaping the harvest of our forefather's sin?

O Soul, why did it take you so long to discern the truth? Why did it take an old French priest to teach you that the Devil has been a Murderer from the beginning?

And is this war, in part, a result of that tragic day when Grandpa Will plunged his sword into the rounded belly of an innocent Indian mother-to-be? That very same sword now lies on the bed across from me, catching on the length of its razor edge the crimson light of a fire-filled sky like a line drawn in human blood, irrevocably binding the past and the present.

God have mercy on the Union and Your people.

KC's living room was dark, save for the flickering brightness from the wide-screen television. She set her beer down next to an open letter from her brother. She picked up the portable phone from the endtable as she pushed herself erect in the leather couch. A soft, Oriental voice spoke from the other end of the line.

"How was your day?" Kim asked.

KC stretched her legs out across the couch. "Everything went as planned. Troy and I had no problem getting into Wertman's room. Tell the Sponsors I'm impressed with the package. The quality of the evidence should present an open-and-shut case against Wertman—as long as he doesn't come home before tomorrow morning and find the stuff."

Kim laughed quietly. "He's watching television in the living room, waiting for me. You do not need to worry about where Harold will be tonight. What is your expression—safe as in his own mother's arms?"

"Safe isn't exactly the word I'd use. I hope the Sponsors know what they're doing."

"We always know what we are doing, KC," Kim purred. "Good night."

"Yeah, sure." KC frowned cynically and severed the connection. She returned the phone to the table and picked up her beer.

She glanced down at the letter from her brother. In exactly ten days Jamal would meet with the Lorton parole board. And if his review went as she expected it would, he'd be a free man once again.

KC guzzled her beer. It was divine justice that his letter arrived the very same day that she and Troy skewered Fletcher. Internal Affairs was having a field day with the videotape of him leaving the witnesses' townhouse. If everything went as planned, Fletcher Rivers' career with the MPD was history.

She crumpled the empty can, her grin spreading into a smile.

Katie snuggled close to Mark, resting her head against his chest. The fireplace glowed unevenly and cast a warm semi-circle of light that reached to the edge of the couch.

On one end of the living room table sat empty plates and glasses from a late dinner and on the other end, Sam's fourth journal.

Mark slipped his arm around her shoulder. "Now we know why Grandpa Kyle had so much trouble with the journals. Sam sees the Devil everywhere! Even behind a flag!"

Katie sighed. "I know what you mean. It's a lot safer to look back through the lens of classroom history.

"On the other hand," she added thoughtfully, "I think we're seeing that if we don't face the evil of past generations, we'll wake up one day and discover that it has caught up with us in a big way."

Mark separated himself from Katie and sat forward on the edge of the couch. "You sound like Sam! Isn't that how the Devil deceives us, by blinding us to who he really is and what he's trying to do? I think that's part of the answer to *unde malum*—whence comes evil."

Gently squeezing her arm, Mark let his gaze slide down into the fire. Seconds later, his head snapped up. Meeting Katie's quizzical stare, he took her hands and pulled her from the couch.

"What are you doing?" she asked, chuckling uneasily.

"Wrong question, honey. What are we doing," Mark quipped. "Marriage is a partnership."

He led her toward the hall tree and their winter coats.

"OK. What are we doing?" Katie asked.

"Just what you advised," Mark said, heading toward the kitchen.

"We're going to face the evil, just like Sam did."

"Stress leave." The devasting turn of events made Fletcher's stomach knot painfully. A cold wind swept past him, down the once-royal tiers of steps in the park's center, darting through winter-bare trees and dense shrubs, in and around neglected statues and fountains, along sidewalks, rustling the stiff, frozen grass.

Fletcher sat on a folded blanket against the pebble-aggregate wall, and shivered. He hadn't noticed the cold until the thermos of cocoa had run out. With bleary eyes he watched the slowly moving lines of traffic descend the steep hill on 16th Street.

He lowered his head. He had been careless. No, worse. Foolish. He should have made arrangements to meet Mark MacDonald and his wife somewhere other than at their home. Couldn't he have guessed that someone might be following him, tracking his involvement in the case? Hadn't he seen the broad-shouldered fellow with blond hair more than once? His stubborn, defiant attitude and self-determination to see Jimmy's case through had finally caught up with him. Fate had dealt him a risky hand, but instead of making a conservative bid, he had upped the ante and played his cards as if there were no tomorrow. There was no tomorrow, not for Detective Fletcher Rivers, anyway.

His two-week suspension—officially designated as stress leave—awaited a more final judgment after the investigation by Internal Affairs.

The wind slipped in under his hood, sliding long, frigid fingers down the middle of his back. Fletcher shivered again, nuzzling his chin into his coat's fur lining. He glanced at his watch and then at Larry and Glenn. Filled with fried chicken, mashed potatoes, oreo cookies, and hot cocoa, they'd endure the frigid January night.

Pushing himself from the blanket, Fletcher gathered up his empty grocery bags. Stress leave! Two weeks! A lot could happen in two weeks. And if he let himself slip back into the depression that clawed at his heart, then KC and Troy—and whoever was responsible for the clinic vandalism and dumping Jimmy's body—might go undiscovered. Too much had happened in just five days.

Too much, too fast! Something was terribly out of whack; he was sure of it! Maybe there was something to Mark's theory about the clinic vandalism being linked to the upcoming pro-life march. What if something bigger and more sinister was developing and what happened at the clinic was just the tip of the iceberg?

Those questions had to be answered quickly—regardless of the suspension. His conscience wouldn't let him quit now. He would use Botello to introduce whatever evidence he uncovered.

The cold invaded the cracks in his coat, chilling him. Determined, he sucked in his breath, patted his friends on their shoulders and said goodbye for the night.

Tomorrow morning, he knew exactly where he would begin, with a phone call. It would be another high risk move, another toss of the dice. But what did he have to lose? He'd already lost everything important to him: his daughter, his wife, his friend, and quite possibly, his career.

As Fletcher walked briskly down the steps and out the south entrance of the park toward his car absorbed in his plan, he passed by the broad-shouldered man in the blue jogging suit who sat attentively on the end of a low wall where Jimmy had sat so many days and nights.

Fletcher paused at the curb opposite his TransAm, lowered his head, breathed slowly, and then crossed the street to his car.

A faint smile etched its way across the man's face as he followed the detective's shifting emotions and demeanor. Though his charge's sudden resolve could never overcome his remorse and guilt, it did provide impetus, propelling him, as it were, down a highway through the wilderness.

Fletcher Rivers' journey was far from over.

The evening had progressed better than Michelle had hoped. After a quiet dinner together, she and Julie had gone to a nearby mall for dessert. Their discussion of Julie's love life had been frank.

Michelle's eyebrows folded into a sharp V as she put the last of the clean dishes away later that evening.

For really the first time, she thoroughly regretted being a "mole." If she openly shared her faith or her morals, her carefully constructed reputation as a progressive liberal would be shattered. So, instead, she focused on Julie's own reservations, encouraging her to follow her conscience and refuse to have an abortion. While at the mall, she bought Julie a book on pregnancy. Pictures of babies in the womb helped reinforce Julie's intent to see her pregnancy all the way through. And Julie had been encouraged to hear that there were hundreds of childless couples in the Washington area anxious to adopt.

At first Julie had seemed surprised at Michelle's support. She had worked long enough at AFI to realize that the feminists rhetoric did not truly support a woman's right to choose.

Michelle sat on her kitchen stool and watched a pot of tea brew on the counter nearby. She paused and listened.

Julie was still upstairs, showering. It hadn't been hard at all to convince Julie to spend the night. She was lonely and unsure of herself.

In the end, books on pregancies and the possibility of adoption would not be the deciding factor for Julie. Abortion was an easy way out if you could not endure nine months of being an unwed mother —particularly if you worked for an organization like AFI!

What she really wanted to share with Julie she couldn't. To tell her about Anne would only end up in an emotional discussion about her beliefs—including Julie's need to know the healing and forgiveness of Christ.

If Julie learned of her fabricated pro-choice position as a mole, Michelle knew that her hopes of exposing AFI could be jeopardized. And with her new revelations about the checks, she could not afford additional risk to her plan. She had already taken a huge gamble talking to Julie about alternatives to abortion. Yet despite the risk, Michelle felt drawn to become more involved. Julie was fast becoming a close friend. Julie's openness had made her feel useful. In some ways, Julie had given her more than she had been able to reciprocate.

Michelle cocked her head. The shower squeaked and stopped running.

She wasn't sure how much longer she could keep juggling her plans and Julie's needs. The two were at odds, moving in opposite directions, getting farther apart and out of balance.

Balance. Maybe Dan was more right than she'd been willing to admit. Sometime ahead, the odds were better than even she would drop one of the criss-crossing, high-arcing balls.

As Michelle filled two cups with tea, Julie padded barefooted into the kitchen, wearing a pair of borrowed sweats. She stopped at the end of the counter. The pant legs were baggy and bunched around her ankles, the too-long shirt sleeves hung down from her arms like handless tubes.

"Well, what do you think?" she asked with a smile, pulling her wet hair from her face.

They laughed and carried their cups of tea into the living room.

The gusting winds calmed abruptly as Mark and Katie crossed the street into the park. In one hand Mark carried a quart-sized aluminum can that he brought up from the cellar, a couple of old rags in the other.

"I can't believe I'm out here with you doing this." Katie stopped and crossed her arms. Puffs of white air drifted slowly away from her mouth.

Mark gently took her hand, his nod an unspoken request to follow. He knelt by the statue, unscrewing the top from the can. A shadow from Cardinal Gibbons' upraised hand fell across him.

"I don't know why I didn't think of this before. I guess that's why a man's wife is his better half. This is really your idea. You just didn't extend it to its logical conclusion."

Katie glanced around. "What if someone walks by and sees us?"

Mark carefully poured some of the liquid onto the rag. "Look at it this way, we're saving the city some money."

"But we could be mistaken for vandals."

"You and me? Not likely. The mayor would appreciate this clean-up measure."

Katie stuffed her hands deep into her pockets and stepped back to avoid the fumes. "I hope you won't damage anything."

"Trust me; it'll be fine."

Katie looked toward the townhouses apprehensively as Mark scrubbed the statue with the rag. At least the tall row of pines on the north side of the park mostly blocked their neighbors' views.

"Just because I can't figure out how this happened, doesn't mean I have to sit back and act like it's something sacred," Mark explained. "Besides, something that can be defeated with a little paint remover can't possess all that much supernatural power."

Mark paused and grinned up at Katie. "Done. You were right this morning when you said that Kyle, Sam, the baby, and our move to Washington are linked. Maybe the vandalism and Fletcher, too. I'm sure of it—we just haven't seen or found all of the connections."

Katie bent over and looked at her husband's handiwork. The confidence in Mark's voice and what she saw made her smile at last. It was as if *unde malum* had never been there at all.

24

Tuesday Morning

Zipping up his coat, Harold Wertman turned and faced Kim in the foyer. Dressed in a bathrobe she leaned against the wall to the right of the front door and smiled. He was running out of time. He had to get home and change for their meeting with the Sponsors. Why he needed to wear a sport coat and tie was beyond him, but Kim had insisted. If changing into some dress clothes would help him collect his twenty thousand dollars, it was a small inconvenience to bear.

As he reached for the door knob, Kim stepped forward and kissed him, then just as abruptly backed away, her dark eyes sparkling, almost jovial. "The meeting begins at 8:15, Harold. Look nice—OK? Today is your big day."

Harold shuffled his feet as he opened the front door to her townhouse. There was something in her dark eyes and smile he did not like. It was as if she had made a joke and he missed the punch line.

"Today is our big day, isn't it?" was all he could manage to say. He pulled his van keys from his coat pocket and stepped outside, the door closing silently behind him.

A car bearing a white-haired woman in a nurse's uniform pulled off to the side of in-bound Route 50, about three miles west of Key Bridge just inside Washington's city limits. Her left rear tire was completely flat. She had driven so far on the tire that the rim to her wheel had been damaged.

She turned on her emergency blinkers, and then the radio. Her face did not show even a hint of concern. Tapping her fingers in time with the music, she glanced at the clock in the dash and waited patiently for someone to stop and help her with the flat.

Shifting gears, True Believer accelerated and expertly maneuvered his Ferarri through the slowly moving traffic on south-bound 16th, crossing the bridge guarded by ornate marble tigers.

The witness' row house, the clinic, and the incendiary bomb were only three blocks away.

On the leather passenger seat beside him lay the hand-sized transmitter. He had purchased both bomb and transmitter from the Irish National Liberation Army via mercenary NATO personnel in West Germany. The military issue explosive had been created for covert operations—easy to conceal, easy to use, yet possessing maximum destructive power. And the fact that Harold Wertman would soon be discovered to have had access to this specific plastique would only add to the image that he was a sophisticated functionary in a well-funded, pro-life terrorist organization. A well-worn Bible with its plethora of yellow-highlighted verses about God's judgment against evildoers was one of a dozen carefully planted pieces of evidence.

He stopped at a red light at Crest and 16th. To his left was Mark MacDonald's row house. Across the street and to the right was the clinic. A slender teenage girl headed up the sidewalk toward the entrance, backpack over her shoulder. At 7:30 A.M. the clinic was already bustling with business.

The cross-street's light turned yellow. A school bus swung around the corner to beat the light but took the turn too wide. True Believer watched with dismay as the front right tire rode up over the curb and burst. The school bus quickly came to a stop.

The traffic light above True Believer turned green. With the bus blocking the right lane, he was forced to wait as a line of cars passed him on the left. He cursed—not at the traffic, but at the foolish school bus driver in front of the clinic—and with a full load of young children!

Cars honked behind him. True Believer swore, pulling out into the lane. He accelerated slowly past the bus. Children moved inside, animated by the flat tire and the prospect of being late for school.

As he passed by the front end of the bus, True Believer watched as the door opened and the driver stepped down onto the curb to look at the tire.

True Believer picked up the radio transmitter and flipped a switch. A rush of adrenaline spread like wild fire through his body. Images of Londonderry, Northern Ireland, superimposed themselves over the Washington cityscape. The four-lane asphalt road narrowed dreamily into a cobblestoned street, an office building into a row of shops and pubs and the smell of burning petrol.

True Believer lowered his thumb toward a small red button. The desire to detonate the explosives was stronger than he had imagined. He visualized the clinic erupting in a tower of flame, bricks, and shards of glass rocketed into the street, killing not only everyone inside, but ripping into the school bus and the children.

Then his thumb froze a quarter inch above the button.

Filling his mind's eye was a small stone church with a steeple that seemed to reach to the sky, a broken fountain adorned with cherubim, the clash of protesters and British paratroopers, and a bottle arcing over his head. His cousins sprawled in the gutter, the front of their sweaters a matching red...

The school bus—the children! Children, the age of Coleen and Aiden! Killing them was not in his plan!

Sweat formed in tiny beads across his thumb. He watched, eerily detached, as his thumb disobeyed, edging downward toward the button. True Believer flipped the switch that turned the transmitter off, then dropped it into the passenger seat. He rubbed his jaw, and then stared at his hand.

True Believer spun the wheel hard and turned the Ferarri down a side street. He pulled over to the curb and slipped the car into neutral. He could not drive and fight memories at the same time!

The troubles of his beloved Ireland had come to haunt him— Coleen and Aiden!

He wiped the sweat from his forehead. His emotions stabilized. He realized that there would be no second chance—such was the nature of his scheme. Less than five minutes from now Harold Wertman would be arrested, but the clinic would remain standing. The timing had been planned to the minute.

Now, his initiatives for Saturday morning would be lost, months of meticulous planning radically altered by a stupid school bus driver trying to beat a yellow light! True Believer knew that his superiors would not tolerate failure. What could he do to minimize his mistake?

True Believer leaned back and slowly flexed his thumb as an alternative plan formed slowly in the chaos of his thoughts.

Perhaps... all was not lost. Not if the city could be made aware of an attempted terrorist attack.

What did he have to lose at this point, anyway? Fate had foiled the original design. His new plan would capitalize on heightened tension and fear, then swiftly allay it. Just as the public's anger and anxiety began to calm, a second successful strike would occur! The city and the nation, poised to celebrate their peaceful transfer of power from one adminstration to another, would be outraged by the senseless, utter destruction of property and life! And Wertman would be blamed for it—he and the pro-lifers. Support for AFI's opponents would vanish. Congress would find it hard to be sympathetic toward the political and judicial goals of a group who used terrorism to coerce and intimidate.

True Believer closed his right hand repeatedly into a fist, staring at his disobedient thumb. Regaining his composure, he shifted the car into gear and promptly pulled out into the street. He knew he'd have to hurry to make his second checkpoint. He lifted his car phone to his ear and dialed a number.

With a squeal of burning rubber, the Ferarri responded. As the car pulled away from the corner, a broad-shouldered man in a blue jogging suit rose from his seat on the curb and headed back up 16th Street toward the broken-down school bus.

In his dream, Mark stood behind Sam on a grassy knoll overlooking Charleston Harbor and defiant Fort Sumter. It was early morning, and though the sun was hidden beneath the rim of the ocean, scores of lanterns illuminated the bustling soldiers at Cumming's Point. In one hand, Sam held a journal book and pen, in the other, his Grandfather Will's long knife. Without looking at his watch, Mark knew the war was about to begin.

As if on cue, Cumming's Point and the other batteries surrounding Charleston Harbor exploded with a round of cannon fire that shook the ground, lighting the sky with long trails of fire and smoke. The sound was deafening. Mark turned away only to find himself staring at a small white church on the other side of the knoll, and in the flashing red-orange light of the discharging cannon, a small cemetery.

The scene changed abruptly and he found himself standing in front of the cemetery's black wrought-iron gate. But unlike the cemetery he remembered reading about in Sam's journal, this cemetery had but seven graves. The headstones were draped with dark shadows.

Mark reached for the gate, but found it already open. A blood-red light now flashed behind him, illuminating the white, round-topped headstone to the far left.

Nikitchecame. Born 1770. Murdered 1836. The light moved to the right, crossing the grass to the next headstone. Sarah MacDonald— Sam's mother! Born 1795. Died in childbirth 1820. After pausing only for a brief moment, the eerie red spotlight slanted to the right. Victoria MacDonald. Born 1830. Murdered 1853. It continued down the row of headstones even more quickly.

Angelina MacDonald. Born 1850. Died 1934.

Mary MacDonald. Born 1878. Murdered 1917.

Mark's knees weakened at the sight of the next name. Evangeline MacDonald. Born 1922. Died in childbirth 1961. His mother—the mother he had never known! His memories were borrowed ones, from old photograph albums and stories his father or relatives had told.

The spotlight did not hesitate. To his mother's right was a freshly-dug grave and headstone, the name and date clearly visible in the red light. Mark stumbled back into the gate. No! It couldn't be!

Katie MacDonald. Born 1962. Murdered...

A loud, dull pop from outside the bedroom window made Mark lurch erect in his bed, his eyes snapping open. Katie lay sleeping at his side. The busy sounds of traffic along 16th Street played in the background. The digital clock on the nightstand read 7:29 A.M.

No Civil War. No cannons, no graves. No names on marble headstones. He pushed himself from the bed and shook the cobwebs from his head. It was the second time in three days that he had disturbing dreams, both of them involving Katie.

Rubbing his eyes, he stood next to the window.

In his dream had he morbidly twisted linkages to Sam's writings? Or was it something else? A revelation? A warning?

The light at 16th and Crest turned green.

Mark watched a fancy, silver Ferarri accelerate slowly and pass a school bus that had stopped directly in front of the clinic. A broad-shouldered man in a blue jogging suit walked parallel to the Ferarri, his head turned toward the car. And coming across the park by the statue of Gibbons was the familiar, shuffling homeless man with jet-black hair and a tattered coat.

An unexpected shiver worked its way down Mark's back as his thoughts returned suddenly to the dream. He could still visualize the bizarre inscriptions. Nikki. Sarah. Victoria. Angelina. Mary. Evangeline. Katie. Death by fire, by childbirth, by murder. Seven women with a repeating pattern, excluding Angelina, whose tombstone gave no clue as to how she had died.

Mark massaged his face. Angelina? Why did her name appear with the others? He shook his head. There were other more important considerations—like Katie's grave!

But Katie had survived her accident! The hit-and-run had been a tragic accident, not an attempted murder.

Accident. Murder. The image of Victoria's wagon tumbling down a ravine flashed through his thoughts. Was it a coincidence?

A second shiver made Mark rub his arms. He started to turn away when a siren wailed below. A police van and two squad cars with lights flashing screeched to halt in front of the clinic. Doors flung open and six policemen streamed up the walk. Four wore uniforms, two wore heavily padded suits and carried large aluminum suitcases. One led a German Shepherd on a leash. Two more policemen from the squad cars ran toward the school bus and ushered children down the sidewalk and away from the clinic.

Katie rolled over on her side. "What's all the noise about?"

Mark glanced back as he ran a hand through his rumpled hair. "I'm not sure. But whatever it is, it doesn't look good."

"Yes, Mr. Peters. I'll put together the media kits ASAP. When Carmen gets in, I'll coordinate with her to get the press releases into the kit. And I have the name and number of your contact at the District Building. I'll have the latest information on the aborted bombing when you arrive." Michelle listened intently as Mr. Peters cleared his throat on the other end of the telephone line.

"Very good. A last point. Your participation in our response to this terrorist act will give you an opportunity to practice the discretion required at the highest levels of our organization."

Michelle lowered her eyes to her desk, searching for an appropriate reply as if one could be found somewhere among the scattered computer printouts.

"I appreciate the vote of confidence."

"Good. I should be in the office in less than an hour."

Michelle said goodbye and slowly hung up the phone. Conflicting thoughts vied for attention. Her unexpected trip with Mr. Peters to the District Building would keep her in touch with the developments, but the analysis she completed just prior to the telephone call from the police had turned up crucial details on Parallax and Harbinger Ltd. For the past two years, both companies had been paid $100,000 in two payments of $50,000 each. Checks given to the same man. Same man—two companies—a highly improbable situation.

Michelle turned toward the computer screen. She wanted to compare the signatures of the man who had endorsed them. As she placed her hands on the keyboard, the phone rang again.

She waited through four rings, then reached for the phone, keeping her eyes on the monitor as she scrolled a second screen of information into view. "Good morning, American Family Institute."

"Yes, hello. Good morning." The male voice carried a noticeable edge of concern, just like the police lieutenant who had called to inform AFI about the bomb threat. "I'm with the Police Department, and I need to speak to someone who can give me information about the incident at the clinic."

Michelle turned to her desk, grabbing her pen and notepad from the earlier conversation. She frowned. Bureaucracies—why didn't they share their information? "I'll help you the best I can. I spoke with Lieutenant Davies about twenty minutes ago about the bomb threat. For the record, could I have your name, please?"

She wrote down his name beneath the lieutenant's. "Thank you, Detective Rivers. I'm Michelle Willoughby, AFI's Controller. What can I do for you?"

Harold Wertman waited for the silver Ferrari to pass by, then pulled into the empty parking space directly opposite Mrs. Grimwald's row house. What luck! He cut the engine off. He glanced at his watch—7:50 A.M. Thirty minutes to shower and change. He still didn't understand Kim's big rush to get him out of the apartment.

A silly grin spread across his face as he thought about his $20,000.

His rising excitement was abruptly shattered as his driver's door unexpectedly popped open.

"Freeze!" a male voice screamed in his ear.

Startled, Harold halted in his turn toward the door and found himself staring straight down the barrel of a police revolver. The officer's face behind the outstretched arms was intense, the eyes locked on Harold's.

"Raise your hands and climb slowly out of the van—now!"

Dazed, he did as he was commanded, dropping one foot, and then the next, out onto the pavement. His motions felt stiff and clumsy, like those of the tin man in *The Wizard of Oz*. Mrs. Grimwald's row house, which framed the plainclothes police officer, slid out of focus into a watery blur.

"Why? What did I—" Harold started to ask, his voice breaking.

The gun seemed to arch upward out of sight as four hands seized him forcefully and pulled him face down onto the street. Harold's cheek pressed against the gravel. Quickly, his arms were twisted behind his back. He felt handcuffs slipped over his wrists and tightened, hands ruffling over his upper body, and his legs. In the background, he could hear the doors to the van being opened, the hustle of feet over the pavement.

Harold opened his eyes. A policeman knelt on one knee just two feet from his face.

"You have the right to remain silent. Anything you say can and will be used against you...."

Fletcher leaned forward on his kitchen stool. Lieutenant Davies? A bomb threat? He gathered his thoughts. Too much, too fast—his fears came rushing back. Stay focused and answer her question—now!

"Rivers—Detective Fletcher Rivers."

Thank you, Detective Rivers. I'm Michelle Willoughby, AFI's Controller. What can I do for you?" Her reply was slightly stilted; she must be writing down his name.

"I'm tying up the loose ends with the vandalism, I'd like to meet with the AFI person or persons who went to the clinic the day following the vandalism. We have reason to believe that this person may have unintentionally withheld evidence in the case."

The line went silent.

Fletcher rubbed his forehead, hoping the woman would buy his line and not ask questions.

"Detective Rivers, I can arrange such a meeting." After a moment's hesitation, she continued, the sound of resignation in her voice. "You're speaking with that person."

Fletcher could hardly contain himself. Little material damage—the words of an accountant, just as he had deduced! He forced himself to remain calm. He sensed a high level of anxiety couched behind her words. If she panicked and refused to meet with him, he might not get another opportunity.

"Don't be alarmed by my statement, Ms. Willoughby. I'd like to get together with you, one-on-one, and clarify a few issues. First there was a vandalism, now a bomb threat.

"Pro-lifers are being implicated for crimes. What's next? Our conversation will be held in the strictest confidence."

Surely her answer was going to be no. Fletcher squeezed the telephone and closed his eyes. Oddly, an image formed suddenly in his mind of a young boy kneeling by his bed, hands folded and offering his bedtime prayers—and he was the young boy!

On the other end of the line, he heard Michelle clear her throat. "OK. But only you and me."

Fletcher smiled and glanced out the kitchen window, lifting his eyes to the cloud-swept sky.

Mark leaned forward in the wing chair, his mouth open in surprise. He glanced at his watch, and then back to the television as a reporter for Channel 4 continued his news-breaking story on Harold Wertman.

"Harold Wertman?" Katie paused as she entered the parlor. "So it appears." Mark glanced a second time at his watch and scratched his chin. The camera zoomed in for a close-up of Harold's face as he was led handcuffed into the District Building.

"According to official police sources," the newscaster explained with somber undertones, "evidence has been found at Mr. Wertman's southeast apartment and in his van linking him directly to the bomb threat uncovered this morning. Mr. Wertman has been the subject of an ongoing police investigation since last Thursday when the Crest Road clinic was vandalized."

The scene cut from a frontal shot of the newscaster to a red brick row house. "Paraphernalia for the construction of sophisticated explosives were recovered from his apartment. In addition to the explosives, police report that they found literature linking Mr. Wertman with an anti-abortion organization. Among other items was a Bible marked with verses that called for God's judgment on the wicked."

On the television, the rowhouse was replaced by a still shot of a gray van, the rear door still open from the arrest and search. "The van, identified by an eyewitness late last Wednesday night, ties Mr. Wertman to the vandalism. The van contained additional evidence."

Katie looked to Mark. "That's you he's talking about."

Mark raised his eyes. "That's not the gray van I identified. I don't know why, but the way this whole thing developed really bothers me. And something else—it's only 10:35—about three hours since the bomb squad arrived. They already have Harold in custody. The police have barely finished sealing off the clinic grounds and Wertman's already been judged guilty by the media."

Katie cut in. "At the start of the news brief, the reporter said the police were already on their way with a search warrant."

"Yeah, that's awfully coincidental, too." Mark suggested. "If someone wanted to point a finger, Wertman's a perfect fall-guy. He's blustery and extreme. He's been in several confrontations with the clinic staff. I can imagine what the media's going to do to him—and to the pro-life groups preparing for next week's march. Like sharks that smell blood, they'll be in a frenzy."

Katie grabbed the remote from the living room table and turned off the television. They lowered their heads and began to pray.

⊰⊱ **25** ⊰⊱

Tuesday Afternoon

TRUE BELIEVER HUNG UP THE PHONE and rose from the couch. He yanked off his sweatshirt and headed for the bedroom.

New York had reluctantly agreed to set up another conference call with Geneva and London. Would they accept that their ultimate purposes could be served just as effectively by an alternative plan? It was a risk he would have to take.

He would not tell them his rationale for sparing the school bus full of children, how his conscience was already burdened with enough innocent blood for a hundred lifetimes.

Mr. Peters touched a button on the driver's arm rest and the passenger side door unlocked. Michelle opened it, slid inside, and set her briefcase on the floor by her legs.

"You have the press releases?" he asked as he adjusted his patterned silk tie.

"Yes, sir, and the history file on the Crest Road clinic vandalism. Nurse Rollins will meet us downtown with the records."

"And our attorneys? Were you able to reach them?"

Michelle nodded. "Christine and Sonya will meet us at the District Building. They highly recommend that you refrain from making any statements, on or off the record, before they arrive."

She folded her hands circumspectly in her lap and stared out the window as her thoughts turned to her research. The records showed that Mr. Peters' involvement with Brian Fein had been ongoing for over two years, to the tune of $400,000. By staying exactly at the $100,000 threshold per year, each account could be expensed without the Board of Director's approval.

Michelle looked up. Without lowering his eyes, Mr. Peters touched a button in the middle of his steering wheel, surrounding them with classical music. He, too, was absorbed in his thoughts.

She glanced back out the window as they turned onto 16th Street and headed south toward the White House. They were only six blocks away from where she had agreed to meet Detective Fletcher Rivers at 5:00 o'clock.

Though the Cadillac maintained the temperature at a steady seventy-two degrees, Michelle felt hot. Her eyes peered ever so slightly to her left, to Mr. Peters. Behind his stoic features, did she see the strained emotions of a man starting to come unglued?

Without warning, Mr. Peters turned his head and met Michelle's gaze solidly. The sensation of raw heat magnified as a rosy blush spread quickly across her cheeks and neck.

She looked away, turning her head casually toward the traffic ahead of them while fighting down the fear that her stare had telegraphed her misgivings and disgust, had warned him that she knew his secrets.

Keeping her eyes on the back of a metro bus directly ahead, Michelle could not see the white knuckles that wrapped themselves tightly around the steering wheel.

Troy Martin raised his huge hand, looking first to the pretty blonde-haired woman who sat pensively across from his desk, red winter coat across her lap, then to her husband, who was growing more frustrated by the moment.

"Mr. MacDonald, just like I said in our first meeting, you're jumping to conclusions. I understand your misgivings about the suspect's guilt and your concern over the use of your testimony by the media, but you'll just have to accept it. Remember, we didn't ask you to come in here and make a statement, you did it voluntarily."

Mark shook his head in dismay. "All I want is the record to show that the eyewitness disagrees with the interpretation of his testimony. After all, we're talking about the possible conviction of an innocent person."

Troy penciled a short sentence on a sheet of paper in the open file folder before him, then smiled. "I've got it all down."

"Do you?" Mark asked forcefully. "Do you have down that he's an old hippie from California who attended Cal-Berkeley and has been involved with a number of protests—save-the-whale kind of stuff, ERA protests? Do you have down the possibility that somebody else is responsible for the vandalism and bombing and that they could have set Harold up to take the blame? Do you have down that somebody may want to discredit the Christian pro-life effort and hinder next week's March for Life?"

"Anything else, Mr. and Mrs. MacDonald?"

"How about ten minutes with your superior?" Mark took Katie by the hand and stood up.

"That's your call. I can direct you to Captain Conran's office right down the hall. Whether or not he'll see you this morning is another issue. Things have become very hectic around here."

Frustrated, Mark stuffed his hands into his coat pocket. "Too busy? Well I'll tell you what. I'll give you until Friday to talk to your superiors about my problem. Otherwise, I'll just give one of the local TV stations a call. Like you said, they'll use every juicy piece of information they can get their hands on. I'm not going to let this thing rest."

The detective shifted his large frame in his chair. He started to speak, and then stopped.

Katie grabbed Mark's hand and edged him toward the open door. She smiled. "Officer Martin, thank you for your time."

Troy pushed back his chair and stood up. "No, Ma'am, I thank you both for taking the time to stop by. You've been more helpful than your husband might suppose, believe me."

He smiled and waved goodbye as they closed the door to his office, then sat back heavily into his chair. He tapped his pencil on the stack of papers on his desk and reached for the telephone.

The phone rang twice before it was answered. "We've got a problem. A real problem."

The deli's frosted glass door opened inward and Michelle stepped inside. The smell of garlic, fried meat and vegetables was pervasive. Across from the door was a large, olive-skinned man behind a counter. Two men in their early twenties in overalls and heavy work boots waited impatiently for their order. A row of four small booths lined the left wall facing the street and sidewalk.

The only occupied booth was at the end. A man in his late forties with shoulder-length gray hair and a neatly trimmed beard was making notes on a yellow legal pad. He wore blue jeans and a navy crew neck sweater. A briefcase stood on the floor by his feet.

As Michelle made her way down the short aisle, he glanced up.

Standing, he smiled and extended a hand. "Detective Fletcher Rivers. Pleased to meet you, Ms. Willoughby."

She shook his hand firmly, slipped off her coat and promptly sat down across from him. "Call me Michelle. It makes conversation a lot easier." Looking at him now, face to face, she immediately noticed the deep lines beneath his eyes. She saw not only physical exhaustion but sadness, too.

"Can I offer you something to drink? To eat? A gyro or a salad?" he asked.

"I'll have some coffee." Michelle avoided staring at the yellow legal pad. She had no doubt that the interview was related to her anonymous tip. Hadn't his words implied as much? And from the look on his face, he seemed aware of her discomfort.

He held up two fingers and signaled the man behind the counter. Michelle noticed that he wore a thin gold wedding band.

"This is not easy for either of us," he said with unexpected softness in his voice. "Only one thing brings us together—a desire for the truth. You and I want to see the real perpetrators of the vandalism brought to justice."

Surprise registered across Michelle's face.

He paused briefly as the owner approached and placed two white ceramic cups on the table in front of them. Fletcher locked his eyes on hers.

"The fact that you submitted an anonymous tip to the police department is important to me, but not perhaps in the way that you might think. I'm not here to discuss your motivations for turning against your employer. You must believe that."

Michelle lowered her eyes and pulled her cup of coffee toward her. She wondered how much she could trust him. He seemed sincere. "Then you don't believe, as the police and the broadcasters portray, that Mr. Wertman or a pro-life organization is guilty of the vandalism and placing the bomb in the clinic?"

"No, I do not. I'm convinced there may be collusion between two police officers and those responsible for the crimes." Fletcher sipped at his cup. His conscience chided him, reminding him that he needed to tell her the truth about his two-week suspension, regardless of the effect. He tried to rid himself of the thought, to buckle down mentally and manipulate the conversation to his advantage. He had done it before many times. Was he growing soft?

Without warning the image of a little boy on his knees, hands folded and face upraised, intruded into his thoughts, followed by the memory of his desperate prayer earlier that morning as he spoke to Michelle over the phone. His conscience argued for honesty. With the feeling that God was somehow watching and listening to all that he said, Fletcher took a deep breath and made his decision.

"Actually, I'm not officially involved in the case. Technically speaking, I've been placed on stress leave. But the effect is the same as suspension from duty."

"Excuse me?" Michelle asked, leaning slightly forward. "You're not offic—"

Fletcher cut in. "I was put on leave for overreaching my jurisdiction in a personal attempt to solve this case. It's a third offense. My pigheadedness finally caught up with me. Does that change your decision to answer my questions?"

Michelle leaned back. "No, it doesn't change my decision. I appreciate your integrity."

For a moment they both fell silent.

Michelle lowered her cup to the table. "Earlier, you said that a desire for the truth is why we're here. Well, here's the truth about me: I'm a Christian pro-life activist and I've got a score to settle with AFI."

She laughed uneasily. "I can't believe I've told you this."

Fletcher's street-wise, tough guy, undercover cop exterior began to give way. She, like himself, walked a razor's edge. He didn't know why, but he felt as unexpectedly comfortable with her as he had with Mark and Katie MacDonald.

He shifted his gaze from his cup of coffee to Michelle's face. Fletcher folded his shaking hands.

"Let me tell you about a friend I once had named Jimmy."

The discount electronics store was busy. A dozen teenagers and adults milled in and around the long rows of wide screen television sets, compact discs, and boom boxes. At this particular moment, however, most of the salesmen and customers stood side-by-side, eyes glued to one of thirty televisions that all displayed the same channel, the same male, fortyish face with madman eyes and greasy shoulder-length brown hair.

Harold Wertman's face was replaced by a close-up of an open Bible with apocalyptic verses highlighted in bright yellow. The close-up was followed by an interview with one of the police officers from Tobacco, Alcohol, and Firearms who explained in detail how the military issue explosive would have brought the building to the ground, not only killing everyone inside, but also injuring passersby in the immediate vicinity.

A picture of Harold's van appeared briefly, then footage from the previous year's March for Life. A dense line of protesters paraded down the middle of Pennsylvania Avenue shouting anti-abortion slogans and carrying vitriolic signs denouncing abortion as murder, followed by clips from Operation Rescue's "Summer of Mercy" in Wichita, Kansas.

A young woman with a baby cursed audibly. An elderly white-haired man frowned angrily and thumped the floor with his walking stick. A young businesswoman made an obscene hand gesture and was cheered loudly by the crowd.

All except for Mark and Katie.

The young businesswoman folded her arms across her chest and lifted her chin in disgust as the spokeswoman for the March for Life forcefully refuted the newscaster's implications that any pro-life organization was involved in the bomb threat.

Katie sighed. "You're right. They're sharks; they've smelled blood and are homing in for the kill."

Mark checked the price on blank tapes. "And with Harold refusing counsel, he's not only complicating things for himself, but for everyone else. He's got a shady background as it is. Now it looks like he's got something to hide."

"Speaking of Wertman's background," Katie said in a questioning tone, turning to face him, "I've been meaning to ask you about something all afternoon. How do you know so much about his life? You rattled off his bio like it was common knowledge. I don't remember hearing that he was from California or that he went to college at Cal Berkeley."

Mark crossed his arms and chuckled quietly. "Funny. I don't recall where I heard that."

"And it's not just the details that struck me as peculiar, it's that same focused look you had yesterday afternoon." Katie cocked her head. "Know what I mean?"

Mark nodded distractedly and paid for the tapes. As they headed out the door, another round of boos went up from the crowd. Once outside, he paused, glancing over his shoulder, the change from his twenty dollar bill still in his hand.

Katie stopped in front of the Blazer and turned around. "What's wrong? Cashier give you the wrong amount?"

Mark stuffed the bills in his pocket. "No. She gave me the correct change." He opened her door, smiling weakly.

Katie climbed in and snapped her seatbelt. "Did you have another insight about somebody in there?"

Mark started the ignition, then drove the Blazer out of its parking space. "Yes—no. Not about anyone in particular. I just started thinking about Father Gibault's account of the frenzied crowds at King Louis' beheading in 1793. I've never seen such an ugly, simultaneous reaction from such a diverse set—those people in there wanted Wertman's head, plain and simple."

"People are getting edgy," Katie agreed. "Let's hope nothing else happens this week to heighten the problem."

Mark nodded as the image of the executioner and his son, the guillotine and a pool of blood spreading across the scaffolding stayed fixed in his mind. What had been the date? January 21, 1793? He made a quick calculation: January 21, the two-hundredth anniversary of the Devil appearing at King Louis' beheading, was only ten days away!

Mark shuddered and merged the Blazer into the right lane with the late evening traffic.

Michelle unlocked the door to her Toyota. "Thanks for walking me to my car. Two blocks at this time of night feels like two miles."

"Anytime," Fletcher replied as she slid into the driver's seat. "Now remember, we need a boat-load of evidence to build a case that will stick. Showing financial violations of the tax code is one thing, but connecting those violations directly to a crime is entirely another. And then tying a crime to specific individuals—including bad cops— is even more difficult. But it's not impossible. I think you've just uncovered the tip of the iceberg."

"I'll keep digging," Michelle replied. Looking up, she waited until she had caught his eye.

Fletcher glanced down at his feet, then at his watch. He stepped away from her car. "Hey—it's getting late. I'm sorry I kept you out so long."

"No problem. Now we have a plan for working through this."

"Let's not take this 'together' thing too far," Fletcher added, wagging his finger.

"Keep a low profile. Dig all you want, just be creative with the dirt. Don't leave it lying around for somebody to notice. The people we're dealing with play for keeps. Framing Harold Wertman took a lot of money and a lot of smarts. They're not going let small fries like you and me get in their way."

"I'm no hero," Michelle replied as she put her key in the ignition, "just an everyday accountant-type mole who promises to stay completely underground. I'm more than happy to leave the dirty work up to you. All I want is a little justice and, if only for once, to nail the bad guys."

"Good," Fletcher said with a smile as he pushed himself off the car. "Tomorrow I'm going to meet with an old buddy and have him run the name of your consultant through the computers. Meanwhile, I'll keep working my side of the tracks. I'll call you in a couple days to compare notes, unless something turns up sooner. OK?"

"OK."

Fletcher started to turn away, and then paused. "By the way, you're sure that this guy is also the manager of a rock group?"

"Pretty sure. Saw the posters for their upcoming performance. The group's name is Legacy."

Fletcher nodded. Leaning her head out the open car door, Michelle watched him walk slowly around the car to the sidewalk, hands thrust deeply in his coat pockets, his head slightly lowered.

"Fletcher!"

He stopped and faced her. The street light overhead partially illumined his sober face.

"I've got a good feeling about Jimmy."

From the distance she wasn't sure, but she thought she saw a smile break across his face. "Did God tell you to tell me that?"

Michelle shrugged her shoulders exaggeratedly, then shut and locked her car door.

⊰⊱ 26 ⊰⊱

Tuesday Night

A S MARK AND KATIE DROVE HOME, they prayed. The quiet time
brought with it an intense perception of God's presence.

The fireplace in the study now burned brightly. Mark leaned
against the mantle, his eyes running the length of Will's Long Knife.
Katie sat in the cushioned chair to the right of the desk, an open
journal across her lap. A half-circle of amber firelight merged with
the glow of a tall lamp on the desk behind Katie's shoulder.

The straightened stacks of materials were just as Mark had left
them Monday afternoon. Katie grinned as Mark handed her the
leather-bound journal.

"Ready?" Katie asked.

Mark nodded, touching the pommel of the sword. "More and
more I'm starting to think that we've been caught up in an orchestra-
tion of events, just like Sam—on a smaller scale. He had a bloody
war to live through."

They were silent for a moment as the fire crackled and popped,
launching a small, winding plume of orange sparks up the chimney.

As his eyes followed the plume, Mark became aware of the
images that continued to haunt around the edges of his conscious
thought—his dream of Charleston harbor, a graveyard, and seven
white tombstones.

He pulled his hand away from the sword. Turning around, he
forced the images back into the darkness. With the problem of *unde
malum* on the statue finally behind them, he didn't need to get Katie
worked up about something else....

Loud music blared from speakers suspended in each corner of Max's
Seafood Grill; the smell of cigarette smoke, spicy steamed crabs, and
shrimp was heavy in the air. The rowdy fraternity group that occupied most of the tables in the center of the long rectangular room
made conversation in the last booth toward the back extremely private, which was all the better for KC and Troy. The pitcher of beer
in the middle of the table between them was almost empty.

"There's no way around it," KC argued. "We must tell Kim about Mark MacDonald's threat."

Troy rubbed his jaw. "If the Sponsors think we've blown it, they might decide to withhold payment until he's dealt with—and if Kim's superiors do something rash, the entire case could be blown back open. But if they don't do something, the witness might just decide to go ahead and blab to the media. I couldn't believe how close his guesses were to the truth. It was kind of spooky."

"More like Catch-22," KC said, downing the last of her beer.

Frowning, Troy turned and sat sideways in the booth. He nestled his mug of beer in his lap. "Maybe we should deal with this ourselves and threaten MacDonald anonymously."

KC laughed cynically. "Yeah, right. Then what do you think he'd do? He'd be right back in your office demanding to meet with Captain Conran. I say we contact Kim. Let the Sponsors figure out a way to deal with Mark MacDonald. Besides, the clinic case is out of our hands anyway. There's nothing in the files you gave the FBI that incriminates us in any way. Let's keep it that way."

"I suppose you're right. But I warn you, if things start going down, I'm bailing out."

"Bail out? What's that supposed to mean?" KC asked, leaning forward.

"It means I'm not going to let the Sponsors flush us down the toilet while they walk away smelling like roses. I've been doing a little investigating of my own. I've put together a couple files, photos, phone numbers and a tape. It's enough to give us leverage with Kim if push comes to shove."

KC's expression was grim. "Troy, you're fooling with fire. We're dealing with people who have power and money. I'd bury those files if I were you."

"They're safely hidden." Troy returned his mug to the table with a bang. "Besides, if we don't do something to cover ourselves, we could end up rotting in some jail cell just like your brother."

KC thought about Jamal's letter. In nine short days he would be up for parole. What an irony it would be for them to switch places! The thought chilled her to the bone.

Glaring, Troy grabbed his coat. "Well? Are you going to make that call to Kim or what?"

20 August 1862, 7:45 P.M.
Near Ashby's Gap, Virginia

I am behind Union lines, near the enemy camp, hiding in John Kline's circuit cabin. I am momentarily safe from peril. I am sitting up for the first time in nearly twenty-four hours. The aroma of dried beef grilling in the skillet, the skillet that saved my life, fills the air.

Though I thoroughly cleansed the bullet wound in my left arm late last night, I fear I already suffer from infection. Sharp pain precludes sleep, so, I shall use these hours to record my insights into the war, the war in unseen realms led by that Thief and Murderer, the Devil. If my strength permits, I shall also record my recent confrontation with Beaumont and his associate, the scar-faced man, and my miraculous escape from their hands and the hangman's noose.

Blood at Sudley Church

At the conclusion of the Battle of Manassas, as the Yankees were in full retreat to Washington, I followed a straggling brigade of Rebel infantrymen north along Sudley Road through the cloying July heat.

When I was a youth my father brought my brother and me up this very road every Sunday morning to Sudley Church. Now the road is worn deep by the feet of soldiers and horses, the wheels of cannon, the wagons of war.

Above me, tall irregularly shaped clouds moved steadily across the sky; suddenly their peculiar forms struck me, coldly, chilling me to the bone. What did I see behind those behemoth conformations? Did my eyes play tricks on me? Were they clouds or dark, angelic armies maneuvering toward another bloody contest for the souls of men?

Filled with trepidation, I was compelled forward by the Spirit of God. I approached the building where my young voice had so often joined with others in praise. Now I heard only the dirge of men in agony. Screams, moans, and shrieks pierced the walls of this infirmary that was once a sanctuary.

Two ragged soldiers wheeled a cart toward the church's front door. A wounded Confederate soldier lay on his back in the bouncing cart, writhing in pain, his legs twitching uncontrollably. A Union Minie ball had struck him in the neck and torn a gaping hole in his jaw.

I trudged forward, crossing the bloodied threshold into the rectangular, one-room structure. The bustle of soldiers and doctors and the moans of the dying nearly overwhelmed me. I gasped in horror as my eyes beheld the communion table where my father, once a deacon, had often helped the pastor to serve the body and blood of our Lord.

Surgeons were using the table for amputations. In the corner where my prayerful father once sat on the deacon's bench, the bloody limbs of soldiers were piled five or six deep. A rancorous odor filled my lungs.

I knew I could not escape my responsibilities. My medical training in Philadelphia had been ordained by Providence for this occasion.

The next three days were indeed the most traumatic of my life. I took upon myself the grisly task of removing the severed limbs and expired bodies of soldiers, stacking them in neat piles along the exterior wall behind the church. God also granted numerous occasions for me to serve when one of the surgeons grew faint from exhaustion. I have carefully detailed the amputation procedure in the Rebel Heart Journal and in articles submitted to Mr. Pitkins. I had never wielded a surgeon's saw on a living man before, and once the ordeal was over, I prayed that God would not require it of me again.

Such a profitless petition!

Aftermath

What lessons can be learned from the blood on the table of the Lord? Is such bloodshed the price for our national guilt? Was it You, Lord, "trampling out the vintage where Your grapes of wrath are stored" and was it You "loosing the fateful lightning of Your terrible swift sword?" Is this really, as Julia Ward Howe's Battle Hymn of the Republic claims, the glory of Your coming?

How can one know the answer? Perhaps there is another principle at work. James 1:14-16: "But every man is tempted when he is drawn away of his own lust and enticed. Then when lust hath conceived, it bringeth forth sin: and sin, when it is finished, bringeth forth death."

Is not war yet another bloody facet of unde malum?

Enemy In The Camp

Following the fight at Kernstown, Mr. Pitkins reassigned me to Major General Stonewall Jackson's army. I rode with Stonewall as a reporter for the Observer and an assistant to the field surgeons through many campaigns. I saw battles in Winchester, Harper's Ferry, Port Republic, Richmond, Cold Harbor, and Malvern Hill. The detailed accounts of our many campaigns are well documented in the Rebel Heart Journal, and the Observer.

Following the Malvern Hill campaign, we received orders to Gordonsville, a town near my Culpeper rendezvous with John Kline. Revival came to our camp. On the evening of August 15th, we gathered at our campfire to meet with God. A full moon lit the clouds as they danced across the sky, reminding me of my experience at Sudley Church. I pondered in my heart if they were unseen spiritual forces arraying themselves once again against God's people.

The deaths of many friends had softened hearts. Our time of fellowship consisted of Rebel fight songs followed by Christian hymns. We ascended into the presence of God, carried upon the sweet offerings of praise and prayers for the families of those who had died. We were about to begin our time of testimony when unexpectedly, a strong tenor voice audaciously sang forth.

Rebel is a sacred name;
Traitor, too, is glorious;

By such names our fathers fought,
And by them were victorious.

The song disrupted the spirit of our meeting, pulling men's attention away from Christ and onto themselves and the false belief that their hearts were right and that this bloody war was justified. But even as I sought to halt the chorus, the voice leading them suddenly rang with a certain familiarity. I rose to my feet and turned to see if my suspicions were correct, but as I did, the soldiers followed my lead and stood up!

The familiar voice faded as the chorus ended. The sense of God's presence departed. After a few weak attempts at another hymn, the group dispersed. Our meeting concluded and the troublemaker escaped unseen.

Discouraged, I returned to my tent and sought the Lord with great fervor. I sat upon my bedroll, knowing that the voice that led the chorus had belonged to none other than Seth Beaumont.

During my time in Charleston with Victoria, Seth had attended the same church we did, often occupying a seat in the pew directly behind us. I struggled to combat my rising anger and fear. Beaumont had come to the Shenandoah. He was somewhere in this camp seeking to undermine my work. I considered this a dangerous turn of events.

Why had he come?

A Sentence of Death

The next morning, before dawn had broken, I discovered the reason for Beaumont's presence. Awakened from a restless slumber, I was curtly informed by Captain Pendleton that Beaumont had a warrant for my arrest. I was accused of stealing General Lee's orders and passing them northward.

I followed Pendleton out of my tent. Burly, sandy-haired Beaumont stood imposingly before General Jackson. He wore his nefarious grin and displayed a cunning cock of his eyebrow.

It was then that I noticed Beaumont's companion, standing twenty yards arrear beneath a copse of trees. He was as I remembered him from the dream: thin and wiry with a ruddy scar.

Formal charges of treason were laid upon me. His evidence: testimony from Captain Pendleton that I had rendezvoused with a Northern sympathizer, a circuit rider by the name of John Kline, the very day that Lee's orders were stolen. It did me little good that John had been arrested several times on foundless charges of spying.

Beaumont continued his accusations, further claiming that I was also wanted in Charleston for the brutal murder of Miss Elkin, a boardinghouse owner.

I was dumbfounded as these gross misrepresentations and lies were leveled against me. It was with Captain Pendleton's permission that I had visited John Kline, a man who had no allegiances, North or South.

But Beaumont knew that Jackson had no jurisdiction over civil affairs in South Carolina and on this charge alone he could assassinate my character. No one in camp could challenge Beaumont's testimony; as a high-ranking member of Jefferson Davis's Secret Service, his wartime powers were immense. I did not doubt that I would be tried and found guilty.

After a half an hour of this madness, Captain Pendleton escorted me back to my tent. I sat on my bedroll and closed my eyes. Why did he want me dead? What threat did I pose?

I sat for several hours in prayer and meditation, calling upon the Lord for His intervention. Yet with each passing hour in the darkness, the inevitability of my fate became increasingly certain. I reflected upon Christ in the garden, the night before His death. He, too, wanted to live, yet He possessed a heart that was willing to face death. "If it be Thy will Father, let this cup pass from me. Nevertheless, not my will but Thy will be done."

The answer to my prayers came miraculously and unexpectedly.

The Escape

Before dawn, I felt a tap on my shoulder. I looked up, startled. I had heard no one enter my tent. Standing above me was a broad-shouldered man with close-cropped blond hair. He wore a Confederate officer's uniform and identified himself as Major Michaels, a name I had not heard before. Like Jackson, he possessed a most commanding presence. I rose to my feet.

"Samuel MacDonald, your death is imminent, yet you shall not die. The enemy's testimony against you will not succeed. I have been ordered to make arrangements for your escape."

I stood silently as he handed me a set of traveling papers. "Should you be stopped, these documents provide you with free and unquestioned passage."

He handed me the uniform of a Confederate Lieutenant. "Your horse is saddled and ready to go, along with your books and other personal items. Change your clothes. Rest assured, the guard will not be looking when you leave your tent. Even so, do not look to your left or your right."

He then announced, "You must head north, Samuel MacDonald. To the west, south and east, you will surely be captured. Armies on both sides are maneuvering for a major battle. Take your civilian clothes and change immediately upon reaching Union lines and most of all, place your trust in God."

Was this an answer to my prayer? Or was I being led like a fool into a trap? I mused on the possibilities and soon realized that it made no difference. If I stayed, I was a dead man for sure. I followed his orders and, true to his word, my escape was uneventful. Within a few brief hours of certain death, my horse, James Madison, and I were on the road north out of Gordonsville, my guitar strapped to my saddle-bag, with my two army medical knapsacks and journals secured across his back. The Long Knife hung from my belt in its sheath, and my orders identifying me as Lieutenant Elijah of the Confederate Secret Service were tucked in my jacket.

I should have paid greater heed to Major Michaels' words. Knowing that I was in a precarious position, I decided to proceed to John Kline's cabin in contradiction to my rescuer's warning.

I spent the night traveling toward the upper portion of the Shenandoah Valley. By morning I was no more than an hour from the cabin. As the rising sun sent its first yellow rays peeking through the tree-tops, sounds of intermittent cannon fire began off to my right somewhere beyond the forest.

Less than an hour later, after crossing a shallow creek, a cluster of birds broke noisily from a stand of trees, slashing upwards into the sky directly above my head.

As I glanced up, the loud bark of a pistol pierced the air.

James Madison buckled beneath me. As I tumbled to the ground, I heard a second clap and a round ripped through my left arm, spinning me onto my back. I heard the gallop of hooves as the barely distinguishable colors of Union blue emerged from the dusk lighted edge of the wood.

The Union scout dismounted. My fate was now certain. I was either a dead man or a Union prisoner. I lay helplessly in the road, knowing that each breath might be my last. As the scout approached, he yanked his pistol from his holster.

I found myself eyeball to eyeball with the barrel of a Union pistol. He drew back the pistol's hammer with a click—which was followed immediately by a dull thwack.

The soldier's eyes rolled back in his head and he toppled to the ground beside the main road.

Soul, did not the hand of my Maker dispense grace and providence upon me? Was I not tempted to disbelieve the familiar figure standing behind the fallen Union soldier?

Before me stood an old friend, Toby Sikes, the free Negro from Mrs. Sheppard's boardinghouse. He wore a huge smile on his face and held an oversized skillet in his hand. Toby served as a cook in one of Pope's regiments. He told me that we were ten miles behind Union lines and dangerously close to roving Union Cavalry units. He'd been cleaning his cooking utensils when he saw me ride by, asleep on

my horse. At first he didn't recognize me, but then, catching sight of
the guitar, he remembered our time at Mrs. Sheppard's Boardinghouse.

Glancing at my bloody Lieutenant's uniform, I realized the careless
mistake I had made.

While recounting his story, he bound my wound, then transferred
my many belongings to the Union officer's horse, helped me up into
the saddle and tied the skillet to my pack.

"Sam, I don't know what you're doin' here but someone heard
them shots. They'll be comin'. You best be movin' quick."

"Why the skillet?" I asked, clutching my arm.

"So you won't ever forget how God used Toby Sikes to save your
life. Strange thing is, I've got a feelin' he's gonna have us meet again!
Now get on outa here!"

Moving On

The infection in my arm continues to spread. I am in poorer condition now than when I first arrived. I must resume my trek. The sound
of cannon tells me the conflict is moving slowly northward.

But the real war is not one between men in blue and gray. No, it is
between forces of Good and of Evil, between angels of light and principalities of darkness. Both North and South were swept up with
pride and made captive by the Serpent, the Devil. Now he freely
stalks the land, seeking to complete his plan to destroy the Nation, as
Father Gibault so clearly forsaw. The Devil aspires to extinguish the
torch of freedom held forth for nearly a century by its guardian and
defender, the Church.

John Ezra's farm is less than a hundred miles away, but it is far
behind Union lines. I will be safe there and able to escape Beaumont's
crazed pursuit. May Your grace go with me.

If this is my last journal entry and I should expire on the road, I
request the finder to please forward my possessions to my brother:

John Ezra MacDonald
Old Mill Crossroads
Gettysburg, Pennsylvania.

⟨⟩ 27 ⟨⟩

Wednesday Morning

FROST BLANKETED THE GRASS IN MERIDIAN HILL PARK. At 7:00 A.M. the sun had not yet crested the horizon of three-story and four-story buildings lining the park's eastern edge.

Fletcher looked down at his shoes. They were coated white around the edges with tiny ice crystals. He glanced back over his shoulders. His footprints were visible all the way down the hill to the park's southwest entrance near the corner.

He passed under a stone archway leading to an ornate marble fountain that had been dry for as long as he could remember. Just as expected, he found his friend and former partner sitting on a marble bench beyond the fountain.

"Botello! It's good to see you, man."

They greeted each other with a solid pat on the back and a handshake. Botello's big black hand wrapped easily around Fletcher's smaller white one.

"Things are getting hot and heavy. You've been caught sticking your finger into somebody's fresh-baked pie. I got a call from Internal Affairs yesterday. They wanted to know if you've been pumping me for information." Botello laughed. "Bill and his boys aren't dummies. They know where I stand. Let's hope I don't get cut off from my source of supply."

Fletcher grinned. "I'm sorry you're catching my heat."

Botello waved him off. "I'll bet. You didn't ask me to meet you out here in the freezing cold just to say thanks. I know you too well, ol' buddy, ol' pal."

"Now that you mention it, I do have something I'd like you to check out—just for your own satisfaction, of course." Fletcher unzipped his coat, then reached inside for a piece of paper. "Can you run this guy through the computers? I've got evidence that he's directly involved with the Crest Road vandalism and the bomb threat. And I think he set Wertman up for a fall."

Botello stuck the note into his coat pocket, exchanging it for a thin sheaf of folded photocopies that he handed to Fletcher. "The bomb business's one hot potato right now. I haven't seen so much activity since the Barry trial. Wertman struck a raw nerve. Lucky it didn't blow or this town would've had themselves a lynching."

Fletcher stared briefly into the distance, then looked back to Botello. "Is Troy still pursuing the vandalism separately, or has it been absorbed into Wertman and the bomb?"

"Funny you should ask. Troy put together an airtight package for the DA and the FBI, linking everything together. In my opinion, maybe it's just a little too airtight. I know his work habits."

"What about KC?" Fletcher added.

Botello rolled his eyes. "Need you ask? Your suspension just whet her appetite. I've seen her down in Internal Affairs a couple times already this week."

"She wants my badge, plain and simple." Fletcher patted Botello on the shoulder. "Thanks for all your help."

"Anytime, my man. And I'll try to get those computer results to you by this evening."

"I appreciate it."

"You think they're all involved, don't you?" Botello asked. "This dude you want me to check out—Troy and KC."

Fletcher pointed at his nose. "Something's spoiled and it's stinkin' up the whole refrigerator—and it ain't my special omelette. We've just got to find what it is."

"I'll poke around in the fridge as quietly as I can."

They shook hands and left the frost-covered garden and fountain in opposite directions.

At Katie's request, Mark rolled over in the bed and placed his hand on her warm stomach.

Katie placed her hands over Mark's. "It's really too early for you to feel the baby move. Still, I wonder what he's doing in there—moving an arm, wiggling his toes."

Mark chuckled. "He? Where'd that come from?"

"I think the Lord's going to give us a boy to continue the MacDonald line and to make up for the accident. He didn't forget that we lost a boy."

The dream image of a tombstone flashed into Mark's thoughts. After several quiet minutes, he gently slid his hand away and climbed out of the bed.

"Getting up so early?" Katie asked, snuggling up to Mark's pillow.

"Early? It's almost 7:30. I've been awake for over an hour and done some hard thinking about our first full week in the house and Sam's journals."

Katie sighed. "How did I know that you were going to mention Sam?"

Mark opened the closet and reached for a flannel shirt. "You make it sound like I was the only person in this house who was compulsive about reading Sam's journals last night."

The rustle of sheets and blankets was followed by bare feet padding across the floor. Warm arms wrapped around his waist.

"I was just kidding," Katie said laughingly over his shoulder. "I'm in deep, too. Holding his journal in my lap, reading those handwritten pages—it was like I was right there beside him in John Kline's cabin as he penned his journal by firelight. And when he described the dark clouds marching across the sky, a shiver ran down my spine. It was just as if—"

Mark buttoned his shirt right over the top of Katie's arms.

Larry and Glenn snored antiphonally. Fletcher left the bag of food by the feet of their sleeping bags. He returned to the park entrance, paused on the steps and stared at the low wall where Jimmy probably sat just one week ago. One week? It felt more like a year, like he left a part of himself somewhere back in the past, a part of him that would be lost forever. Whether that was good or bad, he did not know.

He breathed deeply, turned his head and glanced up the hill and sidewalk bordering Meridian Hill Park. Traffic moving both ways on 16th Street was heavy and slow. Even with the traffic, however, he was only five minutes away from the MacDonald's. Mark and Katie. Thinking about them made Fletcher smile. Last night's conversation with Michelle in the deli had been enlightening in more ways than one. The fact that she, Mark, and Katie attended the same church was coincidental enough. The fact that Michelle submitted the tip and that Mark saw Jimmy's body being dragged away was almost—

Providential. Yes, that was the word Michelle had used. Providential. And she was dead serious when she referred to his friendship to Jimmy in the same way. Why had she included him in her list of miracles, he had asked. Her reply: because God works all things for the good of those who love him.

Michelle's peculiar way of evaluating circumstances reminded him of the MacDonalds. Now, after the bomb attempt, Fletcher was sure that Mark would have a theory on Wertman's innocence. He had a theory for most everything else, including how the Devil came from France to America.

Fletcher shook his head slowly as he continued down the steps and out of Meridian Hill Park. He turned left on W Street away from 16th Street. His car was parked halfway down the block.

Sam MacDonald. Mark's ancestor's name came back in a flash. Fletcher was sure that Mark fancied himself to be like Sam, a man of unsolved mysteries.

After waiting for a trash truck to rumble by, Fletcher jogged across the street to his car. He would get a bite of breakfast and take a look at the case notes Botello had slipped him in the park. Then, around 9:00 A.M., hopefully Mark and his wife would be up to a second visit.

A flat gray cloud cover hung low over the city. Wind rippled through the fir trees lining the park across from Mark and Katie's townhouse. Heavily bundled pedestrians on 16th Street moved briskly. Two young women had entered the women's clinic without resistance. There were no picketers. A judge had approved AFI's injunction and brought the picket to a stop.

As Katie entered the parlor, she saw a neat stack of logs burning in the fireplace. Mark looked over his shoulder. "Hi, Babe. Thought I'd get a fire going." Katie chuckled.

Mark sat down on the hearth. "So, how should we pray this morning? Should we start with Dan and Kent and the others at Agape, or how about the judge who shut down the picket and wants to put limitations on the March for Life?"

Katie sat in the wing chair across from the fireplace. "Let's not forget Detective Rivers. I also think we need to pray about what we're reading in Sam's journals. I can't get that image of the demonic spirit looming over Sudley Church with his sword out of my mind—it reminds me of Will standing over the Indian woman with his Long Knife. It's so gruesome and yet it seems so important somehow, as part of our MacDonald legacy."

Mark stilled. Breaking into his thoughts was a cone of red light that flashed over seven, rounded tombstones with seven names. Then Grandpa Kyle's troubled face, followed by his own—as clear an image as if he stared into the bathroom mirror.

Their legacy?

He breathed deeply as they bowed their heads to seek the Lord.

Kim looked out over the sleek, right wing of the British Airways' Concord Flight number 343 for London. She watched the runway and treetops fall away swiftly. Dulles Airport and the rolling Virginia countryside shrank rapidly beneath her. Speeding cars and tractor trailer trucks became tiny crawling miniatures.

She pulled a mirror from her purse and checked her makeup. The bruises around her eyes and mouth were barely distinguishable. Her long-sleeved cashmere sweater hid the darker ones that were beginning to appear on her arms.

She pondered what she had done to deserve the beating. Going to his penthouse without authorization? Telling him the truth about the phone call from KC about Mark MacDonald? Kim's hand rose to the corner of her mouth, where the back of his hand first struck her, cutting the inside of her lip and drawing blood. A solitary tear trickled down her cheek.

"Excuse me, is everything OK?" asked a stewardess passing by.

Kim wiped the tear from her cheek and forced a smile. "Yes. I'm fine, thank you."

The stewardess nodded and continued down the aisle.

Kim fell back into her reverie. No—what had incited his anger was Wertman's bedtime confession to her that he knew their Sponsor's identity, a young Irishman from his college days at Cal-Berkeley.

True Believer had exploded with rage, his hand arcing to her mouth. He accused her of carelessly providing Harold with details about him—and worse—he accused her of being Geneva's ear within his operation and for feeding Geneva information about his plans!

She had pleaded with the taste of blood in her mouth. But again and again he struck her, punched her, until she had dropped weeping to her knees on the carpet in front of him.

"Get out of my sight!" he screamed. "And take your whoring ways with you!"

As she grabbed her coat and staggered toward his front door, she recalled his final words. His voice became calm, cold.

"Fools! I will handle this problem myself."

Kim held her breath as the memory of her last moment in the apartment replayed itself in her mind. In the semi-darkness of his living room, she had seen the strange illusion a second time. Only for a split second, then it was gone, a shadow angled across the left side of his face.

Had she seen a shadow or a scar—a long, dark scar?

She shuddered and returned her mirror to her purse.

Sitting on his bunk in solitary confinement, Harold Wertman crossed his legs in the lotus position. He closed his eyes and shut out the many troublesome thoughts that besieged his mind.

Even though it had been ten years since he dabbled in meditation, the techniques he memorized came back quickly. He breathed slowly and deeply, letting the tension drain straight down through his body, through the blanket and bunk, through the thick concrete floors and into the earth. He concentrated on the darkness that he had created by closing his eyes, moving through his boundless inner domain like a spaceship in flight.

His days as a social warrior were over. He played his part; he'd run the race set before him; he fought the good fight. Regardless of his captors' threats, he was determined to protect the Sponsors and their plans. He would remain true to the end, even though he'd never collect the twenty thousand that was due him. He didn't need the money—he never had. The prize he sought could not be found in this world. Somewhere inside himself was a treasure beyond compare. And, unlike ten years ago, he would now search until he found the Mystic Plane of Immortal Light and the Eternal City.

Now that search was feasible. He had free room and board; the food was good. After the trial, he would settle into a daily routine that would include exercise and access to a library.

The darkness of his inner domain deepened. He moved faster now, at warp speed. However, even at this speed, it might be an hour before he began to see the first glimmering sparks of the Plane's farthest outpost where Elana, his spirit guide, dwelled. It had been almost ten years since he last spoke with her. And to find the Eternal City, he would first have to find Elana.

Harold smiled and pressed on into the star-swept blackness.

Katie settled into the wing chair as Mark turned to the first page in the new journal.

As Mark opened his mouth to read, Katie leaned forward in her chair, a wrinkle forming between her eyebrows.

"Do you think we might have our own modern day Beaumont or scar-faced man running around Washington? We both believe that Harold was a pawn for somebody else."

Shifting his weight in the chair, Mark considered her question, his expression sobering. "That's a good question. There might be."

Katie nodded, folding her arms across her Washington Redskins' sweatshirt. "Sorry, but I've been thinking about it ever since we prayed."

Mark fingered the old journal, cleared his throat and lowered his eyes to the page.

Michelle opened the blue file folder in front of her. She glanced up at the open doorway separating her office from Julie's. She could hear Julie's fingers clicking rapidly on her keyboard.

"Julie, would you mind closing your door, please?"

The keys stopped clicking. "Sure," came a cheerful reply. Julie stepped briefly into view. She turned and smiled at Michelle before returning to her desk.

For the moment, Julie's crisis and the budding friendship had come into a useful harmony. Julie broke off with her boyfriend, packed her belongings, and accepted the offer to move in with Michelle until the baby was born and she was back on her feet. Michelle was glad. The extra bedroom was only used when her parents visited once or twice a year. Now it could be put to good use.

Michelle returned her attention to the open folder. The initial results of her vendor analysis had been fruitful. During the past calendar year, seven companies—all of which were marketing, advertising and consulting entities—received $100,000 in payments. Yesterday, she gave Julie a printout of the AFI check numbers and had her dig through storage box after storage box of canceled checks until she found all fourteen on Michelle's list.

Michelle studied the checks in the blue folder one last time. *For Deposit Only* had been stamped on the back of each one, and below it the company name. On each of the sets of canceled checks were seven different account numbers. When she first looked at the checks, the different account numbers seemed to destroy her theory that the companies were related. But her sharp eye found the link. There were seven different account numbers, but only one bank identification number. That meant the companies not only used the same Washington bank, but it was the very one where AFI held its main accounts!

Dig deeper, Fletcher Rivers had encouraged her. So she had. Stepping out on a limb of her own, she placed a discreet call to a friend at the bank and uncovered the fact that though each company was registered for "Doing Business As" under a unique corporate name—Parallax, Harbinger LTD., New Age Images and four others—the seven accounts were electronically linked to a common, high-interest money market fund under an eighth company name.

Michelle closed the folder. She drew a deep breath. She'd finally hit the jackpot. She uncovered a minimum of $8,000 in tax-exempt status violations directly implicating Mr. Peters. She contemplated her next step. She still had four more days until Carol returned, four days to dig deeply enough to expose Mr. Peters' empire.

Four days. It would be close, real close.

26 September 1862, 7:50 A.M.
Old Mill Crossing, Gettysburg

I am feeling better today. Angelina, Thomas Peter, and Elizabeth have all taken turns staying by my bedside during my recovery.

Apparently my arrival created quite a stir. All three insisted that I swayed so severely in the saddle that they were certain I would tumble to the ground. Elizabeth was the first to reach me. She says I was incoherent and that I resisted their efforts to help me down, flailing my arms wildly and growling. What a spectacle I must have been! Twice this past week I caught glimpses of Angelina and Thomas Peter, straddling the split rail fence between the house and the barn, swaying back and forth and trying to make deep noises with their voices, imitating me.

My health is returning. The wound in my left arm is almost healed.

My twelve-year-old nursemaid, Angelina, has appeared in the doorway, arms crossed. The look on her face informs me that this day's writing is drawing to a close. Her almond colored skin, slightly thickened lips, and wavy dark hair reveal her guiltless mixture of race and culture, embodying the bewildering perplexity of our bloody sectional conflict. She is an innocent, caught between two worlds, both white and black, much like the very issues surrounding this war.

She embodies the war that works within me. I, too, am a mixture. I advocate autonomy for the States as do my brothers in the Confederacy. Yet, I proclaim the urgency of overcoming the great evils of slavery as do my brothers in the North.

Angelina refuses to leave the doorway, watching me with a smile behind her eyes.

Very well, I shall put away the pen for today, with the promise that you must let me continue my writing as God permits. I will use these days to focus upon the <u>Rebel Heart</u> and Founding Fathers' journals.

My brother John Ezra, Captain of the 63rd Pennsylvania volunteer regiment, is on the move again with an offensive in Virginia. Elizabeth is not certain of his whereabouts at this time.

"Somebody knocked on the front door," Katie said, interrupting her husband as he read.

Mark closed the journal and rose from his chair. "I'll go down. Maybe it's Fletcher!"

Less than a minute later she heard the sound of footsteps on the stairs—two sets of footsteps. Mark reentered the study with a dining room chair, and behind him, an apologetic Fletcher Rivers.

"Really, it's no problem," Mark explained as he positioned the chair to the left of the fireplace. "We were right between journal entries."

Fletcher, dressed in Dockers and a long-sleeve cotton shirt, accepted the seat nearest to the fireplace. He smiled at Katie. "Nice to see you both again. But really, I feel like I'm intruding."

Katie shook her head. "Don't. We were talking about you earlier this morning, half-expecting you might stop by now that Harold's been arrested."

Fletcher looked admiringly around the study, first at the fireplace and the sword, then to the stacks of Sam's journals and letters, his eyes finally resting on the antique desk. "I probably shouldn't be here. I've been placed on stress leave for sticking my nose into someone else's case—a preliminary move to an investigation by Internal Affairs that might cost me my job."

"So, what can we do for you?" Mark asked offering Fletcher a seat.

"I was wondering if you had anything to add about Wertman's arrest?" Fletcher asked.

"Well, I guess the most important thing is I went back down to see Detective Martin."

His statement struck Fletcher like a splash of cold water, bringing his ingrained professionalism to bear. "Tell me about it."

Mark described in detail his frustration and the ultimatum he levied on Troy, and then his concern that Harold was being set up. In fact, he wasn't even sure that anyone ever actually intended to blow up the clinic. Faking the bombing would save a lot of money and grief but would still generate tons and tons of vindictive sentiment in the public and press.

Katie sat up straight and stared questioningly at Mark.

Fletcher nodded occasionally. He listened patiently until Mark had finished. From their first meeting he knew Mark possessed a keen, deductive mind; still it surprised him that they had both come up with a similar, unified explanation of the events. Folding his hands together, Fletcher looked up, keeping his concern from expressing itself through his words.

"Did you tell Troy you thought the bomb attempt was staged?"

"No. I don't think so. It's a much more recent theory," Mark replied nervously as he glanced over at Katie.

Fletcher noticed Katie's expression of genuine surprise before asking several questions about what they saw Tuesday morning. Mark gave him the scanty details.

Even as he wrote down Mark's statement, the final pieces of the puzzle fell into place and a picture formed clearly in Fletcher's mind. One corner piece to the puzzle was KC's warning outside the elevators by the morgue. Another was Troy's reaction to Fletcher's probing questions in the office. A third was Carlton Glaze's murder. The fourth and final piece was his videotaped meeting with Mark and subsequent placement on stress leave.

Bad cops—the unspoken words tasted bitter on his tongue. Bad cops were dangerous cops. When Fletcher finally lifted his eyes, he knew from Mark's and Katie's sober faces that he had not been able to hide the alarm he suddenly felt.

Mark frowned. "Threatening Troy got us in trouble, didn't it?"

Fletcher's lips flattened into a severe line. Feeling the tension, he raised a hand and rubbed the corner of his mouth. "I'm afraid it may have—how seriously I'm just not sure. Regardless, you and Katie have got to lie low for a while. And whatever you do, don't follow up on your ultimatum. In fact, it would help considerably if you called and told him you've reconsidered."

Mark sighed. "I don't know if I can agree to that."

"Then let me explain it this way," Fletcher said, sitting forward in his chair. He recounted how Carlton Glaze died and what his death revealed about their opponent's fear of discovery.

For several moments the study was totally silent, save for the soft crackle of burning oak. Fletcher leaned back. He wanted Mark to understand that this was not a game, that their lives could be in jeopardy if he continued to press the matter with Troy.

"My husband will do exactly as you ask," Katie said at last. "You have my word."

"That's what I needed to hear. I don't want you to underestimate the seriousness of what's going on. I don't want you to get yourself into any deeper trouble." Fletcher started to rise from his chair. "Well, that's about it. I plan to keep in close touch. You have my beeper number; call me anytime, day or night."

A smile returned to Mark's face as he crossed the room. "Since you're on stress leave, why don't you hang around awhile? We're reading my ancestor Sam's journals. I think you'd find his perspective on history—"

"Mark! Give Fletcher a break!" Katie interjected, eyeballing her husband as he approached the table where Sam's journals were neatly stacked. "I imagine he has a few more important things to do than sit around and listen to us read!"

Fletcher chuckled and glanced at the floor. "I'd love to stay—and that's the truth. But today just won't work. I'll take a rain check, though."

Mark nodded. "Great. A rain check it is."

Rising from his chair, Mark led Fletcher back downstairs.

⟨⟩ **28** ⟨⟩

Wednesday Afternoon

23 October 1862, 9:50 P.M.
Old Mill Crossing, Gettysburg

Summer has departed and a brilliant autumn has arrived. We have no word from my brother. It has been six weeks since his last letter. Elizabeth informs me that John had been writing two or three letters a week. We are all very concerned.

<u>Unde Malum</u>

Angelina and I are becoming good friends. I finally learned the peculiar details behind her letter to me dated nearly a year and a half ago, though my chance to meet her mother, Violet, has come too late. Violet died two months before my arrival. Elizabeth, who knew firsthand of my pursuit to expose the Devil in history, helped Angelina tell her mother's story of their family and how they came to America.

It is such an incredible story, both precluding and confirming all that Father Gibault spoke to me that cold December day in 1859 at John Brown's hanging. That I would be granted to learn of Violet's story is surely the work of an All-Knowing God.

<u>Journey's West</u>

Angelina's grandmother, Marie Charbonneau, was born of wealthy French parents in 1785 and was among the thousands who witnessed King Louis XVI's beheading in 1793. To avoid the terror that followed, her family left France. Her father and his older brother crossed the Atlantic to Haiti and became plantation owners; her father's younger brother continued onto Charleston, South Carolina.

In 1797, the terror found them again when a bloody slave revolt struck the tiny Caribbean island. Only twelve-year-old Marie and her older brother escaped, crossing the mountains to Hispaniola. Ten years later, the flames of revolt that swallowed their parent's plantation clawed their way over the mountains. Marie's brother was killed; she was beaten and raped in her own home. She would never forget that dark night, when her former slaves danced on the lawn chanting the name of Ogu Loa! Ogu Loa! A beak-faced old man in tattered clothing stood among the burning timbers without being consumed.

At the age of twenty-two, Marie gave birth to a mulatto girl she named Catherine, after her mother. Fifteen years later in 1822, Marie and Catherine departed Hispaniola for her uncle's plantation in South Carolina. While aboard the ship, Marie contracted pneumonia and died three months later, in Charleston. The family confiscated Marie's assets and forced Catherine from the house because she was a mulatto. Without protection, she fell into the hands of a local banker who renamed her Violet and took her into his house.

The banker was Angelina's natural father. In 1858, he died, and his son sold Violet and Angelina to a ship's captain from Alexandria, Virginia. In the summer of 1860, the captain went down at sea. Violet and Angelina returned to the auction block. A merchant from Gettysburg, representing several families, came to the estate auction that year and purchased them both for the purpose of granting them freedom.

Providence

Upon reaching Gettysburg, Violet and Angelina were taken in by John Ezra and Elizabeth. Now I know why God sent Angelina to me. She is only twelve, yet she has insight into the spiritual beyond what I can anticipate. Not only that, but her brief family history has given me insight to understand how the Devil drew his bloody trail of oppression, rebellion, and violence from Europe across the Atlantic and through the Caribbean on to America.

Earlier this evening we sat on the front porch and watched a crimson sunset behind Big Round Top. While I wrote notes on the Rebel Heart, Angelina sat on the top step, my family journal open across her lap.

She looked up at me, her eyes brimming with tears. "Grandma Nikki died in your arms?"

I closed my notebook. "Yes, she did."

Angelina scrunched her dark eyebrows. "She was a woman of God, wasn't she?"

I recalled Grandma's face, determined and purposeful, with sparkling eyes. "Yes, she was."

Angelina drew her finger across the journal page. "'Out of your loins will come two men with strong medicine. With their lips they will drink from a bitter spring. With their ears they will hear the cry of the blood. With their eyes they will see the dark root of evil in men's souls.'"

She turned around, her face bursting with awe. She climbed to her knees and edged close to my chair.

How disarmed I was by this precious girl! And how unprepared for the revelation she would so casually offer! Truly, "Out of the mouths of babes and infants You have ordained strength, because of Your enemies, that You may silence the enemy and the avenger."

Angelina studied my face. I do not recall having ever seen such a sober visage in one her age.

"Sam," she said, placing her hand over mine, "you're gonna be like my Grandma and my Mamma, aren't you? God gave you special eyes to see Ogu Loa, the Devil, too."

My body tingled from head to toe, and the hairs on my arms and the back of my neck stood on end. Never once since Grandma Nikki spoke the prophecy to me in the barn had I considered interpreting her words in such a literal manner.

Stunned, I squeezed her hand. To Angelina, the Devil was not a clever theological dissertation on moral corruption. To Angelina, Evil was not an intangible force, but a living, visible power.

We sat quietly and watched the sun disappear behind the crest of Big Round Top.

Morning of Darkness

Twelve hours have passed since the close of my last entry.

It is as if winter's icy breath has come early to this house, and no fire can warm the chill now set into our hearts. Tears hide behind every eye. Broken hearts are held together with the everyday motions of a busy fall morning.

This morning, shortly after dawn, a rider approached the house. We thought him to be another Union supply officer seeking to purchase horses or perhaps cattle for beef. He was not here to purchase supplies, but to be the bearer of tragic news.

John Ezra has been killed in battle.

Our hearts went numb. After the sympathetic officer left, our stunned silence turned to tears. I comforted Elizabeth, holding her in my arms. The children gathered to us, clung to our legs, and cried, too.

Breakfast was a plate of tasteless pancakes and eggs. Thomas Peter ventured outside to the barn where he could be alone in his grief. Elizabeth poked about the kitchen, cleaning the table and sweeping the floors, then retired to her room. Angelina sits on the corner of the hearth, quietly reading my journals, her eyes pools of sadness.

I sit in the kitchen, alone, struggling to write these bitter words.

O Lord, why John and not me? I have no purpose here! I research and reason; I seek to know the truth; I record my thoughts for posterity. To what end? Will my words ever reach anyone who might find meaning in them? I carry an old sword to remind me of the power of evil in men's hearts. I record tales of guillotines and hangmen's nooses, of a wiry old man shuffling like a serpent across the ground. Am I a madman or just a fool?

I am drinking from Tecumseh's bitter spring once again. My wife was murdered, my brother has been killed. Where now is Your redemption? Your power? How many men will lay down their lives for this impotent vision of a just war?

We cannot cleanse ourselves in its bloody flow! O, the futility of shedding our own blood!

As Mark closed the journal, his eyes were red. Toward the end he found it difficult to keep his voice from cracking. He looked at Katie. She lowered her Kleenex and stared quietly at the dying fire.

The one-hundred-thirty-year-old journal page and its passionately penned script still burned with Sam's devotion for the Lord and his fervent desire to embrace God's will, even though the Devil and his war had claimed another life in the MacDonald bloodline.

Mark exhaled deeply, closing his eyes. Now, only Sam and Thomas Peter remained to carry on the family. How many other MacDonalds had the Devil taken before their time through violence and murder? Will's wife Nikki? Sam's wife, Victoria? Kyle's wife, Mary?

No! Mark cut short his line of thought and forced open his eyes. He removed his hand from the open journal and looked up.

Katie's eyes locked on his, her mouth partially opened with concern.

"Honey, is something wrong? You're as pale as a ghost."

"Hey, Mike, what's up?" Fletcher cradled the phone in his shoulder, and pulled a small notebook and pen from his pant's pocket. He walked across the kitchen and sat down on a stool at the bar.

"I've got good news and I've got bad news," Botello explained. "Which do you want first?"

Fletcher shrugged. "Your call."

Botello continued. "All right, how 'bout the bad news first? The computer cranked and cranked and couldn't find a single match— zippo, nada. Fein's clean. Now, here's the good news."

Fletcher recognized the tone in his ex-partner's voice. He'd heard it before—mostly when they'd busted someone, catching them red-handed with incriminating evidence.

"Somebody's been very, very naughty. I was sitting there at the keyboard typing in his name when I remembered a bust I'd been involved with almost a year ago. Get this—a rock band got caught with ten thousand bucks worth of crack. Their promoter got involved and worked out a deal with the DA's office. In return for naming their distributor, another unsavory and criminal fellow, charges were dropped against the band. But here's the catch—I remember running several reports on those guys. Fein's name was in the computer a year ago—but not now."

"Somebody's wiped him from the database!"

"You got it," Botello said gleefully.

"What's next then?"

"Means a delay while I find someone to quietly run him down using another source. You know, Fletcher, somebody's playing for keeps. Wiping out computer files is a major league offense."

"In a few days. We don't want to scare the fish away by firing up the motor, not yet. Let's just paddle around a little longer."

"You've convinced me. I'll call you when I've tracked this guy down. Take care!"

"Adios, amigo." Fletcher rose from his stool and hung up the phone.

29

Wednesday Evening

THE PHONE RANG TWICE before the woman whose code name was Geneva retrieved it. She lifted the receiver and sat down behind her desk at one end of the laboratory, and then continued typing on her computer keyboard with her free hand.

A ripple of alarm shot across her face, drawing her eyes away from the screen. "Yes, I'll take the call. Thank you, Marna. Put her through."

Shaken, Geneva sat erect in her chair. It was 11:00 P.M. "Hello—Kim? What's going on? Why are you in London?"

Geneva listened quietly as Kim explained. Her neck and cheeks turned a deep red. "Catch the next flight available. I'll expect a full report when you arrive. I'll be waiting."

As soon as Kim hung up, Geneva depressed the button, then punched in an international code. She looked at her watch a second time and made a calculation. U.S. Eastern Standard Time was six hours behind—that would make it 5:00 P.M.

The call was systematically routed through several sterile lines. Thirty seconds later a connection was made. She did not wait for someone to speak. "This is Geneva. Give me New York, immediately!"

Despite her insistence, she was put on hold. She breathed deeply and considered her options with True Believer. She stared at the computer screen in front of her. The gray-green map of the world was dotted with twelve, tiny red triangular symbols that marked their network's key data centers.

A spike of anger flamed Geneva's cheeks a second time. Who did Fein think he was, dispensing Kim without clearing his decision with Bonn or her first? And the abuse! His actions were reprehensible!

Fein was not really the only true believer as his code name implied. He was a mercenary, plain and simple—hard, relentless, and unforgiving. She, Bonn, London, New York, and the other eight contributors—they, too, were believers. They would usher in the new world order and cleanse it of all that was weak—and corrupt. Fein was not fit to rule. Men like Fein were dispensable, purchased and traded like chattel—throwaways if need be.

The telephone line clicked and the transfer was completed.

Geneva exploded.

11 July 1863, Saturday, 9:15 P.M.
Gettysburg, Pennsylvania

The battle outside these walls ended eight days ago, but the battle within these walls continues.

I finally calmed one of our young amputees. Unlike the other four, his infection has diminished greatly. I suspect he will live to use his remaining arm. I gave him a draught of whiskey to aid his sleep.

Though I am weary, I must record a brief personal account of our current trial. Elizabeth and Thomas Peter are asleep. I am responsible for the first watch as we tend the wounded who fill this house. Angelina refused to leave me alone. She sits across the table from me writing in her own journal.

After the bloodiest warfare ever on American soil, our home became one of the first ancillary hospitals in Gettysburg. Since the first night, when I brought five young Southern boys from the field, our home has been a citadel against the Dark Root who seeks to steal, kill, and destroy. Bodies battered, broken, and bandaged are spread throughout the house, thirty-two at last count, and mostly Confederate. I have heard doctors say the number of wounded on both sides is approaching thirty thousand, some three-fifths of the total casualties. The number is staggering, unimaginable: sixty wounded soldiers for every healthy townsperson—man, woman and child. Most will die where they lay unattended on the hills and fields.

Horsemen In the Sky and Devil's Den

Many accounts of this bloody contest will be written. I suspect that my perspective of the conflict will be different from those of my fellow journalists. I begin with the 19th of June. Our entire family spent that evening on the porch. A crescent moon provided little light so we brought out two lanterns, so Elizabeth could see to mend Thomas Peter's trousers and Angelina and I could read.

At 8:30 P.M. we heard loud rumblings from the east. We assumed it to be the Union Cavalry on night maneuvers, but we saw nothing on the road. The sound came from above. Angelina grabbed my hand. We rose and moved to the edge of the porch, our heads tilted toward the clouds, watching the tall, oddly shaped moonlit columns, their twisted and contorted forms passing swiftly overhead.

A rumble like the sound of hoofbeats passed over us in a clamorous uproar, gradually moving northwest and ending with a solitary, blistering flash of lightning just beyond Big Round Top.

I shrugged off the display as an atmospheric occurrence, an odd mixture of dry summer heat and pressure in the air, producing thunder and lightning without rain as July evenings often do.

The following evening, Angelina called to me as she ran toward the front porch. Elizabeth pulled the wagon into the barn.

"Sam! Sam!" she shrieked, "It's him! The old man! Just like Mamma saw! A red sky—a crescent moon!"

I put my arm around her as she told her story.

On their return trip from town, they had made a visit to the Rose house, delivering several items from Fahnestock's store to the elderly Mrs. Rose. While Elizabeth helped Mrs. Rose, Angelina hiked through the woods, as she often does, to the home of young Melanie Timbers, a friend who lives on an adjacent farm.

Just before she reached Melanie's house, she saw an old man shuffling along the precipice above the rock known locally as the Devil's Den, near the west side of Big Top where lightning struck the night before.

There was a crescent moon that evening and a rosy sky, but at the time, I unfortunately dismissed her account for a more practical explanation.

"It was probably just old man Timbers," I said, "shuffling after his turkeys on his gimpy leg. Besides, it is I who have been given the ability to see the Devil. Am I not right?"

My spirit was not sensitive that evening. Had it been, I would have connected the two events and read the portent for what it really was.

The Devil's Harvest

Two weeks have passed and our time is now spent tending to the wounded and dying. Angelina has gone to bed. Sitting alone in the kitchen once again, I partake firsthand of the bitter fruit brought forth by sin.

What my spirit was amiss in discerning on those two evenings I now understand: Angelina had not seen Old Man Timbers. She had seen the Devil, directing his henchman, a grim demonic Power who sits upon a throne of Violence and Murder and reaps a bloody harvest from this peaceful market town.

Outside, the familiar stillness has only recently begun to return to the pastures and forests of Adams County. Fields and meadows, charred by thousands of cannon salvos and trampled by the feet of 160 thousand soldiers, are now quiet.

I consider the glistening bloodline that is being drawn through the heart of our Nation—Manassas, Shiloh, Antietam, Chancellorsville, Vicksburg, and Gettysburg. Such death and destruction! What lies ahead for this torn and bleeding land?

The cry of another soldier in pain compels me to place my pen in its well.

A Seamless Union

The house is silent again. I return to my journal having witnessed the departure of yet another soul. I consider John Kline's words from our last meeting: "Verily, the sons of men sink into the grave like raindrops into the sea and are seen no more. As a pitcher is broken at the fountain even before it is filled with water, unexpectedly does death come to man."

One broken pitcher, Tommy Alexander, an infantryman from Surry, Virginia, resisted the Gospel's call to the bitter end. An ardent foe of Lincoln and everything Northern, his dying words to me and the young Union amputee beside him were simply, "Us Rebs hate you Yanks more than you hate us."

Refusing to surrender his life and hatred to Christ, I fear he cast his soul into the sulfury fires of Hell.

What might have been if Tommy, and others like him, had not met such an untimely end? Perhaps the Spirit might have slowly softened his hatred and the grace of God might have visited him later in life. Now the opportunity has passed forever and the door to heaven has been irrevocably shut by the Devil's bloody sword.

Such a premature harvest of souls can only be the present fruit of man's stubborn defiance and the selfish ambition of him who is the true Enemy of both man and God.

Unde malum: is it not collusion, a seamless union between the Devil and the unrepentant heart of man?

True Believer hung up the phone, then returned to the leather high-back armchair across from Mr. Peters' cherry desk.

Mr. Peters, still listening on his extension, nodded twice, and then slowly hung up, his eyes moving from the phone to Brian Fein's sober glare. He straightened his tie and tugged at the lapels to his suit coat, the blush slowly fading from his neck and cheeks.

"Now that you've heard about this part of our problem first hand, do you understand the seriousness of our position?" True Believer asked, his voice quiet, deliberate.

Mr. Peters did not answer his question. To do so would have been superfluous. "Do they think this MacDonald fellow will really follow through with his threat? What must we do?"

"You will do nothing. MacDonald is my problem. Focus on your Controller. As I asked you at our last meeting, have you found any additional evidence that she's passing information to the outside?"

Mr. Peters shook his head. "I'm still not convinced she authored that anonymous tip. She's one of our hardest workers and—"

True Believer's gray eyes were emotionless as he raised a hand and cut the Director off. "Did you know that she attends a fundamentalist, born-again church?"

"No, but going to church doesn't mean—"

A sharp wave of the hand cut him off a second time. "The same fundamentalist, born-again church that the overly inquisitive Mac-Donalds attend?"

Mr. Peters eyes opened wide, his mouth started to open.

True Believer shook his head, raised his hand and pressed a forefinger to his lips.

19 November 1863
Gettysburg, Pennsylvania

I went walking late this afternoon in Gettysburg's newly dedicated cemetery, mourning our dead soldiers and weeping for our lost nation. The sight of so many gravestones reminded me of John Brown's prophetic words: "the crimes of this guilty land will never be purged away but with blood."

The Scriptures teach that the life of the flesh is in the blood. If the flesh of man is corrupt, then is not his bloodline corrupt also? How then can the blood of man redeem?

Visit With an Old Friend

This afternoon, a crowd of about fifteen thousand gathered as one, proceeded to Cemetery Hill to dedicate the new cemetery, and settled in for the oration by Edward Everett. His speech was classic in style and about two hours long. All four of us were there, Thomas Peter and Angelina taking turns on the shoulders of a friendly, likable behemoth named Clyde, a brawny blacksmith from town.

At last Lincoln stepped onto the platform and approached the podium.

To my great surprise, his message was short and concise. The brevity of his speech caught everyone off-guard. His words had no time to sink in as he stepped down. As the stunned crowd disbanded, a smartly dressed Union officer grabbed me at the elbow and introduced himself as Colonel Grigsby.

He led me through the crowd toward the platform. A lanky gentleman in a stovepipe hat came into view. He had aged considerably and grown a beard that followed his square jaw line.

Had my letters really reached him? I had put the thought so firmly out of my mind, I hardly remembered corresponding!

"Sam," President Lincoln exclaimed, his handshake firm, "how good to see you. I got your note yesterday. What are you doing here? Your last letter placed you south of the Mason Dixon line."

"I was, fifteen months ago." I said, stumbling over my words.

He still carried himself in a familiar manner. To me, he was still Abe of Illinois, the man I first met at the Young Men's Lyceum in 1838, the lawyer my father hired to resolve his land disputes. A younger Abe was the first man who had aroused the passion of patriotism in me. I told him of my unfortunate confrontation with Jefferson Davis's nefarious secret service agent, Seth Beaumont, my miraculous escape, and my recovery here in Gettysburg at the home of my late brother.

His eyes brimmed with tears and he expressed his condolences at the loss of John Ezra. "I have heard and read too many tragic accounts of lost loved ones, husbands, sons, and brothers," he explained, his face revealing the remarkable weight he has borne these three years, laboring to hold the Union together. "And surely I will hear or read too many more before this war is over."

I gathered my thoughts and responded. "Mr. President, do you remember your words at the Young Men's Lyceum, when we first met twenty-five years ago? You said that 'danger would spring up from amongst us, not come from abroad,' and that we 'as freemen must live through all time or die by suicide.'"

"'If destruction be our lot, we ourselves must be its author and finisher.'" Lincoln replied artfully, his eyes twinkling.

"I guess you do remember," I said. His words summed up the conundrum <u>unde malum</u>. How I wanted to say so! But, I restrained my anxious tongue.

Our brief conversation turned to the problem of reconstruction. He said he appreciated my views of reconciliation and expressed his desire for me to serve in his administration after the war ended, as a speech writer and aide. It was a cordial conversation holding much promise for the future.

I wandered up the hill and along the edge of the new cemetery. Most of the celebrants had departed, although some strolled slowly among the graves, heads hung low, eyes red with tears. I paused and stood silently among the freshly dug graves and white headstones set flush to the ground. There, the Lord brought to mind Lincoln's address and opened my heart to the Truth concerning the blood.

Revelation

Lincoln's address assures us that history will not forget Gettysburg and those three tragic days in July. And yet, as I consider his words, I must ask: what will future generations learn from them?

> ... But in a larger sense, we cannot dedicate—we cannot consecrate—we cannot hallow—this ground. The brave men, living and dead, who struggled here, have consecrated it, far above our poor power to add or detract...

Lincoln, like John Brown and Webster before him, called our attention to the sacrificial offering of the "honored" dead's blood. But will their sacrifice, offered in behalf of the Union, bring reconciliation and deliverance for our national sins against the black race?

I say no! This land cannot be purged with the blood of men! It is true, we cannot "dedicate," "consecrate," or "hallow" the ground. But neither can the "honored" dead! Only the blood of Christ can purge men of their sin and its evil fruits; only the blood of Christ can purge this land, this ground, of its bloodguiltiness.

We have accepted the Devil's lie, rejecting God's marvelous provision in the blood of Christ. Do the rows of white headstones mark a savior's grave? Or do they mark only the graves of mortals who will not rise again until their final judgment at the last trumpet?

> ... that we here highly resolve that these dead shall not have died in vain—that this nation, under God, shall have a new birth of freedom...

If the deaths of these men mean anything, it is that a race of people has been freed from over two hundred years of bondage. And we should not take this benefit lightly. But we as a people are not free. We can have no "new birth of freedom" in this bloodied Nation until we corporately and individually yield ourselves to the living Christ. Instead we have yielded to our lower natures and contracted with the Devil. We have slipped more deeply into bondage because of our hatred. I fear we shall now be bound with even stronger cords of self-deception.

O Rebel Hearts, Sons of the South, see how dark is that root of sin, your pride and your peculiar institution called slavery!

The Spring from which we now drink is most Bitter and the Cry of the Blood has become deafening to those who have ears to hear. Gettysburg's ground has not become hallowed, but profaned, now crying with a voice louder than the death shouts of those tens of thousands who perished in battle.

Pushing his dinner plate to the side, Fletcher swiveled on his stool and faced the pile of mail at the other end of the counter. The pile was six inches deep and a foot across. He'd been shrugging off the task for over a week, letting it build up into a small mountain. He pulled it across the counter and began sorting—junk and advertisements to the left, bills and letters to the right.

His thoughts drifted back to Mark and Katie's cozy study, to the fireplace and the antique sword, to the leather-bound journals and the fabulous antique desk. He could see each of the details clearly, down to what type of clothes Mark and Katie had worn, how Katie had pulled her hair back into a loose braid.

Fletcher sighed as he continued to sort the mail. The terrible feeling of emptiness from Melissa's and Susan's absence, activated once again by his time with the MacDonalds, returned to batter him.

He tossed the last piece of junk mail to the side and slipped off the stool. He popped open the refrigerator and grabbed a Coke. In his heart of hearts, Fletcher knew that something outside his everyday experience was at work inside him, softening hard places, making him feel vulnerable.

What it was he wasn't sure, but he knew it began with his first visit to the MacDonald's on Monday, when Katie shared about her brush with death and her miraculous healing. The feeling was reinforced during his conversation with Michelle at the deli Tuesday evening.

Here were people who had suffered through some tough trials, too. But what a different response! Instead of turning inward and internalizing their grief and their pain as he knew he had done, they claimed they had turned and yielded their lives to God. And even though Michelle was angry and had a score to settle, she had a soft spot that wanted what was right and best for others.

Fletcher passed through the kitchen and into the living room, snapping on the stereo. The gentle sounds of violins and cellos suddenly filled the room. He retreated to his sectional couch.

He leaned his head back onto the cushions, slipped off his shoes, swung up his legs and reflected on all that had happened the last seven days, all that he'd learned, all that he'd heard.

And strangely, for the first time since Susan had packed her bags and departed with Melissa for Iowa, he did not feel alone.

Katie slid beneath the covers.

Mark appeared in the door, standing in his new, oversized Washington Redskin boxer shorts, arms slightly raised and bent, muscles flexed in a classic weightlifter's pose.

His lightheartedness was a welcome relief from the soberness

Sam's writings had brought to their hearts. Katie couldn't help but chuckle. "Nice, honey. But for home viewing only. I wouldn't recommend them for the beach. They make your legs look skinny."

Mark grinned, relaxed his pose, picked up the iron poker and opened the fire screen. He prodded the logs. A golden spiral of sparks shot up the flue. He refused to let the images of the seven tombstones and names have any place in his thoughts.

He climbed onto the bed and across the blankets to Katie, burying his face in her neck. He kissed her, working his way softly across her shoulder.

Katie pulled back. "Sam might be watching from heaven."

Mark glanced up at the ceiling, then kissed her again. "Ah, yes, Sam would agree on the blessings of conjugality."

Punching him lightly in the arm, Katie sighed. "I'm glad you didn't live back then—what a pair you two would've made."

Mark's countenance stiffened. He rolled over onto his back. A puzzled look swept Katie's face. "What's the matter? Did I say something wrong?"

"No. You just got me thinking about Sam."

Katie patted Mark's chest. "Sam did take some pretty hefty shots at Lincoln."

Mark laid flat on his back and folded his hands behind his head. "But you know, Sam was right. We studied the Gettyburg Address from elementary school all the way through college and never once questioned it."

"Well—at least this entry ended on a positive note," Katie added, "President Lincoln offered Sam a position in his post-war cabinet."

Mark's eyes narrowed. "I guess it depends on how you want to look at it. I think history proved pretty unfair to Sam."

Katie rubbed her hand across Mark's chest. Before she could ask him what his last remark meant, the phone rang noisily, startling them.

Mark rolled over and grabbed it quickly. "Hello?"

"Hi, Mark?" asked a woman's voice.

"Yes, who is this?" Mark glanced at Katie and shrugged.

"Michelle Willoughby, from Agape Christian Fellowship. I hope I haven't called too late."

"Oh, hi—no problem. From the church? What can I do for you?"

"We've never been introduced, but we almost met—last Sunday. I sat in the row directly opposite you and your wife. Then, when we were in line waiting to leave, I was right behind you."

Mark thought back. He did remember an attractive young woman with short brown hair.

Michelle continued. "I'll be blunt. Kent and Dan are out of town for four days. They encouraged me to call you. I've already met with

Fletcher Rivers. I'd like to talk to you about the vandalism, and if you don't mind a little mystery, I'd prefer to talk in person rather than on the phone."

"Hold on a second." He explained the situation to Katie. She nodded and offered a suggestion.

"Katie wants you to come for dinner tomorrow night," Mark explained enthusiastically. "What time do you get off work?"

"Anytime between 5:00 and 6:00. But dinner? Are you sure?"

"We're sure. How about 5:30?"

"Sounds great. Thanks for accommodating me on short notice."

"Like I said, it's no problem. Do you know where we live?"

"Yes. Last townhouse on the end across from the park."

"Exactly."

"Well, thanks again. Good night."

Mark hung up the phone.

Katie slid over. She snuggled against his back and legs. "It'll be nice to meet someone else from the church."

Mark considered Michelle's comment.

If you don't mind a little mystery.

He reached over to the nightstand and gently yanked the braided tassel, turning off the lamp.

⪻ **30** ⪼

Thursday Morning

FLETCHER KNOCKED SOFTLY on Mrs. Grimwald's apartment door. He adjusted his tie and quickly rehearsed his lines. It was another risky but necessary move. The door cracked open a hand's breadth. Fletcher saw a puffy cheek, one red rimmed eye and disheveled, frizzy gray hair.

"Who are you? Police?"

Fletcher smiled and displayed his badge. "Yes, Ma'am. Sorry to bother you so early."

Her face moved behind the narrow opening.

"I imagine you've had enough of the police, probably up to here." Fletcher raised his badge and held it level with his eyes. "And in part, that's why I'm here. I'm with Internal Affairs. Speaking plainly, Mrs. Grimwald, I police the police. It's my job to make sure that suspects are given a fair trial. Make sure there's been no rough stuff, that kind of thing, from our side."

Fletcher watched Mrs. Grimwald's face as he spoke. From the narrowing of her gaze he could tell she was carefully weighing his words. She would either help or shut the door in his face.

"Just a second," she said in a monotone, disappearing as she walked away from the door.

She returned moments later, stuck her hand out through the crack in the door and held out a key. "Up the stairs. Apartment number two."

Fletcher thanked her and took the key.

Mrs. Grimwald brought her face close to the door. "While you're poking around up there, if you find any money, it's mine. Wertman owes me three weeks' rent. But if you find a silver and blue sports bag, take it. It's yours."

"Mine? How's that, Ma'am?" Fletcher asked, pausing on the step and turning to face her.

"The day before Wertman was arrested, I let two detectives in his apartment. They left it behind."

Two familiar faces popped up in Fletcher's mind's eyes. "Wouldn't have been a tall black woman and a really big guy that looked like a football player?" he asked nonchalantly, turning the key over in his hand.

Through the crack in the door, he could see Mrs. Grimwald nod.

Fletcher grinned and waved, then bounded up the stairs. On the second floor landing there were two rooms, one on the left and one on the right. KC and Troy. A gym bag. On Monday.

Secured across the door to the left were two yellow plastic strips with big black words that read: Police Line Do Not Cross.

Fletcher walked up to the wooden door and slipped the key into the lock. If KC and Troy had been inside and planted evidence, then where had Harold been on Monday? From the case notes Botello had given him, most of the evidence was found in plain view. Had Harold returned home, he would have discovered that he was being framed.

Ducking under the yellow strip, Fletcher slipped inside, quickly closing the door behind him.

The apartment was a one-room efficiency: kitchen on the left, separated from the living room by a long bar-like counter. Furnishings were sparse: a sagging forest green sofa, a bean bag chair, a crate with a lamp on it. Grungy yellow curtains hung crookedly over the two windows. Opposite the couch were eight feet of books lining the far wall.

He entered the kitchen area. On the long bar separating the kitchen from the living area was a cereal box, a plastic bowl, and a spoon. Beside the spoon was a felt-tipped pen with its cap off. Empty, crumpled soft drink cans and crumbs of varying size and shape littered the counter by the refrigerator. Lying in the sink were a few odd pieces of dirty silverware. It was a spartan lifestyle, to say the least.

As Fletcher turned around, the left curtain moved slightly. Was the window open? He crossed the living room. Kneeling down, he edged back the curtain and felt a stream of cold air on his face.

The window was open four to five inches. It had no lock, but the position of two deep indentations in the wooden sill indicated that leverage had been required to open it. Peering closely at the indentations, Fletcher could tell they were fresh. But how fresh? Were the marks made before or after Harold Wertman's arrest or the subsequent search of his apartment by the police?

As he let the curtain drop back into place, a gust of wind slammed violently into the window, billowing the curtains and into his face. Off-balance and surprised, Fletcher fell straight backward, crashing into the row of books against the wall and then plopping heavily to the floor, his tie flung over his shoulder, his legs spread wide in a V.

Fletcher pushed himself erect. The feel of cool smooth paper under his left hand made him glance down.

In falling backward against the row of books, he had knocked the end of the pile away from the wall. The book on the far right end had popped open. He stared at the open page. On it were two old photographs and a title: The Harper's Ferry Raiders. Harper's Ferry. The name sounded familiar.

Fletcher picked up the black hardcover book, slipping two fingers between the pages to hold his place at the photographs. He read the gold leaf lettering on the spine.

To Purge This Land with Blood. A biography of John Brown, the abolitionist who had attempted to rouse the slaves into rebellion at the small town of Harper's Ferry.

The flap of cloth and cool air brushing his face snapped his attention back to the situation at hand. He tucked the book under his arm, then crossed the room to the front door, opening it slowly and peeking out into the hall.

The hallway was clear.

Michelle opened the blue file folder.

It was time to resume placing her calls to the remaining State Corporation Commission offices on her list. Yesterday afternoon, she was able to make good headway, working through the alphabet all the way to Illinois.

Glancing down at the blue folder, Michelle moved the thin, stapled stack of canceled $50,000 checks to one side, exposing her three-page computer printout listing the fifty states and their associated Commission offices. She had already discovered the states in which two of the seven companies had been incorporated—Florida and Delaware—and been given the names and phone numbers of those two companies' corporate agents.

Michelle sat back and frowned. As significant as her discoveries appeared on the surface, after calling the corporate agents she had run into a dead-end. Both agents, one a man, the other a woman, had given her the same reply: the corporation was being run by "undisclosed principals."

Undisclosed principals! Legitimate and impenetrable, the legal mechanism kept the corporation's controlling interests' identity a secret. However, the information was still useful. It confirmed her belief that Parallax, Harbinger Ltd., and the other five companies that had received payments of $100,000 had something to hide. She picked up the telephone and looked at the next state—Indiana. Though she feared each of the remaining five companies would only lead to more undisclosed principals, she had to try.

Michelle sat up straight as the outer door of the secretarial area adjacent to her private office opened. She kept her eyes level, avoiding the open folder and its contents.

Julie waved and disappeared to her desk around the corner. "I'm glad that's over with," she said, her chair squeaking as she sat down. "I really don't like working that crazy switchboard."

Michelle's shoulders sagged with relief. She hung up the phone and closed the folder.

The squeak of a chair preceded Julie's appearance in the doorway. Julie crossed her arms in front of her sweater dress, her eyes meeting Michelle's squarely. "Are you all right? You've cloistered yourself with those files for almost two days."

Michelle grinned, folding her hands.

Julie sighed. "Let's be honest, OK? From the things you've shared with me and all the checks and files you've asked me to dig up for you, I have a good idea what you're doing. Why you're doing it, I don't know."

Michelle felt the Holy Spirit's gentle prodding. Julie needed to know the whole story, not just bits and pieces. Anne and her abortion. AFI's corruption. Everything. "Tell you what, when I get back from my dinner engagement tonight, I'll tell you what I am working through."

With a smile and a nod of her head, Julie put her hand on the door and started to back away—nearly colliding with Mr. Peters.

Michelle's hands froze above the stack of cancelled checks. The Commission Office report was to her right—and in plain view.

Mr. Peters put one hand on Julie's shoulder and stopped her from retreating. He smiled at Julie. "Just one question…"

He turned his attention abruptly to Michelle. "Have you spoken to the police department about the clinic vandalism and offered information outside of your job responsibilities?"

Prickles ran along Michelle's forehead and down the sides of her face. She forced her eyes to stay level with his as the pointed question tried to burrow through her conscience and expose her.

She couldn't admit she'd spoken to Fletcher——but if she hesitated a second longer, she would not have to admit to anything, her faltering would answer for her!

Mark looked out over the park and statue of Cardinal James Gibbons, then beyond to the vacant church. The irony! His eyes followed the familiar, steady flow of traffic on 16th Street to the Crest Road Clinic. Only two days had passed since Harold Wertman's arrest, and it was business as usual once again for the busiest abortuary in the District. Thinking about what transpired behind those gray stone walls darkened his countenance and soberly brought to mind several passages from Sam's last journal entry.

His next journal, however, would have to wait a few hours. Katie had already planned their day: eat breakfast and then head out early to the Smithsonian Air and Space Museum.

"We can read Sam this afternoon," she'd said as they'd made the bed. "But this morning we're going to get out and do something. I've never been to the Air and Space Museum."

Mark didn't argue.

Their trip earlier in the week to the Jefferson Memorial and Lincoln Memorial had been fun. Next in line—the Washington Monument—another place she'd never been.

A gray and white spotted pigeon landed adroitly on the head of Cardinal Gibbon's statue, catching Mark's eye. Seeing the statue reminded him of Sam and his world of the 1860s.

Mark allowed his head to dip forward against the cold window pane. Sam's world: seven and a half painful years had passed, compared to only seven and a half days in his own!

And how violent were those years, not counting the war. Arsons, murders and lynchings often went unpunished. Men, women, and children were sold on public auction blocks. A horse had more legal rights than a black man!

Compared to the present, life in nineteenth-century America was brutal and unforgiving.

Or was it?

The hair on the nape of Mark's neck stood on end.

He lifted his head from the window, his eyes moving from the pigeon and statue of Cardinal Gibbons back across 16th Street to the grim stone building on the corner. A young teenage girl, a hot pink backpack slung over one shoulder, strolled up its long sidewalk toward the front door.

Two worlds a century and a half apart collided in a bloody mist of revelation as two Latin words resonated loudly through his thoughts.

Julie's face fell as Michelle answered Mr. Peters.

"Yes, I did," Michelle said as casually as she could. All she could do was hope that Mr. Peters' own startled reaction kept him from noticing Julie's.

"When I went to the clinic last Thursday morning to meet with the insurance company about the vandalism, I spoke with the nurse and the two policemen. I told them that I didn't think that the pro-lifers that Nurse Rollins was accusing would be that blatantly violent just a couple weeks before their annual march."

Michelle folded her hands over the cancelled checks and tried to ignore the implications of Mr. Peter's visit and question.

"Was my comment out of line? I hope I didn't say something that confused the investigators."

Mr. Peters cleared his throat and quickly composed himself. "No, I think not. You're very close to the clinic situation. I'm just reminding everyone involved that all information about the vandalism is highly confidential.

"That will be all. Continue on with whatever you're doing."

❦ 31 ❦

Thursday Afternoon

THE PARKING SPACE DIRECTLY ACROSS THE STREET from the Greek deli was empty. Fletcher smiled, spinning the steering wheel sharply to the left and making a quick U-turn at the intersection.

His morning had gone well, beginning with his discovery that KC and Troy had been in Wertman's apartment and Mrs. Grimwald's disclosure of the gym bag.

Unbuckling his seatbelt, Fletcher thought about his stop in the park to deliver food to Larry and Glenn. Since Jimmy's death, their relationship had changed. In the past seven days he had spent more time with Larry and Glenn than he had in the last year. Their conversations had taken a more intimate turn. Hearing Larry tell about his fall from Superintendent of Public Works into two decades of depression and alcoholism had been painful.

As Larry's balding head drooped lower with every downturn in his story, Fletcher saw clearly that in transferring the anger and pain of alienating his wife and daughter into concern for Jimmy, he had been compulsive and selfish. He had satisfied his own internalized sense of failure, never considering Larry's and Glenn's deep-seated hurts and lack of self-worth. Trading money and food for information that made him a successful detective had been the foundation of his concern, not care or compassion.

How mercenary he'd become! His attempts at goodness and kindness had gone awry, twisted into something divisive by his own inadequacies and misdirected motives. Guilt, not love, had been the driving force behind his attachment to Jimmy.

Fletcher sat back as tears gathered in the corners of his eyes. He leaned across the seat and scooped up the stuffed yellow mailer and the book with one hand, then shut the car door with his elbow.

Mark handed Sam's journal to Katie, and then returned to his arm chair near the fireplace. The burning logs had warmed the parlor quickly upon their return from the museums and a walk across the Mall. Gusting winds had chilled them to the bone.

251

"Here's journal number nine. There're only two left."

Katie pushed herself into the corner of the couch and crossed her legs. She opened the brown leather journal and glanced at the first page. "Oh my!"

Mark slouched down in the arm chair, folding his arms. "Hey— you're the one who complained about me stopping to read ahead."

Katie grinned. "You'll like how Sam opens—"

"Honey!"

"I've been waiting for this the last two entries—"

"Wife!"

Katie, keeping her eyes glued to the page, held back her laugh. She rubbed the end of her nose, then began to read.

Christmas Eve 1863, 3:30 P.M.
Old Mill Crossroads

"Sam, I don't want you to leave, but it is not appropriate for us to continue living under the same roof."

Elizabeth's unexpected words last evening pierced my heart. I have benefitted from this arrangement more than Elizabeth. In this world, a woman's reputation is more easily tarnished than a man's. I have taken advantage of her kind hospitality, deceiving myself, I suppose, with the flawed argument that she and the children could not handle the farm without me. I failed to discern how "inappropriate" she has thought my prolonged stay to be, although nothing inappropriate ever occurred.

O Lord, what is Your will in this matter? It is indeed a delicate situation with Elizabeth. And concerning Angelina, should I adopt her? I know that she desires it to be so.

Lord, guide me in these matters.

The December ground is lightly dusted with snow. I am reminded of my wintry heart, made cold by the loss of my dear Victoria over ten years ago. My heart has begun to thaw, warmed by the affections of Elizabeth, Thomas Peter, and that special child, Angelina.

I see a wagon approaching up the Baltimore Pike, accompanied by what appear to be three Union cavalrymen. Why would they visit our farm today, on Christmas Eve? The images evoke poignant memories of a fall day a little over a year ago, when we learned of John Ezra's death and when You, Lord, tilled the soil of my heart.

Elizabeth, Thomas Peter, and Angelina call with one voice. What a cheerful racket! I must lay down my pen and see what develops.

The Grace of God

Twenty-four hours have passed.

Lord, how shall I compose my joyous thoughts? Should I not let the account of those first moments tell their own story?

"Sam, Sam, come down right now!" Angelina had clamored, wrestling me from my chair to the top of the stairs.

What a sight! Framed by the doorway and backlit by the late afternoon sun, I beheld John Ezra wrapped tightly in Elizabeth's arms! Behind him stood a Union officer.

I bounded down the steps two at a time as she buried her face in his neck with tears of joy streaming down her cheeks.

"We thought you were dead!"

John smiled as he glanced down at his wife's deliriously happy face. "I thought I was dead, too. But it wasn't God's time for me—as it was not God's time for you. My wife tells me God's grace and a sturdy horse saved you from a life-threatening wound and brought you here."

For several moments, the room grew quiet. Thomas Peter clung to his father's arm. Elizabeth struggled with a question that would not make its way through her tears. She seemed overcome.

"What happened?" I inquired, sensing what she wanted to ask. "How could a year pass with no one knowing you were alive?"

"There was a mix-up, to say the least. The army believed that I had died at Bull Run—blown to pieces by a Confederate cannon."

John coughed and wheezed. "Instead, I was taken prisoner at Manassas Junction. They took me to Richmond, to Libby Prison where they packed a thousand of us into an old tobacco warehouse."

The Union officer patted John Ezra on the shoulder and looked to Elizabeth. "Captain MacDonald's a real fighter, ma'am. Most men wouldn't have made it. Then again, seein' what he had waitin' for him I can understand why he didn't give up."

John coughed again and nodded. The officer saluted him, then turned and let himself out the door.

I helped Elizabeth get John upstairs to bed, and then retreated to the kitchen.

A half hour later, Elizabeth came downstairs. She sat at the table beside me and gently touched my arm. "It's a miracle, Sam. The Lord has given me back my husband."

Her eyes still brimming with tears, Elizabeth drew close, kissed me on the cheek, then rose from the table and went back upstairs to be with John.

The company-wide memo from Mr. Peters arrived on Michelle's desk at noon. Its message was simple: all employees would attend Saturday's pro-choice counter-rally or be subject to disciplinary action.

Michelle crumpled the memo and tossed it into the trashcan.

Frowning, she dug into her skirt pocket and pulled out two quarters for the soft drink machine.

As she did, she thought about Mr. Peters' question and whether or not he believed her answer. At least she only received a stupid memo and not a pink slip!

Pumping her quarters into the drink machine, she glanced at the poster on the wall—the same poster she had seen last week in the conference room. Legacy, a heavy-metal band noted for its controversial lyrics, would be performing at the AFI weekend counter-rally Saturday at the foot of the Washington Monument. The concert was being promoted by AFI and Parallax—one of the seven companies she was investigating.

She used her fist to make her selection. It still remained to be seen if she would be continuing her investigation—or be out on the street looking for a new job.

Michelle pulled the soft drink from the machine and then glanced at her watch—3:30. Only two hours to go until she met with Mark and Katie. She knew her carefully fashioned, liberal feminist alter-ego was just about ready to fall completely apart.

And what of the vow she made to herself to avenge her sister and expose AFI? The deeper she dug, the more she realized the scenario had changed. If she still had her job—Mr. Peters could be pulled down. Unfortunately, AFI could survive his scandalous behavior by denouncing him as a spirited anarchist with a private agenda. Once the political and criminal fallout had settled, AFI would continue its deceptive onslaught against the American family.

"Anne! I'm so sorry!"

Michelle popped open her drink and blinked her tears away.

KC slipped into Troy's office and closed the door behind her. She walked straight to his desk, slammed her hand down on the corner and accidentally knocked a tall stack of his file folders to the floor. There was anger in her eyes. And fear.

"What were you thinking about when you called the Sponsors? Now they'll know you've been following up on them."

Troy looked at the jumbled pile of papers by his feet, then at KC. He met her gaze squarely, then shrugged. "That's exactly the point I wanted to make! We're not his lackeys."

KC backed away, her lips tightening into a thin line.

Troy noticed her rigid stance. "Relax. Now he knows we're not playing games. He's agreed to pay us off—tomorrow night, at the Bayou. Seven o'clock sharp."

He rose from his chair and stepped around the desk. "Everything's OK, believe me. It's all over—for both of us. We're out of it. For good."

Troy smiled. "Come on, brighten up! I've saved the best news for last. A little birdie told me the Review Board's going to grant Jamal parole next week. He's as good as out."

He cupped her chin in his huge hand and kissed her.

13 June 1864, 5:30 P.M.
Charleston, South Carolina

In the five months following John's return, he has slowly recovered his strength. When Mr. Pitkins' letter arrived two and a half weeks ago, John planted his fists on his hips and insisted that he and Elizabeth were capable of handling the farm without me. I thank You, Lord, for permitting the letter from Mr. Pitkins to miraculously find its way to Adams County.

Accuser of the Brethren

Leaving Old Mill Crossroads was difficult. I prepared myself to reenter Charleston, a bitter fountain of rebellion and Beaumont's diabolical den, by reading of Paul's return to Rome. I felt a kindred spirit with the Apostle Paul, as though destiny had appointed me to this journey, a man already in chains.

Now, looking out the small window in my cell, I see the Union fleet stretched across the rim of the harbor. Their floating batteries continue to bombard this indigent city with a vengeance. What an ironic contrast to that morning three years ago when the Confederates fired on Fort Sumter.

Mr. Pitkins informed me that Seth Beaumont's estate was among the first to be destroyed by the fierce cannonade. His letter related Victoria's mother's situation, how Mrs. Moore, having no heirs, had devised her real property estate to me. Beaumont immediately laid claim to Moore Hill, attaching the land by a judicial order as payment for a lien he claims to have placed several years ago for a bill never paid by Mr. Moore. There is no such lien. I checked the courthouse records myself three days ago.

Am I ambitious to possess Moore Hill? No! I simply decided that the time had come for the treacherous deception and thuggery of this evil man to be halted once and for all. Mr. Pitkins, who alleges that I still retain a good reputation, encouraged me to come swiftly. My article, "Behind Union Lines," was well received. When I arrived yesterday he paid me nearly two years back wages. He is such an honorable man. So I left the offices of The Observer in a happy mood, proceeding toward Broad Street to find temporary lodging until the dispute over the Moore estate could be settled.

As I stepped into the street, three men intercepted me, one at each elbow, the third in front of me.

At first I did not recognize Beaumont. He wore a patchy beard. His left ear was mangled and missing the lobe. The left side of his neck was withered and brown from a severe burn. His nose had obviously been broken and healed improperly; a dark pink scar stretched fully across his left cheek to the corner of a black patch that covered his left eye. His left arm hung limp and obviously useless.

His singular, hateful eye stared loathsomely into mine. It wasn't until he spoke that the face and voice matched his name. "MacDonald, I will have that land and you <u>will</u> hang for treason against the Confederacy <u>and</u> for the murder of Miss Elkin!"

That was eight hours ago. Now, the evening sun has set and I write by candlelight at a small wooden table in my cell. In two days I shall go before a judge to be charged with treason and murder. My accuser, Seth Beaumont, will make sure that I do not escape the hangman's noose a second time.

My sole regret is that I shall never again see Angelina, my daughter-to-be. May she continue to find comfort in the love of John, Elizabeth and Thomas Peter. O, Lord, grant me the faith that I might continue to love unconditionally, even Seth Beaumont who seeks my demise.

Forgive us our debts as we forgive our debtors.

⊰⊱ **32** ⊰⊱

Late Thursday Afternoon

T RUE BELIEVER SLAMMED THE DOOR OF HIS PENTHOUSE. He was dressed in black—shoes, slacks, turtleneck, leather jacket and gloves—with his hair pulled back into a ponytail. He hit the down button by the elevator, the muscles in his face taut, his dark gray eyes seething with anger.

He could not fathom Detective Martin's stupidity! The complications his telephone call created were staggering. Friday's highly structured and critically timed activities didn't allow for a meeting at the Bayou! How foolish was the faithless American, breaking protocol, demanding payment and damnably worse—tracing Kim's phone number, then locating and searching her apartment! Now there were two couples True Believer would have to deal with—the detectives and the MacDonalds.

A small bell sounded and the elevator doors slid open.

He stepped inside and pounded the button for the lower parking level, his already stormy countenance darkening the harsh red line that stretched from the corner of his mouth to the corner of his left eye.

16 June 1864
Charleston, South Carolina

Three days ago, while waiting for my trial to begin, I took comfort in the Bible's account of Paul and Silas in jail. Hearing footsteps, I closed my Bible and stood up. My time had come. To my surprise, I saw not only the deputy, but Seth Beaumont, his officer's cloak slung over one arm. The deputy let him inside.

Seth looked awful. The flesh around his good eye was dark and puffy, as if he had not slept. His hair was matted to his head. A dirty lock curled down onto his eye patch. The long diagonal pink scar on his cheek seemed hot, infected. His Confederate grays were stained with grease and food. He reeked with the smell of liquor and an acrid scent emanated from his clothing.

"MacDonald, I must have a few words with you before the trial," he said, his eye avoiding mine.

I replied with a nod of my head. The moment was most peculiar. His voice was cold and angry. The anxious expression on his face belied an emotion that I could not readily distinguish.

He crossed the cell and leaned heavily against the opposite wall. His movements were sluggish. I was tempted to hate him but God's grace prevailed. The Spirit of God pierced me with pity.

His eye met mine. "My time is short. Grant me, MacDonald, a chance to speak."

I was dumbfounded and sat down on my cot. My action seemed to please him. He bobbed his head. A thin, pale smile formed briefly, then vanished.

"I've hated you from the day you set foot in Charleston."

I flinched at his straightforward words.

He grimaced, pulling his gimpy arm and cloak tightly to his body. "Now, I'm going to tell you why." He took a labored breath, looked directly at me, and spoke.

"I loved Victoria Moore."

My shoulders sagged. The dream of Victoria's tumbling wagon lashed through my mind. I remembered the image of Beaumont standing beside his dark-haired companion.

"Yes, I loved her since she was a child. I always fancied us getting married someday. She was only sixteen when I left Charleston in '46 to fight the Mexicans, and when I returned a decorated hero in '49, old man Moore had packed up his family and headed west to find his fortune in gold. Victoria was gone from my life forever. But then in the spring of '50 she returned—only you, MacDonald, were with her!"

Beaumont's eye narrowed, the sides of his neck and cheeks shading red. "It was wrong enough that she didn't marry a true Southerner, but to use her father's influence with the state legislature to approve the release of her slaves—well, that made my blood boil! I couldn't allow such a thing!"

The foul vengeance in his voice faded abruptly. His eye filled with tears. "I always loved her, MacDonald, believe me! I never meant for her to die! You can't imagine the pain of seeing her with you. She was the one hope I had of pulling myself out of the mess I had made of my life and of restoring honor and decency to the Beaumont family!

"I knew Victoria was a religious woman. That's why I sang at the top of my lungs every Sunday. I wanted her to notice me, to think I was religious, too, like her. Don't you remember how I sat behind both of you in church? Even after she was married to you, I still loved her.

"When I met her on the road that day, it was just to talk, that's all. I encouraged her to leave you and return to her Southern roots. We had words; I got upset. I don't know why but I fired my revolver in the air. The horses bolted and Victoria's wagon ended up in the ravine. I rode down to help her but she was dead! Beautiful Victoria, dead! I was scared—scared, bitter and angry—angry at myself, angry at her, angry at you, and angry at God for ruining my life!"

He trembled violently. His bitterness and jealousy had killed Victoria and robbed me of a wife. In my mind's eye I imagined him riding away from the overturned wagon, his face as grief-stricken as it was now.

In my spirit, I knew the time had come for the truth. So I asked Beaumont about the scar-faced man.

The corner of his mouth began to twitch. "How do you know about him?"

I told him about my letter from Mrs. Doyle and Father Gibault's account of John Brown's hanging. I recounted my dream, how I saw Victoria's tumbling wagon, how he and the scar-faced man watched on horseback from the edge of the ravine. And finally, of that day in Jackson's camp when Beaumont sought to have me hanged the first time for stealing General Lee's orders.

Beaumont's countenance darkened. Leaning back into the corner, he slumped slowly to the floor, dropping his cloak into his lap. I remained motionless on my cot.

He raised his good arm and hand, lightly running a quivering finger along the dull scar on his left cheek. His eye met mine briefly, and then closed. Horror swept his face. He clenched his teeth, and then opened his eye, forcing himself to look directly at me.

"Sam, don't hate me for what I've done."

For the next quarter hour, he wept like a troubled child. From his mouth poured forth an excessively emotional and disjointed account of his ruinous family history. What follows is my straightforward recounting of his story, his flood of tears and tortured expressions set aside.

Seth's Bloodlines

He began his story in 1675. He spoke in detail of several Beaumont generations. His ancestors include a pirate, a slave runner, a wealthy Charleston plantation owner with over two thousand slaves, and his grandfather, a mean spirited politician. Seth's father, a veteran of the War of 1812, died prematurely in 1822, killed in a scuffle with one of his own slaves. The slave was lynched that very afternoon—a lynching Seth would never forget.

That same afternoon, Seth's twelve-year-old uncle, Nicolas-Eugene, a stowaway on a French frigate, set foot on Charleston's docks.

Seth's mother was frightened when Nicolas appeared at the lynching.

As Seth thumped the horse's rear and sent the slave to his death, he remembered catching a glimpse of his young uncle's face. Seth did not describe exactly what he had seen that day, but as he rubbed his hand over his left cheek, I could tell that whatever it had been still had power over him.

Seth's mother refused to give Nicolas a place in her home, a decision which Seth did not understand. And for several months following her half-brother's arrival, she was plagued with severe fits of depression. When Seth asked about her unhappiness, her half-brother, or her family in Paris, Seth's mother refused to answer. Her countenance would darken and an acute nervousness would overtake her. Her formerly cheerful disposition never completely returned.

Nicolas left Charleston in 1822 and headed west. Fourteen years passed before the two met again. Nicolas, a vocal southern sympathizer, worked under the guise of a gambler with his own private riverboat. He ran the Mississippi from New Orleans to St. Louis, serving the violent interests of wealthy men and organizations whose existence depended on the availability of Negro labor. He gleaned huge profits for threatening and beating abolitionists, Northern sympathizers, and conductors for the Underground Railroad, and for burning their houses and businesses and hunting down runaway slaves.

It was only a year later, in 1837, when Seth and Nicolas conceived their diabolical plan.

After being involved in the attack and murder of a prominent black abolitionist printer, Elijah Lovejoy, from Alton, Illinois, they observed how effective carefully selected violence could enrage large sections of the population, either North or South.

They quickly put their plan into motion: find a radical abolitionist, fuel his political and social fires, further inflame the South against the North and create a bloody breach that would further divide the nation and insure the creation of a Confederacy.

Shortly afterwards, Nicolas and Seth met John Brown.

Playing the part of an abolitionist, Nicolas became a go-between for several monied backers. He worked behind the scenes with Brown for a number of years, encouraging him toward violence and bloodshed as a means of freeing the slaves. It was Nicolas who gave John Brown the idea that the nation could not be purged but with much bloodshed.

A Heart of Darkness

Beaumont finished the story. The dark circle around his eye seemed to deepen. He tossed his coat from his arm. To my surprise, he clutched two ragged-edged journals.

"Sam, these are yours."

My surprise turned to shock. My journals? Then I remembered. My journals had disappeared on my return trip from the hanging of John Brown!

He studied my reaction and nodded. "You wonder why I have them, don't you? The answer is quite simple. My uncle was there for Brown's hanging. He recognized you—even after six years, from when you lived in Charleston, South Carolina."

Again, Beaumont carefully watched my reaction. I sat silent and immobile on my bunk. My hands and feet felt as if they had been nailed down. Had Seth's uncle ridden with him the day of Victoria's death?

"My uncle saw the priest approach you at the hanging. He followed you to the chapel. He figured that you were a journalist of some kind. After you left the chapel, he followed you again to the hotel, and, the next morning, onto the train for Baltimore. Absconding with your journals was child's play."

I listened but could not fathom any logical explanation for his uncle's actions. Why steal my journals?

Beaumont spoke slowly.

"Four nights ago I found my uncle dead in his hotel room. He'd shot himself in the head with a revolver. He was slumped over his desk... and over your journals."

Beaumont wore a pained expression. The lines in his face were raw, harsh. "After I buried him, I came back and cleaned out his valuables, including the journals. Read 'em myself. It's irony! It was in your journal where I finally learned the truth that my mother kept hidden to her dying day, the truth about her family. The old French priest's story helped me finally understand why my mother despised and rejected Nicolas."

I was taken back by an incalculable sadness in his words.

"Sam, that's why I'm asking you... begging you... to forgive me for what happened to..."

His voice faltered for a moment. He swallowed hard. "What happened to Victoria. Read the letter. I stuck it in here..."

He tapped the top journal with his finger. Strangely, his eye now seemed to be pleading with me.

"In this world I've received my just rewards, and being here with you, I'm still receiving them. Only God knows what reward I'll receive when I pass beyond the veil."

Beaumont began to shake all over. He bent at the waist and reached into his boot, pulling out a revolver. He raised his head. I gasped. The scar on his left cheek seemed to flame bright red.

I felt the palpable presence of evil, like an oppressive summer heat. Never before had I experienced the demonic so strongly, so intimately, so physically. Sweat popped out across my brow and trickled down my nose. I did not move, but pleaded silently to God that His will be done and not the Devil's.

As if responding to my prayer, Beaumont relaxed. Slowly, he lowered the revolver, staring incredulously at it, as if it had a life of its own.

Seth's moment of decision had come. My spirit responded to God's prompting. "Seth Beaumont, choose this day whom you will serve. As a boy you first yielded to your hatred when you helped to hang that slave. You've heard the truth of the gospel—yield now to Christ's Lordship. Only His blood can save you."

A frightful shriek unlike anything I had ever heard before broke from his lips. I heard the jailer shout for help as he ran down the hall toward my cell.

Seth's eye glazed over. He raised his pistol and placed it against his temple.

"No!" I shouted. "In the name of Jesus, no!"

In that instant, I thought my eyes were blurring. I saw a strange double image of two Beaumonts sitting in front of me, one clinging to the other. Beaumont squeezed the trigger and the pistol sounded painfully in the tiny cell. He slumped to his side, the pistol still clutched in his hand, the journals across his lap.

My heart pounded as a shadowy, human-like figure hovered over him, staring me straight in the eye, its mouth twisted into a hideous mocking smile. Across its opaque left cheek was a long, diagonal scar.

The jailer threw open the cell door. His assistant was in the hall behind him with a shotgun. They watched in shock as the apparition passed through the wall of the jailhouse and disappeared from sight. This is the truth as I saw it, and not only I, but the jailer and his assistant. Later that day, they presented their testimony about Seth Beaumont's suicide to the magistrate. Their testimony regarding the ghastly appearance of a demon spirit, coupled with Beaumont's letter in which he rescinded his accusations against me for treason and confessed to the murder of Miss Elkin, secured my freedom.

I was released and all of my belongings were returned to me, including the two journals that Seth had brought into the cell with him.

A Secret Revealed

I now sit alone in the Moore house.

I understand why Mrs. Doyle saw a scar-faced man in Kansas, why Father Gibault saw a scar-faced man beneath the gallows at John Brown's hanging. It was Nicolas, the man with Beaumont at Victoria's death, the man with Beaumont at Jackson's camp.

On the table nearby lay my stolen journals, stained with Seth's and Nicolas' blood. On the pages at the end of the journal, following the account of my meeting with Father Gibault, Beaumont's uncle wrote about his own tragic bloodline. All has become clear at last.

History has opened itself and yielded up a dark secret.

Nicolas was the son of Henri Sanson, the son of Charles-Henri Sanson, chief executioner of Paris. Henri, on that January day in 1793, lifted the king's decapitated head from the basket and paraded it around the scaffold for all to see.

Henri, Charles-Henri, and four generations of Sansons before them—over two hundred years—have been human instruments of torture and governmentally-sanctioned death. Nicolas sought to escape his heritage, hoping to find refuge in the home of his older stepsister, Seth's mother. His hopes were dashed. Seth's mother had fled France, like Nicolas, fearing that if she bore a son, he too would share in the Sanson's bloody heritage. Nicolas' arrival in Charleston in 1822 only revived her fears. Unable to bear even the sound of his name, she rejected him and turned him out into the streets.

The Beaumonts, unlike the MacDonalds, were a two-fold cord of godless strands. Both of us had murderers in our family lines, but Seth had no one in his line who had experienced the cleansing, redemptive work of Christ. Without an Advocate to plead their cause before the Accuser, a heritage of sin passed from one generation to the next.

And except through the blood of Christ, Seth never had a chance.

I believe he knew that the crimson scar on Nicolas' cheek manifested a frightening and dark reality. The scar had not been drawn by man's instruments, but by an indwelling presence, a demonic spirit who inhabited the Sanson line for generations. The spirit came to this country with a singular hunger, like that of his master, the Devil, to shed blood. Lord, whence has that spirit fled? And what evil shall that Devilish prince yet contrive against me, now that I have discerned his identity?

Michelle walked up the steps onto the MacDonald's front porch. She knocked twice on the door.

After waiting a half minute, she knocked again, this time a little harder. About the time she was going to knock a third time, the door creaked open.

"Oh, hi. You must be Michelle. Hope you haven't been knocking too long. Katie and I were upstairs, reading," Mark said, stepping back and running a hand through his short hair. "Come on in."

Michelle wasn't sure what expression rippled across Mark's face. "That's OK."

As she crossed the doorstep, a small gust of wind swirled up the front steps and across the porch behind her, darting inside around her ankles into the hall.

$\ll \gg$ **33** $\ll \gg$

Thursday Evening

FOR THE ENTIRE AFTERNOON Fletcher forgot that he was sitting in a Greek deli. From his place in the last booth, with his back to the busy counter, little interfered with his immersion into Stephen Oates' biography of John Brown and pre-Civil War America.

And the more he read, the harder it became to put the book down. John Brown was not only a schemer who had a penchant for using and losing other people's money—he was a determined and self-appointed soldier of God, a doomsayer who believed that it would be better for a whole generation of men, women, and children to die than for slavery to continue.

Fletcher shook his head. This compelling account of the person behind the headlines of history actually shed light on his own situation. His hypocrisy with Larry and Glenn had struck home even harder. Like John Brown, Fletcher realized that he had tried to convert his failures into more lofty motivations of self-sacrifice and heroic determination—ultimately at other people's expense.

Fletcher sat up straight in the booth, put his hands behind his head and stretched. While he was in the neighborhood, he would stop by the MacDonald's and see how they were doing, show Mark the biography.

Staring thoughtfully out the window, Fletcher noticed but did not register the broad-shouldered, blond-headed man sitting on a bench at the bus stop. The man ignored the cold, hands folded casually in his lap, eyes closed, wearing a most sublime smile.

Fletcher lowered his hands and rubbed them together, then turned his attention back to *To Purge This Land With Blood.*

Mark would enjoy the book, he was sure of it.

"So it was you I saw heading up the walk to the clinic last Thursday morning," Katie said with a look of revelation, returning her steak knife to her plate.

"Yes. I was upset because I knew something was wrong. What really upset me was the animal blood painted over the doorway, an obvious reference to the Passover and the angel of destruction—a contradiction in symbols. A swastika, I could believe. Pro-lifers like to compare Nazi Germany and the abortion industry."

Mark sipped his iced tea. "Your testimony supports the premise that the vandalism and bomb attempt has been a setup from the beginning."

Michelle stared momentarily at her plate and wiped the corner of her mouth with her napkin. She sighed. "I'm pretty close to blowing this thing open—if my boss doesn't catch on to what I'm doing and fire me first. When all's been said and done, I'm going to nail him on numerous violations and criminal charges. What hurts most is that AFI, as an organization, will be able to avoid culpability. I'll be long gone before I can complete the research needed for my exposé."

Mark glanced at the clock on the dining room wall. A quarter after six—it seemed that they had been talking for hours, not forty minutes!

Katie set her elbows on the table and folded her hands beneath her chin. "We appreciate your openness, sharing with us about Anne's situation."

"For the better part of three years, I've lived a dual life. Not everybody in the church agrees with what I'm doing. Dan and Kent said you'd be good for me, someone I could share with—come out of the closet with—so to speak. And to be perfectly honest, it's hard keeping up the charade."

Mark spoke up. "Earlier you mentioned that you met Fletcher Rivers. How's he doing, anyway?"

Katie rose from the table and gathered their empty plates. "Let's move this conversation to the front room. How's that sound?"

By a quarter of seven the table was cleared. Katie and Michelle shared the couch. Mark sat on the corner of the warm hearth, facing them.

Michelle explained in detail about her and Fletcher's theory on the interconnections between Mr. Peters, Brian Fein and the seven companies. Peters had funneled hundreds of thousands of dollars to Fein. They believed that AFI was secretly backing a heavy metal band called Legacy, financing the attempted bombing of the clinic, buying off detective Troy Martin and a female undercover policewoman, and fronting Harold Wertman.

Mark thought back to his and Katie's discussion about Wertman being a pawn for others—how there might be a conspiracy developing right here in Washington. They had been right!

He propped his elbows on his knees and leaned forward. In his mind's eye he saw Sam, sitting on a low wall at the hanging of John Brown. At that time, Sam had not seen the connections between

Nicolas Sanson and Seth Beaumont, and how they were behind John Brown and his failed insurrection to create a bloody rebellion throughout the South.

But that was just the visible layer of a more frightening conspiracy —as Father Gibault's story had revealed. The old man, the Devil, had come from France to America to use a conflict of government to draw his line of blood through the heart of the nation and the Christian Church.

The result was a civil war and death on a catastophic scale.

The red pickup truck was right next to the dumpster just as his contact had promised. True Believer walked across the poorly-lit parking lot, his portable telephone clutched in his gloved hand.

True Believer knew his coming and going would go unnoticed and unrecorded. He opened the door to the truck, ran his hand over the floor under the seat and found the ignition key. The first step was complete. Now it was almost time to place the telephone call.

True Believer smiled and breathed in deeply at the raw excitement at having his plan back on target again.

He was in control, his mind and body working harmoniously toward one end. How many times had he experienced this rush of emotion? Fifty times? One hundred times?

Londonderry. Dublin. Belfast. London.

Soon that part of his past would be behind him forever.

Katie rose from the couch and started toward the kitchen. "Anyone want a refill?"

"I do," Mark said.

Michelle nodded as the telephone rang.

Mark glanced toward the kitchen. Moments later, Katie called out. "It's for you, honey. Someone from the police department."

Surprise flashed across his face as he placed the journal on the floor beside the hearth. He jumping to his feet.

Katie handed him the phone. "It's a Captain Williams."

Mark put the phone to his ear as he leaned back against the wall. "Yes, sir. What can I do for you?"

Katie turned away from the coffee pot to watch Mark's face. His anxiety faded.

"Yes sir, we can. What time?" He nodded. "Sure, that'll work just fine."

He nodded a second time. "Having someone meet us at the lobby sounds great to me. Thank you very much for the opportunity to present my side of things."

Mark grinned. "Right, I won't forget. 8:15 to 8:30, at the front desk. Bye."

Hanging up the phone, Mark took the tray from Katie and started for the living room. "Looks like we're going to get a chance to make our case. And the captain wants to hear it straight from the horses' mouths, so he's asked us to come down tonight."

"Tonight?"

"Yep. He said that too much was riding on this case to let things drag out another day. They've been working around the clock. He promised he'd only keep us for a half hour or so—once they got to us."

Mark set the tray on the table and looked at Michelle.

She rose to her feet. "I guess I should be leaving."

Thoughts of Ireland and the dream of his young cousins lying dead in a Londonderry gutter had plagued him for three consecutive nights.

As True Believer pulled the red pickup into an empty space on Crest Road adjacent to the church, he cut the engine, checked his watch, then looked up the street. His eyes darted to the row house, then to the vacant park.

Though he had been in the park early Saturday morning and stood directly in front of the statue, his focus had prevented him from paying much attention to it. But now...

... Nearby street lights illuminated the reclining figure of the priest, one hand upraised, the other clutching a crucifix close to his chest.

The crucifix!

True Believer gripped the steering wheel as a severe sadness stabbed into the center of his soul. He leaned forward and lowered his head onto his whitening knuckles.

His cousin had died clutching a crucifix to her chest! Waves of sorrow spilled through his heart as he remembered the dark stain on the front of Coleen's pale blue sweater. He had knelt at her side, unable to staunch the flow of blood. Her life had drained away right before his eyes.

Now, at the pinnacle of his career, when he would at last regain his freedom from Bonn and her order, a young man by the name of Mark MacDonald jeopardized it all!

The agony in True Believer's heart flared painfully. He would have his freedom! He had worked too hard to have his opportunity for personal liberty sabotaged by Mark MacDonald, Troy Martin— anyone! It had taken him four years to cultivate his successful dual identity of Brian Fein, the successful music promoter whose independent net worth could approach one million dollars this coming year when Legacy made its first national tour.

He stared out the driver's window at the deserted church on his left and scowled bitterly. God had failed his father, and then his mother, allowing them to die without peace. Turning his attention back to the statue of the priest, to his upraised hand of blessing, to the crucifix clutched close to his chest, True Believer waited silently, yielding to his anger, smoldering like a red-hot coal about to burst into flame.

Fletcher carefully folded the yellowed newspaper page between the pages of *To Purge This Land with Blood.*

He ran his finger over the top of the book and touched the protruding edge of the folded newsprint. As he did, an electric sensation vibrated up his fingers and through his arm.

The word conspiracy flashed before his eyes like a storefront neon sign. He reached into his coat pocket for a ten dollar bill, and then tossed it onto the table by his tab as, one by one, faces appeared behind the flashing word.

Fein. Peters. Wertman. Daniels. Martin. The last face to pass by was Jimmy's. Jimmy and his wide smile, his bright eyes, his scruffy face. Jimmy was an unexpected stone that fell between the slowly turning cogs of the conspiracy's machinations, threatening its existence. The cogs had easily crushed the stone and disposed of the remains—all except for a barely discernible trail of dust.

Fletcher rose from the booth, staring momentarily at the biography. That trail of dust had ultimately led back to the cogs.

On the way out the door, Fletcher stopped and snapped his fingers. Mark and Katie—he'd almost forgotten!

He jogged to the corner and joined two elderly black women waiting for the light to turn red and for a pause in the crowded but quickly moving line of traffic.

Mark closed the front door behind him and smiled. Katie, her hands in the pockets of her red coat, waited at the edge of the porch under the light.

Michelle waved goodbye and crossed the street to her car.

Halfway down the walk, Mark stopped and turned around, Katie in tow. He stared up at the three-story Gothic structure with its conical roof, green fish-scale shingles and triple bay windows. The nearby street light cast shadows across its facade.

"Seems like the Lord's using this old house to bring a bunch of hurting people together... you and me, Michelle, Fletcher."

Katie pulled at Mark's arm and nodded.

They started back down the walk toward the street. Squeezing Katie's hand, Mark stopped at the curb directly across from their

Blazer as a line of cars hurried by from left to right to make the green light at the intersection of Crest and 16th.

The last car in the line of traffic passed by Mark and Katie Mac-Donald.

Pumping the pickup's gas pedal, True Believer shifted gears and accelerated from his parking space next to the church. They were less than a hundred feet away, just beyond the street light.

As the man paused and looked back up at the townhouse, his wife stepped down off the curb into the street, pulling playfully at his arm.

Now! Adrenalin surged through True Believer. He floored the red pickup and focused on his targets through a deepening red haze. Raw energy coursed down through his shoulders and into his arms and hands.

The engine roared. The pickup leapt forward down the street.

Michelle unlocked the door to her car and looked up.

Mark and Katie stood at the curb beneath the street light, Katie in her red coat laughing and yanking at Mark's arm.

The sight brought a grin to Michelle's face. They were good medicine for her—Mark and his enthusiasm at one extreme, Katie and her quiet determination at the other.

She started to get inside her car when a loud noise off to the right made her look up.

As Fletcher slowed his car and pulled into a parking space on 16th Street near the corner of the park, he noticed Mark and Katie standing by the curb in front of their townhouse. He only needed a minute to show them the old newspaper picture with Fein and Wertman and arrange a later time for them to meet and talk.

He opened the car door, biography in hand.

Squealing tires and a gunning engine snapped his head to the opposite corner of the park near the deserted church. A red pickup truck darted down the narrow street as if to beat the changing traffic signal, and then swerved to the right around the light pole and up over the curb.

Fletcher tossed the book into the car and broke into a sprint around the corner.

Mark's nightmare replayed itself in vivid detail—not in his mind, but right there on the street in front of him. Just like in his dream, Katie now stood with one foot on the curb, wearing the same red winter coat and snow boots. A gust of wind snapped her hair back from her face. She was turning, laughing, pulling on his hand, the traffic light above her shoulder changing from green to yellow.

Out of the corner of his eye to the left, Mark noticed an old red pickup racing down Crest Street to beat the yellow light.

Images—past and present—crashed together. Mark spun and without warning jerked his wife toward him with all his might.

Uncontrollable urges forced a blood-red rage through the tortuous streets of True Believer's memories. Belfast! Londonderry! Dublin! Sounds of explosions filled his ears. Broken and bleeding bodies lay strewn on the sidewalks.

He angled the pickup sharply around the light pole then up over the curb. Only then did he finally notice the No Parking sign that had been hidden from his line of sight.

True Believer plowed over it.

With the red pickup racing straight at them, Mark thrust himself backwards from the curb, pulling Katie down on top of him. Falling heavily to the sidewalk, Katie crashed onto his chest. Mark ignored the pain and loud metallic bang to his immediate left, rolling and pushing Katie toward the house as he simultaneously drew his knees up close to his body.

The truck roared by, its tires brushing the toes of his sneakers. Mark watched from his side as the pickup continued straight down the sidewalk and skidded across the corner at Crest and 16th Street. Horns blared as the screeching truck fishtailed onto 16th in front of a slowly moving line of traffic.

Katie! With a sharp pain in his lower back, Mark pushed himself to his knees. He crawled the three feet to Katie's side. She moaned lightly, propping herself on an arm and rubbing her forehead with her free hand. The patter of feet from two directions preceded helping hands. Fletcher Rivers dropped to one knee beside Mark, Michelle beside Katie.

"I'm OK," Mark blurted, shocked to see Fletcher but thankful he had showed up. "It's Katie I'm worried—"

Katie waved Mark off. With Michelle's help she turned and sat up. "I think I'm all right. I landed on top of you and we banged foreheads."

"I'll call an ambulance!" Fletcher said, assisting Mark up from his knees.

"Don't! I'm not going to any hospital!" Katie replied sharply as Michelle helped her to her feet.

Mark noticed that her eyes had taken on a steely edge. She ignored his pleading stare. Unspoken communication flowed between them. Resistance.

Visibly concerned, Fletcher turned to Mark. "What do you say?"

Mark studied his wife as she brushed the dirt off her coat. She lifted her head and their eyes met again. Though her chin trembled slightly, her gaze was resolute.

"Let's go inside. But honey, you've got to let us know if you feel anything at all."

She nodded and started up the sidewalk with Michelle.

Fletcher put his hand on Mark's arm and held him back. "What did you see?"

Mark breathed deeply as he glanced at his watch. He noticed that he was trembling.

"Not much. It happened too fast. We were on our way to police headquarters to see Captain Williams. He wanted to talk with me."

Fletcher stiffened. "Captain who?"

"Captain Williams—I'm sure that's what he said."

Fletcher breathed deeply. There was no Captain Williams in the Washington MPD.

The drive from downtown Washington across the Potomac River to National Airport in nearby Virginia took True Believer only twenty minutes. However, the twenty minutes seemed interminable, each stop light and stop sign another obstacle to his retreat.

He pulled the pickup into a long-term parking lot on the northwest side of the airport and headed toward its upper end and a thin line of barren trees. He cursed loudly, slamming his fist into the rearview mirror and snapping it off. He had missed his targets! Impossible! Turning the steering wheel sharply to the left, he angled across the lot to the corner. A row of three cars and two vans caught his eye. He slowed the pickup and carefully pulled into a space. It would be days, maybe weeks, before someone figured out that the old pickup had been abandoned. He reached over and picked up his portable telephone from under the seat, stepped out and locked the door. He tossed the key over the concrete wall bordering the parking lot.

Nothing had gone as planned. Not only had the MacDonalds survived, but that irksome Fletcher Rivers had turned up and witnessed everything. Now he could only hope that they would stay put for two days, at least until Sunday. He needed them out of the way just long enough for him to complete his task.

True Believer approached a blue van, reached into his pocket and removed a key. He unlocked and opened the back doors, then reached around to the left and pressed a small, carefully hidden switch. Disarmed, the van was now safe to start.

Drawing a deep breath, True Believer stepped up into the van, closed and locked the doors behind him. The heavily tinted windows effectively blocked any light from outside. He reached up and felt around the ceiling until he found the custom light switch.

A dull red glow filled the van, illuminating four, large identical metal cases, two on each wall. The cases, like the door, were locked and booby-trapped. He continued to the front of the van. At least this phase of the operation had gone without incident. He was now the possessor of four hundred pounds of the U.S. military's most powerful explosive and sophisticated electronic surveillance equipment.

When he spoke with Geneva and New York in their final conference call late Friday night, he would thank the coordinator and the banker for the flawless execution in delivering these crucial resources.

True Believer climbed into the driver's seat, put a second key into the ignition and looked out the driver's side window. His body stiffened, his only movement was the sudden narrowing of his eyes as he read two words that had been fingered on the dust-laden window. The words were difficult to make out, reading them backwards from the inside.

Then he understood. Sweat lined his temples. He rolled down the window, wiping the words away. He started the engine and backed out of the space. He tried to imagine how the words *unde malum* had found their way onto the window, but no explanation would come. Who else could possibly know about those two obscure, Latin words?

He had no time for mysteries. He pushed the thoughts aside and started the engine.

As the van pulled slowly away toward the exit ramp, a man watched with keen interest from a nearby hill behind the row of barren trees bordering the parking lot.

Gusting winds swept over the crest of the hill, rustling the grass, the branches of the barren cherry trees and the legs of his blue jogging suit. The wind swirled up around his thick torso, snapping his jacket and his blond hair.

Unfolding his arms from across his chest, he said soberly, "Does not God require that which is past?"

He turned and strode down the hill toward the parkway below.

PART

❧ III ❧

❧ 34 ❧

Early Friday Morning

THE WALL CLOCK IN THE DINING ROOM chimed midnight. Mark sat down and rubbed his face. He looked up at Katie, stretched on the couch with a pillow behind her head. Michelle and Fletcher sat in wing chairs at the edge of the flickering firelight, their faces serious and their mouths downturned.

As the clock sounded its final chime, Mark's eyes fell to Michelle's briefcase and file folder. Her research successfully linked AFI to seven tightly held and highly secretive corporations. One of the corporations, Parallax, promoted a heavy metal band called Legacy. Brian Fein was Parallax's chief executive and financial officer.

On the opposite end of the table from Michelle's folder was a book that Fletcher had brought: Stephen Oates' biography of John Brown. On top of the book lay a magazine photograph from the early seventies. The caption beneath the picture identified three Cal-Berkeley student-writer prizewinners. On the left, Harold Wertman, on the right, a young man by the name of Brian Fein.

Michelle broke the silence with a long, embarrassing yawn. She put her hand over her mouth. "I think it's time for me to head on home. I need to be back at my desk in less than seven hours."

"Mark and I'll walk you to your car," Fletcher suggested, uncrossing his legs. "But before you scoot out of here, let's take a second to review where we ended up."

Fletcher glanced over at Katie. "How are you doing?"

"Fine," she replied, resting her hands on her stomach. "By God's grace."

"Amen to that," Fletcher said as he sat up in the wing chair, turning his head toward Mark. "The most important thing that happened tonight is what didn't happen. A hit-and-run attempt failed. Though we have no proof, this action could be the result of threatening Troy Martin."

Fletcher's eyes darted to Michelle. "I've no doubt that when Botello finishes his background check on Fein—we'll hit paydirt and establish a solid connection between him, Troy, and KC."

Fletcher lifted his glass of diet soda from the table. The only sound was the clink of ice in the glass and the soft crackle of burning embers.

"Fein and Peters were afraid Mark would force attention back to the cases and the evidence that Troy used to frame Wertman. They just couldn't afford to let Mark do that."

"The good news is that Fein's failure will give us the time we need to tie the loose ends together. And if Troy and KC are involved like I think they are, they'll try to find a safer method to dispense with your statement. If they do, I'll have Internal Affairs chop them down at the knees. Even if some of the evidence we bring to the District Attorney doesn't hold up in court, it will shut them down."

"We need to pray that you're right," Mark said, standing up and stretching.

"Trust me in this," Fletcher said with all of the conviction he could muster. "We'll wrap this thing up in a couple of days."

Michelle nodded and closed her briefcase.

After walking to the front door, Mark helped her into her coat. A quiet Fletcher was right behind. They stepped outside onto the porch. The air was cold and still, the sky clear. Pale moonlight bathed the neighborhood.

Her Toyota was parked directly opposite the townhouse. They crossed the street to her car. Michelle climbed in, then paused, her hand on the door. She looked up at Mark and Fletcher. "I'll give you both a call tomorrow."

Mark nodded. "Thanks for sticking around. I'm sure Katie appreciated your being here as much as I did."

"I'm glad I could be of help and I hope we get to spend more time together." She locked the door and started the engine. "Including you, Fletcher."

"Likewise," he replied, his voice wavering. He patted the rear fender as the car eased out of the space. Crossing the street toward the townhouse, they watched the Toyota all the way around the corner onto 16th.

Fletcher stopped Mark. The shadows cast by the streetlight exaggerated his foreboding expression. "I wanted us to walk Michelle to the car so we could have a minute to speak in private. Inside, I wanted to paint the most positive picture for everybody."

"Are you implying that we may be subject to another reprisal?"

"No—not necessarily. But if things don't break open soon, we may have to take stronger measures—force Botello's hand and start talking with people at higher levels and get police protection. The report Botello gave me indicated Fein is an accomplished terrorist—bombings, that kind of thing. He's probably the one who set up

Wertman. This conspiracy could be a lot bigger than we thought."

Mark nodded, rubbed his arms and started to head back inside. "I agree—but for different reasons than you or Michelle. I think there's more behind Fein's attack than politics. I believe there are spiritual forces at work against Katie and me."

Fletcher followed. An image of Fein's face appeared in his mind. Should he tell Mark what he'd seen or not? Wouldn't it only feed Mark's imagination?

Fletcher hesitated as a gust of wind ruffled his pant legs and jacket. He shook his head, then reached out and put his hand on Mark's shoulder.

"When Fein drove his pickup by you and Katie, I was less than fifteen feet away and got a real good look at him. I can still see him through the driver's window—chiseled face, hair pulled back. He was angry—explosive—like a hunter who had missed his prey from point-blank range."

Then Fletcher told Mark what he had seen.

Mark's eyes narrowed sharply; his lips turned downward. He shuddered and rubbed his arms a second time. Suddenly, he looked weary, resigned.

"Let's go inside. It's time I introduce you to somebody."

His face in shadows, Mark pulled the sheet and blanket up around Katie's shoulders.

"I'm not sure when I'll be to bed. If Fletcher and I stay up much longer, I'll ask him to spend the night."

Mark leaned down and reached his arms around his wife, and then gave her a long hug as he pictured Fletcher's description of Fein and the dark scar that angled across his cheek.

He closed his eyes and winced.

Katie laid back onto the pillow.

Mark kissed her softly on the forehead. "I love you."

"I love you, too."

Fletcher sat in a chair to the right of the fireplace, the journal across his lap propped against the arm rest.

As Mark leaned against the mantle, Fletcher turned a page and glanced up. His wide eyes revealed his reaction to Sam's journal entry about his confrontation with Beaumont and an evil spirit. He started to speak, then stopped. His eyes moved from Mark to the fireplace.

Mark cleared his throat. "My sentiments, exactly. How about a soda?"

"Sure, thanks. I could use something cold about now."

Mark returned with two frosty cans, popped them open and handed one to Fletcher.

Fletcher looked up questioningly. "What was that thing in Sam's cell?"

Mark rubbed his chin. "If you believe what the Bible says about the Devil and the supernatural, you'd call that thing a demon—and a powerful one, too. You haven't read the half of it."

"No offense," Fletcher said, placing the journal on the table, "but to a biblical illiterate, Sam reads more like a Stephen King horror story than reality."

Mark sank down onto the hearth. He sipped his soft drink, and then rested his head back against the bricks. His eyes focused in midair as he considered Fletcher's comment. *Horror.* His dream of the racing red pickup had been fulfilled.

"I need to tell you," Mark said, gripping his drink tightly, "why I believe what happened tonight was a spiritual attack."

By the time Mark finished telling his story of the red pickup, the women's tombstones and the curse that an old frontiersman and his sword had brought upon the family, a single chime sounded from the clock in the parlor.

"It's taken me a while to face up to the truth of what's been happening to my family," Mark said as he rose from the hearth and moved to a chair.

"After reading Sam's writings and thinking about my own experience, I'm convinced that an evil spirit—a familial demon that can be traced back to eighteenth century Paris and at least five generations of executioners—is after the MacDonald women."

"My mother died in childbirth with me, just like my ancestor Sam's mother did with him. His wife and grandmother were killed by pro-slavery men. I don't know what happened to my grandmother and I'm not sure I want to find—"

Mark stopped in mid-sentence. His eyes focused on the stack of journals, then pulled away slowly before returning to Fletcher.

"Finding out about this legacy is frightening enough. Losing one child and almost losing your wife—twice—it's just too much to bear, alone."

For a long while, only the crackling of the fire could be heard. With a lump in his throat, Fletcher stared at his hands. He was trembling.

Mark's frankness, like Michelle's at the deli a few days earlier, touched him on a level little else in his experience ever had.

What kind of people were these Christians? Riddled with hurts and victims of injustice, Mark and Katie and Michelle defied the stereotypes he had formed for so many years. They weren't holier-than-thou, nor were they callous, right-wing bigots—they were genuine. In many ways their suffering had been far more painful than his. Getting to know them had resurrected not only his hunger for friendship, but a yearning to be with his wife again.

Fletcher's eyes glistened. And yet, there was more to what was going on inside of him than just a desire for human friendship—and he knew it.

Too much to bear, alone. Mark's words cast light upon a hurting place deep inside him, a place he knew he had no power within himself to heal. He had tried to compensate by helping Jimmy, but even that ultimately failed.

Fletcher was suprised as he once again remembered that summer years ago at the Methodist camp. A scene unfolded: a young boy with a crewcut stepping out from between a row of chairs and walking up an aisle to the front of the chapel, joining a growing circle of elementary school-age children. "If you confess with your lips that Jesus is Lord and believe in your heart that God raised him from the dead, you will be saved," the youth minister said, holding an open Bible in front of him.

A second image came to mind, one that he hadn't thought about in many years. Standing quietly behind the youth minister was a tall, broad-shouldered man with blond hair. How odd was his presence, his shoulders so straight, his smile—how big and bright! If demons really existed, as Mark believed, then what about angels? Had God been watching over his life all these years, a patient, caring father, waiting for the day when the grownup young boy would finally let go of his guilt and his pride...

And come home.

Fletcher picked up his winter coat and reached into a pocket. Tears welled in the the detective's eyes as he placed something on top of the open journal.

The movement caught Mark's attention. He leaned forward. On the journal lay a picture of a young girl—four or five years old—and her mother. The girl was dressed in a pink snow cap, a long winter coat, and boots. A little girl!

The missing piece in Fletcher's life?

A soft sob caused Mark to look up.

He saw a weary, broken man. Fletcher's whispery voice cracked as he folded his hands, lowered his head and began to cry.

A piece of Tecumseh's prophecy popped into Mark's thoughts.

Whatever happened with Fletcher's family, that bitter spring had grown into a dark and deadly root of guilt and self-loathing in the center of his soul.

Fletcher needed strong medicine, medicine strong enough to cure a sin-poisoned heart.

Mark reached forward and clasped his hands over Fletcher's.

❧ 35 ❧

Late Friday Morning

THE AFI OFFICES WERE PRACTICALLY DESERTED by 10 A.M. Mr. Peters had announced, via the intercom and then formally by memo, a liberal leave policy on Friday due to Saturday's pro-choice counter-rally on the Mall.

Julie entered Michelle's office with a cup of tea and a wide smile. "I just knew that you had found something crooked," she said quietly.

Michelle shook her head. "Has it been that obvious to you what I've been doing?"

Julie nodded and turned to leave the room.

"Thanks for the tea," Michelle added, reaching for her cup and taking a sip.

Her young assistant paused for a moment before closing the door. "Thanks for taking me in."

Michelle blushed slightly. She had held so much back from Julie —Anne's problems, her faith and life in Christ—all to maintain her cover as a loyal AFI employee. But that was going to change. Her days as a mole were numbered. One look into the books on her desk could forever seal her future with AFI. To acknowledge that she had taken advantage of her temporary position to examine ownership records and investment portfolios would be, as her boss would say, a CTD—a career terminating decision! However, losing her job—even the directorship she was so close to attaining—didn't seem nearly so tragic. For the first time in two and a half years, her emotions concurred with her thinking over the issue of her job.

She was closing in on the truth. The paper trail was almost complete. The checks connected Mr. Peters, Brian Fein, and the seven corporations.

Her intuition and training told her there was more yet to come. Money out meant money in. Conventional expenditures came from conventional funding which came from government entitlement programs, private industry, or personal contributions. But what of illicit expenditures? Had Mr. Peters found an illicit source of funding for his plans? Somewhere on her desk were the answers.

Setting the mug off to the side, Michelle's expression hardened. She dismissed the fear that wanted to creep in and narrowed her attention to the investment portfolios.

She opened the book marked "Domestic" and started scanning the pages, one by one.

Fletcher pulled back the curtain and stared out of the study's third-floor window at the streets and park below.

The sky was a lead sheet except where the sun peeked over the red tile roof of the church to the left of the park. The forecast called for cloudy skies and the possibility of rain. The sunlight breaking over the church painted the tops of the trees a pale gold, in striking contrast to the dull cloud cover.

When was the last time he had taken a moment to appreciate the morning's artistic play of light and color?

He inhaled slowly, deeply. He felt completely relaxed, no tension around his eyes or temples or shoulders. For the last several months, mornings had always been lonely, his steps the only sounds in an otherwise silent house. Stressful, too, as he compensated for the loneliness by directing his thoughts immediately to the day's itinerary and upcoming problems facing him at work—worrying about an upcoming court case, an uncooperative judge, planning a dangerous bust.

But not this morning. Everything seemed fresh. Vital.

Yesterday he had been drowning, spiraling downward in a bottomless pool, dragged into darker and darker depths by twin weights of guilt and failed self-determination. And just when the light above his head had nearly faded, God somehow reached down from heaven—through the living hands of Mark MacDonald—and pulled him up and out of harm's way.

A wide smile lit up Fletcher's face. Today he would face his life free from himself and the Devilish powers of remorse and guilt that for so long stalked his soul. He liked Mark's explanation from the Bible that, when we surrender our heart to Christ, our old life dies and is buried. Then our new life—a totally new creation—begins, washed in Christ's blood, forgiven, free from the burdens of the past.

What had Mark called Christ's blood—strong medicine?

Medicine strong enough to take care of Melissa and Susan and even Jimmy. Fletcher smiled again. In his heart, he felt assured that Jimmy was with God.

A splash of sun caught Fletcher's eye and reminded him of the new spark of hope he had for reconciling with Susan. The fear of divorce had vanished.

And with Melissa, a supernatural peace now defended his heart from gnawing dread and uncertainty. Indeed, the illogical quietness in his soul over the well-being of his daughter was the greatest miracle of all. Her safety and future were in God's hands.

His eyes moved away from the park. He turned toward the desk and the open Bible he had been reading.

He was under no illusions about his confession of faith. He had opened the door for Christ to enter in. The world had not changed, he had. His problems had not vanished, but he had been released from their deadly power.

He sat down and found his place in the Gospels. In the two hours since he was awake, he finished the Book of John and was ready to begin reading Luke.

His beeper sounded. He pulled it from his belt, turned it on end and read the row of familiar red numbers.

Fletcher rose from the chair and quietly headed downstairs to the phone.

Turning the three-pound brick of C-4 in his hand, True Believer grinned as broadly as his taut, muscular face would allow. Sitting on the aluminum packing case in the back of the van, he stared at the pliable gray compound as a miser would stare at his treasure. In its own way, each block of plastic explosive was worth far more than its weight in gold.

Four hundred pounds of C-4 was a means to buy his freedom: freedom to choose and freedom to be his own man for the first time in his life! For Bonn, Geneva and the AFI, the C-4 would usher in a new age of legal sanctions against the radical Christian Right. For Mr. Peters and the others on the speaker's platform at the counter-rally, the playdough-like bricks would be the unexpected and tragic cause of their deaths.

True Believer's grin vanished as a steely sheen fell over his face. Mr. Peters was too great a liability, knew too much about the man Brian Fein. In the aftermath of the counter-rally and the ensuing investigation, their intimate working relationship would surely be brought to light. And that was not acceptable. New York would be furious—even vengeful—but that was Bonn's responsibility. It was she who made the final decision that Mr. Peters was a replaceable commodity.

He rose from his seat and returned the explosive to its case. Everything checked out. The electronics, the explosives, the magnetic labels for the doors and sides of the van, his uniforms and IDs. Now, all that was left was his trip to the mall and a day's worth of sightseeing, maybe even a ride up to the top of the Washington Monument.

He chided himself—business before pleasure. Maybe the workers erecting the speaker's platform at the base of the monument could use a little help....

Expressionless, Kim Park stared down through the light cloud cover at the dark green forests and the thin, sandy edge of the Atlantic seaboard. The Concord was descending, beginning the first leg of its approach to Dulles Airport in Virginia, just west of Washington, D.C.

The bruises on her face and arms were nearly invisible, but the wounds in her spirit were just as painful as the day True Believer slapped her to her knees on his penthouse floor.

Her baggage consisted of her purse and a carry-on. Her visit to the States would last less than thirty-six hours. She would see the arrogant Irishman one final time and then, only from a distance.

Kim closed her eyes and rehearsed the details over and over again.

"Done." Katie rinsed the last of the breakfast dishes and handed it to Mark. He wiped it dry with the dish towel and put it back on the shelf.

Mark leaned back against the counter. "Are you sure you don't feel anything from our fall last night? You're not sore anywhere?"

"Nope. Not a bit. I said I'd let you know immediately if I felt anything."

As they passed by the stairs on the way to the living room, they could hear Fletcher talking on the telephone from the bedroom on the second floor. Katie sat down on the couch. "Seems like forever since we read Sam's journal."

"Only twenty-four hours," Mark said, sitting on the hearth and rubbing his shoulders to fight off a chill. His eyes narrowed pensively on the brown, leather-bound journal resting in the middle of the table.

The sound of feet on the stairs preceded Fletcher's entrance into the parlor. "Botello's got a folder filled with goodies on Fein, our secretive Irishman. And there's more on the way."

"Goodies?" Katie asked.

"That's his favorite word for hard evidence. He's going to pick me up here in a couple hours. Things are still hot around the district building."

Fletcher sat in the chair near Katie's end of the couch. Mark stared thoughtfully out the front window.

Katie smiled and handed Fletcher the journal. "Then I'd say it's time to cash in that rain check."

Michelle picked up her purse and headed for the door. Julie scurried to the ladies' room. They would meet by the elevators and then head out for a long lunch.

From her new vantage point, she could see that Mr. Peters' scheme was actually quite simple. Annual stock transactions between a New York bank and Mr. Peters pumped $700,000 dollars per year of tax-deductible monies into AFI which could then be dispersed into seven tightly-held corporations, all managed by the dark-haired Mr. Fein.

Michelle shook her head. For three years she had combed the records to find tax violations—excess contributions, prohibitions on self-dealings, investments jeopardizing exempt purposes—all to no avail. Then, after an hour of looking at the corporate stock and investment portfolios, the answer had fallen into her lap.

AFI's ownership in unrelated businesses—the seven companies—exceeded the limits allowed by their tax-exempt status. All the IRS would have to do to challenge AFI's tax-exempt status was to establish a direct relationship between the seven corporations and AFI. The bank in New York had been the missing link.

The click of heels on the tile floor brought Michelle out of her reverie.

"Ready at last," Julie said with a cheery smile.

Michelle could not help but return the smile as she punched the down arrow for the elevator.

❧ 36 ❧

Friday Afternoon

Easter Sunday 1865, 1:30 P.M.
Sheppard's Boardinghouse, Washington, D.C.

Customarily, I do not write on the Lord's Day, but this morning the Spirit of God prompted me to recount the events of a week that will change this nation's course forever.

On Palm Sunday, just one week ago today, Lee signed surrender documents in Appomattox, Virginia.

After hearing news of the war's end, I proceeded from Richmond, Virginia immediately to Washington, arriving mid-afternoon Monday at Sheppard's Boardinghouse. I found it overrun with returning soldiers. Mrs. Sheppard expressed regrets at having to turn me away as she handed me the unexpected letter from John Ezra. It detailed the arrival of his family on Tuesday afternoon by train from Gettysburg. John will also return my two matching knapsacks.

So I left Mrs. Sheppard's with a spring in my step. Joy filled my heart as I looked forward to my promised staff position in Lincoln's second term and a reunion with John Ezra and his family. Now, only a few legal details remain to complete my adoption of Angelina.

I crossed Pennsylvania Avenue and walked to the edge of the marshy tidal basin. Viewing the unfinished monument, birds roosting in her scaffolding, and pigs wandering about her base, I wondered if our national government would enjoy greater success at reconstructing our broken nation than those who attempted to raise this edifice.

I found lodging late Monday night at the Herndon House, a boarding facility run by Mrs. Murray. I experienced the most restful sleep since the beginning of the war.

Tuesday morning, parades and marchers filled the streets and numerous speeches were offered. That afternoon I spent five minutes alone with Lincoln. His face was haggard and tired. We discussed his plan to restore the South. He assured me that he would clearly define my role in his administration and scheduled me for a more detailed briefing the following Monday at 2:00 P.M. I was exuberant.

I wrote most of the day Wednesday, my door and window open to take advantage of a slight breeze. As the hours passed, a peculiar character caught my attention, a Mr. Payne. He kept the room across from mine. At noon, Simon, a free black of many years, brought my lunch. "Mr. Payne likes to eat by hisself every day, too." he explained. "Mostly stays away from Mrs. Murray, myself, and the rest of the boarders."

I passed Payne in the second floor hall about an hour later. A young man in his early twenties, he had broad shoulders, a clean-shaven face and thick lips. Something about his countenance unnerved me, the furtive look in his eyes, his tight, serious mouth.

That afternoon and evening, an odd collection of folks came and went from his room, further awakening my inquisitiveness. I began to suspect that Payne was conducting some sort of illicit business.

Late Wednesday evening I picked up a small piece of paper from the floor in the hall. It was a letter addressed to "Friend Wilkes." It spoke of an oil deal, of stock worth eight thousand dollars, of sinking the well deep enough, and of a supposed escape route through Capon and Romney.

As I read it, Payne's door burst open and a mustachioed man wearing an open-necked, long-sleeved white shirt with fancy gold cufflinks stepped out and snatched the letter from my hand. Our eyes met. "That's mine!" he snapped.

I concluded that these folks were involved in some sort of oil speculation. But in retrospect I now see that a deadly intrigue was brewing.

On Thursday evening, several of these same gentlemen gathered at Herndon House to share a meal. Uncharacteristically, Payne ate in the dining room. I sat at the far end of the table. They carried on a hearty discussion amongst themselves, highlighted by catlike glances and knowing looks. It was an odd meal, unlike any of my fond memories of dinner at Mrs. Sheppard's. I retired early with a dark foreboding in my spirit.

Good Friday

The day that would undo the bindings on this bleeding nation finally arrived. I awoke from a troubled sleep, ate breakfast, and continued work on the Rebel Heart.

At noon, Simon brought my lunch. On the tray stood an envelope. Simon smiled proudly.

Inside was a theatre ticket for the play, My American Cousin and a note from President Lincoln requesting my attendance at Ford's Theatre on Friday evening. I wrote all afternoon with added vigor. Following dinner, I donned my Sunday best and prepared to leave for the theatre.

As I stood before the mirror adjusting my tie, I noticed out of the corner of my eye that the door to my room was ajar. Before the oddity had fully registered, I was walloped ferociously on the back of the head.

I remember falling, watching the room skew sharply to one side. Sometime later I awoke slowly, dazed, confused, and tied to a chair. My head ached. It was dark outside. My watch rested on the nightstand in front of the mirror but I could not see its face. I waited for a few moments and allowed my throbbing head to clear.

Who had done this deed? And why? In my mind's eye I replayed the scene. I was staring at myself in the mirror adjusting my tie, then the door ajar—yes, and for the briefest moment, a second image in the mirror: a jacketed arm and a white cuff with fancy cufflinks.

Like a flash it came to me. The white cuff, the fancy cufflinks— they belonged to the man called Wilkes. The face and the name merged. John Wilkes Booth—a respected actor from Maryland who often played at Ford's Theatre. I had seen him at dinner just the night before! I had read about him and heard rumors that he was a Southern sympathizer and Lincoln-hater. Surely he was on his way to the same play as I, in his best attire.

But why was I knocked out and tied up? Was it the letter? What had it said? "When you sink your well, go deep enough, don't fail; everything depends upon you and your helpers." The words came back to me then, just as they do now, without struggle. Was it an illicit oil deal? Or was it something more sinister?

I prayed vehemently. "O God, if ever You've helped me, help me now!"

My legs were tied to the bottom of the chair legs. I could not tap the floor with my boots. My mouth was bound with a handkerchief. There was only one hope—knock myself over onto the floor, and pray that the crash would arouse Mrs. Murray or Simon below. If my plan failed, I would be totally immobile.

I rocked back and forth until I felt the front legs lift from the floor, then I threw my weight backwards. I fell like a cut tree. The jolt was severe and more painful than I had anticipated, while the bang of the chair against the oak floor generated less sound than I had hoped for.

Minutes passed and no one responded. At last I heard footsteps coming up the stairs and a knock on the door.

"Mr. MacDonald, is everything all right?" The voice belonged to Mrs. Murray.

I yelled through the handkerchief; my cry was indistinct but loud enough to be heard. The door opened and she appeared.

"Dear Lord, Mr. MacDonald, what happened?"

She pulled the handkerchief from my mouth. I offered my explanation. She called for Simon; together they cut me loose.

"Was a man by the name of John Wilkes Booth here early this evening?" I asked, rubbing my wrists.

"Yes, Mr. Booth left with Mr. Payne about two hours ago. I believe they were going to the theatre."

I grabbed my pocket watch from the table and read the time. It was 9:35 P.M. Instinctively, I reached into my knapsack and pulled out the Long Knife and attached the sheath to my belt. At the sight of the sword, Mrs. Murray put her hand over her mouth. Simon whistled.

Ford's Theatre is only three blocks from Herndon House. I decided to leave Andrew Jackson in his stable and run.

Breathing heavily, I turned a corner. My passage through a narrow alleyway was abruptly halted by a brawny Union soldier on horseback guzzling down his last swig of whiskey. He threw the bottle to the ground, shattering the glass. His horse bucked, but he fought it down with a sharp jerk on the reins.

Then he reared his horse, backing me against the alley wall.

The soldier slid from his saddle and lumbered toward me. His horse, snorting and kicking, galloped madly away down the alley toward 5th Ave. The horse's reaction paralyzed me. I could smell liquor on the soldier's breath as he grabbed my shirt.

With one hand he lifted me from my feet and pressed my back against the brick wall. His eyes found the Long Knife on my belt. He yanked it from its sheath with his other hand, whipping it wildly in the air. I was dazzled by his strength—my toes didn't touch the ground.

"I'm going to kill you, Sam MacDonald!" he snarled, his black eyes blazing.

Shocked by the sound of my name, I could not reply. Yet he answered the question that darted through my mind as if I had just asked it.

"I've known you from birth." He waved the tip of the Long Knife in front of my face. "You can't escape me, just as Will MacDonald could not escape.

"I waged a war in the heavens over Kentucky, locked in bitter contests with the heavenly hosts—the cheled and the shinan, ser-

vants of El and his Son. I fought them for the right to make this
sword shed blood."

The soldier's fist tightened on my shirt. I feared for my life. I was
not in the grasp of a drunken Northern soldier but a dark power
from Hell itself. My heart grew faint, my arms and legs numb. I
prayed. Unable to utter words aloud, I called upon God. No sooner
had my heart whispered the name of Jesus than did the Holy Spirit
rise up within me.

"What is your name?" I asked, fighting for breath and focusing
my thoughts on the grace of God.

He sneered, turned his head to the side, stared at me out of the
corners of his eyes, and cocked his brow. The dark spirit lowered
me to the ground, my knees nearly buckling beneath me.

"Your grandmother's offense to me shall cease here. The prophecy shall fail. Though I cannot have your soul, I will dispatch your
flesh from this earth."

He raised the Long Knife, circling it in front of my face. Grabbing
my left wrist and slamming it against the wall, he jabbed the sword's
point through my left palm. Blood trickled down my arm, turning
my white shirt sleeve a dark red. My hand pulsated excruciatingly
as he released his grip and brandished the Long Knife in front of my
eyes once again.

The soldier glanced at my bloody sleeve. His eyes grew wide. A
diabolic grin blossomed on his face. "The sins of this land will never
be purged away!"

Grabbing my neck and firmly pressing my head against the wall
with his right hand, he choked off my air. He raised the Long Knife
toward my chest. As he did, I noticed the scar, a thin pink line running from the corner of his mouth to the corner of his eye.

"Lord, I'm Yours," I prayed without breath.

To my astonishment, the soldier's head jerked back, his grasp on
my neck loosening.

At that same moment, out of the corner of my right eye, I saw
four Union soldiers running toward us from across the street.

My attacker bellowed with an angry voice that was not his own.
His brow tightened into grotesque fleshy folds as he drew back the
sword.

I heard a dull thud.

The soldier toppled face-first into the street, the Long Knife slipping from his hand and landing by my feet. And there, a figure hovered in the air before me, like a replay of that moment in the cell
with Beaumont. Only now, I could see the figure's eyes like deep-set
rubies in a burning red mist. He hung motionless for a fleeting
instant, hatred seething from his ghostlike form. Then he departed,

leaving a gust of hot, putrid air in his wake.

And lingering in my thoughts, like crimson wisps of smoke, was a name. Rasah.

A voice calling my name dispelled the images from my mind.

"Sam? Sam!"

Before me stood an old friend. Holding the butt of a rifle in his left hand, the barrel in his right, Toby Sikes looked as stunned as I felt. Behind him stood three more Negro soldiers, laying their rifles aside and tending to the unconscious private who lay sprawled at my feet.

I slid down the wall and sat on the ground next to my attacker. My left hand throbbed.

"Seems like I'm always getting you outa some kinda mess, Sam. But this time I don't rightly know what kinda trouble I've saved you from!"

Then he saw my hand. "Looks like you need a doctor—now."

"Don't have time," I said. I picked up the Long Knife with my good hand and tried to stand.

"Just hold it right there," Toby said, trying to push me back down. "You need to see a doctor."

"Later," I said, sensing that Booth and the spirit's appearance were connected. I wasn't sure how, but I knew a murder was about to be committed. I feared the worst.

"We've got to save the President."

Three sets of eyes darted to mine, their faces registering shock as Toby pulled me up.

I raced down the block to the side door of Ford's Theatre; Toby gave his men orders, then followed. Not knowing exactly where the President would be, I opened the door and saw a stairway that wound upward to the balcony. Laura Keene and her leading man stood facing each other on the stage.

We raced up the stairs, only to find a closed door at the end a narrow hall. Toby pushed on the door.

It would not open.

Without warning, like some grim and fantastic nightmare, the spirit's scarred and hideous head protruded through the solid door! His face was an eerie, disembodied red mask, half human and half mist, his eyes filled with malice.

Toby gasped and fell backward against the wall. From below, I heard a man call out, "It is now ten minutes after ten!"

The spirit laughed mockingly and disappeared.

Toby and I threw ourselves into the heavy door as a pistol shot rang out. We pushed open the door to the box seats adjacent to

Lincoln's in time to see a man drop from the balcony to the stage below.

It was Booth!

Mrs. Lincoln screamed, "They've killed the President!" Her cry was followed by a man's frantic voice, "Stop him!"

Booth ran across the stage and cried out, "sic semper tyrannis!" For the briefest moment there was complete silence, shattered by a woman's long, piercing scream. Mayhem broke loose on the floor of the theatre.

As men surged to break down the locked door, my gaze was drawn to the stage. Standing behind Miss Keene was an old man in a tattered waistcoat. He had raven hair and a nose like the beak of a bird. He lifted a hand and pointed at me. The hairs on my forearms and neck stood on end.

My mind was barraged with hateful thoughts—vile, vindictive thoughts aimed at my faith, my belief in God.

Men trying to get to Lincoln knocked me to the floor. I scrambled to my feet, but when I looked back to the stage, the old man was gone. I looked at Toby. He turned his head toward me, his eyes wide.

A Murderer From the Beginning

President Lincoln died at 7:22 A.M. Saturday morning. Reports indicate that a single bullet entered the base of his neck three inches from his left ear and passed obliquely forward through his brain, lodging somewhere beneath his right eye. Washington City spent Saturday in sober reflection. For Toby it was a time of repentance and a personal reckoning with God for the rights to his soul. For me it was a day of tending to the wound in my hand and the wounds in my heart.

Last evening I returned to Mrs. Sheppard's Boardinghouse. This morning Toby and I attended Easter services. The church building overflowed with saints who offered spiritless thanksgiving for the war's end, as they mourned their fallen leader. Communion was presented and I received the elements. O, how my heart wrestled with You, God. I have endeavored to keep my soul free from unforgiveness' hold! But its power has again nearly overwhelmed me!

In my short lifetime I have danced with the sultry spirit of revenge, courted the loathsome whore called hatred, and nearly consummated my betrothal to a bride named bitterness. When these sins could not overtake me, the Devil sought to put me in the hangman's noose, twice, and then, even more directly, to slay me with Grandpa Will's Long Knife.

Friday's encounter confirms that he seeks to defeat God's purposes revealed in the prophecy. O God, may I, and those who follow me, continue to be delivered fully from our darker nature, from evil men and from the Devil, himself.

A New Chapter

Outwardly, Washington's unfinished monument looks the same as it did that day when I opened my first journal upon my return from the Cowger's farm, nine springs ago. And yet, how utterly changed is the world outside my window!

The sun sets this Easter Sunday. A chapter in my life—and in this nation's history—is closing as well. I stand at the edge of a new dawn. Angelina arrives the day after tomorrow, and I shall finally discover what it means to be a father. This is a time of new beginnings, a time for reconciliation, rebuilding, and healing. It is time for books to be written and sermons to be preached. It is time for God's Church, His Holy Bride, to repent and return to her first love.

April whispers her cool evening breezes through my open window, gently brushing the curtain and comforting me. A cardinal flutters outside my window, swooping lazily across Pennsylvania Avenue.

The dinner bell rings its final call; I must close this entry. Toby has already headed downstairs. This evening, of all evenings, I do not wish to be consigned to the kitchen as Mrs. Sheppard is still prone to do with those who think they can come late to her table.

Botello slowed his Cutlass Ciera in front of the vacant church, hunting for a parking space, and then spotted Fletcher on the sidewalk in the triangular park near the statue. He honked, waited for several cars to pass by, turned left and swung his car over to the curb.

Fletcher opened the door and slipped inside.

The broad grin on Botello's face faded. Fletcher was pale and silent. His expressions were a stark contrast to the positive tone of voice Fletcher used on the telephone an hour and a half earlier when he shared with Botello about how he gave his life to the Lord.

Fletcher forced a thin smile. "Let's go somewhere where we can talk. Remember Tripolis?"

"Good ol' Garlic City? How could I forget your favorite hole-in-the-wall? You doin' OK?"

Fletcher answered distractedly, looking out his window, his eyes glancing up at the gathering clouds.

"Of course we knew the outcome all along," Mark said soberly as they sat on the bench. "Like I said the other night, history was always against Sam. Lincoln's assassination could not be undone. Sam could never serve in Lincoln's cabinet."

Katie frowned. "I guess I knew, too."

Sunlight broke through parting clouds and drenched the park with brightness and warmth. Looking up at the statue of Cardinal Gibbons, Mark remembered the two Latin words that had been painted on its base. *Unde malum.*

On the heels of *whence comes evil* came the words of the prophecy: *Out of your loins will come two men with strong medicine.*

When Nikki first told Sam the prophecy, how profound and glorious it had seemed! Little did Sam realize that the prophecy would make him a target of the Devil's wrath.

Though Mark sat still on the bench, his eyes opened wide. No—that was only part of it. Sam wasn't the only target.

A shadowy line moved swiftly across the park. Mark looked up as a thick veil of gray clouds marched overhead and obscured the sun. Katie sat up as a chilling breeze swept over them.

"Brrr..." she exclaimed, standing up and pulling on Mark's arm. "Time to go inside."

Mark dropped his gaze from the darkening sky. He hardly heard Katie's remark.

His thoughts were locked on an image of seven tombstones.

Botello closed the manila folder and stared across the booth at Fletcher. "The way I see it, there's not much we can do until Monday."

Fletcher drained his coffee cup. "What about Internal Affairs?"

"No way! If you so much as set your foot in Gresham's office with allegations of misconduct against Troy and KC right now, they'll toss both you and your evidence out. You're still a pariah, a loose cannon."

"Special Operations, then—"

"Come on, Fletcher! You know that we can't go to them without clear evidence that your man Fein has selected a specific target. They'll treat you like a kid crying wolf. Our best course of action is to let me take this folder to Hardaway at the Bureau Monday morning. If they have something on Fein already, then maybe we can go see Jim down in Special Operations."

Fletcher stared straight at his friend. His frown melted into a half-formed smile. "Before, I never appreciated the fact that you were a Christian. You and your wife prayed for me, didn't you?"

"I knew you were hurtin'," Botello said. "After you got your daughter back, you were as tight-lipped as a clam."

Fletcher nodded soberly. "Funny how it all comes back. Was I really that hard a case?"

Botello smiled. "Let's just say that if you apply yourself as a believer the same way you do at work, that scar-faced demon is in for a real surprise!"

"So you don't think we're all crazy?"

"Not at all." Botello said with sudden conviction and a soberness in his voice. "That old serpent's been on the loose for a long, long time."

⊰⊱ 37 ⊰⊱

Friday Evening

THE VIEW FROM THE WASHINGTON MONUMENT'S observation window at dusk was spectacular, dulled only by the thickening layer of gray clouds that had moved in from the southwest. Five hundred feet of elevation extended the western horizon far into nearby Virginia, beyond the Lincoln Memorial and Potomac River, past Arlington National Cemetery. Visitors walking below looked surprisingly small, like brightly colored ants. The fifty American flags edging the circular sidewalk snapped smartly as the wind swept up the grassy mall, past the counter-rally's now completed stage and around the Monument's base.

Ironically, all of the Park Service's extensive plans—the rows and rows of bleachers lining Constitution Avenue, the thousands of feet of red, white, and blue bunting—for next week's inaugural parade—would not be necessary. He had to admit, Bonn's plan to enrage the Amercian public and the Congress to action against the conservative right was a bold stroke of genius.

True Believer folded his arms across his chest, breathed deeply and took it all in. It was an historic moment and he wanted to enjoy it fully. He had stood at the west window. What a view—and he would be one of the last to enjoy it! At least in its original form...

"Excuse me!" came a deep voice from behind him. The twenty or so visitors in the observation area all turned around at the same time.

"Sorry, folks, but we've got some major difficulties with the elevator, so I've got to ask you to move to the stairs," the young policeman explained with a reserved smile. "I'll be escorting you down—all 500 feet and 897 steps. As I said, I'm sorry for the inconvenience, particularly for those of you with young children. Now, if you please, follow me to the stairs."

True Believer smiled and took his place in line.

Mark faced the table in the third floor study. Evening light filtered through the curtains onto the neat stacks of journals.

He and Katie had read them all, from Sam's trip to the valley in 1856 to his closing entry on Easter day, 1865. He ran his hands over them lightly, then over the old map of Kansas and Shawnee Mission where Sam's father had labored and died.

Lowering his head, he glanced at the small group of miscellaneous letters written to Sam that they had yet to read. Because of his interest in the journals, he had simply collected the letters and placed them off to the side.

Mark glanced at several of them. Two letters were from Mr. Pitkins of the *Charleston Observer*, another from Mrs. Sheppard, the woman who ran the boardinghouse—names that didn't mean anything to him before. Now they were familiar.

All of the envelopes were faded, their edges worn.

All except one.

Mark slipped out a plain white envelope. A small fold appeared between his eyebrows. He couldn't remember where it had come from.

He started to toss it back on the pile when he noticed faint pencil markings in the upper left-hand corner.

He lifted the envelope closer.

Michelle kicked off her shoes and sat down on the end of her bed. She let herself fall backwards, arms outstretched.

Yes! She did it! She'd found evidence so irrefutable that it could stand on its own in a court of law. She hadn't felt this giddy since her college graduation!

Now it did not matter that Carol would return to her position Monday morning. Nothing about AFI mattered any more at all. The date on the headlines that played through Michelle's mind was indistinct, but the message was clear: AFI TAX STATUS IN JEOPARDY! or AFI DIRECTOR RESIGNS! She was going to make sure that Mr. Peters did not escape. Canceled checks, stock ownership records and his distinctive signature would guarantee that his days at AFI were as numbered as hers.

Michelle rolled over and pushed herself from the bed. As she stepped to the closet to change clothes, her conscience voiced itself loudly enough to finally be heard.

Hold it right there!

The capricious sensation overwhelming her dissipated rapidly as the convicting presence of the Holy Spirit entered her thoughts. Yes, all that she'd hoped for, for Anne, now had the potential to come true. But was that what really mattered?

No. God had not put her at AFI to satisfy a personal vendetta, but to bring her, Fletcher, Mark, and Katie together. Though she wasn't sure how all of the pieces in the puzzle they were solving would fit together, or what the outcome would be, she knew she was an integral part.

She had also become an important part of Julie's life.

If the Freedom of Choice Act made it through Congress intact, and all of the restraints and obstacles that existed under Roe v. Wade were brushed aside by the sweeping strokes of the President's signature, then there would be more women like Julie who needed personal guidance and care—real friendship. A friendship that was more than words but included, if need be, a room and a bed, someone to talk to on a lonely night, and someone to adopt the child a young mother might decide she could not keep.

Michelle slipped into her sweats. Her personal battle with AFI was almost over. But in five days, at the Clinton inauguration, the larger war between two opposing ideologies would escalate.

Her peace finally returned. Michelle breathed deeply, stuck her feet into her slippers and headed downstairs to help Julie with their late dinner.

"I feel so stupid," Mark said, plopping heavily onto the sofa as he handed Katie the two-page letter.

She patted his leg and smiled. "Do you want me to read it?"

Mark closed his eyes and nodded his head. "I thought you'd like to hear it the same time I did."

Katie stared in disbelief at the salutation, and then at Mark.

He shrugged. "What can I say?"

"Yes, Troy, I'll meet you at the Bayou at 7:30," KC said sharply. "I just wish you asked my opinion before you told the Sponsors we were dropping out."

"Hey, if you want to stay in, stay in. You'll have a chance to tell the man, yourself, face-to-face, but I'm out for good! I made a mistake getting involved with those clowns. Anybody who thinks he can play god with me can think again. See you."

KC swallowed hard and hung up the phone. Three days ago she felt on top of the world. Wertman was safe and secure in the slammer, Fletcher was forced into "stress leave" pending investigation by Internal Affairs, and she received a letter from her brother. Then Mark MacDonald had come along and stuck his nose into the case, panicking Troy.

Where did that leave her?

She cursed and yanked open the fridge. Grabbing a beer, she headed for the living room and the nightly news.

She had some time to burn. 7:30 was an hour away.

November 8, 1971
Dear Mark,

God has spared me, your Grandpa Kyle, from death, for a season. Three weeks ago, from my sickbed, I gave Aunt Clara what I believed was my final deposition, knowing you were still ignorant of the MacDonald family legacy. Now, with my fever fully passed, I realize that there are certain things that you should know as you prepare to read Sam's writings. Understand, I have read all of them, as well.

First, you should know that your grandmother Mary died in 1917, four months after the fire that nearly took our home. Had it been only the loss of Mary that overwhelmed me so, I might have eventually regained my bearings and put my life back on course. Many who are widowed marry again and find happiness. But it was not her death alone that devastated me. As I reflected on our family history, I realized that Mary was the fourth MacDonald woman within five generations to die tragically. What really happened within my home the night of the fire, I will never know for sure. But I will always suspect the spiritual wickedness that claimed the lives of Grandma Nikki, Sarah, and Victoria also claimed the life of my beloved Mary. The only exception to this deadly chain was my mother Angelina who died in 1934.

Second, I have never had the insights that Sam had, nor a sense within my heart that I was the second man, as my other grandfather, John Ezra, realized early in his life. It has always been this lack of spiritual insight that kept me from wanting to share Sam's writing with the family. If I could not discern the Devil, or his henchmen, as Sam had done, then how could I guide my family to resist them?

This fear paralyzed me for several years. Sam's writings remained sealed up in the knapsacks and hidden from sight. As time passed, I thought less and less about the knapsacks. Your father's and your Aunt Clara's lives were as normal as any parent could hope for.

That is, until your mother, Evangeline, died in 1961, giving birth to you. My fear returned that the Devil was still after the MacDonald line.

Now, at the end, I regret keeping Sam's two knapsacks locked away and withholding his journals and Founding Fathers research from your father. Perhaps you, Mark, will be the man Sam hoped I would be, the man I never gave your father the chance to be. I pray you find your portion.

With all my love,
Grandpa Kyle

Katie leaned forward on the sofa. "Honey, are you OK?"

All Mark could do was hold his head in his hands.

The gray-eyed man pushed a thick white envelope across the shadowed table top. As he did this, the harsh, distorted blare of electric guitars, drums and shrieking voices exploded across the Bayou's dance floor.

KC winced. Troy ignored the dissonant roar and frenetically animated guitarists on the sound stage to his left. He grabbed the envelope, pulled it open and ruffled through the bills inside.

"Excellent. Exactly as I requested." Troy stared the Sponsor in the eye. The Sponsor's gaze was unnerving. Troy looked down at the envelope.

"I've given you everything pertinent to Wertman's case. I'm still the detective in charge, so you don't have to worry about any screw-ups or negative developments from my end. I don't want to get fried for my involvement with Wertman—same as you."

"And Mark MacDonald?" the Sponsor asked, his voice oddly dispassionate.

Troy outlined his plan to dispose of the witness' statement.

KC listened to Troy but watched the Sponsor's face. His gray eyes narrowed; the muscles in his jaw and neck tightened. The diagonal mark on his cheek seemed to darken. KC's stomach flip-flopped. Had she seen that right? Or was it just the play of light on his face?

"Perhaps your plan will work," the Sponsor replied coldly. Without explanation he slid out of the booth and rose to his feet. "But now you will have to excuse me. I have an itinerary that must be kept."

Troy waited for the Sponsor to walk away, then turned and grinned at KC. He put his arm around her and planted a soft kiss on the side of her mouth. "Well, that wasn't so bad. We've got our money and he's got his information. The fact that Wertman's case is still marginally open actually works to our advantage. It keeps everybody honest. One false move on the Sponsor's part and he knows that I've got his number."

Troy kissed her again. "Why don't we go out and celebrate, then head back to my place?"

KC lifted Troy's arm and swung her legs from the booth. She stood up, pulled a five dollar bill from her jeans' pocket, and tossed it onto the table. She turned and walked away.

Troy dropped a ten dollar bill beside her five, grabbed his coat, then pushed his way rudely through a small group of college students heading for their table. He caught up with her outside the front entrance on the way to the parking lot, grabbing her by the arm.

"Hey! What's up with you? I didn't hear you contradict anything I said."

Spinning away, KC yanked her arm free. "Back off, Troy. Way off. I need some time to think, to sort this thing out. I don't know what I want anymore."

Troy studied her face for a moment, and then shrugged. He stepped up close and adjusted the lapel on her jacket. As he did, he slipped the white envelope inside her jacket. "You forgot your share."

He stepped back. "You know where I sleep and where I work. Call me, OK?"

KC chewed on her lower lip, and then nodded.

Troy waved, turned, and headed across the street toward the parking lot underneath the overpass. KC did likewise.

She arrived at her Camaro, draped in the shadows of a massive concrete column supporting the ramp above her head. She unlocked the door and got inside, so preoccupied that she missed the fact that her inside dome light did not come on. Parked facing outward, she could see Troy a hundred feet away unlocking his car and getting inside. As she pulled out her keys and put them in the ignition, KC regretted not having said goodbye.

Troy's Buick Skylark's headlights snapped on—followed immediately by a blinding orange and white explosion. Instinctively, KC raised her arms as the Skylark rose a foot off the pavement, a bright erupting ball of fragmented metal, shattered glass and flame.

Stunned, KC stared at the ring of keys in the ignition.

As she did this, a grim, familiar voice spoke quietly from the back seat. "Don't worry, your car is safe. Turn the key and drive!"

KC shuddered as all control drained from her limbs. She started the engine, pulled from her parking space and turned left. In her rearview mirror she could see the Sponsor's head silhouetted by the burning wreckage of Troy's car.

"Quickly!" the voice behind her commanded.

Cutting sharply out of the parking lot onto the street, KC obeyed, shifting gears and stomping hard on the gas pedal.

"Turn left, then right at the light."

Like an automaton, KC responded. She accelerated up the short hill. The light at M Street was green. Twenty seconds later, the Camaro was just one of a hundred cars moving east through Georgetown on a bustling Friday night.

"You may slow down now," the voice suggested calmly. "We do not need a speeding violation at this time. Continue east until I tell you otherwise."

Downshifting, KC complied, tears streaming down her cheeks. She wiped them away with her coat sleeve. She had to locate a police cruiser and stop it—even if it meant ramming her Camaro.

"Don't grieve for your friend. It is your brother that I would be concerned about."

The words sliced like a sharp, thin knife into KC's heart. Her foot involuntarily touched the brake. She forced words from her mouth. "My brother? What about my brother?"

The voice from the back seat was sober and compassionless. "He suffered a terrible accident in the prison yard while playing football. Someone undercut his legs. He flipped and the concrete was very unforgiving. The doctors are not sure he will pull through. And even if he does not suffer any additional complications, there is the possibility of permanent disability. But mind my words—only a possibility."

The street and traffic seemed to flatten before KC's eyes like a slowly deflating balloon. She fought to control the wheel, to remember which pedal at her feet was which—clutch, brake, gas. She almost hit three teenagers who darted in front of her.

"You are obviously distressed. Perhaps I should get out at the next corner. But do not worry, I will be calling you with additional information about your brother. Until then, I would suggest you go directly home. Shortly, you will be receiving a call about your friend Troy. I recommend you keep your story simple: you had words in the parking lot, then left a few minutes ahead of him. You saw nothing."

KC pulled sharply over at the corner and lowered her head into her hands. She heard the door open, and then close.

Sobbing, she pounded the steering wheel with her fists.

"Why didn't you tell me about your two dreams before now?" Katie demanded from the study doorway. She crossed her arms over her sweater and frowned.

Mark placed Kyle's letter on the desk, and then slumped into the straight-back chair.

"With the baby and all, I just didn't think you needed to revisit the accident or hear about your name appearing on a tombstone. Last night we almost got run down, and Fletcher tells me he saw a scar on Fein's face. Suddenly it was like seeing the words *unde malum* on the statue all over again. That only made me more hesitant."

Mark turned in the chair to face Katie directly. "I'm sorry. I couldn't face the fact that the Devil was trying to end the family bloodline. He's hunting us just like he hunted Sam and Victoria and the offspring of every generation since Will and Nikki."

Katie brushed the hair back from her face. "Now I understand why Grandpa Kyle's letter affected you that way."

Mark rose from the chair and faced the window. He thought back eight days to how excited he'd been as he unwound the heavy wire and opened the box. He heard footsteps behind him, and then felt his wife's warm arms wrap around his waist.

"Your grandpa's letter clears something else up in my mind." Her voice had softened.

Mark sighed. "What's that?"

"The identity of the second man in Tecumseh's prophecy." Katie paused, squeezing Mark gently.

He pulled her arms apart, and then spun around. "What are you saying?"

Katie leaned in and rested her head on his chest. "I think Tecumseh's prophecy has yet to be fulfilled."

A single tear rolled down Mark's cheek as he shook his head from side to side.

Katie grasped his hands tightly. Mark worked his hands free, and then stepped back and turned away. He leaned over the table by the windows, his head drooping.

"Just because Sam turned out to be my great great grandfather by adopting Angelina doesn't mean I have to follow in his footsteps. We've already had our share of tragedy."

Pressing in against his side, Katie could feel the tension in her husband's body. "Remember how the Lord spared John Ezra? How Toby was always there when Sam needed him?"

Mark slammed his hands against the edge of the table. "Forget Toby! The same spirit that tried to kill Sam and assassinated Lincoln shows up in Washington D.C. and tries to run us down with a pickup truck—and you want me to consider if I'm the other man?"

"Yes, I do! Because Grandpa Kyle's letter proves your calling's just not going to fade away with time."

"Then we're doomed," Mark replied, his voice faint. "That spirit's after me if I'm the other man, and after you and the baby if I'm not. It won't quit until it ends our bloodline."

"But Kyle lived to be a hundred! And Sam lived into his seventies—at least."

Mark's shoulders sagged. "Is that what you want for our children? To go through life knowing they're on the Devil's hit list?"

Katie draped her arms around his shoulders. "Four years ago when they wheeled me into surgery, the doctors told you I only had a twenty percent chance to live. They said I'd never walk or get pregnant. I know what it feels like to be on a hit list."

After several silent moments standing by the table that held Sam's journals, Katie kissed Mark on the cheek. She wiped his tears away with her fingers.

"Bottom line is, everyone's on the Devil's hit list."

Mark closed his eyes as she backed away. She crossed the study and started down the stairs.

As her footfalls faded, a tired smile broke across his face. Katie! She was right. Things had often been dark and they suffered through many temporary setbacks, through times of depression and despondency. But the Lord was still there through it all, allowing them to meet their fears head-on.

Just like the Lord had allowed Sam.

He lifted his eyes. He tried to pray at church on Sunday, but the words had been hollow. From his mouth. Not his heart.

Then he remembered the hymn. The three-hundred-year-old melody of another fellow sufferer stirred inside of him.

Be still, my soul, the Lord is on thy side.

The words came back, clear and strong, washing over him like a river of mercy.

Bear patiently the cross of grief or pain.
Leave to thy God to order and provide.
In every change the faithful will remain.

Mark lowered his head into his hands. Heartache poured from his soul and streamed from his eyes.

Be still my soul, thy best, thy heavenly friend,
through thorny ways leads to a joyful end.

He opened his heart and his mouth.

Sam's words became his.

A half hour later, still sensing God's presence strongly about him, Mark snapped off the study light. He paused at the landing.

The mystery surrounding his grandfather's decision to hide the two knapsacks was over. And so was a second mystery.

Holding Grandpa Kyle's letter, Mark thumped himself on the head. Could he have really been that blind?

Details in the letter indicated that he had!

With a gleam in his eye, he crossed the hall to the storage room where he found the box of journals. He opened the door. Bright moonlight fell into the room through open curtains. He stared at the spot on the floor where he found the first medical knapsack—a plain wooden box minus the original canvas cover and shoulder straps used for carrying it.

Four feet away he could see the sharp corner of a second wooden box mostly obscured by a tattered army blanket and a yellowed lampshade.

Sam's second knapsack.

21 January 1893

Crest Road, Washington D.C.

I write at my new desk, a welcoming gift from my nephew and his wife. Kyle has promised to mount the Long Knife above the fireplace. Angelina, ever sensitive to the Lord's timing, urges me to share with Kyle the story of this sword and the prophecy spoken thirty-five years prior to my birth.

Since my confrontation with the spirit Rasah on the night Lincoln was assassinated, the bitter spring within my own life has not seemed so bitter. For the Scriptures teach, "Submit yourselves therefore to God. Resist the Devil and he will flee from you."

However, the cry of the blood is just as loud as it was at Gettysburg thirty years ago, for The War Between the States did not change the hearts of men nor did it hallow the ground. The dark root has never been purged from the heart of our nation and now, the Devil's servants sow a garden of madness, seeding a future far more tyrannical than that which divided our house and I fear, with consequences more dire.

For the time, Rasah, the spirit of murder, is silent. When he speaks again, I fear he will be speaking as legion. He will never stop shedding blood, until men resist him and give him no place in their hearts.

Lord, when my time here on earth has passed, I hope to be buried in Manassas Battlefield, near the place of my birth, along the banks of the Bull Run near Sudley Church. I have asked that these old bones be placed in the soil that soaked up the blood of so many men, North and South. I wish to sleep in that soil where brother slew brother as Cain slew Abel, where blood was poured out that could not redeem, where sacrifices were made that could not cleanse.

This I shall do as a memorial to all MacDonalds who follow, so they shall never forget the lessons that You, Lord, taught me. For as my faithful brother John Kline wrote, "The earth can cover the body, but it cannot cover hope."

Amen.

⊰ **38** ⊱

Saturday Morning

IN THE GRAY LIGHT OF DAWN, the Otis Elevator serviceman pulled his
van into the parking lot on the north side of the Washington Monument. At 7 A.M. there was only one other vehicle beside his own—a
cargo-style van with darkly tinted windows.

The Park Service's work request indicated that the elevator cables
had fouled again. It was a relatively easy fix that required few tools.
If this repair was similar to the last fouled cable he worked on, the
elevator would be up and running before noon. He slipped a pen
into the pocket of his uniform, stepped out of the van with his
checklist, and closed and locked the door. His eyes rose admiringly
to the tallest freestanding masonry structure in the world. He wondered how it had been in the 1840s to pull duty on the monument's
original elevator—a steam-driven hoist. He scratched his sideburns.
As far as elevator work went, a man couldn't hope for a better assignment.

Assignment—the word was jolted from his thoughts by a numbing blow to the back of his neck. He heard the clipboard clatter by
his feet, then the ground rushed hard at his face and exploded into
black.

"Sounds great. We'd love to support Michelle. I know she and her
friend Julie were dreading going to the rally."

Katie switched the telephone to her other ear and listened to
Fletcher's follow-up question, and then smiled.

"The baby and I are feeling fine, really. Besides, I've never had
my own private tour of the Washington Monument. I didn't realize
you could make arrangements like that."

She nodded. "Mark's fine. By the way, you'll never guess what
happened. Last night Mark found Sam's second knapsack."

Katie chuckled at Fletcher's comment, and then glanced sideways
at her husband who was pouring himself a cup of coffee.

"You're right about that. Maybe Mark can start jogging with you.
He's done little more than eat and read for ten days."

Mark glanced over his shoulder and frowned, and then returned the daguerreotype of Victoria MacDonald to the counter.

"OK, 9:00 A.M. See you then." Katie grinned and hung up the phone.

Mark sipped his coffee. "I take it we're going on a tour."

"Yep. Fletcher's got connections with the Park Service. We're going to try to abscond with Michelle and her friend, Julie, and escape to the Observation Deck."

Katie studied the daguerreotype. "It's good timing, too. Fletcher says there's no safer place for us to be right now than out in public."

A large group of high school seniors from Nebraska milled around the entrance to the monument as a young red-headed woman in a green Park Service uniform waved them away.

"Sorry! The monument's closed this morning," the woman explained to the disappointed students. "The elevator should be back in service sometime this afternoon."

The students slowly cleared from the entrance area, spreading to each side around the monument, some snapping pictures, others sitting or climbing on the two concentric rows of benches surrounding the base. A small contingent headed down the hill past the temporary stage toward the reflecting pool.

The Park Service employee walked up to a white iron gate at the monument's entrance. She yanked on a padlock that kept anyone from opening the gate and sneaking inside. As she did, the elevator man exited the equipment room to the right of the elevator doors. He stood in the hallway directly ahead, clipboard and pen in hand.

"Are we still on target for this afternoon?" she asked.

The dark-haired repairman smiled. "I'm making great progress."

"Good! If you don't mind being locked up in here alone, I've got to go back down to the Survey Lodge. Every free Park Service body is going to be needed for crowd control. When you're finished, just give us a call." She reached through the bars and pointed at a wall phone to the left. "Punch the Survey Lodge button. It's a direct line."

"Thanks," the repairman replied. He walked to the phone.

The woman waved goodbye and disappeared around the monument to the right.

The repairman pulled a pair of wire cutters from his back pocket. Smiling again, he reached up and snipped all three of the lines leading into the base of the phone.

Putting the cutters back into his pocket, he turned and walked down the short hall to the elevator doors. From his other pocket he removed a black remote control-like device. He pressed one of a dozen numbered buttons on its face.

The elevator doors slid open.

Good! The transmitter relayed its signals flawlessly!

The repairman walked inside. In the near corner was one of two large, rectangular aluminum cases that he had brought up from the van. The other case was already emptied, its contents strategically placed on top of the elevator cab and around the base of the shaft inside the equipment room.

He pushed a second button on the remote and the doors slid shut. He pushed a third and the elevator began its ascent to the 500 foot level at its perfectly normal rate of 4.8 miles per hour.

Fletcher turned right off 15th Street onto Independence Avenue. The monument was to their right and crowds arriving for the counter-rally swarmed around its base. Beyond a stand of trees, a smaller crowd gathered at the Sylvan Theatre for pre-rally festivities. A quarter of a mile further down, he turned right again onto a narrow service road due south of the monument. Fletcher pulled into a spot behind an orange highway cone near the Survey Lodge, a recently renovated stone steam house, now used by the Park Service as a base of operations. A ring of Park employees and police studied a large map and made plans. A short way off to the left, three Park Police sat stoically on their handsome, brown steeds, scanning the crowd that gathered in the area between the reflecting pool and the sound stage at the base of the monument.

"This is fantastic!" Julie said, opening her door and looking up at the monument.

"Compliments of an old friend," Fletcher said, grinning and locking his door. "Before we head up the hill, I need to stop in and tell Tom we're here, and thank him for saving us this parking place. I'll be right back!"

Mark locked his door and joined Katie who had already crossed the gravel road to the grassy edge of the mall. They stopped beside a wide sidewalk that wound lazily up the slope to the south side of the monument. The sun broke through the cloud cover, dappling the wide, grassy concourse with huge bright spots. Mark wrapped his arm around his wife's shoulders, nuzzled his face behind her ear and planted a soft kiss on her neck.

Michelle and Julie stepped up to Mark's left, their eyes glued to the top of the monument.

"So, what do you think?" Mark asked Julie.

"I've lived in the area four years, but I've never been up the

Washington Monument," Julie answered as the wind brushed her hair onto her face. "It's a lot more massive looking when you get close like this."

Mark pointed at the monument. "See that line in the marble about a third of the way up? From the 1840s to the 1870s, it was nothing more than an ugly stump. Where we're standing used to be a marsh."

Out of the corner of his eye, Mark saw Fletcher jog across the gravel drive behind them.

Fletcher raised his hands apologetically. "Guys—I've got good news and bad news—and the bad news is the elevator's on the blink. They've got a serviceman working on it right now, but it'll be early afternoon before it's operational."

"What's the good news?" Katie asked.

"We'll be the first to go up, before it's reopened to the public. In the meantime, why don't we take a stroll down to the Vietnam Memorial? By the time we get back, it'll be almost eleven and we can check with the serviceman. How's that sound?"

Brian Fein swung his legs over the top edge of the cab, rolled onto his stomach, then lowered himself down the side of the elevator housing. He landed easily on his feet in front of the open doors. For a moment, he had forgotten where he had left the remote control and detonator. He glanced inside the elevator. The small, black plastic remote was right where it should be—on the seat of the old wooden chair next to the control panel.

He took six C-4 bricks from the aluminum case, then walked around to the west side of the monument. He dropped the C-4 on the wooden box beneath the rectangular observation window. Brian walked back to the elevator, then returned with a roll of duct tape and a cardboard box. He taped the bricks to the marble around the edge of the observation window, two above and two below the window and one on each end. From the cardboard box he removed six detonators, stabbing one deeply into the center of each brick. To each detonator he attached a coil of thin, insulated wire.

One window completed, three to go.

Brian paused, glancing down at the milling crowds and the speaker's stand. The flimsy structure would disintegrate into a fireball when the two bricks of C-4 he had planted beneath it were detonated.

The chance that he would actually topple the monument, however, was slim, perhaps non-existent. This target was the greatest challenge of his career and he was under no illusions. Yachts, pubs, and public buildings had been child's play. The Washington Monument would test every aspect of his engineering knowledge. The walls at its base were fifteen feet thick, narrowing at the 150 foot level, the 400 foot level and again at the observation level where the walls were only eighteen inches thick.

His precisely timed detonations would begin with the four windows, followed by a single brick that would break the cables and send the elevator plunging down the shaft. A half second later, the 150 pounds of C-4 wedged in the cross-beams above him at the corners of the elevator shaft would explode. The cumulative effect would be devastating to the observation area. Four gaping, six to eight foot holes would be created at each window. The plastic explosive in the cross-beams would vent its dynamic fury downward, out the windows and down the shaft. The elevator, already dropping at a rate of thirty-two feet per second, would be further accelerated. On its own, the elevator would have reached the bottom in five seconds, traveling over one hundred miles per hour—and that was without the added propulsion of the explosion behind it.

Thus, his second detonation would begin two and one-half seconds later, rather than five, when the elevator was approximately twenty-five feet from ground level. The remaining two hundred pounds of C-4 at the bottom of the shaft would be detonated, their effects more spectacular than the first. The force of a six-ton elevator traveling at nearly two hundred miles an hour in a confined shaft would compress the exploding gases, heat, and flame like a huge piston.

Quite simply, the Washington Monument would become the world's largest Roman candle. The elevator would blow back up the shaft and out the weakened top, spewing a bright red-orange geyser of fire, marble, and metal. Anyone standing within two hundred yards and directly in line with the monument doors would not survive.

The entire country would be shocked and enraged when they discovered that Harold Wertman's Christian terrorist organization claimed responsibility. The Christian Right's future potential for legitimacy would be lost in that terrible, swift moment in time. Organizations who had lost their leaders in the inhuman, unthinkable bombing—not to mention the Senators and Congressmen in town for the inauguration—would see to it that radical conservatives were stripped of any public or political influence.

Bonn, and other invisible leaders like her scattered around the globe, would press forward with their agenda for societal reorganization and the cleansing of Judeo-Christian ethics. They would press for state control and sanctioning of churches and the removal of their tax-exempt status. Ordinations would be monitored and politically active pastors expelled from religious service. The church would be silenced.

Then Bonn would move forward as she had never done before.

A ferocious smile broke across Brian's tense face as he picked up six more of the gray bricks and started for the east window.

Katie sat down on the short flight of steps near the east end of the reflecting pool. Mark approached Fletcher and explained how long, uninterrupted walks were hard on her. The Vietnam Memorial was another half-mile away.

"I understand," Fletcher said with a nod. "There's no need to tire Katie out. We'll catch you on our way back, in forty-five minutes."

Fletcher rejoined Michelle and Julie. They waved as they walked off.

Taking a seat beside his wife, Mark watched the crowds stream onto the mall from the side streets intersecting Constitution Avenue. Placards were starting to appear in thickening streams as busloads of out-of-town protesters were deposited neatly onto the sidewalks. The messages on the signs were varied in size and color but seemed to follow one theme: Say Yes to Pro-Choice!

Mark glanced at his watch: 10:15. According to Michelle, the counter-rally didn't actually begin until 11:00 when Legacy would take the stage for a forty-five minute concert. Several politicians would then make introductions, followed by a half-dozen pro-choice leaders. Following the speeches, a march was planned down the length of the mall and around the Capitol to the Supreme Court building where a Women's Bill of Rights would be symbolically "nailed" to the front doors.

Heavy shadows fell across Mark and Katie. They looked up. The cloud cover had thickened again, the sky now a lifeless gray with only a few scattered streaks of blue. And without sunlight, the gentle breeze turned colder. Katie stuffed her hands into her coat pockets.

She turned slightly on the steps to face Mark more squarely, her eyes narrowing and her mouth curling slowly into a grin as she caught him staring skyward with an absent-minded smile on his face.

"What are you thinking about?"

Mark put an arm around her shoulders. "Everything seems different this morning. New."

Katie's grin widened. "I'm so excited you found the second knapsack. Just seeing that daguerreotype of Victoria made her more real to me. She was so beautiful."

Mark listened quietly, his eyes roaming the sky as he recalled the words of an old Indian chieftain.

Out of your loins will come two...

It was almost 11:00. Brian stared out the west observation window, watching the crowds below pack in closer to the temporary stage. Legacy was warming up, the bass guitarist thumping out a long, fast riff.

In forty-five minutes, their concert would end, and Legacy would turn the stage over to Peters, the old fool, for opening remarks. Legacy would immediately join him in a waiting limosine in the monument parking lot, and then hurry to catch a private jet for a concert in New York. Saving Legacy would not only provide him with a legitimate cover and escape, but would protect his investment in the rockers and their future royalties if they really hit it big.

Peters' fate would not be so fortunate, nor would the Controller's if Peters followed his directions and had her sit with him on the front row. Five minutes into Peters' opening remarks, as Legacy's limo pulled out of the parking lot onto Constitution Avenue, Brian visualized himself sequentially depressing two rubber pads on the remote. His fireworks display would ignite beneath the podium where Peters was speaking.

A fraction of a second is all that it would take! He would be free, free to dictate his terms to New York, London, and Geneva! Even Bonn. And they would listen—he would make them listen! They could not afford to be exposed. The information stored on the computer disks he kept locked away in a local bank safety deposit box would guarantee his freedom. This supreme humbling of Christian fanaticism would be his final service for those who owned the rights to his body and soul. He would buy it back—extort it back if need be! He would publish the names and addresses of the organization's key contacts if he had to! Never again would he allow himself to be purchased; never again would he make himself subservient to anyone!

Liberty—Brian paused and looked out the observation window at the Lincoln Memorial. Liberty was the unrestrained enjoyment of natural rights. Liberty had other meanings, too, but none that gripped his emotions so strongly. How he longed for liberty—for the day he wouldn't need to carry a razor-sharp knife strapped to his calf or a 9mm automatic tucked into a holster under his arm or in the small of his back.

As a young boy, he often prayed for peace—at Mass, kneeling by his bed at night—praying that God would protect his mother and father and family. How futile had been his early years of pleading with God! How distant was the Almighty from Ireland's troubles, refusing to intervene, to make a lasting peace, and to establish justice!

Kneeling in a filthy gutter by his dead cousins had brought an end to his praying and pleading.

From below came thunderous applause as Legacy began to play, the sound of a monstrous human heartbeat echoing over the quieting crowd. Brian moved away from the observation window and began his final inspection of every detonator and every wire.

Liberty! Forty-five minutes and counting...

To the surprise of the onlookers, Fletcher pulled a ring with three keys from his pocket and unlocked the monument's white cast iron gate. He opened the gate wide enough to allow Mark and Katie to enter, then slipped in behind them and refastened the padlock.

"Sorry," he apologized to a group of students. "The elevator's still out of commission."

From outside, Michelle patted the bars. "I can't believe that Mr. Peters actually spotted me in the crowd. He wants me to sit in his special front row seats. But thanks for trying."

Julie put a hand on Michelle's shoulder. "I'll be right there behind you to keep you company."

Michelle frowned. "Why don't you go in with them?"

"Forget it!" Julie chided. "Fletcher's already agreed to take us up another time."

Shrugging her shoulders and smiling, Michelle stepped back from the gate. "Then I guess we better be heading back. The concert's starting."

As if on cue, the crowd cheered. The group of teenagers standing on nearby benches jumped down and ran toward the sound. Michelle and Julie waved goodbye.

Fletcher pulled hard on the padlock one last time. It was secure. Just as he started to turn from the gate, his eyes rose to the wall phone to the right of the gate. He noticed the buttons. One was marked "Survey Lodge," another "Observation Phone." The third was an outside line.

"Hey, Fletcher!" Mark called from down the hall and around the corner. "The elevator door is closed. Does that mean it's working?"

As he turned and walked down the hall, Fletcher admired the marble tile floor and walls. It'd been a while since he'd been in the monument. He'd forgotten about the beautiful craftsmanship.

Stepping around the corner, Fletcher glanced at the elevator doors. Mark leaned against the wall; Katie sat on the bench.

"Hold on a second. Let me check the equipment room; it's back around the other side."

The equipment room was locked. Fletcher knocked on the door but no one answered. He pulled a ring of keys from his coat pocket and unlocked the door. The narrow room was dark. Fletcher felt the wall to his left, then threw the light switch.

To his surprise, the light did not come on. He closed the door. Maybe the serviceman had completed his work and already returned to the Survey Lodge. He locked the door. There was one way to find out.

Returning to the gate, Fletcher picked up the phone and punched the Survey Lodge button. Even as he did, he realized that there was no tone. He punched each line but the effect was the same: silence. Fletcher replaced the handset on the receiver. Odd. He wondered if the light being out and the phone not working were connected—an electrical failure of some kind.

From outside, a dull pounding could be heard, followed by a huge roar from the crowd. The peculiar sound was hauntingly familiar. Fletcher rubbed the back of his neck and turned away, then he remembered—Legacy!

Frowning, he returned to Mark and Katie and found them studying the inscription to George Washington in the marble tiles: *First in the hearts of his countrymen.*

"Well, I'm not really sure what's going on," Fletcher explained. "The phone's dead and so's the light in the equipment room. I guess there's not much we can do but go back down to the Lodge. Maybe we'll find the serviceman there. Without the elevator key, we can't get up unless we walk up the stairs."

"You could take Mark up a few levels," Katie suggested, unzipping her coat. "I don't mind waiting. I know Mark's been drooling about seeing some of the dedication stones."

"Honey, I wouldn't think of leaving you here."

"I know you wouldn't—but I would! Enjoy yourselves. If the repairman returns, we'll call up the stairs to you."

Mark rolled his eyes. Fletcher smiled back and shrugged.

Brian pulled the last packing case from the elevator and slid it to the side as Legacy began their second number. His work on the 500 foot level was almost complete.

He surveyed the observation area. Wires curved around from the right and left of the elevator housing. They connected to a shoebox-sized, battery-driven receiver and power supply sitting beneath the north observation window. Signals generated by his remote from the van would be boosted and then transmitted to the three receivers in the monument, one at the bottom, one directly across from him beneath the window and one on top of the elevator.

All that was left was a final check of the detonators and wire connections in the equipment room.

Brian approached the burnished stainless steel doors and pulled the remote from his shirt pocket. As he did, his finger inadvertently pressed one of the buttons. The elevator doors slid shut.

Aggravated, Brian hastily punched the button directly below it. Wait... but his finger had been too quick. He cursed and slammed a fist against the doors—he pushed the wrong button.

The elevator started down.

And there was nothing he could do until it reached the bottom. Angry at his foolish mistake, Brian turned and leaned his back against the doors. A minute down, a minute up.

He started counting the seconds.

Mark and Fletcher climbed the six-foot-wide stairway, huge blocks of hand-cut granite on their right. They found the first dedication stones at the thirty-foot level. Some inscriptions were ornate, others plain; Maine and Delaware were two of the most attractive. According to Fletcher each stone was made of material indigenous to the state. The forty-foot level held a large and notable stone from Alabama, the first stone to be placed within the monument's walls.

As they reached the sixty-foot level, Mark looked at his watch. "Last floor."

Fletcher nodded, and then turned his head quickly toward the elevator shaft.

The rough sliding sound of cables behind them seized their attention. They turned and walked over to the wall of heavy chain link fence enclosing the elevator shaft. The cables moved rapidly.

"I'd say the elevator's working," Fletcher said. "Let's get back down."

He turned just as the elevator swooshed by, following its swift descent down the shaft. His eye caught something out of place on the cable assembly, but the elevator had fallen too rapidly from sight to identify it. He rubbed the back of his neck.

What had he seen?

Katie rose from the bench and watched the stainless steel doors as the elevator came to a stop. To her great surprise, the doors slid open to reveal an empty elevator. Without first thinking why, she accepted the apparent invitation and cautiously stepped inside.

As she did, the doors closed behind her.

Mark and Fletcher waited at the sixty-foot level and stared at each other as the cables started moving again. Mark turned and faced the tall steps on the landing. Was Katie directing the serviceman to pick them up?

Fletcher's mind sped into overdrive. He pressed his cheek against the wire mesh and focused his eyes on the ascending elevator and its cable assembly.

Up the shaft it came, the spotlight from the landing clearly illuminating the top of the cab. Taped to the thick cables about a foot above the steel reinforcing bars was a gray brick with a wire sticking out from it and running down to a black box resting on the roof of the cab.

Mark's eyes were focused elsewhere. As the elevator passed by, his mouth fell open. Katie was inside the elevator, staring out the small window to the right of the doors, her face sharply marked with worry! And behind her to the left, Mark saw the angular face of an old man with wild, pitch-black hair and a nose like the beak of a bird.

The old man's beady eyes met his.

Mark gasped audibly, his legs buckling. He grabbed for the rail in front of him, and then looked at Fletcher. He had to force the words from his mouth. "Katie's in the cab..."

Fletcher's face paled. "Are you sure?"

Pulling himself closer to the shaft, Mark's eyes darted upward to follow the elevator as it disappeared into the darkness above. He tried to dispel the image of the face he'd seen. "Something's wrong, impossibly wrong—I saw the old man."

Fletcher cocked his head in disbelief. The old man—the Devil? His mouth went dry. "Fein's here, too! There were plastic explosives on the roof of the cab!"

Tossing his winter coat aside, Mark turned and started up the steps, two at time.

Peeling off his jacket, Fletcher let it drop to the steps, then pulled his 9mm Glock from the holster in the small of his back. "Mark! Hold on!"

There was no response, just the quickly fading sound of tennis shoes on concrete. Fletcher froze, glanced to his left and down the stairs. Five flights to the bottom—he swung his head around—forty-four flights to the observation level! What did Mark think he could possibly do?

Each passing second tore at Fletcher's conscience. To reach the Survey Lodge would take five minutes and another ten for the Park Service to formulate a response. By the time Special Operations arrived, another fifteen minutes would pass. Even then, what options would they have? Without the elevator they would have to climb the 490 feet in their heavy gear. A helicopter assault would be useless. And what about Mark's statement that he'd seen the Devil? He couldn't explain that to anybody!

There was only one option. Fletcher threw the safety on his automatic, reached behind his back and jammed the pistol into the holster. He breathed deeply, turned to his right and started up the steps, just like Mark, two at a time, desperate prayers exploding from his lips.

The elevator slowed to a halt. Timidly, Katie turned and faced the door, hoping the serviceman conducting his tests would believe her story.

The elevator doors slid open.

Just as Katie had suspected, the dark-haired serviceman was waiting directly outside. He took a step forward, and then froze, one foot in the elevator, one out. His dark eyes snapped wide open; his taut, muscular face registering absolute shock.

Katie's explanation and apology lodged in her throat as his look of surprise darkened suddenly to anger. The arch of his heavy eyebrows and the twist of his lips were severe, startling—and frighteningly familiar. The serviceman's eyes narrowed calculatingly as he stared up and down, and then closed for a brief, painful moment. He opened his eyes and met hers straight on. A cold, palpable hatred invaded Katie, weakening her at the knees.

Without warning, the serviceman reached in and harshly grabbed her by the wrist. He pulled her from the elevator. His face had the look of chiseled stone, except for a faint, diagonal red line on his left cheek.

"Mrs. MacDonald," he said without emotion, twisting her arm behind her back. "I cannot say that it's a pleasure to meet you."

At the 390 foot level Mark dropped to one knee, raggedly sucking air into his lungs. His calves, thighs, and chest burned, his heart pounded wildly and sweat stung his eyes. A few seconds later he heard Fletcher behind him, grunting for breath.

Fletcher staggered past him to the next flight of steps, then stopped, leaning against the wall and wiping at his face with his sleeve. Words broke from his mouth in short barks.

"Gonna make it?"

"Don't know," Mark gasped, pushing himself to his feet.

Fletcher nodded wearily, inhaled deeply, and started up the stairs ahead of his friend.

After binding Katie's hands and feet, Brian sat her on the marble floor with her back against the east side of the elevator. She had grown strangely silent and calm after an outburst of tears during his interrogation about her companions, keeping her soft blue eyes focused somewhere above his head. Was she praying? Making foolish appeals to God? Didn't she know that she, and any would-be rescuers, were doomed?

Brian moved around the elevator to the stairwell door. Surely her husband and Fletcher Rivers had watched the elevator pass by. Had the policeman spotted the C-4 and the receiver on top of the cab? If he did, he probably sent MacDonald back down the stairs for help. But what of Rivers? Was he on his way up the stairs?

Best to assume he was. Other than to cover the entrance, Rivers would realize that the Park Police wouldn't be able to easily choose a course of action—the rally guaranteed that. No, it would not be the Park Service that responded, but the MPD Special Operations Division. All in all, a good thirty minutes would pass before the first, telltale signs of the S.O.D.'s presence would appear with a helicopter pass and telescopic inspection of what could be seen through the observation windows.

Their inspection would reveal Katie, bound and sitting by the elevator in clear view. And her presence, in combination with the tens of thousands of protesters attending the rally, would complicate their move on the monument. And as Rivers was probably now discovering, so would the 897 steps. Decked in their heavy assault jackets, the stairs would remove every advantage an MPD attack force might normally achieve through surprise and numbers.

Theoretically, he still had time to leave, using Katie as a hostage. But the odds of his survival were marginal at best. And worse, if a sharpshooter picked him off before he could use the detonator...

Sweet liberty! He had come so close!

For the last ten years he'd been playing a deadly game with the deck stacked against him. Three times the Royal Ulster Constabulary should have gunned him down. And once, in Belfast, he found himself staring straight down the barrel of a Loyalist's handgun. Miraculously, the assassin's gun jammed.

And now it tortured him to think he might be undone by an American civilian, his wife and a down-and-out undercover cop.

A bitter, red haze flashed across his vision, and then down inside him, consuming every emotion that stood in its way—hope, longing, passion. A malicious tingling spread down through his arms and into his hands. His hand rose to his shirt pocket, gently feeling for the remote.

If they were going to deny him his liberty, then he'd deny them theirs, each and every last one of them.

The number 490 painted on the top stair was barely distinguishable through the sweaty blur. Fletcher's rubbery legs and raw lungs were on fire; every inhalation through his open mouth and nose tore painfully down his throat. He collapsed by the elevator platform. He tried to rise but his feet felt like they were bolted to the cement floor. It wasn't fear that kept him down, but exhaustion.

Fletcher fumbled for the ring of keys, knowing that even if he could make his way up the stairs to the observation level door and somehow unlock it, he would be physically unable to take on a fully rested and waiting opponent.

He shook his head. The pain in his chest was so great that he squeezed tears out of the corners of his eyes. He fought down the bile in his throat and yanked the keys from his pocket. He rolled over on his side and reached behind for his Glock. The 9mm semi-automatic felt heavy and unwieldy in his swollen hand and fingers.

Still, he knew he had to try. Lives were at stake. If he was right, Fein had Katie. The bomb on the elevator may only have been one of several.

"Dear God—help me!" Fletcher cried weakly, pulling himself forward on his elbows toward the iron steps. He grabbed the rail with his free hand and pulled himself up on one knee.

Pain slammed into his chest like a hammer. Fletcher grabbed his left arm and pitched helplessly face forward onto the steps and blackness. His body shuddered once, and then stilled.

Michael the archangel gently laid his hand on the detective's head. The condition he had forced upon the policeman's weary body would not be permanent; to the contrary, it would save his life.

Thick blond hair framed his sober face as he looked upward. His prayer rose heavenward, unimpeded by the clamor of demonic hordes clustered in the small room beyond the door at the top of the nearby stairs. Both they and their master would be deaf to his urgent plea.

He recited the ancient truths from Ecclesiastes, speaking the Lord's will into fulfillment once again: "I know that whatsoever God does, it shall be forever: nothing can be put to it—God does it, that all should fear before Him."

As Michael rose to his feet, the posture of his broad-shouldered body manifested the acute focus of his spirit.

"That which has been is now, that which is to be hath already been, and God requires that which is past."

Mark shuddered uncontrollably—one more flight of tortuous steps to the 490 foot level.

His prayers for Katie and their child fell out of a parched mouth.

Four flights ago he had stopped running, tripping, and falling on legs that felt like jello. Instead, he took one step at a time, using the rail to help pull himself forward. Between each stab of pain in his thighs and calves, he expelled his agonized pleas toward heaven in jolting bursts. And intermingled with his cries, bits and pieces of Sam's account of his confrontation with the Devil at Ford's Theatre flashed into his thoughts. Sam had tried to be the hero—and failed. Lincoln had been shot. History could not be changed.

Mark kept his eyes on the stairs. And what of the flashing cone of red light and the tombstones? Katie's name had been on the last one and her death prophesied. Would she become part of history, too?

Only three steps remained. Two. One.

He slumped heavily against the wire fencing, locking his fingers into the mesh for support. His eyes followed the fence down the length of the corridor.

Fletcher!

It was as if the fence was electrified. Mark flung himself forward, staggering, sliding to his knees by his motionless friend. He felt Fletcher's neck for a pulse, but his senses were so wasted he wasn't sure what his fingertips told him.

"Come on, Fletcher!" Mark sobbed into his ear. "This isn't your time! Not now, not here!"

Heavy vibrations on the iron steps caused Mark to look up.

"I'm afraid you're wrong about that," Brian Fein explained, stopping halfway down the stairs above him, an automatic pistol held steadily in his hand.

"Dead wrong."

After struggling up the stairs to the observation level with Fletcher, Mark proceeded to bind his friend's hands and feet with duct tape. Every few moments, Mark stole a glance at Katie. She watched his every move through tear-filled eyes.

"That's good enough." Brian rose from his squat and walked to the window. He listened to the crowd roar their approval as Legacy finished another song.

Mark looked up, distressed. "He may die."

"He may indeed. Now, wrap your own feet and back up to the wall beside your wife. Then sit on your hands. If I see your fingers, I'll bind you, too."

Mark turned toward Katie. As their eyes met, a tear tumbled down one cheek. Mark rubbed it away with his fingertips. "You OK?" he asked in a hushed voice. Katie bit at her lip and nodded.

Brian returned his gun to the holster under his arm. "Very touching. I retract a statement I made earlier. I can now honestly say that it has been a pleasure meeting both of you. And Fletcher, too. Now please, remain very quiet. I must place a call to verify that what you have told me is true. Please do not raise your voices—it would prove fatal for Katie."

Brian reached into the cardboard box at his feet and removed a portable phone. He pressed a two-digit number.

"Yes, hello. This is Mr. Alverson, from Otis. I've finally got those cables unjammed. The elevator should be fully operational in about forty-five minutes." Brian's tense face relaxed into a grin. "Yes, I'm already aware that Officer Rivers will be escorting a party for a private tour. Thank you, goodbye."

As Brian placed the phone back into the cardboard box, Mark glanced down at Fletcher. He seemed to be breathing steadily.

"There will be no police intervention," Brian added, "and that buys us all time and will save lives."

"Not ours, of course," Mark said, leaning his head back against the elevator housing. "You tried to kill us once already."

The Irishman turned his head and stared coldly.

"Brian, how many others have you killed—or do you prefer Ciaran?" Mark asked calmly. "We became dangerous to you, didn't we? Was it because I saw you in the back of the van the night of the vandalism, or because we discovered your relationship with Harold Wertman dating back to Cal-Berkeley? Or did you discover that we uncovered your relationship with Peters, Legacy, and the seven companies?"

Mark's words struck Brian like a blow to the face. His head snapped back. His eyes glazed over as he tore his pistol from its holster. He leaned against the marble beam by the observation window. The diagonal line across his cheek deepened in color.

Cat-like, Brian pushed himself from the wall. He dropped to one knee beside Mark, pressing the barrel of his gun harshly up under Mark's chin. His eyes were dark and furious.

"How do you know these things?" he shouted in Mark's ear, yanking on his shirt collar and driving the gun's barrel deeply into the soft flesh of Mark's neck.

Katie cried out. Brian swiveled around toward her.

Mark coughed, forcing his hands to remain beneath him. "No! Katie—I'm OK. Brian, leave her alone. I'll talk."

Brian teetered, as if he had lost his balance. The features on his face exploded with hate. His body shook with rage.

He jerked Mark away from the wall with one hand and forced him face-first onto the marble floor. Katie screamed. Brian spun on one knee and aimed the gun straight between her eyes.

Mark leaned forward, his eyes locked on Brian's. "You can kill us, maybe even get out of here, but your freedom will be short-lived. You're a marked man, Fein."

The Irishman slowly backed away toward the observation window, bumping into the wall, the color draining from his face. With his gun still leveled on Mark, he slumped to the floor beside the open cardboard box.

Brian's dark eyes darted pensively from Mark to Katie, and then back to Mark. "Against the wall! Sit on your hands! And shut up."

Mark obeyed, turning over and pulling himself into a sitting position. He slid over to Katie's side. He wedged his hands beneath his thighs, watching the terrorist's eyes.

Mark held his breath as he watched an eerie transformation of Brian's face. The scar pulsed, its crimson color fading. Hatred! Mark saw it clearly—a dark, bottomless, bitter whirlpool in the center of Brian's heart.

Brian blinked as Legacy's thumping, electronic heartbeat resumed. They had just begun their closing number—a reprise of *Children of the Earth*.

The reality of his predicament became painfully evident. Others besides Mark and Fletcher were involved. And as he had feared, Peters had unwittingly put his trust and sole evidence of their operation directly into the hands of the opposition!

A growing, incandescent fury pounded in his chest as he raised his bleary eyes and focused on Mark and his wife. It was imperative that Peters and the Controller die, as well as the MacDonalds and Fletcher Rivers.

Grabbing the duct tape from the box beside him, Brian sprang to his feet. Pressing his pistol against Mark's temple, he quickly and securely bound his hands, then lowered his mouth to Mark's ear.

"I would shoot you now, but that would waste my magazine. Good luck, Mark MacDonald, in the world to come—if that's what you believe."

Turning his head, his eyes moist with compassion, Mark stared Brian in the face. Memories of Sam and a desperate Seth Beaumont in the Charleston jail cell filled his thoughts. Only the truth could help Brian now—and save them.

"What's going on here is not between you and me and Fletcher. And it's not between Christians and your organization."

Inching the barrel of his gun toward the corner of Mark's left eye, Brian arched his eyebrow as if to ask, who then?

They were so close that Mark could feel Brian's warm breath on his face. Mark refused to lower his gaze. "It's between God and the Devil."

"God! The Devil!" Brian chortled. "I see that you are fooled by my little tricks! Late Friday night, a week ago—I broke into your house. From the edge of the second floor landing, I saw you stop at the top of stairs. I felt your fear! Demons! Hah! Then, after you went to bed, I found your ancestor's journals! I prepared the speech Wertman gave that morning.

"Then you found those two Latin words painted on the statue—another of my ploys to frighten and distract you from the case."

Memories of those dark, terrifying moments on the stairs and the words painted on the statue came back. Mark shook his head and cleared his thoughts.

"You're wrong—you don't pull the strings!"

Mark watched the scar on Fein's cheek redden.

"The spirit Rasah has had both our numbers for a long, long time —only neither of us realized it! Rasah's tearing the heart out of this country, just like it's been doing in Ireland."

Tears welled in Mark's eyes. "It's using your hands to do its work! It wants to divide this country with the same bloody sectionalism that you ran away from in Ireland. Resist it now, while you've still got a chance!"

The granite floor seemed to move beneath Brian's feet and he rolled back on his heels. He fought to maintain his balance, and then realized that he was not falling at all, but that his body had gone numb and he had lost control of his limbs. He felt his mouth twist open oddly to one side and his tongue wipe over his dry lips. His hand still held the gun to Mark's head, but a force beyond himself was slowly squeezing the trigger. Rabid fear merged with seething anger —he was a detached observer, a captive within his own consciousness and body.

His finger stopped a hair's breadth from discharging the gun.

Mark fought down fear as the scar on Brian's cheek darkened to the color of fresh blood. The Irishman's steely eyes brimmed with madness and wild, virulent hatred. His mouth twisted as thick, guttural sounds broke from between his lips. The sounds did not issue from Brian, but Rasah!

As if she heard her husband's thoughts, Katie buried her face into his shoulder, biting her lip.

Rasah moved Brian's body to face Mark and Katie square on, dropping to one knee between them, sliding the gun slowly across

Mark's forehead to a point just above and between his eyes—then lowering it, returning the gun to his shoulder holster with a barking laugh.

Vivid images wedged their way past Mark's own thoughts: Beaumont shooting himself in the head; Sam being lifted off his feet and pinned against a brick wall. The images shifted to a snow-covered glen and a frontiersman who cruelly held a young Indian woman by the throat, his sword brandished above his head, his eyes filled with murder.

The scene faded and Mark found himself staring into Brian's eyes. No—he forced himself to remember—the narrowed malicious stare belonged to Rasah.

Rasah moved Brian backward six feet to the opposite wall and thrust him to the floor, his eyes searching the observation area, following the wires from the molded bricks of C-4 taped around the windows to the power supply on the wooden box behind him to the left. He reached into his shirt pocket and removed the black remote. He studied the small buttons and smiled—a bent, wicked smile pasted over a sweaty face heavily-lined with fear. The incongruous sight was unnerving.

Rasah stared upward, his eyes searching through and beyond the marble. "The heavens above this feeble structure are thick with my *maleak*, my warriors! O that you could behold these mighty ones as I do—then you would fear all the more and understand why I will prevail.

"Where is the great El, now?" Rasah demanded, raising Brian's hand and running a trembling forefinger down the length of the scar. "Where are his warriors—his *cheled*, his *shinan*? Why have they abandoned you to me? Answer that question."

The voice inside Mark's thoughts quietly urged him not to reply.

Rasah toyed with the remote, twisting Brian's mouth to painful extremes, baring his teeth like an animal.

"Though you possess the revelation of my ambition, your knowledge shall come to naught! Once and for all, the prophecy shall finally be cut off."

The spirit's proclamation forced Mark to open his eyes. He resisted the fear clawing for control of his thoughts and instead, yielded his heart and mind to the Holy Spirit, abandoning himself to God's mercy, just as Sam had done in Beaumont's cell. He stared past the seething resentment in the eyes locked on his, past the hatred to the man, Brian Fein. Like a flood, the compassion of Christ poured out from the center of Mark's soul, surging through his pounding heart. It was not the enemy who sat on the floor across from him, but a broken, despairing man.

Rasah raised the detonator. On its face near the bottom were two red buttons.

Mark obeyed an inner prompting, drew a deep breath and concentrated on Christ, on the work of the Cross. In the center of his thoughts a picture formed: two small children sprawled in a nearby gutter. Kneeling beside the bodies was a small boy. Hovering above and behind the boy was a dark apparition. The children were dead, their clothing soaked a deep red. Sobbing, the small boy reached down and lifted a tiny, bloodied crucifix from around the girl's neck. As he did, the apparition wavered, then plunged downward into the boy, rocking him back on his heels. The boy tilted his head, his long, agonizing wail echoing across a body littered square.

Then Mark knew. Rasah had violated the sanctity of a young boy's soul, forging what he hoped would be an irreparable rift between Brian and God!

Mocking laughter and Katie pressing hard into his shoulder caused Mark to open his eyes again.

Rasah forced Brian to depress one of the two red buttons. His face was a patchwork of tortured, contradictory expressions: Brian's stark horror; Rasah's savage delight; Brian's revulsion; Rasah's hunger. Slowly, Brian's forefinger started down toward the second button.

"Brian! Don't! It was Rasah who killed the children!"

Brian's quivering finger touched the button, then paused, his eyes flashing. Mark watched as his warring emotions intensified. Shock and anger collided with venomous spite, grimly twisting his countenance.

Mark looked past the frightening visage and focused on the inner man. "You allowed Rasah to enter. He made his malice yours and sculpted your heart to be like his."

Then Mark saw something else. Dead in the center of Brian's soul, in the middle of a cracked and barren wasteland, was a small, fruit-bearing tree guarded all around by a self-willed, flaming sword. A dozen black-feathered vultures darted in and out, hunting for an opening to steal the last remaining piece of fruit. But the massive sword faithfully maintained its charge, slashing, cutting through the air, keeping the birds at bay.

Mark's and Brian's eyes met. Words rose from deep within Mark's heart. His body shook as he said each one.

"You have one hope, Brian. Only one. Otherwise, Rasah will make you kill us and who knows how many thousands more. This moment has nothing to do with politics or religion—it's about death! The death of innocent children!"

In that moment Mark understood it all. The relationship of two conflicting bloodlines shot through his thoughts like crossing beams of a ruby laser. One line was drawn with the holy blood of the Lamb, one perfect sacrifice for all mankind; the other was drawn with the blood of countless millions, stretching all the way back to Abel. Father Gibault revealed what the Scriptures proclaimed all along—that the Devil was a murderer from the beginning. The Devil not only used individuals but governments and nations to do his work. And the deaths that resulted from wars were nothing compared to his new, vast and constant harvest of innocent blood: the lives of millions upon millions of the unborn.

A spasm shook Brian from head to toe, his face turning a deep red. In one motion he jerked his hand away from the remote, raising it to the open neck of his white shirt. Between his shaking thumb and forefinger was a small, gold crucifix on a thin chain—the crucifix that had belonged to his cousin. He closed his hand around it and snapped it from his neck.

Dropping the remote into his lap, he wrapped his free hand around his tightly clenched fist. He bit so hard on his lip that blood showed.

"Free... your hands... before I lose... control!" Brian stuttered, his body shuddering. Muscles bunched and twitched in his arms and legs.

Mark tore at the duct tape around his wrists with his teeth, then reached down and ripped the tape from his feet. Brian watched with a fevered expression, his hands clutching the cross.

"Knife... strapped to my... left leg. Quickly!" Brian trembled violently as Mark pushed up his pant leg and yanked the knife from its leather sheath. Without speaking, he cut the tape from Katie's wrists and ankles, then from around Fletcher's.

"Take the gun... from my holster!"

Dropping the knife, Mark reached for the remote.

"No!" Brian exclaimed. "Don't! You'll blow this place. Do as I said. Take the gun. Do not delay!"

As Mark stepped close and pulled the heavy gun from the shoulder holster, he could feel the conflict raging in Brian. He was breathing hard, his body hot.

Brian lifted his sweat-drenched head. Mark stepped back, gun in hand. There was a sudden calmness about his face, like a devastated island momentarily resting in the eye of a hurricane.

"Kill me," he said weakly, his knuckles white and locked around the crucifix. "If you don't, we will all die—and thousands below."

Mark glanced at the gun, then back at Brian. He shook his head. "I can't shoot you!"

"You must! There's no other way!"

"I refuse. Only the Lord can deliver you." Mark said quietly, placing the gun on the floor. He looked at Katie. "Let's get Fletcher in the elevator first."

Rubbing her wrists, she nodded. Together, with Mark doing most of the work, they slid Fletcher into the elevator. Mark returned to Brian. The Irishman was doubled over and quaking violently, his body enfolded around his hands and the crucifix. Mark reached down and took the remote from his lap and carefully handed it to Katie. He put his arm around Brian and helped pull him to his feet.

Brian's head snapped up, and Mark found himself face-to-face with pure hatred.

Rasah drew Brian's mouth into a snarl, teeth bared, blood and saliva dripping from the corners of swollen and broken lips. His eyes flashed like razor-edged knives, stabbing fear deeply into Mark's thoughts.

You will die! Your wife and child will die!

Mark stared deeply into blood-red pupils. He saw through the crimson haze to a black, bitter core of resentment. The dark mass pulsed with raw power and emotion so palpable and so frenzied that Mark felt as if someone had pressed a hot iron against his cheek.

"Rasah," Mark whispered, holding his ground and refusing to lower his eyes, "you are now in the hands of an angry God!"

A ghastly, inhuman scream erupted from Brian's mouth. His eyes rolled up, his head arched backwards, but his hands maintained their iron grip on the crucifix.

Mark helped Brian as he staggered into the elevator and sat him in the wooden chair in the corner. After taking the remote from Katie, he studied the buttons and found a downward pointing triangle. He closed his eyes, offered a silent prayer and pressed the button.

The elevator doors slid shut.

Brian collapsed into the corner and watched through a blurry veil of tears as the elevator began its downward descent. The foul taste of bile filled his mouth, and his stomach churned agonizingly, threatening to disgorge itself. His limbs were still not his own. If it were not for the tiny cross, he knew that his hands would obey another master.

He gasped. The cross! He could see it right through his hands! The tiny gold crucifix that had been covered in his cousin's blood was bleeding again!

And growing.

His hands fell away as the crucifix elongated and widened. In seconds, it was as tall as he was, stretching silently, impossibly. Brian felt himself twisting in space. The elevator darkened, and a bitter wind snapped across his face. His arms were pulled apart and back. His feet no longer touched the floor. Excruciating pain flashed through his wrists, up his arms and across his shoulders, then again through his feet, up his legs and into his hips. He felt his left shoulder pop, then the right. He wanted to scream, but his lungs had to fight for enough air just to breathe.

What is happening to me? He opened his eyes. For a split second he forgot the pain, shocked by the scene below him. A crowd milled about on a rocky hilltop. Some wore long flowing gowns and robes; several wore short tunics. A soldier stood almost directly beneath him—not a modern-day soldier, but a soldier wearing a breastplate and helmet with a short, wide sword on his hip. A Roman centurion?

He raised his head. Nearby rose tall stone walls. Behind the walls were hundreds of dusty roof tops and the dome of a temple. Beyond the enclosed city rose a broad mountain.

His fascination was shattered by an explosion of pain from his wrists and feet that stole his breath away. He turned his head to the right. His arm bowed out from his body along a thick wooden beam. His eyes locked onto a horrifying sight—an iron nail as thick as his thumb protruded from the base of his blood-smeared wrist, pinning it to the beam. Sickened, Brian let his head fall to his chest, the pain in his wrists mounting quickly.

A familiar, vile voice barked from his left.

Turning his head, he saw two other men with arms spread wide, their feet and wrists nailed to crudely-hewn crosses. A black-haired man on the cross to the far left, his scarred face a corkscrew of hatred, spat curses at the man between them.

Though racked with pain, Brian recoiled as his eyes fell upon the man Rasah cursed. A ring of thorns was wrapped around his head. Streams of blood streaked his severely battered face, trickling around the corners of his mouth into his beard.

The man to whom the curses had been hurled, lifted his eyes to his accuser. Ah! The gentle, forgiving look on his battered face was disturbing to behold! Purity and goodness radiated from him like light from a beacon.

"Aren't you the Christ?" Rasah asked mockingly through the dark-haired man's twisted mouth. "Save yourself and us!"

The Christ! The stony covering around Brian's heart shattered. The Christ of the crucifix!

Then Brian perceived the names of everything within his sight: the city stretching before him and the rugged mountain behind it, the rocky hill from which he looked down, the middle-aged woman who stood at the edge of the crowd and wept into her hands, and the man beside her with his arm wrapped around her shoulder.

All of my life I have been foolish and blind. I have served those who hate him. How could this man be guilty of any crime? A new kind of anger burned in Brian's chest, stronger than the pain that sliced through every joint and muscle in his body.

"You should fear God," he yelled across at Rasah, "since you are under the same sentence! We are punished justly, getting what we deserve. But this man has done nothing wrong."

Brian fought for enough breath to continue speaking, ignoring Rasah's profane cries. His lungs were filled with fire, his wrists and feet were throbbing, ragged flesh.

Suddenly, the gray sky darkened noticeably. Brian twisted his head to the side and peered upward. The sun had eclipsed! A spasm shook his body. He lowered his gaze.

To his surprise, he found himself standing on a smooth stone floor near the white iron gate just inside the open mouth of the Washington Monument, staring through the bars into the shocked and worried face of AFI's Controller.

Mark fumbled with the key ring while he spoke with Michelle. "I don't have time to explain! You've got to find someone with the Park Police—fast! The phone's dead."

Michelle anxiously lowered her eyes to Fletcher, stretched out on the floor behind Mark and Katie, and then back up to Brian. His face was a grim mask of pain. A thin gold chain dangled from his tightly clenched fists. His tortured gaze was focused beyond her. No—now on her!

"Michelle!" Mark exclaimed sharply. "Please! Fletcher needs medical attention."

Without another second's delay, she let go of the iron bars and started running down the hill toward the Survey Lodge. Julie, who had been watching from the row of benches, followed behind her.

Mark slipped the key into the lock and thanked the Lord that Michelle and Julie decided to return to the monument. The key worked! He praised the Lord a second time and swung the gate open wide. To his amazement the area in front of the monument was clear of tourists or protesters.

A groan from Brian caused him to turn around.

The Irishman shook from head to toe. His eyes were locked on Mark's. Tearful, pleading eyes—they were Brian's eyes, not Rasah's —Mark was sure of it. Brian needed to be freed from Rasah's grip. But how? And Fletcher needed medical attention.

As he struggled with a course of action, Mark suddenly realized he still held the detonator. *Lord Jesus! Rasah could still get control of the explosives!* He darted back into the Monument, past Katie and Fletcher to open the door of the elevator. He glanced at the remote, then pressed a button. As the doors started to close, he bent down and carefully slid it inside.

They were safe—at last! Now it would take someone with a key to the elevator to get the remote.

Katie knelt beside Fletcher. She placed a hand on his shoulder and started to pray.

Katie's gentle, urgent requests reached Brian's ears. His eyes opened wide and the fear and anguish crowding his features retreated slightly.

His hands still gripping the cross, Brian leaned against the iron gate to hold himself up. A wave of relief crashed over him as he realized what Mark had done. The detonator was out of Rasah's hands! There would be no explosion!

In that same fraction of a second, another half of his brain interpreted his analysis in an entirely different way: the lack of an explosion meant he had failed.

Failure. Failure at this level of operation was not only unacceptable, but would demand...

Years of field experience flashed the obvious grim logic through his thoughts. Just as he had done with Troy—Bonn, Geneva, London, and New York would never allow him to compromise the organization if he didn't successfully complete his mission!

He would become expendable!

Brian erupted into two simultaneous courses of action. Information had to be passed and he had to get away from Mark and Katie.

With Rasah's sickening urges still raking his body, he gripped the cross tightly in his right hand. Mustering his strength, he thrust himself away from the wall and plunged his left hand down into his open shirt for the other thin chain that hung around his neck. He snapped it loose with a hard jerk.

As he did, Katie stepped past him out through the gate.

No! Brian's mind screamed. Moving in front of me will put you in the marksman's line of fire!

Brian staggered into Katie, his hands between them, pressing against her and pushing her toward the row of benches to the right. Katie cried out in surprise.

Brian anticipated the precise moment when the marksman would fire and where on his body the deadly round would strike. He turned his body sideways, his eyes scanning the horizon from left to right, past a distant clump of trees, past the concession building due east and across the field to the Sylvan Theatre.

His consummate skills and his keen sense of timing and placement had not lied. A glint of light led his eyes to his adversary. A
woman with black hair perched on the roof of the outdoor theatre
forty yards away! Kim!

Brian flinched, twisting his body even more parallel to the theatre.
The cheering of the vast crowd drowned the crisp bark of rifle shot
that tore through the air and slammed into Brian's chest, knocking
him backward off his feet onto the concrete sidewalk behind the
benches.

Mark stood with one hand on the gate as Katie grabbed the back of
a bench to regain her balance. He saw Brian spin and tumble to the
ground.

The direction of Brian's fall caused Mark to spin in the opposite
direction, toward the Sylvan Theatre, just in time to spot a small,
Oriental woman lower herself over the back of the theatre and disappear from sight. She wore a police uniform and had a rifle with a
scope slung over her shoulder.

Ignoring the potential danger of his action, Mark darted across the
opening to Brian's side. The Irishman's chest and shoulder were
bathed in red. There was nothing he could do but pray.

Brian felt his chest collapse as he was knocked from his feet.
Nothing mattered now, nothing but holding on to the cross! He
opened his eyes, expecting to see one final snapshot of the huge,
stone monument looming above him before he faded into oblivion
and death.

Instead, he found himself staring into the face of the one called
Jesus, the Christ. His arms were stretched across a rugged cross,
framed by a dark, sunless sky. His forehead was scarred and bloody,
yet his eyes brimmed with understanding and compassion.

All at once, Brian remembered everything. The dusty, walled city
and the rugged mountain. The rocky hill. A third cross. And Rasah,
embodied in the thief beyond the Christ. Rasah's cursing was filled
with despair, his visage grim and hopeless, misshapen with bitterness and hatred.

Brian turned his eyes back upon Jesus. Mark MacDonald had
been right all along. He had no other hope. The Irishman let his broken heart speak.

"Remember me when you come into your kingdom."

A caring smile formed on the God-man's lips.

Mark watched as Brian's right hand tightened around the tiny gold
crucifix. He reached down, gently clasped Brian's left hand and

examined the Irishman's wound. Blood flowed freely in a widening stain from an ugly purple hole in his shirt near the center of his chest.

He squeezed Brian's hand and prayed for God's mercy. Brian had deliberately pushed himself away from him and Katie and Fletcher, keeping them clear from the sharpshooter's line of fire.

A hand on Mark's shoulder made him look up. It was Michelle, her face registering horror as she saw Brian's bloody shirt and wound. "Help Katie, will you?" Mark asked quietly. "There's nothing that you can do here."

Michelle nodded.

Mark looked back down. To his surprise, Brian's eyes fluttered open. As they did, a broad swath of sunlight broke across the sidewalk and benches, warming the Irishman's face. All the anger and tension were gone, leaving his features smooth and peaceful.

Mark glanced up at the sky. The cloud cover had broken. As he looked back to Brian, a deep roll of thunder echoed majestically down the length of mall, long and full, crackling with power and strength. The hair on Mark's arms stood on end. Was it thunder or a voice?

Brian grinned wearily. A lone tear trickled down his left cheek where the scar had once been. He squeezed Mark's hand, closed his eyes and whispered two words.

"Yes... Lord."

Mark gently placed Brian's hand across his chest. He lifted his eyes toward heaven, weeping and praising God in holy abandon.

EPILOGUE

Thursday Afternoon
January 21, 1993

THE SKY ABOVE the Manassas National Battlefield Park was clear, the sun was bright and the air felt unseasonably warm. A handful of students and their teacher from a private school stood at the entrance to the battlefield's visitor center. Wearing jeans and heavy sweaters, Michelle and Julie climbed into a Toyota and shut their doors.

Next to the Toyota was a beige Cutlass Ciera. Mark and Katie sat in the back seat. Fletcher buckled his seatbelt and then closed the front passenger door. Botello climbed behind the steering wheel and slipped his key into the ignition.

Exhaust spurted from the tailpipes of the Cutlass and Toyota. The Cutlass led the way out of the parking lot, heading down the hill toward the road on which jubilant Confederate troops had once marched to victory.

A mile away from the battlefield's visitor center, in a small cemetery behind the Sudley Church, a man with blond hair knelt down in front of a tombstone. His blue jogging suit stood out against the winter landscape. He looked up and cocked his head. He could feel the joy of the Lord rise from the new circle of friends who were approaching.

He turned his attention back to the tombstone. Sam MacDonald. January 21—one century ago to the very day, by human reckoning, Sam had arrived at his nephew's in Washington, D.C. His heart had been burdened by the knowledge that Rasah was loosed upon the world, plotting bloodshed and destruction upon mankind just as he had done exactly one century before at the beheading of the French king.

Placing his hand on the rounded stone, he recited another of the ancient truths, speaking God's word into fulfillment. His eyes gleamed with delight.

"Indeed, Sam MacDonald, 'The memory of the righteous will be a blessing.'"

Fletcher lowered the newspaper and glanced over his shoulder. "Nothing in the *Post* or the *Times*. There's a lot about yesterday's inauguration and tomorrow's March for Life—but nothing on Fein. It's as if nothing happened. Doesn't seem possible with the way the media finds things out these days."

Mark sighed. "I guess we'll never know. Somebody in high places didn't want the presidential inauguration disrupted."

Botello nodded as he turned right out of the battlefield access road onto Sudley Road. "The National Security Agency and the FBI seized all of the cases, including Troy's. KC's on administrative leave and in seclusion. No one's sure what's going to happen next. Sometimes a national security case will melt away and never be heard of again."

With a look of resignation on his face, Mark glanced at Katie. "Michelle says the last she heard before being fired was that Peters took an extended leave of absence. Scuttlebutt was he wouldn't be returning."

"There are a lot of things we'll probably never know," Fletcher said, folding the paper and putting it on his lap. "When we signed those non-disclosure forms at the NSA, we lost whatever rights we had to follow up on any of this."

"Maybe it's best," Katie said, folding her hands in her lap. "Now we can get back to a normal life and leave these things in the hands of people more equipped to deal with them."

Botello slapped the steering wheel and grinned. "The only person I know of like that is the Lord!"

"You got that right," Fletcher affirmed as they passed beneath a traffic light near an old stone house with a cannonball stuck in the front wall.

Mark tapped Fletcher on the shoulder, "Rumor has it you called your wife and daughter a couple times last Saturday and Sunday while you were in the hospital."

"Rumor has it right," Fletcher replied with a bright smile. "It's a beginning. Spoke with my little girl for nearly ten minutes. They're calling me tomorrow evening."

Mark nodded. "It's amazing what strong medicine will do for you...."

Michael, archangel of the Most High, stared at the name on the front of the tombstone. A smile broke across his face. A multitude of the heavenly host—*cheled*, the swift ones, and *shinan*, the bright ones—gathered nearby, lifting their powerful voices heavenward in song to the Lamb.

Because of the faithfulness of this man and his seed, the name of Brian Fein would not be erased from the Lamb's Book of Life. By thwarting Rasah's plans, thousands of lives had been spared, and this nation, though deeply divided, avoided another bloody rupture.

Michael shifted his gaze skyward. Perhaps the day was not far off when Rasah's companions, Ashteroth and Molech, would be dealt with as well: more battles were yet to come.

The archangel heard sounds behind him. Tires crunched over gravel. Two cars slowed and stopped in a parking area beyond a nearby stone wall. Doors opened.

The archangel stood up and watched his charges enter the cemetery through a wrought-iron gate and approach the gravesite. He knew them all by name, including the young woman named Julie, whose name would soon be written in the Lamb's Book of Life.

Michael studied Mark's and Katie's faces. He understood their sadness and joy and respect and awe. This was as humanly close as they could get to Sam MacDonald—in this lifetime. The others could not understand the emotions Mark and Katie felt.

The archangel watched as a wry grin creased Mark's face. "Look at the message Sam left his family. He's still teaching us, even from the grave."

"How's that?" Katie asked.

Mark's grin opened into a smile. "Our Father which art in heaven, hallowed be Thy name..."

Katie looked at the tombstone, her eyes widening with delight. "Thy kingdom come, Thy will be done in earth, as it is in heaven."

The others joined in. "Give us this day our daily bread and forgive us our debts as we forgive our debtors."

Overwhelmed with joy, Mark reached out and clasped Katie's hand. "And lead us not into temptation, but deliver us from evil—"

Standing beside Mark and Katie, the archangel listened as the ancient truth coursed through him like living fire.

Michael shook his head and united his voice with theirs.

"For Thine is the kingdom!"

A rushing wind swept through the small cemetery, swirling around the tombstones, kicking up leaves from the ground and rustling the barren dogwood trees.

"And the power!"

A crack of thunder echoed overhead as his jogging suit burst into shimmering white flames.

"And the glory!"

The ring of wide-eyed faces surrounding the tombstone looked incredulously upward at a clear blue sky.

Michael lifted his arms toward heaven and the ranks of heavenly warriors joined their jubilant voices with his own.

"For ever!"

"Amen!"

Other Novels from Servant Publications

The Bird in the Tree
*Book 1 * The Eliot Heritage*
Elizabeth Goudge

In her fierce devotion to the Eliot clan, Lucilla Eliot had worked to make Damerosehay, her home on the Hampshire coast, a beautiful refuge, capable of withstanding any threat to family happiness. Now her lifetimes's labor was about to be destroyed by her favorite grandson, David, in love with the estranged wife of another man. Would he sacrifice his love to preserve his family's integrity? **$10.99**

Pilgrim's Inn
*Book 2 * The Eliot Heritage*
Elizabeth Goudge

This is the absorbing sequel to *The Bird in the Tree*. Nadine and George Eliot had moved into a wonderful old inn near Damerosehay. Surrounded by a wild and mysterious wood, the inn seemed to possess powers for mending minds and healing souls. With singular beauty, we are swept into a story of intertwining destinies, of love lost and love forever gained. **$10.99**

The Heart of the Family
*Book 3 * The Eliot Heritage*
Elizabeth Goudge

Here is the culmination of the story of the remarkable Eliot Family, spanning four genrerations: Lucilla, David, Sally, Nadine, George, Ben, and Meg. Their lives are intricately woven together in a tale of startling beauty and immense depth. **$10.99**